# PRAISE FOR *AMERICAN ADULTERER*

"It seems so obvious that one wonders why no one has done it be-fore—to take a novel, clinical approach to John F. Kennedy as a case study in philandering and psychosexual pathology . . . Mercurio presents JFK as a liberal hero, rather than a hypocrite, just the man for those times, a fascinating synthesis of surrogate motive and po-litical vision."

—Chris Petit, *The Guardian* (UK)

"[A] remarkable new novel . . . [*American Adulterer*] makes the case that Kennedy's vice is worth studying as the tragic flaw in a genuine hero. The man's wit, courtesy, peacemaking vision and cool judg-ment are all here, vividly re-created, as well as his courage in the face of near-disabling infirmity and pain. . . . gripping and thoughtful."

—Hugo Barnacle, *The Sunday Times* (UK)

"The Cuban missile crisis is brilliantly, claustrophobically han-dled. . . . it's hard not to recommend [t]his book to anyone in-trigued by the idea of a necessarily small human being caught by the terrible weight of an office of state. Admirably, even in dealing with historical events of such rare import, the author isn't afraid of using his imagination in pursuit of a more poetic kind of truth."

—Archie Bland, *Arts and Book Review*, *The Independent* (UK)

"American Adulterer: the words sting like two well-aimed slaps . . . Jed Mercurio's compelling third novel . . . is ultimately a sympa-thetic portrait . . . Mercurio shows that a stylish surface matched to an inner seriousness can conceal all manner of blemishes."

—Adrian Turpin, *Financial Times* (UK)

"[Jed Mercurio] writes in brilliantly clinical prose . . . His real suc-cess here is to highlight how JFK moved politics into a culture of celebrity . . . [finding] a truth in JFK through fiction."

—Ben East, *Metro* (UK)

## ALSO BY JED MERCURIO

*Ascent*

*Bodies*

# American Adulterer

## JED MERCURIO

SIMON & SCHUSTER PAPERBACKS
NEW YORK   LONDON   TORONTO   SYDNEY

Simon & Schuster Paperbacks
1230 Avenue of the Americas
New York, NY 10020

First Simon & Schuster trade paperback edition March 2010

SIMON & SCHUSTER and colophon are registered trademarks
of Simon & Schuster, Inc.

For information about special discounts for bulk purchases,
please contact Simon & Schuster Special Sales at
1-866-506-1949 or business@simonandschuster.com.

The Simon & Schuster Speakers Bureau can bring authors
to your live event. For more information or to book an event,
contact the Simon & Schuster Speakers Bureau at
1-866-248-3049 or visit our website at www.simonspeakers.com.

Designed by Davina Mock-Maniscalco

Manufactured in the United States of America

1  3  5  7  9  10  8  6  4  2

The Library of Congress hs cataloged the hardcover edition as follows:
Mercurio, Jed.
American adulterer / Jed Mercurio.
p.    cm.
Includes bibliographical references.
1. Kennedy, John. F. (John Fitzgerald), 1917–1963—Fiction.
2. Presidents—United States—Fiction. 3. Adultery—Fiction. I. Title.
PR6113.E73A825    2009
823'.92—dc22      2009002296
ISBN 978-1-4391-1563-3
ISBN 978-1-4391-1625-8 (pbk)
ISBN 978-1-4391-3732-1 (ebook)

*To my Wife*

# CONTENTS

vii

*Men are such a combination of good and evil.*

—JACQUELINE BOUVIER KENNEDY

# AMERICAN ADULTERER

# THE SUBJECT

THE SUBJECT IS an American citizen holding high elected office, married, and father to a young family, who takes the view that monogamy has seldom been the engine of great men's lives. He has always had women—numerously, sequentially and simultaneously, in the form of family friends, heiresses, socialites, models, actresses, professional acquaintances, colleagues' spouses, party girls, shopgirls and prostitutes—following the youthful discovery that he liked women and they liked him.

Only in the course of longer-lasting affairs did the question of marriage arise; it was not something he took seriously until his political ambitions began to include high office, whereupon it was clarified by numerous colleagues that a good marriage was not merely an advantage but a necessity. A politician must remain publicly faithful to those principles and causes he chooses to follow; whether he remains faithful to his wife is another question.

Seven years ago, at age thirty-six, he married a beautiful young woman twelve years his junior. He will not admit defrauding his marital vows. Before God, he decided not to be derailed by the impossibility of making promises based upon the permanence of love, when it is clear to any thinking person that to guarantee one's state of mind in twenty or even thirty years' time is preposterous. Taking vows is merely etiquette—as is appearing to observe them.

His bride convinced herself that the institution of marriage would wave a magic wand over his catholic libido. Of course, in those days a good part was directed toward her. He refuses to blame himself for her misconception. She was attracted to a man who had his pick of women. If she had wanted the type who struggles to get laid, then she should have married one—certainly there are enough to choose from.

When he sees a beautiful woman, he wants to make love to her. That has been a natural, physical desire he has experienced since youth. If marriage had quelled the impulse, no one would have been happier than he—with the exception, of course, of his wife.

ONCE MARRIED, OBVIOUSLY the subject had to become more discreet. He always denied any wrongdoing, except to essential accomplices. Work occupied him at weekends and in the evenings, and, for many months during that initial phase of their marriage, he impressed on his wife that he was absent in the company of men or in the service of work with females present by coincidence. Over time, his plausible denials failed to disabuse his wife of her suspicions. His periods away from home and his social engagements in the presence of attractive women were opportunities for fornication but only as long as he retained the requisite appetite. Her epiphany was provoked by what she saw in front of her rather than that which he hid behind her back: stolen glances, lingering handshakes, and subtle shifts in the focus of his attention during the telling of an anecdote. No matter how strenuous his denials, the insight that prevailed was that his sexual interest in other women had not expired.

As time passed, he remained convinced his wife was an excellent choice and one he certainly did not regret, save for her lack of accommodation to his need for an independent personal life, so he adopted the stratagem of reminding her constantly of her status. He puts her first in all things, and her place in his life, and in his heart, is unique and secure. It may come as no surprise that these proclamations did not end the matter.

AFTER THREE YEARS of marriage, his wife gave birth to a stillborn daughter, the child arriving prematurely, while he was on vacation in the Mediterranean. There were wild nights on the yacht, and he had sex with four women in total, one of whom sailed with his party for a time and became a short-term mistress. He was reluctant to return home, as he was having such a fine time and the mistress was a stunning blonde, but he made the sacrifice for the sake of their marriage.

Yet, in her distress, his wife threatened divorce. She remained angry and upset for so long that he worried the effort of constant denial would wear him out. Thankfully the subject is convinced his wife has never acquired irrefutable proof of his adultery. His single-minded determination to protect his privacy has allowed their love to prevail.

The obstetrician counseled them to conceive again as soon as possible, for his wife's well-being. Both parties share a commitment to resilience. They have both enjoyed much fortune in their lives, so they must not resent misfortune; obstacles must be overcome and tragedies endured without complaint. So it was imperative that rancor be set aside, though some months passed before his independent personal life could again be a fit subject for rational examination. By then, his wife was pregnant again, and they are now not only blessed with a beautiful three-year-old daughter, but his wife is also expecting their next child.

Fatherhood has been the great blessing brought by marriage. He values the stable companionship of a wife, and also the social and professional advantages that accompany having a consort and hostess, but the emotional core of life lies in his relationship with his child. One might argue that marriage provides a vehicle for such men to father children responsibly. Kings left bastard children scattered throughout their lands, denied their father's patronage, just as common men of weak character drift out of their children's lives for selfish reasons.

The subject intends to provide for his children the safe and loving home only a marriage can offer. In this statement, he considers his own experience: his father traveled a good deal, as is only to be expected of a successful and important businessman and politician, and in his youth he discovered his father was far from a faithful husband. His mother appeared completely faithful; in fact, she was a devout observer of her marital vows. Yet his mother is not a demonstratively loving parent: when he was a child, and often quite sick, she regularly made trips for her own private reasons and he would not see her for weeks. In reflecting briefly upon his upbringing, he concludes that his opinion of neither parent is colored by their fidelity.

His wife's father was also a philanderer. He was a public embarrassment to the subject's mother-in-law, so they divorced. The subject's parents remain married. However, his mother denied his father sex once she'd borne his youngest brother; his father's mistresses served a substitute function, though the subject never formed the impression it was a course of action he pursued with a great many scruples. In contrast, the subject's wife doesn't deny him sex; if that were enough to satisfy him, life would be simple.

Virtually all males possess the sexual impulse, essential to continuation of the species, though they possess it to greater or lesser degrees, and in some cases the urge is not directed toward the conventional model of feminine pulchritude, or toward females at all. The subject doesn't believe such men are morally deviant. They experience desires generated by their bodily hormones. Each of us must take a moral view on the repercussions of satisfying his natural desires, and in the past he's been given to reflecting on his own case. He resists applying the terms "condition" or "pathology" to his behavior, because he believes his libido lies within the variants of normal rather than being in any way abnormal, as would, for example, a sexual attraction to minors or to animals. Past reflections only reaffirmed his conviction that promiscuous sexual relations with consenting partners not his wife are no cause for moral self-recrimination. He no longer examines his conduct, proceeding with a clear conscience.

This point of view is reinforced by his observation that constant desire for women appears both natural and normal. He is not an animal overcome with a bestial urge. He does not rip the clothes from a woman's body and ravish her in public. He asks her about herself. He endeavors to interest and amuse her. When he concludes there is a possibility of mutual attraction, he employs direct but delicate methods of suggesting sex.

That is not to say that he has never practiced restraint. He has desired women who were already taken by another man he liked, respected or feared, or who were confidantes of his wife, or whom he's solely encountered in the close company of his wife. In such cases, he consigns himself to the misery of continence.

It must be understood that his compulsion is more complex than simple sexual release. He gains far greater satisfaction from the pursuit and conquest of a novel desirable woman than from sex with his familiar desirable wife. It is not even the nature of the sex act itself: for the most part he does not act with extramarital partners differently from how he acts with his wife, and for the most part they do not perform with markedly greater alacrity or aptitude (or, for that matter, markedly less) than her, nor does the intimacy of "love" make the physical experience any more (or less) pleasurable for him. Novelty is the most intense sexual thrill: novelty of sexual partner. He compares the experience to unwrapping a present. The anticipation can be breathless.

HIS WIFE DREADS their circle inferring she does not arouse him sexually. Picture one occasion: she holds a gin in her hand, her eyes burn with fury, and she screams at him, "She'd better be gorgeous!" before sweeping out of the room. He's never invited his wife to elucidate this remark. The conclusion he's reached, forming the basis of the first rule of his adultery, is that it would help her to know that a mistress was so beautiful that any husband, however loving, would be tempted to be unfaithful. How many married men would reject the chance to go to bed with a magnificent beauty if they could be sure of getting away with it? Her remark also reflects the importance his wife places, even in betrayal, on matters of taste.

When she suspects his philandering, he will deliberately contract the period of time an affair might have lasted. Though he will always deny the accusation, his second rule recognizes it respects her sensitivities to assume a particular girlfriend is someone he could have been with only once. The more of a habit the subject forms with a mistress, the greater the challenge it poses to the uniqueness of his wife's position, which is a state of affairs both would regard with disapproval.

At the end of lengthy denials, or simply after a refusal to engage with her allegations, he will conclude that meeting the criteria of the first two rules will console her should she remain suspicious, but the reality remains unspoken between them: she has no proof of his philandering, nor does he have proof that she has no proof. He will never hurt or embarrass her by confirming his dalliances, not just to her but to anyone, which introduces the third rule.

Once his wife has exhausted herself trying to provoke a confession, she may say, "If *I* think there's something going on, who else does?" or "If I know" (bearing in mind she doesn't, for sure), "who else knows?" It is insufficient for his wife not to know—*nobody* must know. In the old days, he would be most content with women who had the most distant possible connection to his work, his family or his wife. The less they knew about him, the better. He kept many a girlfriend out of town who had only the vaguest idea of his identity, who would know nobody that could start a chain of gossip linking back to his wife. Even if he was open with the girlfriend, he could discount the probability of running into her at a social engagement in the company of his wife. This rule was the "nobody knows" rule, and he was never more secure in his philandering than when a mistress assumed he was single and childless, barely knew his name and therefore had no telling details to broadcast to anyone else, but now his new position makes it extremely unlikely a woman won't be familiar with the principal biographical facts.

Therefore, for the first time in his adult life, he must consider curtailing his sexual adventures, though he endeavors to convince himself there must be hope. Perhaps on foreign tours he will encounter moments of privacy with a willing secretary, or on the campaign trail with a discreet former girlfriend. But the machinations of adultery take their toll on one's concentration. While he regards the prospect of monogamy as one would a prison sentence, a man of his resilience must concede that it might require that he approach the coming years with the serenity of one facing internment, and find some solace in being spared the stresses of seduction, fornication and concealment under what will certainly be the most challenging of circumstances. While he's certain that the question of temptation will arise at some point, it is by no means predictable how he will answer it.

IN THE PAST, the subject has been an expert in concealment, yet he is not a conniving philanderer: he doesn't tell women that his wife doesn't understand him, or that she denies him sex, or that he's a doleful figure daily on the verge of suicide on account of being trapped in some loveless marriage from which only the willing tenderness of another female soul will save him. Instead he says simply that he has the best marriage practicable for a man like him, but that monogamy is quite impossible; he needs more, bigger, faster sex than decades with the same woman can ever provide, and, to the woman in question, the one before him whom he's aiming to seduce, he reveals that he has chosen her from all the others at the dinner or the party or the rally because she is the one whose sex lures him.

*"Altiora peto,"* he whispers: "I seek higher things." But no place exists in the seduction for the promise of an enduring affair, the office of mistress or the prospect that he will fall in love and divorce his wife. Surely all the indications must self-evidently point toward the contrary. Yet, to his dismay, often this woman cannot bear to see her delusions of romance remain unrealized. She threatens to tell his wife; she may threaten to sell her story to the press, but the newspapers have no interest in the private life of a public figure.

When the subject pursued an affair with an aide in his previous political post, the relationship was discovered by her pious land-lady, who subsequently launched a volley of letters on the subject to the press, even snapping a photograph of him leaving the apart-ment in the middle of the night. The lady took the view that his appearance of being a devoted husband and father was a sham. Hers was the simplistic fallacy of the moral monogamist, but the gentlemen of the press never ran the story, showing the more so-phisticated understanding that there is no inherent contradiction between loving one's wife and child and keeping a mistress.

Making love with Pamela, the aide, a couple of nights a week didn't discourage him from treating his wife and daughter with love and tenderness. In fact, as his irrepressible urges enjoyed an outlet, his wife and daughter were spared the short temper of the frustrated male, and certainly there was no question of the girlfriend suffering in the slightest, apart from the inconvenience of the move when she wisely sought a new apartment, and subsequently he arranged a new appointment for her (as his wife's Press Secretary).

That affair occurred at the time he and his wife were attempting to start a family, soon after they settled into their marital home in Georgetown. Sex shrunk to a medical process; the deed had to be done, so to speak, rather like pulling a tooth. By comparison, the successful experience of lust is abundantly invigorating, though he did receive his therapeutic courses with extreme circumspection for the sake of his wife's fragile emotional condition, and they successfully produced their daughter at the end of the following year. She was handed to him bundled inside a blanket, and he cradled her at his wife's bedside, this tiny crying thing more animal than human.

On a tranquil sea, he had sailed across an invisible equator and would remain oblivious till the moment he changed course: only then would his compasses spin, only then would he realize he was lost. He broke off with Pamela and resisted other temptations. His fear lay in the uncertainty of how his wife, now a mother, now the apex of their little triangle, would regard his independent personal ventures, and whether this successful transcendence into family life would galvanize her into adopting a less capitulatory position. At times it felt like his life had been taken over by a creature who could only communicate by crying. And there was also the baby. He had grown wearily accustomed to the occasional instances wherein his wife's suspicions seethed into a crisis of anguish and insecurity, but now he feared the prospect of their daughter being yanked into these melodramas. Yet he needn't have worried, because in the end such anxieties played more tellingly on his wife, who foresaw that, though the necessity to protect and provide for their daughter fell on both of them, she was the one who had in larger measure surrendered her independence. After her parents' divorce, her mother found herself seeking remarriage as the sole means of restoring domestic stability to her children's lives. She would only be forced to pursue elsewhere the comfort and security the subject provides (in addition to social standing and companionship), with the possibility that the new man would be a less loving father to their daughter and perhaps even possess the same vices as the subject, if not greater ones.

This deduction did not wholly deliver him from fear. He became unusually tense, convincing his wife he was concealing a relapse of the back condition that had necessitated major surgeries three years earlier and which augured incapacity, plus the abrupt termination of his ambitions for higher office. Although the true cause of his irritability was the caesura in his womanizing, he would regard the prospect of losing the capacity to vent his sexual impulses with the same despair as he would losing the ability to walk.

While his daughter captivated him, he was becoming resentful of his life condensing into a suffocating matrix. Fidelity was making him a worse husband and father than when he was philandering, to the extent that he feared becoming as austere to his child as his own mother had been to him, and therefore some months following the arrival of their daughter he resumed his customary pursuit of additional sexual partners, discovering to his utmost relief that he could continue in this vein under the same conditions as prior to his daughter's birth. He could be an object of greater constancy in his daughter's life by virtue of the freedom not to be a constant presence in their home every night and every weekend, and a greater support to his wife because he no longer resented her as one resents a prison warden. Monogamy and parenthood were invented by moral authorities to sublimate the male sexual urge, but in his case the effect resembles pressurizing a gasoline tank.

Today he would regard theirs as an exceptionally happy family. Their daughter enjoys the love of two parents, the comfort of a secure home, and the constant attention of a doting father. When he looks back at those first moments he held his daughter, he realizes what he experienced was impotence, in the form of a repression of his freedom to fornicate, but resilience has won through: he did not desert his responsibilities to his family, nor did he destroy himself in the slow, withering bitterness of monogamy. Free from the dread and resentment of three years ago, he is able to welcome the birth of their next child.

HIS WIFE GOES into labor three weeks early. On account of her obstetric history, the doctors take no chances and deliver the baby, a boy, by emergency cesarean section. Named John after his father, their son appears healthy, but as a precaution due to his prematurity he is placed in an incubator. His mother remains in the operating room while his father trails the pediatricians, the boy cradled by a nurse, and then the father gazes at the son as he is sealed inside the warm glass box, where he wriggles and howls, a pink quiver of life. When the subject returns to his wife, they share tears of joy; the families gather, and soon the hospital is inundated with gifts for their son, toys and clothes, bouquets for his wife, from friends, celebrities and dignitaries.

The subject's visits to the hospital represent the first normal social encounters since the election two weeks ago. A few months earlier, he would have appeared a man of some distinction, but no one would have known his name, even if the face appeared somehow familiar. Now people respond to him in quite a different manner. They are nervous; they stumble over their words; they blush when he looks at them; some, he worries, go out of their way to avoid him, while others slink into nooks to watch as he marches within a phalanx of crew-cut bodyguards.

Naturally he's curious about the women. A year ago he would have anticipated a certain reaction. He's come to appreciate that he wears the demeanor of an alpha male. He stands just over six feet tall, with a tanned complexion that conveys rude health and sharply tailored suits that flatter his trim physique. He is blessed with thick, light-brown hair, in contrast to the grey heads and receding hairlines of many men his age. It is no vain posturing but a self-evident fact that he is a physically attractive man for his age, and exceptionally so for his status.

In the past, he could have expected some nurse to glance admiringly as he strolled by, or to smile if he caught her eye, or even to flirt a little bit if he happened to engage her in conversation, but today none of them show any such signs, instead dropping their eyes like Victorian servants if he so much as glances in their direction. A gulf has opened. He has become remote from women, an austere figure with whom sex is unattainable, and in these first encounters of this newest phase of his career as a philanderer, he experiences a plunging despair, not only because he is never unwatched, but from the realization that the nurses of Georgetown University Hospital must stand for all women the nation wide in that it appears not one would dare abandon her obeisance and go to bed with the newly elected President of the United States.

# THE GULF

O N ACCOUNT OF the cesarean section, the doctors advise the First Lady–to-be to avoid activity that might strain her abdomen, and, though the President-elect is deeply grateful for the well-being of his wife and newborn son, the resumption of marital sexual relations is denied. Throughout his adult life, the subject has become accustomed to regular sex, interrupted only by illness and service at sea. While we can debate the definition of "normal" activity, there can be no dispute over the subject's habitual promiscuity, and therefore abstinence constitutes a dramatic change in his sexual routine.

Since his late teens, the subject has suffered toxic accumulations. Clearly it is a simple matter to achieve release single-handed, but he does not obtain much gratification from this practice. Afterward his spirit is withered by shame at a man of his age and status indulging in these tawdry acts instead of seducing a living, breathing woman. Seduction is a far more stimulating experience and thereby a more cleansing act of release.

As his wife's convalescence continues, the denial of a sexual outlet challenges the subject's emotional and psychological well-being. Within a few short weeks, the subject becomes depressed. First his prostate, already chronically inflamed following multiple venereal infections in his youth, grows tender from retained juices. He feels weak, and day after day a headache builds. His endocrinologist notes a tremor and a drain of energy, so he suggests increasing the subject's cortisone dose and adjusting his thyroxin prescription. It is important that the President-elect appears energetic and vigorous at all times, so he complies with the physician's instructions, swallowing pills morning and night in an effort to replace the natural flow of hormones his body is unable to produce as a result of Addison's disease and an underactive thyroid gland. Replacement steroids cause water retention, making his face swell, so he calls Dr. J., a physician his wife nicknamed "Doctor Feelgood," whom they've been consulting since last year, and the good doctor prescribes amphetamines, which boost the subject's energy without the side effects he experiences from cortisone, conveniently leaving a supply of syringes and vials so he can self-administer shots to counteract the episodes of listlessness that overtake him in the afternoons following long and demanding meetings.

The closed sessions in such meetings allow him to focus on work, but there are women everywhere. Today he glimpses a pretty secretary through a doorway, sitting at her desk, lifting a telephone to her ear, and the idea appeals to him of strolling out at the end of the meeting and finding a quip to make her smile, after which her hand might run self-consciously through her hair, while he watches the sway of her breasts; she'd recognize his need, and perhaps eventually submit in a closet someplace, letting his hands work open the buttons of her crisp, white shirt. But she remains at her post, lost in the halls of his transitional offices, the

President-elect gazing at her across an impassable gulf. And, though he is alone, he is never alone, not for a single minute, as even in his office he is under surveillance by the Secret Service agents, and the casual opening of conversation with anyone, let alone an attractive young woman, is consigned to his past. His secretary used to leave spaces in his diary for assignations, but now it is only crammed with political appointments.

Today's meeting concerns an island nation and its anti-American dictator against whom his predecessor struggled but never triumphed, thereafter approving a scheme to overthrow the new regime by plotting an invasion, though at this juncture he's unable to influence progress to any significant extent, a power he will only acquire on taking office next month.

Just as the President-elect looks ahead to that day with anticipation, his daughter is excited in the way only a three-year-old can be, and her parents stress that helping her baby brother settle in will be a role of national importance, with the hope that this shameless favoritism will somehow compensate for his arrival overshadowing her birthday only two days later, since when she has veered between curiosity and jealousy for her infant sibling. She worries, for example, that her father will no longer read her bedtime story, to which he assures her that he will continue, though his new job means that he might not be free to do so every night, but on those nights that he is free she will hear two stories to make up for missing out. Later her questioning, which he regards as a far more challenging interrogation than the press ever mounts, branches into other areas of immediate concern regarding their move, such as, "Where will I play?"

The President-elect states, "I can assure the young lady that under my administration play will improve," but, more fearful of being caught out by this election promise than by any other, he instructs aides to make contact with the relevant people at the White House to ensure a room is converted into a play-room and to order the construction, at his personal expense, of some form of playground. When he receives confirmation that this will indeed happen as forecast, he breaks the news to his daughter with great pride, before proceeding with her bedtime story.

As she receives her goodnight kisses, she peers up curiously at his face and brushes her fingers on his cheek before he stands back in embarrassment, and he still feels his daughter's curious touch as he and his wife ensure their son is sleeping soundly in the neighboring bedroom. The President-elect stands over John Jr.'s cot, gazing down at him, touching his own cheek as their daughter did to explore its unnatural fleshiness and praying that his children do not inherit his curse.

The side effects of the increased cortisone dose include re-tained fluid, which puffs out the subject's jowls so he remarks that he resembles "Philipon's cartoons of King Louis-Philippe metamorphosing into a pear." He feels ugly but manages to joke with his secretary, Mrs. Lincoln, a middle-aged lady who's worked for him ever since his days as senator, that he wonders if the President's fat face can be grounds for postponing the inau-guration. "They say the camera adds fifteen pounds," he says, "and with the number pointed at me that day I'll look like the Graf Zeppelin."

Mrs. Lincoln laughs. "Just so long as it isn't the *Hindenburg,* Mr. President," she says.

Long ago the subject could have chosen to make his ailments an alibi for ambition, but instead he has chosen concealment, for in overcoming them without pleading special treatment he has earned the right to be considered the fit, healthy, vigorous man he appears, while the truth would merely be exploited by opponents and doubters to bar his entry to office, reverting him to the lonely little boy reading history books in his sickbed while the other children got to run and play in the fresh air.

Similarly he presumes he's not one of those men bound to soldier on to a ripe old age, given that his health has continued to deteriorate, with his back becoming increasingly tender and inflexible, his bowels prone to bouts of bellyache and bloody diarrhea, and his body in general exhibiting greater signs of Addison's disease, as exemplified by his Palm Beach tan, which in certain lighting doesn't capture quite enough brown to hide the yellow tinge. The reason he sought the presidency in his early forties, when his youth has been a disadvantage, is that his doctors cannot predict his physical state in four or eight years' time. Ever since the mixed results of spinal surgery, the prospect of relentless deterioration has hung over him, and on days when the condition is so severe that he needs a painkilling injection every six hours to spare being crippled by discomfort—on days like those he recognizes the possibility that it might not be many years before he's wheelchair-bound, paralyzed, incontinent and impotent, and given that he cannot alter the future, he must derive as much as possible from the present in regard to the pleasures of physical capability.

But, rather than his denial of infirmity giving license to romp though the wet grass, he commits himself to a schedule of meetings stretching from morning till evening. The President-elect aims to assemble a court of the best and brightest in the land: to slow down, to take a long lunch and then spend the afternoon in a warm bath unlocking the seized hinges of his back might mean he would miss out on one of those brightest and best, as would the country, so in this cause he invites intellectuals, historians, economists and more to his transitional offices or calls them personally, sounding the same clarion call to each, that he intends to use his time in office to establish a partnership between the world of power and the world of thought, since the men who create power make an undeniably important contribution to the country's greatness, but the intellectuals who question power can make a contribution just as important, as they can help determine how that power is used. Soon the word is out: the drab, grey days are fading and spring is coming, a spring in which the most colorful flowers can bloom: and even the most cynical in the universities and corporations feel the pull toward public service, a sensation they've never experienced before, but one the President-elect has borne all his adult life, which now climbs toward its zenith. One after another these men feel the pull, and they join.

THERE ARE WOMEN in the workplace, and the smart ones realize a woman's sex can overcome even the most powerful man, that in fact the two attributes, female beauty and male power, are often an equal and felicitous match. He would imagine there must be some of those secretaries who believe they've got enough to tempt him into bed, if only he could get through the phalanx of bodyguards to send a secret signal that he is not a tedious monogamist.

He welcomes an assignation being initiated by the woman; in fact, he regards a moment of eye contact, a smile, or a greeting to constitute "initiation." Equally the subject is not at all reticent about being first to suggest sex: ordinarily it is his modus operandi. But he finds himself imprisoned. Sexual toxins circulate in spiraling abundance, causing headaches, nausea and muscle spasms, and the occasional sight of a physically appealing woman releases a spigot somewhere inside that pours more of the effluent into the subject's system, inflaming his already inflamed genital tubing, so that his prostate surgeon prescribes him a short course of antibiotics to ward off infection of the urinary tract, while Dr. Feelgood advises him the best remedy is ejaculation, not through facile masturbation, but through the process of full sexual intercourse with a stimulating partner, as the only certain method of releasing the suppurating juices that have been accumulating for weeks without remission.

Dr. Feelgood is alone among the subject's physicians in comprehending that the subject is experiencing withdrawal symptoms, an observation diagnostic of addiction.

THE PRESIDENT-ELECT AND the First Lady–to-be resume sexual relations, but what is a medical tonic for him is an insult for her, the cesarean scar remaining sore and her womb bruised, causing her to find the experience too uncomfortable to bear, so he must apologize and kiss her on the cheek, while she reassures him that she has not been injured, only suffering a transient discomfort, and he shuffles off of her and limps to the en-suite, where he discharges the suppuration before flushing with a bitterly ungratified pull of the chain.

One must wonder why his wife does not gently probe the subject's practices, and that is because the newspapers are not alone in maintaining decorum. Even between husband and wife, there remain grounds not to be trespassed; the subject never took a vow, marital or otherwise, to forgo privacy. Just as children will misbehave, men and women will have affairs: the trick is not to give them attention. A spouse shouldn't need to know what goes on in the privy, so he or she doesn't open the door, and ignores the noises.

He returns to bed unable to sleep, because the toxins are already reaccumulating, pounding his head and inflaming his back and bowels and tubing. It is the night before his inauguration, with heavy snow falling, an excuse to escape parading his steroidal face before the world, but he doesn't want an escape—he is ready to take office and begin the great work of his life. Before he slumbers, his mind, descending to unconsciousness, imagines a field of lights going dark, and then in his dreamlike state he realizes phrases from his predecessor's valedictory address are becoming confused, as he pictures the Old Bastard recalling his vision of our country as a thousand points of light. The Old Bastard floats on a podium, in some kind of auditorium filled with men in uniform, saying, "I am about to get on with the rest of my life," but then the image changes, like a TV changing channels, and he is seated in the Oval Office, his eyes probing a TV camera, saying, "We must guard against the acquisition of unwarranted influence, whether sought or unsought . . ." before he disappears in a fog of interference, while the President-elect wonders to whom he addresses this caution, if anyone, or if it is merely a message he has imagined. Then he sleeps, as the missiles in their silos sleep.

* * *

THE MORNING IS bright and freezing cold, with snow decking the capital, and up on the Hill the low winter sun blinds the masses, as the new President swears his oath:

> "I, John Fitzgerald Kennedy, do solemnly swear that I will faithfully execute the office of President of the United States, and will to the best of my ability, preserve, protect and defend the Constitution of the United States."

Coatless, he appears impervious to the weather, in contrast to the chill bones of old men who surround him, but in truth his furnace is fired by shots of painkillers, steroids and amphetamines as he addresses the crowd below the Capitol:

> "Let the word go forth from this time and place, to friend and foe alike, that the torch has been passed to a new generation. In the past, those who foolishly sought power by riding the back of the tiger ended up inside. The world is very different now. For man holds in his mortal hands the power to abolish all forms of human poverty and all forms of human life. And yet the same revolutionary beliefs for which our forebears fought are still at issue around the globe. Let every nation know, whether it wishes us well or ill, that we shall pay any price, bear any burden, meet any hardship, support any friend, oppose any foe, in order to assure the survival and the success of liberty.
>
> "To those nations who would make themselves our adversary, we offer not a pledge but a request: that both

sides begin anew the quest for peace, before the dark powers of destruction engulf all humanity. Let us never negotiate out of fear. But let us never fear to negotiate. Let both sides seek to invoke the wonders of science instead of its terrors. Together let us explore the stars, conquer the deserts, eradicate disease, tap the ocean depths, and encourage the arts and commerce. All this will not be finished in the first one hundred days. Nor will it be finished in the first one thousand days, nor in the life of this administration, nor even perhaps in our lifetime on this planet. But let us begin.

"The energy, the faith, the devotion which we bring to this endeavor will light our country and all who serve it—and the glow from that fire can truly light the world. And so, my fellow Americans: ask not what your country can do for you—ask what you can do for your country."

The crowd applauds, and the new President is attacked by an octopus of handshakes. One of them must be the Old Bastard— he was only a few feet away, on the podium—but, when the President scans the faces, he can't see the grey old man anywhere, so he has uttered his last and melted into history, a curtain of snow falling across him as it fell across his image blanked by interference on the TV screen in last night's delirium, and the President is escorted back to the motorcade, his sojourn in the open air having been all too brief. He would have liked to have walked back to the White House, but pain revisits his back as the anesthetic injections wear off, and nowadays he can only walk a hundred yards or so at most, so he bends into the limousine and the agent closes the door on the clear, cold air, which now turns to leather.

The President occupies a box, waving out through glass, but he feels a great sense of hope for his country and for himself. He believes the work carried out in the next few years will change the whole world for the better. He has an idea for an organization called the Peace Corps, which will give idealistic young men and women the chance to dedicate their skills abroad, to carry his message to the poor and dispossessed of the world that the great powers must hold out a hand not a gun, and perhaps he should have mentioned it in his address, but he's merely being jittery, because he knows the speech went well, and the First Lady smiles at him proudly as they glide along Constitution Avenue to their new home.

Later, in the Oval Office, secretaries unpack boxes while workmen maneuver his desk into place. His wife brings the children to see him, and he plays a game with his daughter that's a hybrid of hide-and-seek and peekaboo, Caroline being too young to obey the rules of the former and too old to be entertained by the latter, and then, when his wife says that she ought to take them away, he asks them to promise to return soon, because this office resembles yet another cell, another interior, and he wants them to have the run of the place so he doesn't feel so isolated. He places his arm round his wife's shoulders, kissing the side of her thick dark hair, smelling it, and gazing down at their son, whom she cradles.

The President's first executive order doubles the federal food ration to the poor, a secret promise made to himself when campaigning in West Virginia, where he and his wife were shocked by the sight of countrymen who appeared to live as if in the previous century or on an undeveloped continent, whose children brought home food from school to share with their hungry families. By the end of his first full day, he suffers dry eyes, a runny nose and a sore throat, triggered by his allergy to house dust, which customarily flares up quite severely during initial habitation of a new home or office, it being a straightforward matter to take antihistamines until his immune system becomes desensitized.

As the real work begins, the President discovers that the country really *is* in as big of a mess as he claimed in his campaign, so he orders his team of close advisors to compile a list of all the idiots, obstructionists and deadwood in every division of government, which the President dubs the "shit list," but soon the mandarins of intelligence and the military distract him with bulletins on their force of fifteen hundred exiled freedom fighters training to carry out an amphibious landing from which they will stir an uprising against the dictator of a certain foreign power. Naturally the President would like to see the downfall of every tyrant, and he possesses no obstructive affection for this particular republic, his days long gone of vacationing on the island for the purposes of gambling, whoring and screwing the Italian ambassador's wife (or was it the Spanish?), but he's equally opposed to the idea of our own military participating in the operation, given that his quest to win the respect of peoples of alien ideology has only just begun, and it would advance his cause not one jot to be seen interfering in the self-determination of a sovereign state with the odious violence of an imperialist, particularly given it's plain for the world to see that this particular dictator is better characterized as a thorn in America's flesh than a dagger through our heart.

But the Central Intelligence Agency and the Joint Chiefs of Staff are convinced the operation will be a surgical decapitation, after which the citizenry will gladly embrace the freedom with which it has been presented.

As the President sits in his rocking chair with a face waxen at the effort involved in concealing the agonizing spasms down his spine, he asks, "How do we know the people will welcome the postinvasion regime?"

The CIA Director says simply, "Why *wouldn't* they, Mr. President?"

Afterward the President struggles to his feet and presses his palms hard against the lower portion of his back brace as he attempts to arch rearward, but there is no relief, only unremitting pain, so he asks Mrs. Lincoln to contact the First Lady urgently, while he stumbles through to the small private study adjacent to the Oval Office, wherein his wife arrives a few minutes later to discover him prostrate on the floor struggling to untie the seam of his back brace.

She helps him release the brace, and then they pull down his pants to give a painkilling shot in each buttock, after which she kneads the hollows of his lower back, endeavoring to pry open the iron grip of muscle spasm, while he waits for the anesthetic to take effect.

Then he returns to work.

That evening, in the Residence, his wife insists he receive a visit from a doctor. Instead he summons two. Adm. B. advocates surgery as the only definitive treatment, followed an hour later by Dr. T., who declares surgery will almost certainly render the President a cripple. If one laid all the physicians in the world end-to-end, they wouldn't reach a conclusion, this being the subject's reason for being as promiscuous with doctors as he is with women. He goes to bed with painkillers, but wakes in the night, his back in spasm again, so he slides out onto the floor, trying not to raise a sound that might disturb the children sleeping in the next room, but the gasps of pain from stretching and bending wake his wife, who puts his favorite record on their old Victrola, the music turned down to a whisper, as she rubs muscles that are hard as the stone-cold floor underlying the bedroom carpet.

THE SUBJECT MET his future wife at a dinner party hosted by a mutual friend when he was a junior senator and she was employed as a roving camera reporter, an occupation that involved approaching strangers on the streets and in the meeting places of the capital, with the purpose of capturing their reactions to the lighter news stories of the day, which he purported to find admirable, as is only sensible when meeting someone for the first time who also happens to be a beautiful young woman, to which she responded that it was a temporary diversion, as she wished to pursue a career in serious journalism but her youth and good looks were obstacles to being taken seriously. "Then I'm certain to go far," he joked.

Her name, Jacqueline, she pronounced in the French style. She was intelligent but shy, a luminous presence that outshone everyone at dinner that night, so first he asked her for the asparagus and then for a date. They saw each other on and off for the next two years, during which he often worked evenings and weekends, while her wanderlust took her to Europe for a time, so their courtship was intermittent, weeks often elapsing between dates, though, when it got late in a bar somewhere, he'd fish a fistful of coins from his pocket and, despite frequently going home with some girl he'd picked up, there was only one woman he kept on calling, and one woman he ever seriously considered for the permanent position.

He lies face down, feeling her hands squeeze his flesh but blind to her expression, and remembers he could never be sure in the early months of their relationship whether she understood the depth of his compulsion, but even at that stage she must have capitulated to the fact, almost as if she expected it in a man like him, an expectation developed from her father's philandering, and possibly finding herself subconsciously attracted to a similar type. Whatever her reasons, she decided marriage was worth the risk of heartbreak, just as he now lies twisted in agony from an office he has craved but that rides him harder than fitter men.

She is the only woman he's let witness his vulnerability. Because he's suffered sickness all his life, he's been taken ill in the presence of girlfriends before, and there have been times when his back interrupted sex, sometimes with consequences that in retrospect were comical, but on those occasions, rather than admit his infirmity, he preferred to leave the girl believing she was to blame, unless she happened to be a particularly decent type, in which case the story of a back wrecked by a war wound might be acknowledged in a superficial sort of a way, rather like the fellow in *The Sun Also Rises*. Only the subject's wife is fully *au fait* with the complete extent of his infirmities, alone against the various members of his family who have witnessed his episodes over the years but no longer receive his intimacy, and alone against the various medical professionals who have come, scratched their heads, argued among themselves and done precious little, none ever quite grasping the whole story of this body lurching into premature decrepitude. Although no doubt she would wish for a husband blessed with rude health, his wife has learned to accept her lot, as has he. Where perhaps they might differ is that he would include his sexual proclivities within the spectrum of his physical stigmata. He can no more dispel his compulsively active libido than he can wish hormones from his adrenal glands.

In the morning, however, he must act as though his glands are pumping, his intestines carrying out pain-free digestion and his back providing solid support. The subject continues to suffer a mild allergic reaction to the dust and dander of his new surroundings, stimulating a dry cough that particularly troubles him in the evenings.

At 7 A.M. he enters the family dining room in the Residence, where they breakfast together; he explains to their daughter he was unable to read her a bedtime story last night because of work but makes it up by walking hand in hand with her along the West Colonnade, where she spends a few minutes exploring the Rose Garden, excitedly crunching tiny shoe prints into the frosty lawn, and then they continue into his office, where the acts of concealment begin, as the steroids, painkillers and amphetamines flooding his system permit him to project an image of vigorous health. He allows Caroline the run of the Oval Office while he finishes reading the newspapers, then he lifts her up onto his knee to kiss her bye-bye before the nanny conveys her back to the Residence, so he can study the latest set of documents relating to the invasion.

The Joint Chiefs of Staff of the Army, Navy, Air Force and

Marines troop into the Oval Office, followed by the Director of the CIA and his Chief of Operations, to give a progress report.

The President says, "The code name Bumpy Road sounds unwelcomely prophetic, gentlemen. I wonder if this is some form of reverse psychology on the part of the CIA, and in future I can expect to be advised of Operation Abject Failure and Operation Political Suicide."

They chuckle, and then continue to persuade the President that the surgical excision of the dictator will be a great success.

The President asks, "How many men do you estimate he can mount in a counterattack?"

"Twenty-five thousand, Mr. President," answers the Director of the CIA.

"Mr. Dulles, it doesn't take Price Waterhouse to figure out twenty-five thousand against fifteen hundred amounts to pretty good odds for him and pretty rum ones for us."

The Director describes how the invasion will lead to a popular uprising, yet the President treats his argument with the same suspicion he regards the term "military intelligence," the most mordant oxymoron in the idiom of government, because the CIA and the Joint Chiefs are cut from the same cloth as the men who killed his elder brother, a pilot blown to smithereens flying a mission carrying an explosive payload primed with a hair trigger that could be tripped by a bump of turbulence, who equally resemble the generals and admirals who prosecuted the war in the Pacific, safe ashore, pursuing strategies that caused thousands upon thousands of needless casualties, among them the crew of the President's own command, a torpedo boat ripped in half by a destroyer, ruining the President's back and drowning two of his men. Now the generals begin a discussion of exact numbers and how the uprising will unfold, while the President wonders if any of these men, despite the fruit salad splayed across their chests, has spent nights on the black ocean listening out for the rumble of vessels a hundred times your size, if any of these men have seen comrades consumed by fire. Their conversation halts abruptly, and the President surfaces from his reverie hearing his own fingers drumming impatiently on the arm of his rocking chair.

Alone again later, the President limps to the window and stretches his back, peering over the South Lawn toward the Washington Monument, tracking the vehicles sailing along Constitution Avenue, but he hears not a sound through the bulletproof glass, nor feels a breath of the wind that choreographs fallen leaves into a thousand dead hands waving.

At the end of each working day, the President leaves the door into his secretary's office ajar as a signal he's available to the staff, and through the gap he observes his Press Secretary talking to an attractive young woman in the hall outside. Mrs. Lincoln presents the President with tomorrow's engagements for approval, and lastly she hands over some personal letters, one of which bears a sender's address they both recognize, though Mrs. Lincoln discreetly lays the envelope on his desk as if it carries no significance, the envelope remaining sealed unlike the rest of his mail, which she quite properly vets, then she withdraws to her office, shutting the interfacing door to grant privacy for the President to do what he will with the letter, which, after a moment's hesitation, is to open the envelope, to slide out a colorful card of "Good Luck in Your New Home!" with a short greeting on the back that appears to be written with lipstick and her name signed in the bottom right corner.

The President hasn't seen Marilyn since a few weeks before the election, initially giving her the excuse that he'd become too busy with the campaign, and thereafter being noncommittal when she telegraphed CONGRATULATIONS! which she followed by placing a call to his transitional offices, though it was never clear to him how she obtained the number, but obviously during that time he wasn't so busy that it would have been impossible to manufacture an assignation, either at Palm Beach or on the West Coast, instead the issue being the magnitude of Marilyn's celebrity and the concomitant challenges to a discreet liaison now he's been elected, the bittersweet irony being that, had he lost, he could have spent any number of blissful days in Beverly Hills screwing her brains out and no one would have cared a damn.

Truthfully he was seeking an exit, as she was beginning to resent her role in the chorus line of casual lays and wanted to audition for the lead, the prods, hints and neediness of which were becoming somewhat of a drag, climaxing with their assignation the night he secured the nomination, such that it was becoming quite the challenge for him not to appear as if he didn't really give a damn for her, which might sound incredible given her status as the country's foremost sex symbol, yet one of the lessons learned in a career of fornication is that one mustn't be intimidated by a woman's beauty, and certainly not by her overt sexuality, since the appearance of such is a clear statement of her insecurity. A woman like Marilyn is so accustomed to every man in the room wanting to sleep with her that she is imbalanced when they don't, becoming anxious that her face is no longer fresh or her figure no longer firm, to the point where one must tread the fine line between appearing to want to sleep with her while also appearing not so very desperate to.

In Marilyn's case, he found himself adept at striking this balance, for it has been his practice for many years now to treat every woman the same—with the obvious and magnificent exception of his wife. Moreover, it would appear that if one sleeps with one actress or model, it secures a pass to such encounters with their peers. These women receive so many advances in the course of their average week that their methodology for selecting the appropriate suitor appears to be fashioned from herd mentality, where what's good enough for one is good enough for all, and it is also possible that, once a man has secured a liaison with one of these starlets, the others regard him as a means by which to legitimize their status within the herd. Strict adherence to a policy of treating all women the same, however beautiful, necessitates the corollary of not appearing unduly diminished by the fact that one particular starlet or another proves impervious to his charm—or a political aide or a housewife, for that matter—because the smooth cogs of philandering turn on the grease of inconsequential encounters, the gears crunching if rejection is given undue importance. Instead each tooth must turn over in smooth rotation, he to the next model or aide or housewife, and the starlet, who regardless of their conversation has been scanning over his shoulder for the bigger, better deal, to her next sugar daddy.

None of this invective should necessarily be construed as a description of Marilyn, certainly not in her current incarnation, having been a starlet ten years ago but long since having surpassed the diminutive (in any sense of the word), and, on that evening in Los Angeles last July, when, having secured the Democratic nomination to seek the presidency, the subject addressing eighty thousand supporters in the Coliseum, it was abundantly clear there was no bigger, better deal in town. His wife was unable to fly to the convention, in accordance with medical caution regarding her pregnancy. His unaccompanied status ordinarily affords an opportunity to call up some old girlfriends and find a couple of new ones, but the intense, round-the-clock workload of horse-trading old votes and campaigning for new ones took precedence, so that he found himself in that dangerously vulnerable state of being alone in a hotel room late at night, ingesting painkillers with whiskey shots, each day growing more tired and more horny, till fortunately he encountered a coed volunteer: later, in private, taking her by the hand, she responded eagerly to the signal, after which he unzipped his fly and apologized that, owing to the convention schedule, there wasn't time for foreplay.

The invigorating effect of her company was short-lived, however, and he continued to tire, to the extent that he became less forceful in his delivery on the convention floor, this weariness being an intractable problem at that time, prior to receiving the services of Dr. Feelgood, a problem irrecoverable by the roar of the crowd or the excitement of the occasion, since the adrenal surge that his rivals experience never visits him, so instead he relied on the sluggish metabolic shove of cortisone tablets, and in victory he was as much drained as elated, the ascent to the podium sapping his final reserves, whereupon, at a celebration thrown by mutual friends, Marilyn made a surprise appearance and in the possessiveness of her first kiss he understood she regarded his victory as hers too, and, though he should have known better, the subject was in no condition to resist. When a man grows accustomed to a woman sexually, he takes her for granted, beautiful or not, sex symbol or not, and, by virtue of his strict adherence to a policy of not being dazzled by her, he should not be blind to the reason for dumping her, which, in Marilyn's case, was simply that she was the most photographed woman in the land and he was seeking election to its highest office.

But, now, in reading her card, he strives to recall that body, that face, those lips, feeling a surge of desire and curiosity as one would in discovering buried treasures. Though he doesn't generally forget the loot he's uncovered, as time passes, the memory becomes less vivid—less vivid visually but not semiotically—so that he can still ascribe the attribute but can't quite picture it: the sharpness of her cheekbones, say, when he associates cheekbones with her beauty or the trimness of her stomach when he recalls her athletic figure, perhaps because these memories reside in the primitive pathways of his brain, where they made their first impression, and over a period of absence then a reversion occurs toward their first encounter when, in noticing the girl's breasts or her rear, he felt that first surge of desire and curiosity. With Marilyn, although he does not deny being motivated partly by the challenge of bedding a sex symbol, an entry underlined on any womanizer's curriculum vitae, irrespective of how good a lay she was per se: notwithstanding this consideration, the surge he felt in that moment of first meeting and later that moment of first intimacy was still the commonplace desire to explore what lay beneath the surface, but now, as he holds the card in his hand bearing her lipstick greeting, those wondrous discoveries have faded to a dim library of volumes he's eager to reopen, once more bathed by a gush that ignites his inflamed tubing.

IN THE HALL, he sees the pretty young aide again, advancing with a file of papers from the direction of the Press Staff offices, so he smiles and says, "Pierre's working you too hard," to which she blushes and halts in the guilty embarrassment of being caught by the hall monitor, while, presumably on hearing the President's voice, the agent stationed outside his office turns to check to whom he's talking and, hearing his name uttered by the President, the Press Secretary ventures out from his office, all of which causes the President to respond with embarrassment that propels him swiftly through the most immediate exit, the Fish Room (so named as President Roosevelt kept an aquarium here, and the President continues the tradition with a stuffed ten-foot sailfish he hooked off Acapulco—on his honeymoon, an auspice of bountiful catches untrammeled by married life), wherein he finds himself in yet another box, with yet another erection, contemplating how he's fallen from a man who's lain with goddesses to one forbidden to utter two words to an intern.

The subject has not suffered this degree of sexual abstinence in twenty years, causing headaches, nausea, diarrhea and urinary inflammation. That evening he hosts a diplomatic reception, with the First Lady resplendent in a new ball gown, charming as ever toward their guests, after which she helps him off with the back brace in their bedroom. He swallows two painkillers, plus his nightly cortisone dose, an antibiotic and a sleeping tablet, the last prescribed by Dr. T. because it also bears muscle relaxant properties. He brushes her belly but she winces, then she kisses him goodnight and rolls over to sleep, while he lies awake, coughing.

In the morning he's desperate for fresh air, his clothes reeking of liquor and cigar smoke from last night's reception, but he trudges along the West Colonnade hand in hand with his daughter, where she asks why the pond at the foot of the South Lawn, which has risen with melting snow, is not home to any ducks, because she remembers feeding the ducks when they lived in

Georgetown, but what she doesn't like about her big new house is that the ducks have gone away, so, after he's kissed her bye-bye, he asks Mrs. Lincoln if they can't get some ducks for the pond, to which she says, "What breed of ducks, Mr. President?"

"Ones that go, 'Quack,'" he says before proceeding into the Cabinet Room.

According to the CIA, the Joint Chiefs and some Cabinet members, a threat to national security is gathering abroad, in the form of dangerous and extremist ideology. They seem so strongly convinced the President begins to wonder if his toxemia has enslaved him to a delusion that the rationality of government has been usurped and the mice have taken over the experiment.

In the Residence that night, the President reads Caroline a bedtime story, while the First Lady tends to John Jr., who won't settle, and, once he's finished the story, the President goes to his lad, grateful that he's awake so he can hold him while his wife kisses Caroline goodnight and turns out her light. The President carries John Jr. through to the Oval Room, wherein his wife sits on one of the central sofas and he slowly eases himself down into one of the chairs with a rigid, upright backrest, rocking the baby and letting him suckle his finger until he falls asleep, after which the President and the First Lady take supper in the dining room, the First Lady enjoying a glass of sauvignon with their meal, then a cigarette.

After dinner, the press aide returns to the President's thoughts, leading him to fantasize he is back in his previous life, where such issues could be addressed so simply. He would send an invitation through the Press Secretary for the staff to come for drinks at a comfortable bar nearby, at which he would make the acquaintance of them all equally, thereafter grouping with the senior males, a calculation to project to his target the boisterous humor of a man's man combined with vividly comparing the superior physical attributes—height, trim figure, lush hair—of the alpha male, only later in the evening involving her in direct conversation, first by noting some good work she has carried out, then asking her about herself, then making physical contact to gauge whether she might be receptive to an advance, and finally, as he drinks little on such occasions (liquor inflames his stomach lining, causing severe heartburn and peptic ulcers), he will offer to drive her home. Usually, to spare the mutual embarrassment of ending the evening on a rejection, he will signal his sexual interest before they get in the car or, at the latest, before he walks her up to her apartment, with the final proviso being that in prior exchanges he has ascertained her domestic arrangements in case he needs to borrow a colleague's apartment or check them in to a hotel. But such an evening is denied—the presidential motorcade snaking back to a Georgetown apartment block at midnight would hardly allow for a discreet assignation—so the subject suppresses thoughts of the pretty young press aide and retires in a delirium of frustration.

IN THE MORNING Caroline wakes to a surprise: instead of their customary walk along the colonnade to the West Wing, they stroll across the South Lawn to the pond, leading her mother who conveys her baby brother in a stroller, where she is delighted to discover a small colony of ducks, and, to add to her delight, the President produces from his pocket a bag of bread bits. She feeds the ducks while John shifts snugly in his chariot, and, when the President returns to the Cabinet Room, some of the members are already discussing how the invaded land can be carved up into lucrative contracts for American corporations.

Toxemia keeps bubbling in the President's head and gut and back and bladder. His dry cough is keeping him awake at night. He lays out a rainbow of pills and ingests medication to dull the headaches and quell the inflammation, but gets no relief. The next morning delirium fogs his perception of the generals; he cannot distinguish the elephant of analysis from the tiger of advocacy. A woman crosses the hall as he walks out of the Cabinet Room with his advisors, and for a moment he contemplates what it might cost him to follow her into an office and draw the blinds. Instead he spends the afternoon in closed meetings with senior officials, but not one is opposed to the idea of invasion, not one believes it will be anything other than a resounding success, and so he gives the order for the army to cross the Gulf.

# THE FIRST LADY

ALMOST AT ONCE the news from Cuba is bad. The popular uprising does not occur, and, despite his delirium, the President is first to comprehend why. He is much traveled, like the military commanders, but they have only seen the world from a bunker, steadfastly incurious of foreign culture and ignorant of contrary ideology. Cultures will not bend painlessly, and Americanism cannot be exported like Coca-Cola.

Cuban aircraft begin bombing the beaches, destroying the ship carrying ammunition, while tanks and infantry surround the freedom fighters, so the President orders a further air strike from Nicaragua covered by unmarked U.S. Navy jets, but no one coordinating the operation appreciates that the jets fly from a different time zone than the strike bombers, so the bombers cross the Gulf of Mexico an hour before their cover and are shot down.

Throughout this time, day into night and back into day, the President cannot be still, cannot sleep, because those men are pinned down on the beach being blown to bits. The President calls off the invasion, ordering the men to save themselves by dispersing into the mountains to live to fight another day.

A ghastly silence descends on the Oval Office.

"What's the matter with you?" the President says. "Send those men into the mountains!"

Mr. Dulles clears his throat nervously. He says, "The mountains are too far away."

"How far?" the President demands.

The Director says, "The Brigade would have to cross swamps, they're under fire—"

*"How far?"*

"Eighty miles."

The President can barely speak, he can barely look at the CIA or the Joint Chiefs or any of them, and, swallowing a gob of vomit that leaps into his throat, he waves them away, out of the room, so he can lean against the desk for support, in case he falls, because those insane, incompetent bastards have done what they've always done, only this time he's the one who gave the order, he's the one who's condemned brave men to death in some ill-conceived, ill-planned escapade, and he is so fearful he'll choke he steps out into the Rose Garden.

His back throbs. His cough set in at midnight and now his ribs ache from hacking. Agents watch him from the colonnade as he paces the garden, giving the appearance that he's stretching and exercising, but in truth he's struggling for air, choked by the fumes of murder on an industrial scale, poisoning his kidneys and adrenals and gut and bladder, and he tastes the sting of it in his tears.

He can't sleep. He intends to explore all the options that exist for saving those men. His aides and advisors say the same thing as the CIA and the Joint Chiefs: "Escalate." He refuses. Invasion won't save those men now; it will only cost more lives.

Eventually he returns to the Residence, where his family lie asleep. He lingers beside the children's beds, reaching out to touch their skin and their hair but stopping himself, stifling his cough, for fear of waking them, but grateful they are alive, grateful they are safe, and not being blasted like those Cuban sons and brothers on the beach condemned to death or imprisonment. Then he swallows more painkillers, steroids, antihistamines and sedatives, promising himself every single one of those mad, murderous chiefs will be gone from their jobs in the coming weeks and months.

After three hours' fitful sleep, he wakes almost unable to move. His back is so stiff that his wife and a nurse are needed to maneuver him out of bed, yet at the press conference that morning he stands and states: "I'm the responsible officer of the government. Victory has a hundred fathers but defeat is an orphan. I bear sole responsibility. I am strongly opposed to anyone within or without the administration attempting to shift responsibility."

The President returns to his office, where he stares past the Washington Monument at dense white clouds scudding through the blue spring sky. He tries the latches on the patio doors, but they seem to be jammed. The effort of attempting to release them summons the two agents stationed on the colonnade, whom he waves away, turning from the windows rather than press on out into the Rose Garden and be a spectacle.

Later the President is shocked to learn that members of the Cuban Revolutionary Council, a committee of exiles who would have formed the new government and some of whom had sons in Brigade 2506, are being kept under house arrest by the CIA, on the basis that they are a "disposal problem." The President orders their immediate release and transfer to Washington, where he meets with them personally in the Oval Office. By now it is late into the next night, as they sit on the sofas and he in his rocking chair, in constant motion to ease his back and with a fist to his mouth to stifle his cough.

The President says, "The operation was my decision. I am very sorry that it has failed, but the Brigade fought gallantly. Your sons were proud to fight for their country. I know you want to know why I didn't commit our forces to support them, and the reason is that, in the struggle against tyranny, I cannot be hypocritical; I cannot condemn our foes where they interfere in another state's self-determination yet expect the world to turn a blind eye when we do the same. It was not a decision I took lightly. I have fought in a war, and I have seen brave men die. My own brother was killed. I understand your pain. That is why I will send ships and aircraft to rescue survivors. But the last thing I say to you is this: you are all free men in this country—free to go wherever you want, free to say anything you want, free to talk to anyone you want. That is what your sons were fighting for, and you have those rights here, and one day soon I hope you will have them again in your homeland."

They leave, muted, mournful, and soon he's alone again, rocking, with the sun rising on a new day and his expectation that so much must have changed, so much goodwill has been depleted, his reputation rock-bottom, but the city appears the same, the faces in the halls the same, his little girl's ducks and his son's teddy bears. He passes the press aide in her first hour of work and asks her name, and, when she answers, she sounds almost embarrassed for him, prompting him to move on quickly, sick with this poison seething deep inside, though the criticisms of the operation, domestically at least, are milder than he fears, some even laudatory, making him think he's already emulated his predecessor, in that the worse he does the more popular he gets. The cycle of government continues—meetings are scheduled, conferences, public appearances, pros and cons balanced and decisions made—but the President cannot shift the images of those men on the beach, the din, the screams, the blood and blast of it all, then the fall of night, dark and choked with terror, before it all begins again. He realizes his aides are staring at him, in a meeting, just a handful of them in the Oval Office, where he faces what appears to be an embarrassing silence.

"You spoke, Mr. President," one of them explains.

"Did I?" he says.

The President has no recollection of uttering a word, but, after the others have left, the Defense Secretary says, "You were thinking aloud, Mr. President."

"What did I say, Bob?"

"You said, 'How can I have been so stupid?'"

Only a few days have passed since the fiasco, but already the indicators of failure seem blatant in retrospect. The President hears rumors that some lobbyists had been counting on a limitless bounty for their corporate interests in a newly annexed Cuba (after they've first won contracts to clear up the rubble and the corpses). While some parties do appear to lament the President bungling the chance for a lucrative victory, others remain optimistic another opportunity will present itself in short order.

Meanwhile the President wanders the halls between meetings, from his office to the Cabinet Room and the Fish Room. Mrs. Lincoln becomes concerned about these lonesome interludes in his schedule and ensures that meetings are scheduled back-to-back so his mind can't wander toward its shameful self-interrogation. Pretty soon the only time the subject is alone is for his midday swim, the water heated to ninety degrees in an effort to relieve his back, and in the restroom, which is becoming a source of considerable embarrassment. The President has been ingesting large doses of Lomotil to control the diarrhea that afflicted him severely during the invasion, with the result that now, following a return to more normal hours and stress levels, he is severely constipated, for which he's prescribed Metamucil by Dr. T., with painful abdominal cramping, for which Adm. B. is giving Bentyl, but, in spite of frequent, long visits to the head, which do not go unnoticed by Mrs. Lincoln and the Secret Service, the President feels unable to expel the blockage, a situation compounded by a recent exacerbation of urethritis and prostatitis, both of which make urination excruciatingly painful (the subject is on penicillin from Dr. T. and Furadantin from the Admiral), so he voids as infrequently as possible, the resulting condition now being one of great discomfort, particularly when seated, whereby his full bladder presses on his inflamed prostate and also on his loaded bowel, which swells against his sensitive lower spine.

When Dr. Feelgood pays a visit, he prescribes various tonics for the President's back and bowels before making a direct enquiry about sex. "Are you enjoying normal activity, Mr. President?" he asks in his accent.

"Who's to say what's normal?" the President answers.

The doctor says, "A subject accustomed to frequent sexual activity may suffer drastic psychological withdrawal. Concentration and judgment may be severely impaired."

The sense of choking follows the subject in an invisible cloud, when he's with his wife, with his children, when he plays golf, unable to concentrate so he tops shots that skip through the grass menacing field mice. When he gets into bed with his wife, he embraces her, and the sorrow for those men dampens his eyes before she tells him everything will be all right, but she can't share his nightmares because she's never seen a man die, never seen a head explode right beside her.

In the morning, he eats a bland breakfast high in fiber, yet still endures a painful, unproductive half-hour on the toilet before tackling his daily schedule, the pressure in his pelvis building till noon, when he's prescribed some additional pills to move his bowels, this new medication exerting no remedial effect, so that evening, after another low-taste, high-fiber meal, he smokes a cigar and imbibes three Bloody Marys, which have no influence except on his heartburn.

His direst complaint becomes headache. When troubled by the cough, the pressure in his skull becomes unbearable. He feels his hair roots being pushed out from the inside. The subject's condition fails to improve the next day, yet, as is his invariable practice, he lets no one in on his discomfort, so not even his physicians receive a full picture of his constellation of miseries, although Mrs. Lincoln notices the set of his jaw and the tightness around his eyes, which most of his aides assume result from the failed invasion.

Mrs. L. gently inquires whether the President feels in strong enough spirits to fly, as planned, to a West Coast dinner tonight, but it is an important occasion, the first official visit to California since the election. When she has returned to her office, he finds the card from Marilyn, filed in his desk, and slips it into his inside jacket pocket.

The President kisses his family goodbye, assuring his wife he's well enough to make the trip, before the Marine helicopter hops across to Andrews Air Force Base, where he boards the Special Air Mission Boeing for the flight west. The speech tonight follows a meal, and the President is wary of being seen in public to eat a restricted diet, so he consumes the steak just as everyone else does, though in his case he suffers a beef intolerance, which exacerbates his abdominal discomfort. The speech goes over well, and he attempts to relax with a cigar and a whiskey sufficiently to propel himself through the customary glad-handing and arm-twisting, then the Secret Service convey him to his hotel, two agents taking their stations outside his suite, while he suffers on the toilet for forty-five minutes. Afterward the President lies on the bed and consumes his nightly regimen of hormone replacers, painkillers, muscle relaxants, germ killers, bowel movers and stomach pacifiers, till his blood simmers with chemicals.

The hour approaches midnight, but he can't sleep. His sinuses feel blocked, something that occurs regularly when he sleeps in a new place, even though it's mandatory for the presidential suite to have been intensively vacuumed of every particle of house dust and any pillows or mattresses containing feathers to have been replaced, the sinusitis and cough and tightness in his chest simply being the result of the indigenous dander of the environment. He puts the light back on and hears the agents come to attention outside the door. The President limps to the bathroom, where he fears he's going to regurgitate the steak dinner, but nothing comes up save a sickly taste. He summons his valet to run a scalding bath, the steam misting the mirrors and chrome of the bathroom, then the President slides under the water, which turns his skin pink and prickly, and here he lies for almost an hour, regularly reheating the water himself with a burst from the hot tap, yet experiencing only minor relief, so, in the end, alone, he struggles out of the water and towels off, returning to his bed from where he studies the agents' movements that break the slit of light at the foot of the door. He goes out in a sweater and slacks and tells them, "I need some air."

"Please hold, Mr. President, while I call that in."

"Just some fresh air," he says.

"Of course, Mr. President, but you understand our orders are to notify your movements."

"I've changed my mind," he says.

"I'm sorry, Mr. President, it'll only take a few minutes to call it in."

"Please don't take any trouble."

The President shuts the door and returns to one of the beds, where his head feels ready to explode. He makes up his mind, and dials a number. There are six or seven rings before she answers in a sleepy voice, then he says, "It's me."

"Jack?"

"I'm in town."

"My God! Where?"

"The Beverly Hills."

"Shall I come over?"

"It's late."

"Tomorrow then?"

"I go back to D.C. tomorrow."

She says, "It's not so late to come over tonight. It's been too long, Jack."

Down the line, he hears her breathing. He pictures her mouth and wonders what she'll wear.

"Come on over," he murmurs.

The President paces his suite. He limps between the two bedrooms and then into the bathroom but is still unable to pass a motion. He puts on a clean shirt, and then a few minutes later he summons the agent and says, "An old friend is coming to pay me a visit."

"No problem, Mr. President, I'll just require his name and address so we can run the necessary checks. It should be all done in time for breakfast, sir."

The President hesitates. "My friend wants to come tonight."

"Tonight, Mr. President?"

"Very shortly, in fact."

The agent shifts uncomfortably. "I have to report to my captain, Mr. President. Visitors to the presidential suite must be given security clearance prior to arrival and that takes time, as you know, sir."

"Well, there isn't time."

The agent studies the President. The President bites his lip, on edge. "What would you like me to do, Mr. President?" the agent asks him.

"I'd be very grateful if you would just let her up," the President says.

The agent notes the feminine pronoun but, as to a backfiring car engine, he's trained not to react.

The President begins to pace the suite again. He has developed a fine tremor in his hands. He is tempted to call the whole thing off but takes a breath and states, "Yes. Please see to it she's let up."

Now the agent glances back toward the door, where his colleague remains stationed. The two men share a look, and then the agent by the door shrugs and returns to staring blankly along the hall.

"Mr. President, with respect, sir, we follow a security protocol with all visitors. This is most irregular, sir."

"I want to see her," the President says simply, with a hint of desperation.

The agent comes to attention. "Yes, Mr. President, I'll see what I can do."

"Relax," the President says. "I intend to search her thoroughly."

The agents don't relax, but Marilyn arrives about an hour later—fifty minutes in makeup, ten minutes in the taxi. The President hears her voice outside, being greeted courteously by the agents, with whom she flirts, and, as he opens the door, the President sees the agents snap back into their disinterested gaze.

The President helps Marilyn out of her mink and then fixes drinks. "It's great to see you," he says.

"It's great to see you, Mr. Pres-i-dent," she says, with a giggle.

"And you're my first lady," he says, though she misses his irony.

He glances at her blond hair and the heft of her breasts, and soon after he coughs his poison into her.

# THE MOON

IN HER TYPICAL needy fashion, Marilyn insists on coming to the airport to see off the President, his polite efforts to deter her making little impact, since she has perfected the heedlessness of the movie diva who only hears what she wants, even if it's bellowed at her through a megaphone. As her President, he commands her not to come to the airport under any circumstances—in fact, she must leave the hotel at once via a back exit. But she laughs, putting a finger to his lips before knotting his tie, promising that, if he prevails once more on the Secret Service to convey her under camouflage to the SAM, she will give him a memorable send-off.

He hesitates. Then he says, "How memorable?"

"Unforgettable!" she says.

The President arranges for her to motor in a separate vehicle and to be smuggled aboard the aircraft. She must conduct herself as if they have not been in each other's company the night before, claiming she has traveled out especially to discuss an important matter with the President before he departs for Washington. In a private cabin shielded from staff and crew, the President confronts the prospect of a return to constipation in its many excruciating forms, and succumbs once more to his libido's treacherous permeability, with the result that the airplane overruns its takeoff slot, delaying other traffic, until Marilyn emerges from the cabin and makes her exit, after which the Commander-in-Chief learns his aides have ascribed the delay to a presidential haircut.

"At least they didn't say I was getting a blow-dry," he mutters.

Once the doors are sealed and the SAM lifts off, the President rejoices in a clear head and sinuses and a pain-free stomach and tubing. He sips an orange juice at his customary window seat and attacks reports on the economy with renewed vim. The tense furrows around his eyes have softened, making him look five years younger. He flashes a smile at a stewardess who has flown the SAM many times before but never with the new President, and she blushes, struck by his bright eyes, his splendid hair and his tan. When he stands to join his aides for an airborne policy meeting, she offers to brush down the ruffles on his jacket.

"Would you mind hanging it?" he says, and she helps him off with it, stepping close enough to his back for him to get a whiff of her Chanel.

Last night he worried that, as he leant to kiss her neck, Marilyn would hold him off, exclaiming, "But I can't! You're *the President!*" When she did say it, it was afterward, with a coo of pride. And now, as he watches the stewardess's chewing-gum walk up the aisle to hang his jacket, he conceives his office as aphrodisiac.

AFTER THE MEETING, he retires to his cabin for a short nap. The President views the prospect of Marilyn ducking in and out of his life with a mortal kind of dread. Last night's tryst has turned him from a man stumbling through the desert dying of thirst into one who happened across a cocktail bar, but he is deeply concerned by the necessary breaches of privacy required to secure a completely gratifying assignation, having only succeeded in upholding two of his three rules of womanizing: one, that Marilyn is gorgeous enough to warrant the risk and, two, that their dalliance does not develop into a continuing affair (his definition of "continuing" being that both parties expect coupling to occur whenever the opportunity arises). The third, possibly most important, rule—and the one by which he has failed to abide—is that no one must know. In the past, he could enjoy a hotel-room encounter with a pickup and no one would notice her go in and no one log when she came out, but his position as President has put an end to the anonymity of traveling-salesman sex.

Because Marilyn is possibly the most familiar female face on the planet, it's of course impossible to go anywhere she is not recognized, so when they met during the Democratic National Convention last summer, there seemed no likelihood of concealment—in fact, such an approach would have aroused greater suspicion—so they dined openly together at Puccini's as if she were lobbying him about some Hollywood pet interest (animal welfare, let's say) and he were patiently indulging her. Even when he smuggled her into his limousine, it could be said he was merely acting the gentleman by dropping a lady at her apartment.

However, the facts of last night's assignation are that an unaccompanied female was admitted to the presidential suite in the middle of the night and didn't leave till morning, and suspicion would be equally uncomfortable whether the lady in question was a mousy secretary or, as she happened to be, the world's most stupendous sex goddess.

The extremely awkward conversation last night with the agent stationed outside his door brought back memories of smuggling girls into his room at Harvard, or in port, where one always ran the risk of encountering an earnest sentry and having to weigh friendly bribery against confident rank-pulling. But in those days, he was a tail-hound in a crew of tail-hounds, whereas last night, when Marilyn presented herself to his suite ready to be unwrapped from her mink, the President read the agent's expression, albeit carefully buried beneath the stone patio of professional disinterest, of betrayal of family, colleagues and voters. It was an unfortunate coincidence that the man on duty happened to be a moral monogamist, but, on the other hand, the President takes heart that his little adventure may have disabused friendlier parties of the fallacy that he's one too. When the stewardess brings his jacket, she slips it on and straightens the collar, expectant he will enjoy physical intimacy with a good-looking woman. He says, "See you on the next flight, I hope," and she replies, "I hope so too, Mr. President."

Whatever the consequences of his tryst, the President feels clearheaded and detoxified by the experience, allowing him to be lucid and decisive with his aides, most of whom deport themselves toward the President in precisely the same fashion as yesterday, which he interprets as proof they agree a man is entitled to his recreation whether he's a longshoreman on the Boston docks or the President of the United States.

THE SUBJECT AND his wife are reunited that evening. They conduct their children's bedtime ritual before sitting down to dinner together. Over the entrée, she remarks that he looks well, then later, over dessert, the same thing: "You're looking well, Jack."

He smiles but doesn't answer, and rather than searching her eyes for a glimmer of suspicion, he is smart enough to peer into the meniscus of his St. Émilion as he swirls the goblet and ask their staff for a petit corona. The First Lady lights her own filter cigarette, saying, "You must have gotten over Cuba."

"True," he says, blowing some fog, "but never their cigars."

The subject appreciates that sometimes the adulterer cannot help but be smug about his conquests. He enjoys the apocryphal tale of a man shipwrecked on a desert island in the company of a beautiful woman, with whom he enjoys day after day of passionate lovemaking, until eventually the man becomes downcast, whereupon he asks the woman to dress in his clothes and meet him the next morning on the other side of the island. The next morning she sees him running toward her, waving happily, shouting, "Hey, buddy, I just gotta tell you about this chick I'm screwing!"

Philosophers dispute whether a tree that falls in an isolated forest makes a sound, and the artless philanderer becomes anxious that his sex is diminished by people not knowing, causing his behavior to adopt the smug semaphore of secret achievement. As the First Lady loosens his back brace before bed, even he experiences a fleeting temptation to proclaim he spent last night with the nation's number-one sex symbol, on the assumption his wife might be proud of him.

She massages his scars and he feels her breath on his shoulder. He turns and kisses her, and she lets him maneuver them toward the bed.

"You're ready?" he says.

"I'm ready," she says.

"Because if you're doing it just for me . . ."

She shakes her head and kisses him. "I'm doing it for me," she says.

One critical element of the subject's sexual psychology pertains to his withdrawal symptoms appearing refractory to relief from his wife, owing to the unique excitement associated with a new or infrequent partner. This relativism would be hard for his wife to comprehend. At least his father had the excuse of a spouse who denied him sex. Worse, the subject takes his wife's sexual availability so much for granted that, perversely, he's often disinclined to avail himself of it.

In the morning, he wakes refreshed and free of the coughing or tightness in his chest. Though he appears to have suddenly acclimatized to their new home, the First Lady seems much less chipper than usual, but, instead of quizzing him further on his trip to the West Coast, she confides a general depression at the prospect of living for the next four or eight years in musty old halls with chipped paintwork, gimcrack heirlooms and tasteless art—furnishings, she complains, that appear to have originated from a thrift store—and it comes as no surprise to him when, over breakfast, she vows to deal with the situation in precisely the same fashion as she has dealt with every period of disenchantment in their marriage, by profligate expenditure on redecoration.

ALTHOUGH HIS OTHER chronic ailments seem to be temporarily in remission, the same cannot be said of the subject's back, which appears to be deteriorating as a result of the long hours and intense pressures of his work, a situation not helped by Dr. T. and Adm. B. disagreeing over management of the condition. It is now being proposed that the President consult with another specialist, Dr. K. The consultation takes place in the White House, as it would if Dr. K. were an academic expert drafted into a briefing on some specialized field of foreign affairs, an arrangement by which the good doctor is both honored and irritated. He has studied the President's medical records—actually, only those selectively relevant to his back—and recaps the history with the kind of crisp brevity the President appreciates: a ruptured lumbar disc playing college football, exacerbated by a severe impact against the bulkhead of his patrol torpedo boat when rammed by a Japanese destroyer, followed by osteoporosis as a side effect of steroid ingestion, leading to collapse of the fifth lumbar vertebra, which necessitated internal fixation by means of a metal plate, the postoperative course being complicated by septicemia—the future President went into a coma and was given the last rites—only to recover and be diagnosed with an infection in the internal fixing plate, which had to be extracted in a second operation, damaging the bone and cartilage into which the plate had been screwed, this damage being only partially repaired by bone grafts.

Dr. K. examines the President in the Residence, appearing as shocked as by the sight of a sideshow freak, because like any ordinary citizen he has no inkling that the vigorous young leader for whom he possibly voted cannot bend or straighten his back, cannot lift his left leg more than the few degrees necessary for walking, cannot put on his own shoes and socks, cannot turn over in bed and cannot sit in a low or reclining chair, after which the good doctor pronounces that the muscles of the President's back, abdomen and pelvis are dangerously weak and he must embark on a daily regimen of exercises to avert permanent immobility.

The President responds to his anxiety by saying, "You may be interested to know, Doctor, that President Eisenhower had a heart attack and a stroke while in office."

"So did the country," the doctor says back.

The President's booming laugh echoes down the hall for all to hear, but, just as the diagnosis takes place behind closed doors, so he carries out the exercises in the privacy of his rooms, his office and at the pool, where the hot water increases his suppleness, or, more accurately, reduces the lack of it.

He takes to inviting close advisors to join him. Occasionally they swim, but mostly they stand at the side of the pool with their ties loosed and sweat glistening on their faces.

Weekly the President pursues the State Department and the Justice Department about the fate of the Cuban internees, the survivors of the Brigade slung in prison, whose release he's ordered them to negotiate with the Cuban government. But today in the pool it's the turn of Justice to burden the President, as a senior official reveals that the FBI suspect a senior State Department advisor of being a practicing homosexual, a matter that has come to light in a routine (i.e., routinely tense) meeting with the director of the Federal Bureau of Investigation. According to the FBI reports, the State Department official has formed the habit of frequenting certain bars, and federal agents have witnessed transient male acquaintances spending the night with him at an apartment he rents on the other side of town from the home he shares with his wife and children.

"He has to go, Mr. President," says the man from the Justice Department. "He's a security risk."

The President struggles out of the pool and towels his eyes. The agent stationed at the shower is the one from the night with Marilyn, and the President greets him warmly. "How are you today, Dwight?" he says.

"Very well, thank you, Mr. President. And you, sir?"

"Well, thank you. Peggy and the kids?"

"They're also well, thank you, Mr. President."

In order to practice successfully as a fornicator, the President has been forced to secure the complicity of others, but, though he would rather act alone, this situation is not unfamiliar. Sometimes one must rely on a certain gentlemen's-club mentality that provides opportunities to hunt in a pack, to provide alibis where needed, and most importantly, to engender a general moral acceptance of infidelity.

The agent stares sightlessly into a nonexistent distance while the President washes and dries, which he does unselfconsciously, as one would after boarding school and the Navy, unselfconscious even of the double foot-long gashes up his spine. The President experiences no shame in his prematurely decrepit body or in his sexual peccadilloes, only in the failure of a promised new age that foundered in the criminal invasion of Cuba.


THE SOVIETS HAVE put into orbit one of their cosmonauts, a young pilot named Gagarin, ahead of our own plans to launch a man into space. Our national prestige has been dealt a resounding symbolic blow, because the simple-minded of the world are liable to become convinced of the superior achievements made possible by the communist system, and the simple-minded of America, always a group to whom one can successfully appeal in times of crisis, to the inferiority of our nuclear missiles, a point the President made repeatedly during the election to stir up mistrust at the shocking complacency of the previous administration, capitalizing on his predecessor's embarrassment when, on the golf course (where else?), he was forced to answer to his Soviet counterpart bathing in the afterglow of *Sputnik*.

"Beep-beep," went the little satellite, to which the Old Bastard answered that hurling chrome balls into space was meaningless.

But the new President faces the mightier derision, because, while a Soviet pilot has orbited the globe, we have had to make do with chimps.

Eventually our own man is ready to fly, and the President decides the launch must appear live on television, so that the nation can share the tension and excitement of the event, though he is warned of the possibility that the nation might also share in the impromptu *son et lumière* of an explosion, but he sticks by his decision, confident that it will help focus the minds of the engineers and that, as he told the astronaut himself, it won't make a damned bit of difference if he's vaporized in secret or in public, the effect on his person will be equally embarrassing.

The First Lady joins the President and some close aides, plus the Joint Chiefs and the Vice President, as they follow the launch on a TV placed in the Oval Office. The President's unadrenalized heart beats normally while other pulses race. The countdown descends to zero, and the little rocket lifts off into the sky and shrinks to a dot riding a plume of vapor. Once our man has safely gone up and safely come down, which only takes a matter of a quarter-hour, the President joins in with the smiles and handshakes in the room. The Vice President punches the air with delight, reveling in the success, and the President asks the VP to join him in telephoning congratulations to Mr. Webb at NASA, then, once the group has dispersed, the President is alone with his wife for a few minutes.

The First Lady is wearing a striking new hat and coat, which reminds the President he's recently received a clothing bill for her account in the sum of forty thousand dollars.

She says, "The news hens never stop clucking about what I'm wearing, how my hair looks . . . Everyone's watching me, Jack."

"I know, Jacqueline."

"Perhaps I needn't have spent so much. I'll cut back."

"That's all I ask," he says. "I know it's not easy being First Lady."

"I loathe that title," she says. "It makes me sound like a saddle-horse."

He laughs loudly and plants a kiss on her mouth. No woman makes him laugh like she does.


THE FOLLOWING WEEK, the President makes a trip to Florida to visit our Space Center in order to give his congratulations in person to the flight personnel and, naturally, to the astronaut himself. That day, he rides with the Vice President and the astronaut in an open-topped limousine, greeting the cheering crowds, at one point remarking to Our First Man in Space that not many of our citizens are aware that the Vice President is the chairman of the Space Committee, but adding, with a glimmer in his eye, that, if the flight had been a catastrophe, he would certainly have made sure that there'd be very few people who didn't know it.

The President feels little bonhomie toward the VP, mainly for small reasons of personal taste and hygiene, having repeatedly witnessed him using one of his giant, stubby fingers to excavate nasal mucus while he talks loudly on his telephone with the door to his office wide open, and having heard from independent sources that he urinates in the washbasin, sometimes doing so during a meeting. The President rarely uses a public urinal lest his inflamed prostate betray him with an unmanly dribble, and he wonders if perhaps this is the reason the Vice President appears to rejoice in the idea that every golden parabola proclaims him the more vigorous and powerful politician.

Before they took office, the VP made so many entreaties for the President-elect to socialize with him that, in the end, he consented to a weekend hunting on his ranch, though the "hunting" element was somewhat artificial, given that their party simply crouched in the undergrowth, armed to the teeth, until a team of ranch hands drove a herd of deer straight into their ambush. The experience epitomizes the President's view that the VP, despite his political artfulness and loyalty, is apt to misjudge a social situation, for which the President feels a measure of pity. But to this day he recalls with a shiver the cruel crack of gunfire, the animals' blind terror, then the bursts of blood before their legs folded. He cannot shake the Vice President's surprising affinity for slaughter.

The President's family owns a compound at Palm Beach, at which they customarily spend winter weekends, and this is where he repairs, after parting from the VP and Our First Man in Space, for informal discussions over dinner with close aides, the topic of conversation on this occasion being the objectives of the space program. Once again the President has the advantage on his aides, by virtue of the ability, acquired during endless days of convalescence in his youth, to speed-read 1,500 words per minute with close to 90 percent retention, being first to identify from the exhaustive documents the twin decisive factors, namely (1) that many of the objectives of space exploration are not of the right nature to capture the imagination of the country and therefore our ultimate goal must be a simply understood triumph over the Soviets, and (2) that, owing to the Soviet Union's lead in certain aspects of space technology, the chosen goal must be so far removed from current capabilities to give our Space Agency time to overtake their rival.

In taking office, the President appealed to the best men the country has to offer to devote themselves to public service, as he has done despite the gifts of wealth and education that would swing open the doors of every corporate boardroom in the land, and now he sees he must galvanize the people in a similar endeavor, to divert everyone into looking up. "We should put a man on the moon," the President proposes, as the single clearest statement of his belief in the limitlessness of American ambition.

THE SUBJECT'S WIFE and children have not joined him at Palm Beach, instead remaining in Washington before spending a couple of days at the ranch the family has rented in Virginia, his wife excusing them because it's too hot for the children this time of year in Florida and Caroline is pining for her pony.

As the sun goes down, the presidential party sits out by the pool. He wears a hot pack inside his back brace and sips a daiquiri. His gut has run the gamut of constipation, diarrhea and colic, now finding itself in a kind of temporary equilibrium before it veers into its next dysfunction. The President has completed the course of antibiotics prescribed for his urinary tract infection, with the result that he's now able to pass water with minimal discomfort. Marilyn may have sucked the poison from his snakebite, but the snake remains, leeching poison via a subtle osmosis involving his shrunken adrenal glands and swollen prostate. The constipatory intensity of his sexual needs has passed, but those needs have been sharpened since his first dalliance in office, and so the question arises of whether it may be possible to return to preelection levels of fornication, most pertinently on this balmy Florida evening, because the party includes the pretty young press aide who has accompanied her boss, the President's Press Secretary, who thought it would be good experience for her to play some small part in the trip, particularly since our first successful manned spaceflight means there's currently a much more favorable mood toward the administration among the news media.

The girl addresses the President directly, the first time she has spoken before being spoken to, saying, "Mr. President, do you mind if we use the pool?"

He says, "See if you can make as big a splash as Commander Shepard," and she laughs, she and some of the other aides taking to the pool while he speed-reads a fistful of reports. He slides the hot pack over to the other side of his spine. Through a shutter of shuffled reports, he glimpses the group in the pool swimming and splashing, his glances focusing repeatedly on the girl breast-stroking down to the shallow end then standing, water dripping from her slick hair, her bathing suit glistening tight against her figure, but, as she turns to swim the return leg, he drops his gaze a split second too late.

The girl is twenty-two years old. As she splashes in the pool with her colleagues, and he is minded that his recent assignation with Marilyn may already have been rationalized by his staff as a singular encounter between former lovers, he ensures that the next time she glances up from the water she observes his departing figure, trudging indoors with a senior advisor, executing a discussion to which she cannot be privy, given her lowly status.

Before bed, he speaks with his wife over the telephone, who updates him on the children's adventures on the ranch, particularly his daughter's pony rides, which he is sorry to miss even though exposure to horse hair can leave him wheezing for twenty-four hours or more, then he carries out Dr. K.'s back exercises, after which he's helped out of his brace and into his pajamas by the valet. The subject's medications have been placed out on the bedside cabinet beside the telephone and notepad, and he takes each dose with a sip of water, checking each drug on the pharmacopoeia prepared by Adm. B., one of which is a sedative that speeds him to sleep before reflections on the press aide's glistening swimsuit turn tumid.

In the morning, the party returns to D.C., where the President conducts a full day of White House business before donning black-tie for a reception at the Smithsonian thrown in honor of Our First Man in Space, at which there is genuine enthusiasm for the proposed effort to land a man on the Moon. Critics believe the objective is beyond reach, but the President wants the American people to imagine there is nothing we as a country cannot achieve if we set our minds to it, and we will only test this belief by applying ourselves to tasks that are hard, not easy, and by turning our best minds toward lofty endeavors rather than the venal accumulation of wealth or weaponry.

The President notices the VP clinging to Our First Man in Space with ingratiating offers of participation in product endorsements and corporate schemes. Political capital has made him an unlikely shipmate. The President cuts in, barely noticing the Vice President's doleful mien on being cast overboard.

"Naturally, Commander," says the President, "you'll be offered a berth on the second voyage to the Moon."

"Not the first, Mr. President?" the astronaut asks.

"That's reserved for the Vice President."

The astronaut laughs, and a waiter glides a tray of champagne flutes toward them. The President barely touches his champagne since it fires up his heartburn and gives him diarrhea for days, but hides his infirmity by saying, "If I have too much, Commander, Soviet spies will send word tonight would be a good night for a surprise attack."

"Who'd have your job, Mr. President?" the astronaut says.

"I hope there are no takers just yet," the President replies.

Then the President catches the astronaut's gaze drift toward the press aide, looking young and lovely in a cocktail dress, attempting to appear not bored by the attentions of one of the Space Agency's senior managers, and, later, after dinner and speeches, seated at the top table, the President risks a cigar, feeling only a minor tug in his gut as he takes his turn to eye her. The men at his table clench whiskey glasses and drift smoke at each other, while the President and the astronaut talk Navy talk. The President has gravitated toward Our First Man in Space in masculine admiration, and the astronaut senses it, because an erstwhile deference has departed from his manner toward the Commander-in-Chief, and now they converse as if equal alpha males.

Our First Man in Space wears a crew cut, is a man of above-average looks, though not as tall as the President, but clearly, after months of rigorous medical testing, in perfect physical condition. The astronaut's gaze turns toward the girl again, and this time the President's look openly follows his. The astronaut says, "They don't make 'em like that in Pensacola."

The President says, "Go talk to her," then measures a pause, before adding, "I forgot, Commander. You've a wife."

Our First Man in Space grins. "She married a sailor. Excuse me, Mr. President." He slides his left hand casually in his trouser pocket, angling his drink in his right fist, and strolls across the room. The President watches her delirious wonderment that Our First Man in Space is regaling her with tales of his fifteen-minute voyage through the heavens, before the President turns away, satisfied all men are like him, or at least the ones who get the opportunities to be.

Yet the subject has never felt more singular than during his short months in office. He might even describe his current emotional deficit as "loneliness," though he cannot mean loneliness in its conventional sense. He seeks company as others crave companionship; he seeks sexual intimacy as others crave love; yet he is not much different from other men of his generation with similar education and professional standing, nor indeed from men throughout the ages, of any class or race, since they all share the same biology, albeit with chemicals in slightly varying abundance and slightly varying potency. What differs between them is a willingness to accept and act upon their own physical inclinations, and, naturally, a wide variation in opportunity, all these contentions finding living proof in the conduct of Our First Man in Space—officer, gentleman, churchgoer, husband and father—currently and avidly endeavoring to secure missile-lock on his apparently receptive target, a young woman who has enjoyed (mostly married) male attention all evening, and now finds herself under seduction by a national icon and hero of the New Frontier.

The President of the United States crosses the floor to join the astronaut and the press aide just as Our First Man in Space is about to suggest a docking maneuver at his pad. The President turns the conversation to the moon landing, which turns the girl's attention toward him, the alpha of alphas, taller (the previous administration gave serious thought to recruiting circus midgets as astronauts), with far better hair, prompting her to ask, "Do you really believe it's possible, Mr. President?"

"I do believe it. And we all must. To quote Anatole France: 'To accomplish great things, we must not only act, but also dream.' And to paraphrase George Bernard Shaw, 'Some see what is and ask Why? but others dream things that aren't and ask Why not?'

"I do believe. We all must. Because America can show the world, and history, our power, our drive, our courage and our ingenuity in a way that doesn't involve weapons and warfare."

Her eyes widen in the face of a future of limitless possibility. Muscles twitch in the astronaut's stony expression, but he knows he can do nothing to prevent the girl from becoming the President's tonight.

# THE TRANSACTION

BEAUTIFUL YOUNG WOMEN sometimes reward men's stations or achievements with sex, which the subject regards as a fitting tribute, more gratefully received than the standard civic medal. It is a custom he questions only occasionally, since, when he finds himself the beneficiary, he considers the transaction natural, appropriate and commensurate. Men of high standing in commerce or the arts will often come by the gifts of a young admirer, and these men aren't all blessed with the subject's looks, though they do often delude themselves with notions of physical or spiritual charisma, as if their wealth and/or power are irrelevant to the transaction.

Yet, while he accepts that he could attract women were he an advertising executive on Madison Avenue or a mechanic on the production line of the Ford Motor Company, he is certainly not foolish enough to believe he would be *as* attractive, probably not even close. A man of high status does well to adopt the philosophy of the Chinese shopkeeper who, in bartering for a bride, does not separate his own character from the appendage of his business, instead embracing it as integral to his eligibility in the same fashion that a handsome face might be or an athletic physique (or any other appendage you care to imagine).

These musings rarely prompt the subject to examine the transaction from the woman's point of view. When he does, he concludes the woman must somehow be biologically programmed to be seduced by peacock feathers, and moreover she must regard her sexual beauty as a precious franchise and derive a sense of power and influence by giving herself to the man of her choice in the manner that she might cast her vote (if she's old enough). In an election, a politician seeks office but lies at the mercy of the voter who, paradoxically, holds enormous potential power in his gift, and this situation is mirrored by the encounter between the elevated man of state, commerce or art and the sexually appealing young woman, who possesses the body to disarm the most potent adversary, and the moment that both parties become aware of this tantalizing reality, and of the possibility of the associated prize, a balance of power obtains that may well weigh toward the otherwise disenfranchised young woman. The subject imagines the woman is not a calculating femme fatale attempting to win favor or influence, rather that she finds a confused expression for her admiration in the language of sex, though he appreciates that part of this expectation originates from the man, who is accustomed to respect from many quarters, to the point where such compliments become redundant, whereas the exceptional tribute that lies in the gift of the beautiful young woman appears, to him, the most sincere act of approbation possible. When these two disparate individuals meet, the man of power and the woman of beauty, there exists in some circles such a convention of sexual tribute that the man comes to regard it as his entitlement, and certainly the subject does find himself somewhat irritated if, having spent no small time and effort giving attention to a young woman of no political or social influence, he learns that she is neither willing nor able to present him with his "civic medal." Happily, no such contractual misunderstandings apply tonight, as the young lady in question appears utterly familiar with the particulars.

The practical obstacles involved in sleeping with her proved far less challenging than expected. At the reception, the President instructed her to make her way back to the White House on the understanding there would be a late briefing involving her boss, the Press Secretary, at which she would be responsible for taking notes, an arrangement an aide conveyed on behalf of the President to the Secret Service, and, when the girl arrived alone at the White House, she made her way to the Residence to await the Press Secretary in the company of the President. However, the President had deliberately omitted to leave instructions for the Press Secretary, letting him return home directly from the dinner. The First Lady having taken the children to Cape Cod, the President and his guest have the run of the Lincoln Bedroom, wherein he spends a few moments acquainting her with the designs crafted in the woodwork of the giant four-poster bed.

The transaction requires only a few minutes. He's spent decades fingering mobsters and licking debaters, so surely the resultant wealth, status and power excuse him the ghastly drag of foreplay. How selfish, if the girl should want even more. Yet the President's practiced insouciance must not mislead us into overlooking his hunter's heart. It beats so hard he hears the blood in his head. This man without adrenaline experiences the surge now, facing a woman's eyes ready to fight and her muscles ready to fly, only now, only at the kill. She is a mouse dropped in with a snake.

Perhaps because the President took the trouble to offer the girl a glass of wine as an aid to seduction, she imagines that he might want to talk, so she begins to tell him nervously about her school, her college, what it means to work at the White House— she was a volunteer for his campaign, apparently, and those who'd worked hard were rewarded with some kind of position, however minor, in her case by the Press Secretary, who found her a post in his office answering phones and clipping copy, a job she wants to discuss with the President now. She and the other girls like her (one will soon be working for Mrs. Lincoln, another at State) attended the same exclusive New England schools and colleges as the First Lady, a fact the President recognizes in her diction and mannerisms. These girls don't need to work for money; hence they're delighted to take an unimportant job for little pay as a passport to high society; and they seem bred to favor older, richer, more powerful gentlemen.

But the President is not interested in her education or her family, which she possibly offers as a means to elicit similar revelations from him; nor is he interested in discussing politics save in the most superficial way, as he certainly has no intention of confessing his deeper feelings about his office to anyone apart from his wife. Perhaps he becomes uncomfortable in the face of a woman's will, when he realizes she is not passive to his seduction, but has made the same calculation as he. He did not, for example, utter a single comment to Marilyn on the subject of the invasion, even though at that time he was afflicted by nightmarish visions of those men's miserable deaths. Tonight the President is only concerned with this girl's body, hence he says quite directly,

"I still have reading, so I'm afraid we have to get down to it straight away."

Afterward she wants to talk again, but he has no desire for such intimacy and calls down to the lobby.

"It seems Mr. Salinger didn't get the message," he says to the duty clerk. "No, don't call him. I'm tired and would prefer to postpone the meeting till further notice. Would you send a car to the North Portico for. . . ?"

*"Jill,"* she repeats, but he will forget it again instantly.

Putting on her coat, she says, "Is it true? Can we go to the Moon?"

He says, "I believe this generation can change things, and achieve things that haven't been done before. It's our world now."

She smiles and goes to kiss him on the cheek, but he completes his emotional closure, as one would expect having being relieved of his sexual need, and sometimes it is an effort of common courtesy for the subject not to view this circumstance after consummation as he regards the period after a productive bowel movement. For the subject, to this day, the sharpest challenge of the sexual transaction is the moment he now confronts, the custom of postcoital partition, when he feels an urgent desire to flush away what's been laid. He's grateful for her prompt exit, his time being better spent carrying out his back exercises, ingesting his medications, and getting off to sleep ahead of his flight out to the Cape in the morning to join the family.

The valet seems unperturbed by the moderately disrupted arrangement of the bedclothes, bringing the President water with which to take his pills and helping him into his pajamas. The President needs not give the condition of the bedroom a second thought, as the sheets will be laundered over the weekend to be replaced by fresh, clean ones for his family's return on Sunday evening.

Before he sleeps, he calculates that, apart from Our First Man in Space, he doubts anyone paid close attention to the momentary intimacy that occurred at the reception as he acquainted the girl with the scheme whereby they would meet later, nor after when she returned to the Residence under the guise of a late meeting. She spent no more than twenty minutes in the Residence before being seen to leave by the Secret Service when the meeting was canceled. All assumptions would surely be innocent, even those of the valet, who must account for the ruffled sheets by concluding that the President alone is responsible, most likely by one or another stretching exercise, leaving the subject confident he's done nothing to create the impression that he will be vulnerable to sexual distraction during his administration, which is his primary concern toward his staff in the question of his fornication.

The subject has been a practicing philanderer for so long now that it hardly constitutes an intellectual or emotional strain—the converse, in fact, as demonstrated by the physical maladies by which he's afflicted when he suffers enforced continence, and, moreover, he would argue that it is less of a diversion in terms of time and effort than a set of tennis or a round of golf. Sex is the subject's golf: a couple of quick holes, getting around as quickly as possible.

THE GIRL LOOKS the picture of discretion when next she meets the President, and he detects no suspicious glances from his aides.

Even the Press Secretary, his unwitting beard, appears unruffled by the meeting that never was. So it's business as usual, followed by a weekend with the wife and children at their rented property on Cape Cod, during which he decides to pursue a short dalliance with this girl from the Press Office. Naturally his principal concern is concealment. His wife occasionally visits the West Wing, though her staff is based in her East Wing offices, and the Press Office staff are usually present at White House functions. The subject worries that a moment of overfamiliarity, or careless discrepancy in an account of their whereabouts, will ignite his wife's suspicions.

Though he thinks about the girl over the weekend, he has long ago learned that the successful philanderer must be capable of strict compartmentalization. Therefore he appears the devoted family man—which, of course, he is—as he enjoys a pleasant sojourn playing with the children, Caroline in particular seeming to find limitless fascination in scooping out holes in the sand down on the beach, Jackie and John Jr. coming and going, but the clearest memories of the weekend are the simple physical moments between them as a family, Jackie lying close by while they both read—a book on antiquities for her, economic reports for him—cradling John on his lap, helping him sit up, feeling his warm scalp against his chest, and Caroline's hand in his as they stroll along the scrub, particularly the moment just before, when she pulls free to explore, and there he remains with his hand held out, his heart almost ready to break, until she discovers it again.

However, the President is beset with the usual number of work calls and briefings. In the house, he takes a call from Justice; they are raising the issue again of the State Department official, and the President resolves to look into the matter, which he does in a spare moment on Monday, after Mrs. Lincoln fetches the file, which summarizes FBI surveillance reports and witness statements to the effect that the official is undoubtedly guilty, with the opinion succinctly stated in the report's conclusion that it is government policy to regard practicing homosexuals as unfit for public office.

The President and the First Lady dined with his family over the weekend, and their first two evenings this week are taken up with small dinner parties in the Residence, which have become something of a social custom now, usually taking the form of the First Couple hosting six guests in the President's Dining Room, most often friends they have known since before the President came to office, possibly a prominent journalist and his wife, or an ambassador, and occasionally someone from outside the political world, such as an artist or a poet. These are relaxed affairs, for the most part, with two exceptions, the first being the start of the evening, when no one, not even one of their closest friends, dares enter the room before the President, this being the protocol appropriate to his office, and the second being that, with the exception of the First Lady, no one addresses him by his first name. Instead, rather than suffering the embarrassment of calling their old friend "Mr. President," they call him nothing at all, although when referring to him in the third person they have nearly all found a way of enunciating "the President" that sounds simultaneously respectful and mocking, which, to be frank, is a combination of which he rather approves.

Guests have also become accustomed to the President swapping an ordinary dining chair for his rocking chair and to the fact that on a good many evenings he is forced to eat a bland repast devoid of meat, vegetables or flavor, and forgo alcohol and cigars, though the First Lady selflessly blows the smoke of her filtered cigarettes in his direction. Sometimes they screen a movie (wherein occasionally faces turn up that he must pretend not to recognize, and sometimes a newcomer catches his eye whose name he might pass on to his Hollywood brother-in-law vis-à-vis the next West Coast party), but, since sitting still for two hours is never a good idea for his back, he often excuses himself at this time to read reports and make telephone calls.

At last, he and his wife get an evening alone together. After putting the children to bed, she drinks white wine and chain-smokes her L&Ms, while his enforced abstemiousness continues, as his stomach has been only a minor problem for the past few days, with only a single bout of colic followed by bloody diarrhea. Things are convivial enough, with shared laughter at the expense of newspaper columnists and po-faced heads of state. His wife gives an animated account of her restoration program, to which he shows appropriate interest. Occasionally he wonders how their exchanges must sound to an outsider, who would hear his solemn appraisal of the situation in Berlin rejoindered by his wife's description of a particularly striking antique chair her staff have uncovered in one of the basements.

Away from the raucous revelry of a dinner party or a cocktail reception, the President and the First Lady revert to a married couple having dinner at home. They talk a good deal, and they laugh, but the President maintains a lookout for any tension that might suggest his wife is harboring suspicions. He reflects on his harmless encounter with the press girl and becomes resentful that he should feel hounded by his wife when he provides so much love and security for her and their children, so he goes on the offensive, as usual pertaining to her fashion budget, which has gone up rather than down since last they discussed the matter.

"I spend," she says. "It's my vice. What's yours, Jack?"

Quickly he says, "I think it must be that I have delusions of grandeur," to which she laughs her beautiful laugh, a girl's laughter, and she tips her head close and they kiss.

IN THE MORNING, there's a call from Justice. The Attorney General wants to know what to tell the FBI because the Director wants to know what's being done about the State Department official, to which the President answers that, having read the reports, the official is more valuable than he expected, based on the briefing, and he needs more time to reach a decision. After he lays down the phone, the President raps his fingertips on his desk for a few seconds, then he goes through to Mrs. L. on the intercom and asks when the next State Department briefing is in the diary, the answer being later this week, and he adds that he would particularly like this certain official to participate, though obviously he does not give his secretary his reasons.

Later, Mrs. Lincoln takes a call for the President, which fortunately, as it's from Marilyn, comes while he's in a meeting. He gave the number of his direct line during a weak moment (of which there were many) in the hotel suite in L.A., ever since receiving elliptical bulletins on an almost daily basis. She leaves messages asking if she should change agents, or to report seeing a darling puppy she just had to buy but now worries about his allergies. Mrs. Lincoln dutifully logs the calls as coming from "Mac," as the subject invents male-sounding code names for his paramours. He has problems remembering their names already, so often the caller's cryptonym must serve as an *aide-memoire,* a buxom girl, say, being christened Tim Todd Smith. So Mrs. Lincoln takes a message and a return number, dutifully logs them under an alias, and lists them without accentuation among his many other calls at their midafternoon update.

Mrs. Lincoln has been the subject's secretary since the beginning of his career in the Senate, and she probably knows more than anyone about his independent personal life, albeit only the names of the women with whom he socializes and possibly a vague knowledge of the duration of the relationship, certainly not any deeper appreciation, as far as he knows, of what he actually gets up to with these girls. They have a reciprocally remote relationship, Mrs. L. and Mr. President, though not without mutual affection and loyalty, which suits them both, rather as his marriage is a marriage of two distant, austere figures who are both, despite being socially attractive, shy at heart and figures to whom outsiders rarely warm. Hence, Mrs. Lincoln would be amused to hear them described as working in a successful professional marriage, particularly given she is a rather matronly woman in late middle age whom he never addresses as Evelyn. The President genuinely has no inkling what Mrs. L. assumes about his extramarital activity. It was never addressed, for instance, in the case of Pamela, now the First Lady's Press Secretary, with whom he had a dalliance at the time she worked in his Senate office as a receptionist on quite a small staff, when the campaign by Pamela's landlady to publicly embarrass the subject could scarcely have failed to escape Mrs. Lincoln's purview.

The subject senses that Mrs. Lincoln's redoubtable discretion is about to be tested once again, since she has now been joined in her office adjacent to his by a new assistant who will assume responsibility over a pile of typing, as well as assisting with other minor administrative chores. This new girl appears to the President to come from the same mold as Jill, a campaign volunteer and Farmington alumna (his wife's school), good-looking, vivacious, unattached and well bred. She is very much his type, if there is such a thing, that type perforce being a woman with his wife's attributes—looks, refinement, education, wit and intelligence—though no woman possesses those attributes to quite the same degrees as the First Lady. The subject soon tires of the empty-headed type of woman: Marilyn, for example, who tries heartbreakingly hard to appear serious and well informed without being remotely convincing. She has developed a delusion that she is both these things due to the numerous men who collude with it as a route to her bed, and he finds himself often in a struggle to withhold his dissenting view because he appreciates how much it will distress her, though if any of her lovers has a right to claim intellectual superiority it would be him over her avid entourage of Hollywood cads and Las Vegas hoods.

The subject diverts himself for a minute or two while Mrs. Lincoln briefs the new girl on her duties. Meanwhile he folds the paper bearing Marilyn's message and drops it in the trash. When he recalls their last time together, his vision of Marilyn is colored by a curtain of delirium. He compares his condition those weeks ago to a physical and psychological toxemia, and now he must recover: he must learn from his mistake in Cuba and reestablish political authority.

While Mrs. Lincoln and the staff take their lunch break, he swims in the superheated pool, the President sticking rigidly to Dr. K.'s exercise plan. The President consults Adm. B. once a week, but he decides to call him in at the end of the day for an irregular consultation, at which the Admiral is pleased to hear that the President is eager for the treatment of his other medical conditions to be reviewed. Adm. B. advises that the priority is to moderate the President's digestive crises since they cause unpredictable disturbances in the absorption of oral medications, though he is not so pleased when the President seeks a second opinion from Dr. T., who argues that the priority is to manage the Addison's disease since the corticosteroid treatment thereof exerts an enormous effect on the workings of the President's digestive system. An endocrinologist, Dr. C., is summoned from New York for a private consultation at the White House, and soon becomes disconcerted by the full inventory of presidential maladies: Addison's disease, thyroid deficiency, gastric reflux, gastritis, peptic ulcer, ulcerative colitis, prostatitis, urethritis, chronic urinary tract infections, skin infections, fevers of unknown origin, lumbar vertebral collapse, osteoporosis of the lumbar spine, osteoarthritis of the neck, osteoarthritis of the shoulder, high cholesterol, allergic rhinitis, allergic sinusitis and asthma.

Addison's disease is an insufficiency of the glands lying atop the kidneys that secrete hormones that together govern a whole array of bodily functions. The President has a layman's understanding of this complex disease accumulated over the past fifteen years of suffering its effects—fatigue, weight loss, abdominal pain, aching muscles, headaches, abnormal skin pigmentation, low blood pressure, nausea, diarrhea and vomiting, weakness, constipation, muscle cramps and joint pains.

The subject was first diagnosed in England following a collapse, but it became clear that he must have had the disease for some time beforehand, as he'd long suffered weight loss, fatigue, fever, digestive problems and a yellowish complexion, but successive doctors had missed the diagnosis, probably for years, by ascribing his ailments to an inflammatory condition of the bowel. On the voyage home aboard the *Queen Mary,* he collapsed again and received the last rites. Dr. C., like all members of that fraternity, closes ranks with his nameless colleagues of yore and endeavors to convince the President that the steroids employed in the treatment of his digestive problems will have confounded the diagnostic picture for any reputable physician, while at the same time possibly contributing to the atrophy of his adrenal glands. The President offers no comment, given his weariness with debating the rank incompetence of the medical profession. Their self-serving obfuscation served him only once, when rumors of his condition surfaced before the election and were repudiated by a physician's statement that the senator did not suffer from "an ailment classically described as Addison's disease," the verbal trickery hinging on the modifier "classically"—classical Addison's being a primary failure of the adrenals, whereas it is scientifically insupportable to exclude the possibility that the subject's condition originated secondarily to prolonged steroid treatments.

One might also consider it pertinent for the subject to ask the specialist whether his hormonal dysfunction may be responsible for his outstanding libido. Before he was married, the subject did once make this very enquiry, only to be advised there is no medical evidence endocrine disease causes satyriasis. Needless to say, none of these considerations enter the remit of today's consultation; if they did, a reputable endocrinologist like Dr. C. would form the opinion the subject's dependence on sex was purely psychological and his withdrawal symptoms psychosomatic.

Dr. C. reviews the President's records and asks the appropriate questions, although the President withholds the irrelevant details such as his daily use of painkillers and almost daily use of amphetamine. The doctor intends to balance out the prescriptions of hydrocortisone, fludrocortisone and prednisolone, and do the same for the thyroid medications, advocating close monitoring of the President's condition. In return, the President enquires how these changes might affect his other medical problems, but the doctor is evasive, claiming he can't be certain of the prognosis for the President's back and digestive system or his urinary tract for that matter, but he is adamant that the key to the President's well-being lies in fine-controlling his Addison's disease. With that, the good doctor returns to New York, and the President returns to preparations for a speech before Congress that will convince them of urgent necessities facing the country.

He tries when possible to take breakfast with the family and then walk with his daughter to the Oval Office, or sometimes they will all visit him when there's a gap in his schedule. His daughter usually waits in Mrs. Lincoln's office, peeking through the door while he plays a game of pretending to speak on the telephone about her.

"Is that the Federal Kindergarten Bureau? Really? Has Caroline been so very naughty?"

Or pretending to read an official report: "Apparently the Secret Service have seen the First Daughter picking her nose . . ."

"Daddy!" she will complain.

He looks up sharply with a loud laugh and claps three times, the signal for her to scoot into the office for a hug and a chat. He makes time to exercise in the pool while the staff take their lunch, and then returns to work until the evening, with the hope he can finish in time to see the children put to bed and read a bedtime story before he and his wife take part in an evening engagement, either a formal reception on the ground floor or a private dinner up in the Residence. But all the time the President is aware of a narrowing around his eyes, a subtle pursing of his lips, that only those closest to him recognize as his suffering, the spastic muscles over the metal plate in his back, the chokingly tight brace pushing against his churning gut, his whole body being squeezed and the pressure flowing up into his head from where it cannot escape.

Sometimes, as he works or transits to meetings in the Cabinet Room or the Fish Room, he glimpses Mrs. Lincoln's new assistant tapping her typewriter keys or stapling documents. She is there, just a few feet away, a gift waiting to be unwrapped, but for now he closes his mind to the possibilities and concentrates on political obligations.

One of the President's meetings this week involves the State Department's latest offerings on the situation in Southeast Asia, in which the senior advisor alleged to be homosexual takes part. The meeting proceeds in a routine fashion, yet the President makes a point of observing the man's performance. The advisor is outwardly unremarkable, but he answers specific points intelligently and offers sound advice on one topic in particular, the guerrilla warfare tactics of indigenous armies. At the end of the meeting, the President dismisses them all with equal thanks, but pauses for a moment before his next meeting to decide the advisor's fate.

WHILE A LACK of hormones gives the subject the advantage of maintaining a calm, even sanguine, disposition, he can never benefit from a sudden boost in physical and mental power as would other men in a similar situation. With his speechwriters, the President toils over an address to Congress outlining urgent national needs during which he tires and weakens and gains new energy only through sleep. In such times, his metabolic engine is fueled by amphetamines and his rest by sedatives, but the speech takes shape, its central ideas expressed in key phrases of his invention and no one else's. He has one single objective: to show the world that he will atone for the bungled invasion.

On the day, a closed limousine conveys the President to the Capitol, where he must confront Congress with the inherited neglect of his predecessor's policies and command a new vision for this new decade, with no adrenaline to drive him forward when he gazes out across the rising rows of critical faces, though his voice holds steady before the hundreds, his palms don't sweat, and he says:

"These are extraordinary times. And we face an extraordinary challenge. Our strength as well as our convictions have imposed upon this nation the role of leader in freedom's cause. The great battleground for the defense and expansion of freedom today is the lands of the rising peoples. They seek an end to injustice, tyranny, and exploitation. But the adversaries of freedom plan to exploit, to control, and finally to destroy the hopes of the world's newest nations; it is a contest of will and purpose as well as force and violence, a battle for minds and souls as well as lives and territory. And in that contest, we cannot stand aside.

"There is no single simple policy which meets this challenge. Experience has taught us that no one nation has the power or the wisdom to solve all the problems of the world. We would be badly mistaken to consider these problems in military terms alone. Military pacts cannot help nations whose social injustice and economic chaos invite insurgency and extremism. We stand ready now to provide generously of our skills, and our capital, and our food to assist the peoples of the less-developed nations before they are engulfed in crisis.

"But while we talk of sharing and building and the competition of ideas, others talk of arms and threaten war. So we have learned to keep our defenses strong. We will deter an enemy from making a nuclear attack only if our retaliatory power is so strong and so invulnerable that he knows he would be destroyed by our response. But this deterrent concept assumes rational calculations by rational men. The history of this planet, and particularly the history of this century, is sufficient to remind us of the possibilities of an irrational attack, a miscalculation, an unnecessary war, or a conflict of escalation in which the stakes by each side gradually increase to the point of maximum danger which cannot be either foreseen or deterred. I cannot end this discussion of defense and armaments without emphasizing our strongest hope: the creation of an orderly world where disarmament will be possible. I am determined to develop acceptable political and technical alternatives to the present arms race.

"Finally, if we are to win the battle that is now going on around the world between freedom and tyranny, the dramatic achievements in space which occurred in recent weeks should have made clear to us all the impact of this adventure on the minds of men everywhere, who are attempting to make a determination of which road they should take. Now it is time for a great new American enterprise—time for this nation to take a clearly leading role in space achievement, which in many ways may hold the key to our future on earth. While we cannot guarantee that we shall one day be first, we can guarantee that any failure to make this effort will make us last. I believe that this nation should commit itself to achieving the goal, before this decade is out, of landing a man on the moon and returning him safely to the earth. No single space project in this period will be more impressive to mankind, or more important for the long-range exploration of space; and none will be so difficult or expensive to accomplish. If we are to go only half way, or reduce our sights in the face of difficulty, in my judgment it would be better not to go at all unless we are prepared to do the work and bear the burdens to make it successful.

"In my judgment, this is a most serious time in the life of our country and in the life of freedom around the globe. In conclusion, let me emphasize one point: our desire for peace. We seek no conquests, no satellites, no riches—we seek only the day when 'nation shall not lift up sword against nation, neither shall they learn war any more.'"

Afterward there comes applause, with congratulations from those nearby, yet the subject cannot experience the visceral signals of an ordeal survived, since there was never a racing pulse now to slow, nor sweaty palms to dry, his chemical disposition constant irrespective of triumph or disaster, and the first physical indication of his performance arrives in the form of his wife, in her embrace and kiss through which he senses her pride.

His political authority regained, the President is expected to make a decision on our course of action in Southeast Asia. The Chairman of the Joint Chiefs represents the majority view when he says, "We need a show." A small, covert action failed in Cuba but a large, overt action will demonstrate our undiminished power. Instead the President informs the Cabinet he will not sanction military action and instead intends to open negotiations designed to achieve a cease-fire in the region. Faces drop, not least the generals', one of whom mutters a four-letter word.

Later his aides bring responses from the press and members of Congress, and he realizes his gamble has succeeded, that his grand vision for a better country and a better world is winning admiration. Yet on occasions such as this one, he finds the approbation of his colleagues insufficient, and even the love of his wife, perhaps momentarily enhanced by his ascendance, seems quotidian. Instead he believes himself most acutely in need of a sexual tribute from an impressionable young woman swayed by his political adroitness to the extent she will vote with her body. He holds that the type of leader required to achieve these goals in so short a time must be capable of magnetizing the human core; to move a whole nation and a whole generation, he must be capable of turning their compasses toward public service with the same gravity that bent him from his erstwhile life of academic rarefaction and material privilege, and the proof of electrifying the hearts of the young lies in the honest currency of a sexual transaction.

Jill is the obvious choice, and he plots to seduce her again to-night, since his wife and children leave today (Thursday) for their habitual long weekend out of town, this time to the ranch in Middleburg, Virginia, where his daughter's pony is stabled. After he sees them off in the afternoon, with an embrace for his wife and for the children a slow disunion of hands, the nanny cradling John Jr. while Caroline clings to the hem of her mother's dress, the President works through till early evening, principally in meetings but alone at sunset, before he suggests some of the staff join him in the pool, knowing that Jill will endeavor to be among them, and subsequently she is, in a borrowed bathing cos-tume, together with Mrs. Lincoln's new assistant, with whom she has formed a little bond.

The President glides through the steaming water, occasionally stopping to small-talk with aides, but no one speaks to him unless he speaks to them first, so he is able to complete his exer-cise program surreptitiously while they bathe in small groups, the girls' faces hot, flushed and gleaming—the only females being Jill and the new girl—until eventually he swims to their corner of the pool and casually inquires about their work.

"I haven't had the pleasure," he says to the new girl, "of knowing your name."

She laughs and offers her hand formally. "Priscilla, Mr. Presi-dent," she says.

Beads of sweat run down their necks and their hair hangs dark and lank. The President expects to have to draw out slow, nervous answers from the girls, but they brim with confidence, only deferring to him with an occasional "sir" at the end of their shorter sentences, Jill in particular having dispensed with the obligatory "Mr. President" in favor of a familiarity to which the

President neither objects nor warms. She leans in his direction, watching her colleagues bid their farewells to him until the three of them are alone—Jill, Priscilla and the President—and her gaze locks with his.

The President chooses Priscilla. He prefers a drug sufficiently novel his body has yet to develop tolerance. The execution is simple, in that the President calls an end to the pool session and advises her she must stop by Mrs. Lincoln's office before leaving tonight as some papers require filing, and, although he half-expects her to arrive with Jill, when he meets her in the now empty office (as he has earlier sent Mrs. L. home), she makes no mention of her colleague, leaving him free to remark that Mrs. Lincoln is no longer available for the filing and perhaps she would like to join him in the Residence for a drink. They stroll under the gaze of the Secret Service and return under the same gaze less than half an hour later, the picture of innocence, but a transaction fulfilled, his poisons expelled and her tribute avidly received.

THE PRESIDENT JOINS his family for the short weekend, slipping back into the waters of family life without so much as a ripple, the serenity of his wife's outlook perhaps due to her certainty in the practical obstacles aligned against his opportunities for fornication. The weekend passes happily between the four of them with the exception of a slight wheeze picked up by the subject, almost certainly due to the transfer of horse hair via his daughter's clothing, which afflicts him gravely if indoors, a fact often overlooked by his wife, who will promise their patronage of some horse show or other without ensuring it is an outdoor event, thus placing him between the Scylla of asthmatic attendance and the Charybdis of confessing his allergic sensitivity. Economists quip that when America sneezes the world catches a cold, and it is equally true that when a President sneezes the press have him expiring of double pneumonia.

Following the First Family's return to D.C., the President gives a perfect impression of incuriosity about his two concubines, the affairs of state naturally taking precedence over such trifles (he is about to leave for a series of summits in Europe) to the extent that there is plausible deniability when he ignores them both, and, to their credit, he detects no stirring from either party that they consider themselves in receipt of unsympathetic treatment.

The subject has learned to treat his younger mistresses with a combination of paternalism and disdain, but in both cases the central message is the same, to wit that their feelings are irrelevant and it is of no influence on his emotional well-being whether they remain sexually attracted to him or would prefer nothing better than he go jump in a lake.

This philosophy arose from his first adventures in the art of picking up girls, when he observed fellow egos crushed by rejection, to the point where they became incapable of approaching the next girl. The subject determined to take rejection with complete nonchalance, to proceed to the next girl without deflection or deceleration, and to do so right there at the same party or with her best friend or whoever presented herself, soon learning that this could be readily effected without fear, shame or embarrassment, and, moreover, would often lead to his seizing the lips of victory from the jaws of defeat.

Looking ahead to the European tour, the President becomes

hopeful that the new treatment regimen for his Addison's disease will thin out his face. Over the years, he's learned to disguise his physical limitations, walking briskly on the flat to give the impression of vigor, talking rapidly, but approaching stairs with an air of languor to conceal his inability to descend or ascend at normal pace, and spending weekends outdoors in the sun, at Palm Beach in the winter and Cape Cod, frequently at sail, in the summer, to top up his "tan."

The President learned physical courage as a young man. Though failing both the Army and Navy medical boards, as the offspring of a rich family he could have secured some comfortable sinecure far out of harm's way, but instead he exploited his connections to win a position on the front line. The President is inspired by the physical courage of Senator James Grimes, paralyzed two days before his vote against impeaching President Johnson, and Senator Thomas Benton, keeping silent for days to save his voice for speeches due to a cancer that made his throat bleed. It is quite commonplace for the President to request painkillers in meetings, wherein he will wave away the concerns of his staff by playing down his discomfort, the word going out to Mrs. Lincoln that the President has a headache or the President has a twinge in his back and she will come through with a couple of pills and a glass of water; but a few days after his tryst with her little helper, he receives a quite uncommon therapy, when Mrs. Lincoln relays that her new assistant has read in a magazine that tension headaches can be relieved or prevented by scalp massages.

At the President's invitation, the girl bounds into the Oval Office, full of the confidence her breeding confers, and demonstrates the technique upon his person.

The next day, the President is asked by Mrs. Lincoln if he would care for another scalp massage, and Priscilla once more applies herself to the task, this time suggesting that she use a gel as both a lubricant and a hair tonic, his hair in her opinion being a national treasure, and when this substance is applied the day after, it is by Jill, who has joined Priscilla in what becomes a daily ten-minute session to relieve him of stress, which it does quite successfully, even though for the first few days it seems too good to be true that these two concubines have developed such a selfless camaraderie, so that the President jokes with them that he suspects they are Soviet spies bent on turning him as bald as Chairman Khrushchev.

He worries that their intimacy is becoming too visible, but, after due soul-searching, the President decides there is no harm in scalp massages. In fact, they are so beneficial to his stress levels that he employs this excuse for including the two girls on the forthcoming presidential tour.

FINALLY, BEFORE HE sets off, Justice presses him on the fate of the State Department advisor identified as a practicing homosexual, to which the President responds that the man should retain his post, on the grounds that he is a valued professional and what he does in his private life is his own business.

# THE BUTTON

T HE SUBJECT'S RELATIONSHIPS with men are far more
important than his relations with women, which, with the
exception of his marriage, have been irrelevant in the progress of
his career, and, sexual desire apart, exert no major influence on
his day-to-day life, although growing up with female siblings did
have a profound effect on his development, inculcating the sense
that having girls around was the norm, something that otherwise
might have been as foreign a concept as it was to many of his
fellows at boarding school, college and in the Navy.

Though naturally shy, he was no shyer around girls than at
other times, and certainly never nervous or intimidated by their
presence. Because women have come to him without too much
work on his part, he has been liberated to concentrate on male
relationships.

The subject boarded at an exclusive boys' school in Connecticut, albeit missing many weeks and occasionally months of the
year through illness, his medical problems repeatedly preventing
participation in sport, so that he was regarded as one of the
weaker physical specimens, but eventually his burgeoning facility

with women overcame the stigma of being Boston's answer to Tiny Tim Cratchit.

Although he is buoyed by female attention, and certainly a visible lack of it puts a hard ceiling on a man's status (though not popularity) within his peer group, he dismisses women's caprice in favor of the logical disinterest of male companionship. When he first sought public office, the subject could not have been elected through flirtation; the youth and material wealth that attracted certain women were vote-losers to a considerable section of the electorate, requiring him to promote the substance of his character and idealism.

Arguably the President's relations with the men in his administration are more complex than those with women; of them all, the most curious is with the Vice President. In their contest to secure the party nomination, the VP conducted a whispering campaign against the President on the subject of his medical health, knowing that the electorate would mistrust the suitability of a manifestly infirm candidate to hold executive office, and, though the doubt was swiftly and decisively quashed by the President's campaign team, the issue resurfaced when the VP haggled over his role in a potential new administration, whereupon this leverage, together with his popularity in the South, persuaded the President to accept his deputyship. But, having recognized the Vice President's electoral significance, the President now does his best to ignore it.

One day the VP appears at the poolside, less jacket, tie loosened, barefoot with his trousers turned up, to discuss the cost of the space program. He studies the President intently while the latter flexes and stretches, with a jealous gaze that takes in the enormous scars on his back and the bruises from injections and blood tests. Before the President leaves for Europe, he jokes, "If anything happens while I'm away, Lyndon, the keys to the Oval Office are under the mat."

THE SUBJECT IS a man's man, who believes there's something decidedly peculiar about men who do not prefer the company of male peers. He enjoys male talk, male humor and so forth, and, although women have a unique sexual appeal, there are a great many of them he finds a crashing bore. His sisters were all hearty, physical sorts of girls who enjoyed the rough-and-tumble of touch football, in contrast to his wife, a dainty debutante who broke her ankle when reluctantly co-opted into a game, hidden physical frailty being another attribute they share.

His elder sister's frailty was more mental than physical, prompting their father to arrange a lobotomy while their mother was on vacation. The subject does not blame himself, of course, but occasionally he wonders if he should have done more to oppose the operation, particularly since the procedure was botched and his sister is now permanently institutionalized. Such is the price of not fitting in.

Despite his advantages as a child, the subject was accustomed to the state of not fitting in, since he lacked the raucous personality that initially wins favor in the locker room. He learned that one should be smart enough to lead but not so smart one won't be followed. But, by the time he ran for President, the subject had become adept at courting favor from potential supporters, through which efforts, with the help of his brother-in-law the movie actor, he extended his Hollywood connections, which had initially been made during his father's brief flirtation with the movie business, and his somewhat longer flirtation with movie actresses.

In Hollywood, the subject encountered men who appeared to have everything he cherished—money, success, good looks and, most of all at that time, women. They were playboys, and partying with them proved he was no longer the bookish, sickly prep-school loner, but a different, more magnetic type of loner, one who lives on his own terms, as exemplified by Frank.

The subject first met Frank a couple of years ago, his father initially making strategic contact in order to curry support from the Italian-American community, via his brother-in-law, Peter, who seized the opportunity to inveigle himself back into Frank's social circle, from which he'd been exiled for the crime of lunch-dating one of Frank's girls. The subject's father was first to accept hospitality at the bacchanalian court in Palm Springs, which naturally piqued the subject's interest, so that his own visits commenced soon afterward. Frank stood out as the alpha, in contrast to the subject's brother-in-law, an inveterate follower, who'd received no formal education in his youth, instead traveling the world with impecunious aristocratic parents who eventually washed up in Palm Beach, from where he leapt to Hollywood and became a leading player in romances and comedies by usurping the roles of wartime rivals who were overseas doing their duty.

Originally, Peter had invited the subject into the B-list Hollywood scene, and it became a perquisite of office, after being elected to the United States Senate, to pluck an orchard of starlets, many of whom gave forgettable performances on- and off-screen, through which he deduced that there is no class of woman more complaisant with the principle of sex as a social transaction than the aspiring actress-model. Yet it was the subject's unexpected rapport with Frank that opened the green door, through which sashayed Marilyn, Jayne, Angie et al.

To Frank, the subject offered the ticket to a rarefied form of power he'd never experienced, and in return Frank offered access to the most glamorous women imaginable. His brother-in-law might have been able to furnish him with the occasional starlet, but Frank could provide any kind of woman he wanted, whether she was a movie star, a model, a dancer or a hooker. Soon the subject was making regular trips to Palm Springs, or to Las Vegas, where they'd drink and trade jokes, and Frank would mention some girl or other, wondering if maybe the subject fancied meeting her, and then one of his stooges would make a call and the girl would join them later at dinner, or for drinks, or sometimes she'd simply be waiting in the hotel room when he went up. It seemed there wasn't any available woman in Hollywood Frank couldn't call. In all probability, Frank had them first, but that never bothered the subject, since he generally believed he created the more favorable impression, and once he'd been with a girl it was up to him and her if they saw each other again, not Frank.

Toward the subject, he acted respectfully, but with his entourage Frank would often vent spiteful character assassinations to which the victim would offer no retort for fear of exile. The subject does not extend himself to Frank's monarchical excesses, yet one weekend at Palm Beach after the election he got the guys doing push-ups, a spectacle he found hilarious, lying on his lounger wearing a back brace, the agent of a bizarre vengeance against the athletic tormentors of his youth. The subject has reached the pinnacle of his social power, but it is the power he wields over men that furnishes its deepest meaning, something he observed repeatedly with Frank, who might sulk with a girl who wouldn't succumb to his bidding, but his retribution would stop there, whereas, in the case of a male who displeased him, ostracism was not enough: Frank had to see the man ruined.

Those Palm Springs weekends were the subject's first insight into the behavior of a king. Frank was not then, nor has he ever been, Hollywood's biggest movie star, and younger, handsomer singers are arguably more popular, yet he assumed the mantle of a king because he conducts himself like one: he runs a court, he gives and withdraws favor, and people fear he can call upon a private army. Most of all, he explores excess as though the rules that constrain ordinary men don't apply. Like the subject, he exhibits a rampant appetite for women. He could have two or three in a day, or simultaneously, and, as the leader of a pack of lions, would roar at any other male invading his territory. The women were more than a little scared of him and would often submit for fear of causing displeasure, but they understood what was expected when they received their invitations, so one feels they had no cause for complaint. When the subject first joined these gatherings, particularly the ones behind closed doors in Palm Springs, he must have been regarded as something of a curiosity—a young United States senator, a war hero, a Harvard alumnus—but Frank and the senator soon developed the lingua franca of fellow fornicators. Possibly Frank expected an ambitious young politician to disapprove of the limitless sexual opportunities on offer, but of course the subject did not, nor did he deport himself so as to convey unfamiliarity with such practices. Those weekends in the desert, where the air was bone-dry and the pools were dazzling mirrors under the immaculately blue sky, proved that man follows a common and predictable path when free to do so, the path of unconstrained sexual predation. Behind the security gates and high walls, Frank and his guests were at liberty to take a beautiful stranger's hand and walk her across the lush lawns, to the pool, to the hot tub, or into the villa, therein to peel away her coverings if any she wore, and gorge on pleasure. Up against such rampant behavior, monogamy appears a dismal state. The sexual profligacy on display at Frank's was neither unnatural nor immoral, nor did it inflict the deleterious effects of bingeing on alcohol, narcotics or even food. The subject reveled. He took a different girl for each part of the day. He made love as a king makes love.

In Hollywood, there is a hot new girl every month, and, when he volunteered to Frank an interest in a particular actress from some movie or other, he could rely on his fellow fornicator to know somebody sufficiently adjacent to offer bald insights into her availability for sex. One night at his place, the subject listed a dozen girls about whom Frank instantly returned pithy assessments: "married," "in love," "insane," till the whole room descended into laughter, the final epithet being "She's a guy!" Despite the bonhomie, there was always a distance between the two of them, albeit the comfortable remoteness of loners unwilling to surrender intimacy to the other.

In Frank's court, Frank was king, but it was apparent to any observer that the subject was the cleverer, and, when he began his campaign for the Presidency, the possibility arose that one day he might be the more powerful, added to which are Frank's deficiencies in the twin departments by which men compare themselves at first impression, height and hair. Frank's hairline has receded to the point where he has begun experimenting with styling and toupees to increase scalp coverage; former teeny-boppers who've cherished locks of his hair since the forties could sell them back to him for thousands of dollars. In addition, he appears to reach middle height, except when one sees him around the pool without his custom-made shoes, whereupon he shrinks dramatically. But one area of competition is far too sensitive for them to have become rivals. Frank avoided competing with the subject over women by presenting them as campaign contributions, and the subject avoided competing with Frank by never making an overt pass at one of his concubines. It would not be worth jeopardizing an alliance unified publicly by politics and privately by relentless sexual predation.

Frank took credit for applying a Hollywood sheen to the senator's campaign, his patronage attracting leading celebrities to fund-raisers, though the senator always felt this benefit needed to be balanced against the potential embarrassment of his putative association with a certain Italian-American subculture. While the long nights of gambling, whoring, drinking and fornicating continued, it was a risk worth absorbing, and it was Frank who first introduced the subject to Judy, with the irresistible taster that "she looks a lot like Elizabeth Taylor." (The subject once suggested Ms. Taylor as a potential Palm Springs entertainment, but Frank felt she was unavailable due to an overzealous obedience to her marriage vows, a state of mind easy to discount when one is so accustomed to socializing with more enlightened individuals.)

Judy is an old girlfriend the President likes to keep warm, so when he hears via Frank that she's going to be in town on a night when coincidentally his wife is staying with friends in New York, the President has no hesitation in inviting her to the White House for dinner, which they share with a couple of presidential aides for the sake of appearances, before the aides retire, allowing the President to escort her to the Lincoln Bedroom, where they pick up pretty much where they left off in Vegas a few months before the election.

Frank follows up the next morning with a telephone call, via Mrs. Lincoln's office, and the two men agree it's been too long since they last saw each other (the Inauguration Ball), whereupon Frank jokes about what happened that night when, en route from one gathering to the next, with the First Lady asleep at home, fatigued by the various celebrations, the President gave Angie and another starlet a ride in the presidential limousine, only to realize the recklessness of being seen cruising through town with two gorgeous young actresses on his first night in office, dropping them off discreetly and sending his driver around the block a couple of times before he made his entrance unaccompanied. The President laughs as Frank reminds him of the girls' dismay at being denied the grand entrance—and Frank being denied the opportunity to witness the subject stroll into the party with a beauty on each arm in a passable impression of Hugh Hefner—and then he switches to the upcoming dates when his diary places him in Washington, which the President promises to pass on to Mrs. Lincoln with the firm intention of extending him an invitation to come visit, but after the call the President hears an echo of his laughter and reacts in a most peculiar way, feeling a surge of antagonism, for which there can be no justification, since Frank paid him the compliment of addressing him as "Mr. President" and the humor they shared was no more irreverent than with any other old friend.

When the presidential campaign gathered momentum, the balance of power between them began to shift. Though the senator constantly acknowledged Frank's contribution to the campaign, he was one of many, and the senator began to suspect ulterior motives when Frank donated women. Perhaps Frank was sensitive to the situation, which both of them appreciated would reach a turning point in Los Angeles that summer, where the senator for Massachusetts would either receive his party's nomination or sink back into his former obscurity. Either outcome would have its own particular effect on their alliance, a matter about which they jested but never discussed seriously, as neither wanted to surgically explore its anatomy.

Frank called a few weeks ahead of the convention, inviting the senator to a dinner he was hosting at Romanoff's, with the enticement of a beautiful actress who was keen on an introduction. "It's someone new, Jack," he said, "but I daren't say who." He laughed. The senator laughed too and agreed to fly in.

The senator had a list Frank knew about, not a formal list that was written down anyplace, rather a bevy of actresses to whom conversation usually turned between the two of them, such as Angie, whom the senator had admired in *Rio Bravo,* and Jayne, whose forgettable movies he'd never even given himself the opportunity to forget, but he'd had them both by then, so the excitement arose of the mysterious dinner guest being one of the other ladies on the list. Frank being Frank, he never let on, so fantasies played in the subject's imagination, and then, at dinner in Romanoff's, Frank introduced him to Marilyn for the first time.

She was a luminous star who professed a fascination for politics. Frank had told her all about the campaign, and she wanted to lend her support. The senator paid courteous attention to her opinions and interests, yet the whole evening Frank must have observed them from a platform of privileged insight, knowing that the subject would immediately be calculating how he might lure the goddess into bed. Though she confessed a degree of estrangement from her own husband, the subject calculatedly disclosed little about his own personal life.

After she left, Frank said, "She's one of them chicks who reckons she never screws for its own sake. It's always gotta be about something."

So, when the senator called her the next day, he explained how much he'd enjoyed their meeting, how flattered he was by her interest in the campaign, and how intelligent and thought-provoking he'd found their discussion. She gladly accepted an invitation to renew their acquaintance when he returned for the convention, at which, when proceedings began in earnest, he soon found himself shuttling from private meetings onto the floor and back, every hour consumed by the effort to secure votes from the Party. With any ordinary girl, the subject would have bused her to his hotel suite, where he could launch an amatory broadside, but he was acutely aware of Marilyn's extraordinary status and the necessity of convincing her she was respected as well as adored. He managed to speak to her on the telephone on the first day, explaining, "I'm somewhat occupied with the business of becoming the next President, but taking you out for dinner strikes me as a matter of equal national importance." They agreed he would call her again when he opened a window in his schedule, but, while the lead he had established over the other candidates in the primaries appeared to be maintained on the convention floor, creating a likelihood of the nomination, this optimism did not create a relaxed atmosphere, instead fomenting an ethos that the campaign should put its foot on the gas to close out the opposition. It soon became apparent that, if he didn't escape that evening, the following evening—that of the final voting for the nomination—would be his last in Los Angeles and therefore the last chance of bedding Marilyn, when the imperatives of politics would no doubt squash sexual exigency. The senator wrestled with the dilemma for some time before informing his staff, to their astonishment, that he intended to exit the convention in favor of a private dinner.

The senator entertained his target at Puccini's, an exclusive Italian restaurant in Beverly Hills, where he succeeded in consuming a mild pasta dish and a glass of wine without precipitating an embarrassingly Augean withdrawal to the men's room. She confided she had suffered a loveless upbringing, never having known her father, while her mother suffered from mental illness, so that she had spent her childhood in foster homes and orphanages. The subject was tempted to respond by revealing his sister's psychiatric problems, but couldn't discuss the lobotomy without betraying his sadness at her resulting condition, so he forbore. He believed she would respond better to the strength of a father figure, offering a paraphrase of Lawrence: one needs to be loving to find love, but too many people insist on being loved when there is no love in them.

She was eager to talk politics. "Will you be the next president?" she said.

"So far, so good," he said.

"Jack, that's wonderful. Let's celebrate."

And so the transaction presented itself, to a man on the brink of the highest public office, with the most desired sex symbol in the land.

Marilyn struggled in modeling and walk-on parts for almost a decade before she became a star, so one imagines the situation at dinner that night was not unfamiliar, but the subject felt his station was sufficiently grander than a movie impresario to permit a tribute from a personage even of her elevation. Offering to see her home, he ordered his driver to set course for her apartment, the sky still cradling enough light to give outlines to the roofs, black on indigo, as their shapes tracked across the limousine windows. She shone, even in the gloom, her hair expertly dyed to the luster of white gold, her cheek and neck of alabaster, above the dramatic swell of her bust. A man might suffer from nerves. But the subject has enough experience to appreciate that one cannot make love to a goddess.

In that crucial moment, he did wonder if Frank had some agenda in introducing him to Marilyn. Certainly he would understand the delicacy of their relationship, his and his as well as his and hers, if the nominee took up with her. But that night such considerations were of secondary importance. As he would with any beautiful woman on the backseat of a limousine gliding through a city on a clear summer night, he laid his hand on hers, and felt it quiver and squeeze his in return.

THE PRESIDENT AND the First Lady cross the Atlantic aboard the Special Air Mission Boeing out of Idlewild, during which they try to spend some private time together. Travel plays havoc with his back, causing tingling and numbness to spread down his left buttock into his ham. Now propped up by four pillows, following the Canadian accident, the President spoons a bland porridge of a meal while the First Lady sips a glass of French wine and chain-smokes a pack of L&Ms. She's not eating because she was a couple of pounds over on the scales this morning and hasn't had time to work off the weight on the trampoline. In her way, she's just as nervous about this European tour as the President.

They dine in the private cabin where he enjoyed the assignation with Marilyn, yet he is unfazed, so long past counting conquests he now discounts them.

The subject epitomizes how a man requires a particular character to be a successful philanderer. He must possess low levels of guilt regarding his conduct—ideally none, as in his case; after all, a man burdened by post-coital angst can hardly enjoy his daliances, which rather defeats the point of them. He absolutely should not be a bad liar, the best lie being a fact one adopts as the truth. And he must appreciate that, while true love demands a certain toughness of character to overlook its flaws and illogic, adultery requires even more.

He is not alone in these attributes. After their first encounter, at a social dinner ten years ago, he walked his future bride out to her car only to find her fiancé waiting behind the wheel. She had the toughness to shed the wrong man and jump for the right one. Occasionally, particularly during quarrels early in their marriage, she threatened to take lovers, but, being a politician, he was careful neither to endorse nor oppose such a course, knowing his reply in the heat of the moment might return to haunt him. His undisclosed opinion was that, if she enjoyed the occasional private adventure, it would carry no consequence were he to know nothing, a condition he would abundantly prefer over a tearful confession, particularly if the affair benefited her mood in some respect, and the man wasn't someone of whom he'd disapprove (a communist dictator, or a Republican).

The First Lady crouches to peer out the porthole, the setting sun providing just enough light to distinguish the dark sky from the blank sea, and he stretches up to cross the cabin and join her, slipping his arm around her narrow shoulders. She says, "Every time I see the size of the ocean, I can't imagine how you did it."

That first night when he walked her out to her car, he shook her hand and studied her nervous glances toward her fiancé, but the subject knew she had weighed up his experience commanding a tiny torpedo boat on the biggest ocean on the planet, and knew he held the advantage over the other man, even though that man was closer in age and probably easier company. She realized he had the toughness she needed, to match hers, the toughness for marriage and parenthood and success. But, then, when they became married, they found themselves out on the ocean in a small boat, and at times she looked like she wanted to fling herself overboard.

The problem in those days was the creeping realization that he could never have enough premarital sex just as one can never eat a big enough meal to fast without eventually getting hungry. He'd been accustomed to so much that, paradoxically, he might have adjusted better had the opposite been true, since he wouldn't have missed it so very much. Married men who don't miss other partners must not have been particularly interested in women in the first place.

But of course, actually, that wasn't the issue. Rather as she didn't understand how a young man could stand on a tiny boat on a vast ocean and swallow his fear, his wife, who didn't crave other partners, didn't understand why his urges might not have been extinguished by connubial attachment. A few weeks into their marriage, after the gourmet bingeing of honeymoon had slumped into the TV dinners of monogamy, the subject's attraction toward other women visibly returned and she responded with a cold, possessive outrage that so infuriated him he made his natural needs more manifest, at parties flirting with other women, on one occasion removing a girl for a quickie that narrowly escaped his wife's discovery. He maintained this strategy of insidious humiliation until her response was no longer controlled and possessive, but shattered and defeated. This was her punishment for failure to comprehend the potency of his urges. He made the point in order to establish a modus vivendi for their marriage. One will had to overcome the other or else they would have split. And he never felt guilty; once a man starts on that road, who knows where he'll stop?

HE LIMPS BACK to bed and she helps with the pillows. The mattress is rigid, and stuffed with cattle-tail hair so as not to inflame his allergies. She helps remove the brace and then injects a painkiller into his back, after which he swallows various steroid and thyroid pills, another to prevent diarrhea, plus an antibiotic and a sedative. She climbs in beside him. He kisses her and holds her close as they listen to the hum of the engines.

The President decided to include his pair of White House concubines on the trip, even though they have little or no contribution to make to the business of foreign policy. But they would help him concentrate. He adopts the converse of Flaubert's dictum to "be regular and orderly in your life so that you may be violent and original in your work." He gave considerable thought to how he might achieve this little coup, yet in the end simply gave an aide a nonchalant order as if booking passage for the presidential golf clubs. He followed Frank's exemplar of the conduct of a king, and the aide reacted as one of Frank's entourage would to an order for a dozen hookers divided equally between blondes, brunettes and redheads. Just as one of Frank's stooges wouldn't dare quibble that his boss was overordering on the redheads, the aide simply nodded and withdrew to deal with his conscience elsewhere. No doubt it was a matter of gossip among the staff, and later the President's suspicions were confirmed when he saw the Secret Service manifest on which the girls were code-named Fiddle and Faddle, though he doesn't recall who was who.

A name that appears on no manifest is Dr. Feelgood, whom the President has instructed to travel by private jet and add the cost to his bill.

Although the exercise program has improved the condition of the muscles around his lumbar spine, the President suffered an agonizing setback on a state visit to Canada two weeks prior, when he participated in a tree-planting ceremony with the Governor-General. Handed a shovel, in front of a large crowd of reporters and photographers, the President faced a challenge to his vim. It was unthinkable he would permit a national embarrassment akin to being found to throw like a girl or to be unable to urinate in front of other men. The Governor-General led, shifting continental volumes of earth, after which the President gripped the handle and planted his feet, before plunging the spade into the soil and heaving. At once, he felt a lightning bolt shoot through his lower back. He straightened slowly, maintaining a smile in the face of ringing applause, but as the ensuing minutes passed, the hinges locked, and by evening he was on triple painkillers and crutches. Away from the public gaze, the President has been employing crutches ever since, and has conscripted Dr. Feelgood to tail the presidential party and ensure the current maladies don't subvert the global impression of our President as the embodiment of American vigor.

The good doctor alights at a private airfield on the outskirts of Paris, claiming to be personal physician to the First Lady. Meanwhile the President's first port of call is a hot tub, in which he's still immersed when Dr. Feelgood arrives. A quick history precedes the preparation of potions, then the First Lady and a nurse help the President out of the tub, laying him naked, face-down on a mat, in the bathroom that stays humid from the steamy bath. Dr. Feelgood begins with some gentle manipulation, but he has weak hands and no feel for it, before proceeding to prepare the lumbar region for a series of injections. His fingers invade the dips and hollows, each of which is so exquisitely tender that the President squeals, each time Dr. Feelgood saying curtly in his accent, "I'm sorry, Mr. President," while the First Lady grips both her husband's hands, appearing aghast at his uncontrollable weeping, before the procedure begins in earnest, a sharp needle being driven repeatedly into the spaces round the discs and ligaments, after which the Old Nazi gives a final injection of magic potion into the buttock.

By the time he faces the crowds, the President is bounding. The French have lined the streets in the thousands for a glimpse of the First Couple as they glide along the Champs Élysées in their motorcade, waving at the myriad Gallic grimaces. The First Lady has dressed with even more exquisite chic than usual, having spent days with designers ensuring she'd travel with the most stunning array of outfits. In this instance, he's been quite permissive about her spending. At home, there exists a school of thought, particularly in what is wryly termed Middle America, that the First Lady is exhibitionist, spoiled, aloof and a *bon viveur*

(euphemism for a lush), these unfair criticisms principally origi-
nating from observers who place themselves in the comfortable
middle of our citizenship, whereas most demographic indicators
would place them at the bottom, their intellectual conservatism
sharing a pew with piety, though it's curious that people with the
least for which to thank God always seem to believe in him
most.

Yet in this corridor of faces turned in admiration, instead of
contorted into customary Old World sneers, the First Lady's regal
bearing pays off in an instant; the years of marriage, of assumed
monogamy, of strife hidden for the sake of appearances, bear
bountiful political fruit. The President has landed in this land of
sniffy haute couture not in the company of a prim little Mid-
western cookie-baker but on the arm of an American princess,
who not only charms the proletariat but, at the reception this
evening, the President of the Republic himself, by conversing flu-
ently with him in his native tongue.

In the French fashion, le President must keep many mistresses. Perhaps while his American counterpart is over here, he'll
donate him one like they did the Statue of Liberty. He is a king,
this French aristocrat with the martial corpulence of a tank, a reminder that great men can change history, within certain obvious
limitations, and many of them are driven to plunder women, and
what a pale and pathetic world we would inhabit were only the
advertently monogamous permitted to run our industries and
govern our institutions, a world inherited by bloodless men
woken from their dreamless sleep by the crash of lovers, racers,
gourmands and warriors, while men with appetites and the appetite for change fall beneath the juggernaut of conventional morality.

Le President must appreciate that the President is a man of equal, if not substantially stronger, appetites. He must see. He must. His snout twitches at the First Lady's perfume as a hound scents a trail, before his eyes glow in admiration, as, to the President's surprise, do his. Yet it is the American President who possesses the queen, from whom so much of the king's status stems, although for some heads of state their choice makes marriage resemble riding a tiger.

Men make their match not with the woman they can get but with the woman they can keep. A man at some point in his life will sleep with a woman far more attractive than his usual quarry, for whatever reason (she is naïve, she is insane, she is drunker than a monkey), and fall instantly in love. But there will follow the woman's epiphany, which may occur the following morning or after their marriage, in which she glimpses the power of her beauty, a point from which he cannot prevent losing her, and men come to understand this fact in their sexual careers. One does one's best to bed beautiful women, and one's worst by becoming attached to them. Yet the subject appears to have mastered the impossible, a fact indicated by the admiring gazes of men as august as le President, and when they return to the embassy that night, the subject remembers first looking upon his bride to be before she embarked on housekeeping and motherhood and her dreadfully suffocating worship of monogamy.

As he soaks in the giant, gilded bathtub, the steam of those days swirls around, when she was the woman a man could get but couldn't keep, as witnessed by her fiancé, in his car waiting for her to walk out from the restaurant on that night of their first meeting, the knowledge striking the fiancé through the rain-spattered glass of his windshield when he saw her strolling out with the then junior senator as challengingly as if she were a bitch marking a tree.

Before marriage, the subject had a longish dalliance with a movie actress, a dazzling beauty separated from her husband. (The husband eventually became the First Lady's clothes designer, a position holding pressures and responsibilities at least equal to the engineers who build our space rockets.) Gene, the actress, was actually someone he seriously considered marrying from their first night together. She turned heads wherever they went. He offered his career as the reason for breaking up, but the truth was every man would kill for her, and she knew it. He couldn't arrive ten minutes late at a restaurant without finding a chancer at her table, her hand in his as she gazed up at him, whether he was or wasn't the bigger, better deal, and through cocktails she'd give a serene stare that warned, "Don't be late, don't put me down and expect to find me where you left me." In a wife, he required a woman who would capitulate for fear of losing him. Given the kind of drab mouse that can be, he's done rather well for himself.

She slips into the bathroom with a daiquiri she's had the embassy valet make. Steam condenses on her face, making her skin glisten. The President can see she's excited about the day that is just ending, and he's proud of her. "They love you," he says, "almost as much as I do."

THE FIRST LADY takes part in a number of solo cultural engagements while the President conducts a crowded schedule of political summits. Dr. Feelgood treats his back in secret before the President competes with his French counterpart in debates on Franco-American relations. The President receives greater respect than advisors predicted. He suspects General de Gaulle has decided he must have something going for him to have kept such a lovely wife.

This afternoon, while the First Lady visits Marie-Antoinette's house in the company of the Minister of Culture, the subject carves out some time between meetings at the embassy for Fiddle and Faddle to administer a scalp massage in the private quarters. It is now nearly a week since the subject last had extramarital relations. He is complaining of a tension headache, testicular aching and incipient sexual toxemia.

Aides and Secret Service agents appear not to notice the girls troop into the room. His crutches stand propped against the wall inconspicuously; perhaps he hopes these young women will disregard his chronic infirmities as they would a pitcher's sore shoulder or a running back's sprained knee, minor injuries that will heal by the weekend, but the girls are shocked by his infirmity. Quickly, the President asks how they're enjoying the trip, and they're agog with questions about his summit with the French head of state.

He says, "He wants Louisiana back but I offered to trade Canada."

Priscilla laughs, and she is the one he asks to stay for a few minutes when Jill has left. He struggles into a supine position, saying, "My next engagement's in ten minutes."

But she says, "Are you sure you're up to it?" As a boy of sixteen, he was confined to a sanatorium in New York City where a battalion of medics probed the mysteries of his dysfunctional digestive tract. After they'd buggered him with an enema, a nurse cleaned him up. Betsy was her name, an apple-cheeked girl from a good family, not a day over twenty herself. When she rolled him on his back, his face flushed beet red, and Betsy stifled a laugh. She quickly tossed a towel over an erection she could have twanged like a tuning fork. "There, there, Jack," she said. "At least there's one part that works properly."

He puts Priscilla's hand to his zipper. "I'm just fine," he says.


WHEN THE FIRST Lady returns, she is brimming with inspiration for her White House restoration, and at their engagement that evening once again she shines in a stunning gown. The President opens his speech by joking that, since no one has noticed, he's the man accompanying the First Lady on this tour.

The next day, the party flies on to Vienna, the journey throwing the President's back into spasm. As soon as they're hidden inside the embassy compound, he demands his crutches and hobbles to their quarters with word going ahead to run a hot bath. Fortunately, Dr. Feelgood's charter flight lands at a private airfield an hour after the SAM touched down. Three people are required to lift the President out of the tub and lay him on a mat, and then the Old Nazi shoots him up with painkillers, muscle relaxants and amphetamine, his favorite cocktail after a daiquiri.

In the morning, the President's back is locked so tight he can't walk two steps. But, thanks to Dr. Feelgood's next course of injections, the Leader of the Free World bounds down the embassy steps to greet the Soviet Premier.

The Premier favors a hat, the great leveler for the short and bald, which is why the subject deliberately eschews them, all the better to broadcast the excellence of his stature and the lush magnificence of his thatch. For the ceremonial handshake, the President stands erect, so Mr. Khrushchev only comes up to his shoulder. The latter clasps his hand so hard the President feels a pop in the base of his spine, but his smile never flickers thanks to the elixirs swirling through his system.

In the private meeting, the Premier sprays the President with vitriol concerning Berlin, nuclear arms and Cuba. He seizes on the President's sensitivity to the last and goes on the attack. In the end, the President confesses the invasion was a mistake, yet his efforts to open meaningful negotiations on nuclear disarmament and cooperation in the governance of Berlin are bludgeoned by a lengthy tirade on the merits of communism and the crimes of Western imperialism. As the meeting ends, the President inquires about the medals on the Premier's jacket, which Mr. Khrushchev reveals are peace medals. The President says, "Well, I hope you get to keep them!" The Premier chuckles, and, at a banquet at Schönbrunn Palace, he continues the metamorphosis, even cracking jokes with the First Lady. His own lumpy spouse is apparently his third, the first one having died during a famine, so he must take comfort in the knowledge that this one looks extremely unlikely to perish from starvation.

As usual, Dr. Feelgood arrives at the embassy early the next day to effect the President's pharmacological transformation from cripple to vigorous Leader of the Free World, while the jocose farmer from last night's banquet has once more reverted to a hard-nosed communist, who scorns suggestions of a ban on testing nuclear weapons as an initial step toward disarmament. The President endeavors to vocalize his fears that nuclear war might arise from unstoppable escalation, or even by mistake, that as the two great powers who hold the fate of mankind in our grasp, we must collaborate in the quest for peace, but the Premier returns to the subject of Berlin, voicing the certitude of a treaty with East

Germany that will lead to Soviet troops taking control of the western portion of the city.

The President says, "The United States must and will honor its commitment to the people of West Berlin."

The Premier says, "We will sign the treaty whether you like it or not. If you use force, Mr. President, then I will use force. If you want war, that's your problem."

His words haunt the President as the party flies on to Great Britain. The fat little peasant without even so much as a high school education is the Russian bear who expects to triumph in the pit because he sniffs weakness. He is wrong, but he doesn't know he's wrong, and he will believe that confrontation will intimidate the President of the United States into making mistakes. As they drive into London, the President sees streets lined with people, not cheering as they did in Paris, but waving BAN THE BOMB banners grey as gravestones.

Rolling two limos behind is a pair of military aides, one of whom wears the Football handcuffed to his wrist. They accompany the President everywhere, usually within a minute's call, never more than ninety seconds away. They rode on the SAM in seats set apart, in their crisp, dark uniforms, sipping mineral water, the black Football granted a seat of its own. Sometimes the President swears he thinks he hears it tick.

Over the English Channel, alone in their private cabin, he peered down into the slate sea and had never been more fearful, not even in the Pacific. We possess in our nuclear arsenals the power to obliterate each other, and his hopes for the future will disappear from this earth just as the wakes of the ships below perished in immemorial waters. He pictures silver darts rising in banks from beyond the Caucasus, blips on radar screens and telephones ringing, blank men in uniforms confirming codes and then our own missiles groaning in their silos, becoming beasts ascending from the underworld. He sees them merge, over the ocean, making ten thousand metal crosses in the sky, each one to mark the grave of a million dead. His hand is on the button, and it trembles.

AT BUCKINGHAM PALACE, the President is received by the Queen, who is flawlessly hospitable, but, despite being a relatively young and pleasant-looking woman, she's so aristocratically buttoned up he couldn't imagine going to bed with her—her Monagasque counterpart being a different matter entirely, however. Sources suggest her consort has felt the same way ever since they were married, and has pursued affairs of such surgical delicacy that the President wants to sequester him over brandy and cigars, as even *he* might have something to learn.

The President notices Jill has positioned herself prominently when he returns to the embassy, and there is a sufficient hiatus before his luncheon engagement with the Prime Minister for her to accompany him to his quarters for twenty minutes, after which he orders an aide to conscript the Secret Service into emplacing security measures for a private social arrangement this evening.

Later, he sees the bed has been made, with not a wrinkle on the cover to betray him, but when the First Lady returns from the V&A, he notices a button on the bedside furniture that is neither hers nor his. He asks her about her visit, but the whole time he's trying to distract her. She wanders around the room, shedding outer garments, until she lands next to the button. She hovers there, relating her tour of the Victoria and Albert Museum, while he would sweat if he had working adrenal glands.

She glances down, her gaze pointing directly at the button. She hesitates over a phrase, and then continues regardless, eventually withdrawing into the bathroom.

The small, pale button comes from Jill's blouse, and he quickly drops it in the trash, after which he endures a minute searching the room for any other incriminating evidence. Still, he hopes his wife imagines, as he once did, that the presidency gives the incumbent as much chance of fornicating as being in jail does, and far less of being sodomized, but for all his past indiscretions he hates to contemplate being accused, since it feels such a long while since they had one of those conversations that he possesses no exact idea how it would go, whether the First Lady requires a higher index of suspicion given his office, or will consider her position inflates the ignominy of the betrayal. He still can't decode her. Her mystery intrigued him from the start of their courtship. Perhaps it wasn't love at all. Perhaps he was just very, very interested. If he thought marrying her would be the best way of getting to know her, he was wrong.

The London papers contain more pictures of the First Lady than of the President, and she looks elegant as ever in the limousine conveying the couple to Downing Street. The President is familiar with the sights from boyhood when his father was ambassador, and he returned after the war. But the memory of being diagnosed here sours his affections for this city.

He'd been sickly all his life but reached adulthood with the expectation of growing out of allergies and respiratory problems, accepting that he might not be able to play football again but believing his back would eventually heal and knowing maybe he couldn't eat or drink freely but medication would bring his digestive anomalies under control. All that changed the day he collapsed and came to be informed he was afflicted with an incurable condition of the adrenal glands for which he would require life-long therapy. He remembers the feeling once the treatment restored a modicum of well-being, as he drove the streets where once he'd been the privileged ambassador's son gazing into a limitless future, the feeling that everyone he saw walking or running or smiling enjoyed an extraordinary gift of good health that he was perversely denied. Already by then, his elder brother had been killed and his sister lobotomized. Like theirs, his life was no longer limitless, and, as if to prove it, his next sister was obliterated by an air crash the following year. In the years that followed, the back didn't heal, of course, nor did the gut or prostate or thyroid—in fact, they all got mortally worse, to the point where he resigned himself to an unfinished life, but it was here it happened, the shattering epiphany that he'd never enjoy the country-club autumn of a sprightly septuagenarian thwacking tennis balls and goosing waitresses.

There's more warmth in the first five minutes with the British Prime Minister than in all his summit hours in Paris and Vienna. The PM is an Old Etonian in his sixties, a decorated veteran of the First World War, and charming company. Their first meeting includes State Department staff and officials from the Foreign Ministry, but he says, "Wouldn't it be less of a bore if it were just the two of us?"

They dismiss their staffs and the Prime Minister adds, "Forgive my suggestion, but you look worn out, Jack. I had them send over a rocking chair." The PM grins. "Your back and my legs." He houses about half a pound of German shrapnel in his legs that moves about at regular intervals, causing him excruciating discomfort.

The President slips into the rocking chair and feels his back ease. A butler pours them both a whiskey, and the conversation swings from world affairs to society gossip. Later their wives join them for luncheon. His wife is great fun, and he seems devoted to her. Before the President leaves, he confides that the Soviet Premier bested him in Vienna. The PM says, "I shall give you the benefit of my long experience, and reveal the greatest challenge facing the statesman of today: events. Events, my dear Jack, events." The President chuckles, and, as they shake hands, the PM adds, "Call upon me any time of the day or night. I'm a light sleeper."

After a week of travel, the First Lady is keen to rest. The President checks with an aide on the progress of the plan to sneak out for a private rendezvous, and he's pleased to learn the Secret Service has grudgingly agreed to watch his back. Their reluctance stems from the President's order that they remain invisible and allow his companion and him to conduct themselves spontaneously.

Finally, Dr. Feelgood makes his customary secret entrance, this time via the garden, having stumbled through the foliage and entered with leaves stuck to the soles of his shoes, and instills his potions into the presidential back.

At different times, both Fiddle and Faddle hover in the halls, looking to catch his eye. He makes his choice and tells her to get ready. "What for?" she asks.

"We're going out," he says.

"Where?" she says.

"On a date," he says.

She gazes at him incredulously for all of two seconds before she bursts into a glorious smile.

When they walk out into the summer air, the patches of sky visible between the buildings are fading to night. She wears a beautiful coat, but the evening is mild and dry so he wears a sports jacket.

"Where's the limousine?" she asks.

"We're walking. Not far."

She keeps looking around for the Secret Service. They're on foot and in crawling cars, but, true to their undertaking, remain inconspicuous as they stroll the couple of blocks to Claridge's. The doorman's eyes widen as the President approaches, but, then, in the classic British tradition he's counting on, the doorman doffs his cap and bids them "Good evening," as he would any other aristocratic couple.

The President's date checks her hat and coat, then he leads her into the Fumoir. The President notices a heavy-set man with a crew cut in the lobby, and another follows them into the bar, but the agents are doing their best to blend in, even ordering drinks, and, though heads inevitably turn as they seat themselves, flawlessly observed British social reserve prevents anyone staring.

A waiter takes their order with such affected nonchalance that, when he walks away, the First Lady bursts into laughter. "Jack, this is crazy!"

But he says, "What's so crazy about wanting to have a night to myself with the world's number-one sex symbol?"

# THE WALL

WHEN THE PRESIDENT returns to the United States, the children have been brought to greet him at National Airport. Caroline scurries across the tarmac and flings her arms around his thighs, the nanny following as she cradles John Jr. His son sits on his lap in the limousine as they coast back to the White House, while Caroline squeezes herself against his side, laying her head on his upper arm. He realizes how much he has missed them physically. Often we think of our children as tiny packages of ourselves, disregarding the physicality of our love for them, but as his daughter presses herself against him he feels an impression of her soft cheek and hair against his arm, as if he's marked by it as one would be by a tightly bound bandage, and his son gurgles when his father brushes his hand against his face.

The First Lady has stayed on in Europe for a short vacation with her sister. She seems rather taken with the regal status she enjoys over there, prompting the President to jest she's hanging around to hook a prince.

In the confines of the West Wing, the President hops on crutches. Dr. T. speculates that the stress of the European tour aggravated the Canadian insult, but the President keeps secret that Dr. Feelgood's elixirs sped him through those summit meetings at an appalling cost to bone and cartilage that were already in a state of severe trauma. For once, Adm. B. concurs, but wants to investigate further with X-rays, wondering whether something has gone awry with the metal plates. Even Dr. Feelgood makes a house call, smuggled in by the Secret Service to avoid the umbrage of Dr. T. or Adm. B.

The quack inquires about the First Lady, whom he occasionally treats for mood. "You will miss her, Mr. President," he says, "and the danger will be a critical buildup of orgone energy. It must have its release through orgasm, or else a destructive endoplasm infiltrates man's mental and bodily processes."

Too infirm to attend social engagements, the President becomes a recluse, relying on the children for company. In the First Lady's absence, he allows them the run of the West Wing, so that Caroline can often be found seated on a chair in Mrs. Lincoln's office, her feet not reaching the floor, playing at typing and, occasionally, but only if she's very, very good, being allowed to stamp envelopes. The President lets John Jr. bring his toy trucks, planes and boats into the Oval Office and is happy for the boy to play quietly nearby, even under his desk, while the President reads reports and letters.

The President becomes attached to keeping his children close by. He knows the perils of the world better than most fathers, and fears for their future. They accompany him to and from the Residence in the morning, at lunchtime, and in the evening. When work keeps him at his desk, he glances out the window to watch them in the playground with the nanny. Like any doting father, he loves them more than he loves his wife.

On the morning of the third day back, the subject wakes with a mild tension headache, for which he takes aspirin, which irritates his stomach, for which he takes antacids, which give him gas. By evening, the headache is almost intolerable. It is not in his character to pay close attention to his maladies, but in this case the subject makes an exception, since he suspects he is suffering a withdrawal syndrome. Fiddle (or Faddle—he has stopped trying to distinguish them) visits him in the Residence that night.

But the President's back is no better, and Dr. T. and Adm. B. prescribe convalescence in Palm Beach. The compound is eerily deserted at this time of year, before the winter migration, folded deck chairs and raveled umbrellas pinned on adjacent estates as he laps the hot saltwater pool.

A skeleton staff accompanies the President—the French chef, the valet, a few close aides plus secretarial support from Fiddle and Faddle, who'll be least missed in Washington owing to their utter lack of usefulness.

On the second evening, the chef excels himself with a fish supper, and, while the diners quaff chilled Chablis on the verandah, the President entertains a journalist. In quiet moments, the President reflects on the Soviet Premier's threats, and the transient loss of confidence allows his back pain to register around the eyes.

"Aren't you enjoying your presidency?" the journalist says.

"I wouldn't recommend the job," the President says, and, as the journalist is about to make a note, he adds, "not for four or eight years!"

The journalist chuckles, but there's an awkward moment after dinner when the President's aides prepare to drive to their hotel, and the journalist offers Fiddle and Faddle a ride. They make excuses, first that they have their own car, and, when he expects them to follow the group dispersing to the vehicles, that they have some more work to do here tonight. His gaze flicks to the President, but he is casually waving off the staff and hoisting himself onto crutches to turn indoors. Whether or not journalistic inquisitiveness has been piqued, it's understood the matter's off the record.

The pair linger like prom girls waiting to be asked to dance, as they did the night before, when he wanted to avoid favoritism toward one but couldn't recall which he'd had last, and again tonight he can't remember whose turn it is. Fiddle (or Faddle) says, "With all your responsibilities, you shouldn't be expected to make *yet another* decision," and then Faddle (or Fiddle) says, "not when you don't have to choose."

The President grins. "I believe I've gone on the record favoring equality of opportunity in all federal employment."

"We'll run your bath," they say.

"Make it hot," he says, and then, as they scoot indoors—"that also goes for the bath."


THE NEXT MORNING, the President rises early to swim, another little compartment in his mind cleared by not having to distinguish between the girls—he now considers them the Fiddle-Faddle duality, but last night's amusements have put another area into spasm, despite their being scrupulously circumspect. Two agents hoist him out of the pool, one in the water hefting his legs and the other on the side hooking his armpits, then he stands in a stoop while they pass the crutches.

He happens to see a woman walking past the perimeter. She's

a voluptuous brunette of about thirty-five. The presence of the Secret Service at the gate intrigues her, and she looks up toward the house. The President calls, "Good morning!"

She smiles, somewhat bemused. "Good morning . . . Mr. President!"

He says, "I hope you're a Democrat," and tells one of the agents to go get her number.

THE PRESIDENT'S EMBARKATION from Palm Beach is shrouded in secrecy, as he is unable to mount the steps of the aircraft, instead being hoisted on a cherry-picker like a tricky item of oversize baggage. The First Lady returns to Washington a week later, and he's so anxious to see her he has the Secret Service run him to National Airport, where, in a rare public display of affection, they appear as indecorous as a pair of college sweethearts. The subject has missed his wife terribly. There has been no one to whom he has been able to confide his pain and despair, especially not the women he's been using.

Even in the limousine sailing back to the White House, the President appreciates a transformation has taken place in the sexual attraction toward his wife, as the deluge of adoration for her looks and sartorial style reveals how other men must regard her. At dinner in London, having gone on from Claridge's, they behaved like a normal married couple in love, oblivious of the agents stationed discreetly in a car outside, inside at the bar and in the kitchens to prevent assassination by poisoning, though he did joke to his wife that at some point they might be disturbed by a commotion in back followed by one of the agents shouting, "Step away from the manges-touts!"

The First Lady was radiant that evening, not least because she appreciated the thought that went into it, namely that she'd spent day after day and night after night under the spotlight, where everything she wore was photographed and analyzed, and everything she did was reported and given an op-ed, always under the constant pressure to entertain but not offend. In that exclusive restaurant, they were the beneficiaries of British aristocratic reserve, allowed to dine without intrusion, the only occasion they turned heads being when the waiter offered the President a Cuban cigar and he boomed with laughter, and, if anyone cared to comment on the First Lady's chain-smoking or the high pitch of her laugh, they did so in the privacy of their own mansions.

Their sexual relationship has followed the natural trend toward diminishing returns, but his wife holds an enduring attraction that ensures the subject remains interested, and perhaps, for a couple such as they, love can be defined as a state of constant curiosity.

She said, "Jack, this is so romantic."

"I thought you said it was crazy."

"Maybe the two words mean more or less the same."

"Then another glass of this Beaujolais and we'll be dancing on the table."

"Now that *will* raise eyebrows."

"I could kiss you right here and now and no one would care a damn."

"Now wherever did you get the idea a girl could fall for all your big talk?"

Outside the restaurant, in the dark, he spun her into his arms and kissed her on the lips. A limousine shot them back to the embassy, where they made their excuses to the ambassador and retired to bed. He wished they could have fallen up the stairs giggling, but he couldn't even crab up on crutches, nor could that night conclude in a gymnastic concerto of squeaking bedsprings and percussed headboard. The subject's wife always becomes concerned about injuring his back, though nonetheless she feels as his life partner she deserves some sexual gratification of her own.

The subject rarely considers the woman's pleasure, preferring to work fast and sleep early. Often in their early days, she would try joking about it, to which he would respond that she should take it as a compliment. A great deal of their lovemaking has been procreational rather than recreational, but recently she has opened a discussion regarding the question of her own sexual pleasure, and so on that night in London the subject endeavored to provide what he could muster despite being *hors de combat*. Theirs is described as a "political" marriage, yet when husband and wife go to bed every marriage becomes political.

DR. FEELGOOD HAS been good enough to adumbrate his medical opinion to the President regarding the natural history of "orgone energy," observing, "As described by Wilhelm Reich, release is essential for cool intellect and balanced mood. A routine of weekly ejaculation is sufficient to prevent a toxic accumulation of endoplasm—sufficient, but not ideal. Ideally the stressed executive must ejaculate twice per week and do so in circumstances of maximum sexual stimulation in order to maximize orgastic potency, to induce the secretion of all potential toxic vectors of orgone energy into his ejaculatory fluid."

And so it follows, at a Wall Street dinner, that the President runs into an old Navy buddy who served him for a time when he was a senator, and asks him to come work at the White House. Only later does the man suspect the precise nature of his duties, when the President suggests he approach a beautiful young woman and ask her whether she'd like to be introduced. Naturally she blushes at the request but then hitches her dress and crosses the room with the newly appointed Beard, who cuts in on the President's colloquy with a dull stockbroker and presents the young lady. They speak for a few minutes during which the President discovers she hails from a wealthy Wall Street family—she could hardly be here if she were not—whose father is someone with whom the President is distantly acquainted, an extremely successful businessman scarcely a few years older than he.

At the end of the evening, the President arranges with the Beard that he will escort the young lady to the White House on Friday evening, when the First Lady and children will have decamped for their customary weekend in Virginia, with strict instructions that she be vetted and processed by the Secret Service as his guest, not the President's, all of which, come the evening in question, goes off strictly to plan.

"I KNOW IT'S going to be hard for you to divorce your wife."

Marilyn has come through on Mrs. Lincoln's line every day for a week, and in the end the President decides the only way to stop her is to take the call. He dodges her suggestions of meeting in New York or L.A., but eventually she wears him down, whereupon she interprets his tense silence not as a desire to escape from her but to escape *to* her.

He stifles a shocked laugh and says, "But I don't want a divorce."

"Of course you don't, Jack. It's not going to look good. That's why we should wait till after you're reelected."

"Neither of us should count chickens."

"I know. It seems like such a long way off. But we can see each other discreetly. You're going to come stay in Palm Springs, aren't you?"

"My schedule has to stay fluid."

"Sure it does, Jack. But you'll call me, won't you, when you're coming out?"

"I don't know. It might not be so easy."

"All I want is at least for you to try."

"I'll try."

"That's great, Jack."

He makes his excuses and signs off. He wants to sleep with her again, naturally, although the emotional overlay is beginning to bug him.

Yet, over the following months, the letters and calls become less intrusive, and he begins to think fondly of her again, particularly on a clear evening late in summer, sitting on the fantail of the presidential yacht sailing down the Potomac with a few chums, including the Beard, who has dutifully added the Wall Street heiress to the muster roll, and, while the President's time in the cabin with her was pleasurable, as he sits gazing downriver he can't help but reflect on how comfortably and conveniently this new concubine has slotted into the harem, with, after some initial bristling, astonishingly little rancor from the dyad, the girls even coming to chat convivially among themselves on presidential outings, although there is precious little else for them to do save wait for a summons to a private "briefing" with the President.

In part, he credits himself for the success of the arrangement, by an overt absence of favoritism, calling upon the new girl no more often than her counterparts even in the early weeks when her novelty made her far more appealing. Now that that's worn out, he's developed a different appreciation of the comfort and convenience of the policy, his downriver gaze drawn not by the calm waters but by the swells and breakers of Chesapeake Bay, a reminder that sometimes a man needs a little danger. Marilyn hooks him with her troubled sexuality and trickier psychology, and, exposed to the elements on the deck of the yacht, it seems a simple matter to throw overboard any concerns about her needy assumptions and become acquainted with the night.

Later, when he stays in Palm Springs, his brother-in-law plays the beard and escorts Marilyn to a party on the second night, after which the two of them spend some time frolicking in the guesthouse. It reminds the President of their first time together in her apartment during the convention last summer, when he escorted her through the door while the driver waited on the curb. She poured a drink, of which he sipped only a little while gazing at her over the rim of the glass. She put on a record and danced to it. Tonight she does the same, and it helps them find their rhythm after the months apart. In L.A., she moved more slowly, as did he, and the first touches were indecisive enough to be laughed away. But tonight she's faster and drunker and spills her martini. He sets it aside and guides her dance toward the bed. Afterward she drinks too much and comes out of the head with white powder on her nose. "You know what, Jack," she says, "I'll make a *great* First Lady."

\* \* \*

THE STAY IN Palm Springs upset Frank on account of its not being at his place, which was a deliberate decision on the part of the President. He had done himself no favors when he finally got his ticket to the White House, to join the cast of a Hollywood movie being filmed in D.C., in which the President's brother-in-law took a supporting role, as did his former flame, Gene. Frank acted as if he were the biggest star in the room, which he might have been, but it was the acting like it that was the problem; he called the President by his first name a time or two too many, which is fine in private, but not in public with people the President has never met before, such as the stars of the movie, which was about the unseemly underbelly of Washington politics, as if such a thing could exist. Getting Frank to leave that night was like getting the Japanese off Iwo Jima, the repeated solicitations for a firm commitment from the President to stay at his place in Palm Springs eventually breaking down in nebulous concerns about security. The President detected that his raucous and overbearing manner at dinner resulted from a belief that he held a special place at the table. But the President no longer requires his patronage, as he does appear to have acquired a considerable pull of his own. Perhaps Frank feels their bond was forged inside the curtain wall of his sybaritic Palm Springs castle where they first twinned as sexual kings, and what continues to exist of that connection is so unutterably intimate that it can only be implied by the periphrasis of coarse badinage.

That night as he lay in bed, flat and unable to turn, as usual, the First Lady having once again execrated "that tasteless show-man," the President might have been tempted to defend his former ally were it not for the nagging embarrassment that Frank could command far more attention in a room than he up until the election and that now, outside of the Beltway, he remains equally if not still more charismatic, and that despite the President's war record, he is tougher, and in all probability a better lover.

The matter reached its crisis when Frank advised the President's brother-in-law to impress upon the President his own ministrations to security, having instructed contractors to install impregnable quarters on his property.

"I don't think I can make it," the President told Peter.

"Jack, he's had men working round the clock."

"It can't be helped."

"Well, I think you should be the one to tell him."

Peter is a fellow fornicator, a characteristic readily deducible when one factors regular exposure to Hollywood starlets plus lengthy sojourns away from home when performing with Frank in Las Vegas or movie-making on location. Adultery as it pertains to his personal life is naturally a delicate matter, given his marriage to the President's younger sister, but the subject would rather he were able to express his innate polygamous urges than become a bitter and resentful husband, and in turn the relationship is delicate as it pertains to the President's womanizing, as he's frequently availed himself of Peter's Hollywood connections to procure women, and occasionally he has performed the same service here in Washington, while at work on *Advise and Consent,* in which he played a supporting role of a United States senator (with too much panache to be convincing), escorting on one evening a studio girl and on another a governor's receptionist to an intimate White House soiree in the First Lady's absence.

He brings the girls as a favor, or in tribute, and often the President chooses his escort service because his brother-in-law's charm, good looks and celebrity will invariably result in a high class of guest at these club dinners, that being the term given to such evenings where one or two close male colleagues will entertain young women with the President, often complete strangers whom he'll never see again once they've returned to the office or department from which they've caught the eye of the brother-in-law, or the Beard, or whoever has sought to entertain the Commander-in-Chief with a gift of female company.

Afterward they are invited to retire to the President's private quarters. Some say, "No," of course, and that is entirely their prerogative—the Beard will summon a White House vehicle to carry them home, though with slightly more strained courtesy than afforded to a young woman more cognizant of the tacitly assumed transaction—yet most are willing, since they have appreciated the unusual nature of an invitation to dine in the company of the President, and an understanding merely suspected at that point will certainly become more obvious as the evening progresses.

Now that he's in office, the President is aware he must proceed with greater circumspection than in the past, only consorting with women to whom he's been introduced by close colleagues he can trust, because, while the woman herself may confide in her friends, which can't be helped, they are usually amenable to showing the necessary discretion. Fiddle, Faddle and the new girl—who may well have been christened Fuddle—understand their responsibility to national security, but this cannot be assumed of all participants; the governor's receptionist, for example, after they had spent some time alone together in the Lincoln Bedroom, returned a blank and puzzled look when, on showing her to the door, outside which the Beard stood waiting to escort her down to the West Gate where a White House car was parked ready to whisk her home, the President said, "And, er, kiddo, I'm sure you understand national security considerations apply."

"Excuse me, Mr. President?"

"Our evening together. Which I enjoyed very much. There's a consideration for national security I'd be most grateful if you should observe."

This time at her bemused look the President gabbled, "I'm sure Mr. Powers will explain," dumping her on the Beard, who would elucidate patiently before he put her in the car.

As a loyal citizen, as a patriot, she had to understand how damaging it might be if she were to discuss with enemies of the state the President's personal habits, which bear no relevance whatsoever to his Leadership of the Free World, but, if discussed frivolously, might undermine his authority, whereupon the Beard would ensure the girl nodded gravely, ideally swallowing a patriotic lump in her throat (in keeping with any other patriotic swallowing she might have done that evening), before she vanished into the night, possibly to swear her best friend to secrecy, or possibly to bear her burden till the day she dies.

The question of how these girls are managed after the event is of more concern to the President than their position beforehand. Initially he wondered if they oblige him out of duty, or even fear that rejection is tantamount to treason, but, before he accused himself of exercising droit de seigneur, he dismissed the question. He is man and President and the girls fall for one and both.

Nowadays the Beard is arguably the President's most faithful aide. From his days under the senator to putting females under the President, the Beard understands that modulating the subject's orgone energy helps him perform his elected duties, and the President is touched that the Beard regards this service as a service to America.

The brother-in-law serves himself. At Cape Cod this weekend, Peter and the President's sister join a family party, and, once the welcoming pleasantries have been conducted, he picks his moment to corner the President on the sands, revealing that his agent has panicked over some holdup in the deal for a supporting role in Frank's next picture, a project he believed was as good as his.

"Frank's pissed at me," Peter says.

The President says, "It was a political decision not to stay at his place."

"I've never seen him like this. It's worse than when Ava left him. You'll have to call him."

The President gazes out to sea. "I'll get someone to call him."

"No, *you,* Jack. Maybe if you could make it up to him . . ."

"Some things matter more than movies."

"Like *what*?"

Aides who'd been involved in planning the West Coast trip had repeatedly raised concerns about Frank's alleged underworld connections, though they sound no murkier than the average congressman's. When the President telephoned, Frank came on the line with a nonchalant air, as if he'd been tipped off.

"This trip," the President said, "I can't see it's going to work out."

"No sweat, man," he said, but there was a short silence—in which the President said, "I'm sorry"—and he said, "Thanks, Jack," and then hung up instead of following the etiquette of waiting for the senior man to do so first, that one small gesture betraying his resentment and defiance in an otherwise classy exchange. The President held the receiver for a couple of seconds, the dial tone humming, as he stared out over the South Lawn, feeling a little shitty, but then he heard footsteps gathering next door, insisting he must move toward the next business of the day, Berlin.

In their meeting in Vienna, the Soviet Premier asserted his intent to sign a peace treaty with East Germany that in his view would supersede the postwar division of Berlin into East and West, after which, if Western forces did not withdraw, he would either blockade or invade the last remaining outpost of Western democracy on his side of the Iron Curtain. In his eyes, West Berlin is an anomaly that threatens world peace and must be neutralized. One side must blink—and, following his verbal muscularity in Vienna, the Premier counts on it being the President of the United States—or else direct military aggression will ensue, whereupon escalation to all-out nuclear exchange would become alarmingly likely. The President asked the State Department and the Department of Defense to prepare contingency plans for the defense of Berlin, and is deeply perturbed that all such plans involved at minimum the deployment of tactical nuclear weapons, a certain prelude if ever there was one to global thermonuclear war.

Consequently in today's meeting the President orders his advisors to explore strategies that will permit a political solution to the crisis and to define military options that are nonnuclear but sufficiently robust to defend Berlin for sufficient time to create a cooling off period during which both sides might return to the negotiating table instead of escalating to first use of tactical nuclear weapons. The President addresses the nation with a message of which the Soviet Premier will read a translated transcript:

"We cannot and will not permit the communists to drive us out of Berlin, but we do not intend to abandon our duty to mankind to seek a peaceful solution. We do not want military considerations to dominate the thinking of either East or West. In the thermonuclear age, any misjudgment on either side about the intentions of the other could rain more devastation in several hours than has been wrought in all the wars of human history. Nuclear weapons would pollute our planet for all eternity. Those children that survive would curse our memories. "

All the time he is talking, the Football perches on a table in the hall outside, today handcuffed to the wrist of an Army captain. Anyone passing who was unfamiliar with the Football would not appreciate its nature, and would walk on by, oblivious.

THE PRESIDENT VISITS Chicago for a Democratic Party dinner, receiving a message via Mrs. Lincoln from Judy, who must have read the itinerary in the press, because she claims to be staying at the Ambassador East on the same night. After the dinner, his limousine transfers him discreetly to her hotel, though he can only spend a few minutes in her room on account of a State Department briefing, but even in that short time her performance persuades him to invite her to Washington.

The First Lady takes the children up to the Cape on Thursday afternoon, while official engagements keep the President occupied till Saturday morning, whereupon he arranges for a car to bring his date from her hotel to the West Gate and then for the

Beard to convey her through the White House to the second-floor Residence while the President swims to loosen his back, before the three of them enjoy a short lunch together and then, as planned, the Beard excuses himself.

The President escorts Judy to the bedroom, puts on a record and fixes some drinks.

"How's Frank?" he says.

"You know Frank," she says.

"He's fine?"

"He's having a fine time."

"Well, that's good to know."

She undresses in the bathroom while he gets onto the bed, and, when she sees him lying flat on his back, she realizes he's not going to be able to contribute very much, as usual, but she conceals any disappointment she may feel and maneuvers into position.

A few mornings later, the President is woken by the phone ringing next to his bed. He can't turn to reach it because his back is frozen solid, so it rings till the First Lady wakes and scoops the receiver to his ear. Overnight in Berlin, East German troops and police have closed off most of the crossing points between East and West. By the next day, the President learns they've closed off all of them and within the week erected a wall of concrete and barbwire to end the embarrassing exodus of refugees fleeing communist austerity. Border guards have begun shooting at anyone attempting to cross, some victims being left to bleed to death in no-man's-land. The hawks in the administration want to bulldoze the Wall and deploy tanks to reopen the crossing points. To avoid direct confrontation, the President argues that it's an internal matter for East Berlin, but, to show that commitment to the Western sector remains firm, he dispatches an infantry division to take up positions in West Berlin, the column passing of necessity through East Germany.

The President sits with aides in the Oval Office, his back numbed by painkilling injections and his attention made acute by some of Dr. Feelgood's stimulants, receiving dispatches every half-hour on the condition of the column. Any attack by East German or Soviet forces would constitute an act of war. Pain gnaws at his stomach, and he must leave the room, first vomiting a small amount of blood-stained gastric contents and then suffering diarrhea so explosive it resembles nuclear warheads dropping from his fundament.

But the column makes it to West Berlin unscathed, though tensions remain high, and the next turn of the screw occurs when Mr. Khrushchev announces the resumption of Soviet nuclear testing, a policy he ruled out in Vienna after both leaders concurred that it only served to boil up the Cold War, prompting the President to conclude that he's not so much testing nuclear weapons as testing him.

The challenge inflames his gut and bladder, but he intends to answer it, and answer it in the front line of the Cold War.

The President flies to Berlin. His advisors worry for his safety, yet he stands atop a guard tower and peers across the ugly concrete Wall to the grimly deserted streets on the other side, seeing people in apartment windows peering back, some even waving, as if they are prisoners in their own homes. In the upper chambers of City Hall, he stares at the carefully diplomatic speech that his aides have prepared, and feels nausea at the prospect of delivering it to the tens of thousands of beleaguered citizens gathering in the plaza below. He recalls the speechwriters urgently and tells them what he really wants to say. They scratch out the words with pencils, and then, clutching them in a fist of notepapers, the President ventures out into the air that bites with a ferrous wind, the crowd's cheers striking him in waves, whereupon, thanks to the limbering effect of painkillers and muscle relaxants, with the added ingredient of one of Dr. Feelgood's inspirational tonics, he mounts a high podium from which he peers out at the masses quarantined in this most precarious bastion of freedom.

The President says,

> "There are many people in the world who really don't understand, or say they don't, what is the great issue between the Free World and the Communist World. Let them come to Berlin."

The crowd roars, the sound hitting him in concussive waves, and he knows he is sending a message to the world, and to his enemies. He looks out toward the grey concrete divide with its cruel barbwire traps where dozens of Germans, young and old, have been cut down by Soviet machine guns as they vainly sprang toward freedom, and, for a moment, he disregards the raw notes screwed in his fist.

> "Freedom has many difficulties and democracy is not perfect—but we never had to put up a wall to keep our people in."

Another of wave of cheers strikes him.

> "Freedom is indivisible, and when one man is enslaved, all are not free. You live on a defended island

of freedom, but your life is part of the main. So let me ask you to lift your eyes beyond the dangers of today, to the advance of freedom everywhere, beyond the wall to the day of peace with justice, beyond yourselves and ourselves to all mankind. When that day finally comes, as it will, the people of West Berlin can take sober satisfaction in the fact that they were in the front lines for almost two decades.

"Two thousand years ago the proudest boast was *'civis Romanus sum.'* Today, in the world of freedom, the proudest boast is *'Ich bin ein Berliner.'* All free men, wherever they may live, are citizens of Berlin, and, therefore, as a free man, I take pride in the words *Ich bin ein Berliner!*"

A few days later, the Soviet Premier renounces his intent to agree to a treaty with East Germany that would signal a communist effort to take West Berlin by force.

ON MONDAY MORNING, the President telephones the British Prime Minister, and they return to the subject of nuclear tensions between East and West, agreeing to a summit, which, since London and Washington have grown equally wintry, they site in Bermuda. The President flies down with a small party of close aides, advisors from the State Department and the Department of Defense, together with Fiddle, Faddle and Fuddle, an arrangement that can now be made without embarrassment, as it is all left to the Beard, who dubs them the President's "hand luggage," but, owing to a packed schedule of briefings on the flight, the only presummit free time he gets is in the limousine conveying him from Kindley AFB to his first meeting at Government House, so the President asks Fuddle to ride in the backseat, remarking to her as they pass through the lush, tropical countryside that he came here a number of times as a young man, once nearly getting himself killed by falling off a friend's moped, before he confides that he needs to be put in a relaxed mood before the summit, drawing the curtain that divides them from the driver as she slips off the seat to kneel in the well.

Meeting the PM, though, is one of the few examples of contact with a foreign leader where the President doesn't require particularly strict modulation of his orgone energy, which is just as well, as the deepest release comes from sex with a brand-new partner, a fact verified by Dr. Feelgood himself, and that evening, the PM and the President relax on the verandah of Government House, sipping cocktails while the squawks of birds fade with the setting sun and the scratching of crickets becomes the music of the night.

"How's Lady Dorothy?" the President enquires.

"Very well. Very well indeed." He shifts in his wicker chair. It seems like the only slightly uncomfortable moment of the evening. He says, "I miss her frightfully when I travel."

The President gazes out toward the setting sun. He has been keeping track of his withdrawal symptoms, which used to trouble him after a week, but now they seem more acute. "I wonder how it is with you, Harold?" he says. "If I don't have a woman for three days, I get terrible headaches."

The Prime Minister grins mischievously and says, "You have her for three days?" and the President splutters with laughter. The PM says, "If I spent three days with a woman, it would be more than my head that would ache terribly."

They laugh so loudly that one of the cocktail waiters ventures out onto the verandah to check if the two principal leaders of the Western alliance have taken leave of their senses, but they merely wave at him for two more and he withdraws, and once they've finished jesting, they begin designing a practical proposal on nuclear testing with which to present the Soviets, their conviction being that a moratorium on the development of new weapons will slow the arms race and lay the ground for meaningful disarmament.

Back in Washington, the news of progress with our key ally in negotiating a test-ban treaty with the Soviets is greeted with appreciation by aides, but a few days later the Defense Secretary requests an urgent meeting. There are rumors within the Pentagon that Strategic Air Command have flown B-52 training missions inside Soviet airspace, the last occurring to coincide exactly with the President's trip to Bermuda. The President demands an urgent meeting with the Chief of Staff of the Air Force, who defends his policy shamelessly.

"These training missions prepare my crews for war," he says.

"I'm concerned they might start one, General."

"They prove to the Soviets we hold strategic air superiority."

"They encourage brinksmanship, General. Are you familiar with *The Guns of August*?"

"I'm not, sir."

"The path to war is paved with avoidable error and miscalculation. Given the stakes, I hope you'll agree that we should not precipitate a nuclear war with the Soviet Union because a training mission strayed over enemy territory."

"And I hope you'll agree, Mr. President, that my appreciation of the uses of strategic air power probably exceeds that of a Navy junior-grade lieutenant."

The President says, "You're familiar, General, with the story Lucius Lamar told of Sailor Billy Summers."

"No, sir, I can't say I am."

"Senator Lamar was aboard a Confederate blockade runner sailing for Savannah Harbor, the senior officers insistent it was safe to proceed, but the captain ordered Sailor Billy Summers to the crow's nest, and Sailor Billy Summers reported ten Union gunboats in the harbor. Yet the senior officers claimed they knew exactly where the Yankee Fleet was and it couldn't be in Savannah Harbor, so the ship should sail on. The question, General LeMay, is not who holds the highest rank, but who occupies the best vantage point to judge the way forward. And I no longer hold the rank of lieutenant. Mine is Commander-in-Chief. These missions will stop."

The President turns and punches the intercom, asking his secretary to send in the next meeting. She opens the door and the general marches out without a salute.

The President gets through the next meeting with a raw stomach until he can sit in the head for ten minutes, passing scorching diarrhea. That night, he takes Lomotil and codeine, and falls asleep dreaming of American bombers pointing like daggers at an angry Russian Bear.

For breakfast, he eats lean bacon and fruit juice, but his stomach rejects them violently, and he needs antiemetic injections from Adm. B. before he can face the business of the day.

Through official channels, the Director of the FBI has requested a private meeting, which the President decides to take in the Cabinet Room since the enormity of the table will create a desirable barrier, and when the Director arrives, he sees the room and says to the Appointments Secretary, "The President understands this is a *private* meeting?" to which the Appointments Secretary is spared a patient answer, as the President enters via Mrs. Lincoln's office, inviting the Director to sit eye-to-eye across the chamber.

Without preamble, the President says, "What do you have to tell me, Mr. Hoover?"

"I regret, Mr. President, that I must report a delicate matter of national security involving a high-ranking government official."

"The matter being?"

"Fornication," says the Director.

"I see," says the President.

"The man is conducting immoral extramarital relationships."

The Director has run the FBI since before the war, contaminating its policies with his own phobias and paranoia, and now the subject begins to fear he has uncovered the reason none of his predecessors dared dismiss him, despite allegations of homosexuality and transvestism. The consensus of informed opinion is that, if the Director is homosexual, he does not practice. A lifelong bachelor, he is one of those tragic individuals living in denial of his own natural urges, with the consequence that his face has turned into something resembling a twisted little fruit. Yet he has exploited all of the Bureau's capacity for surveillance in order to gather sensitive information on the nation's leaders.

"And who might the man be?" the President says.

"Do you require me to say, sir?"

"Are you spying on me, sir?"

"The Bureau confines itself to conducting operations in defense of national security, Mr. President."

"What I do in my private life is no concern of the Bureau's, nor of yours, Mr. Director."

"Except where private conduct impinges on national security, Mr. President."

"That would appear to be a definition over which you and I might be in dispute, Mr. Director."

The Director says, "Aforesaid high-ranking government official is involved with one woman with un-American sympathies and another connected with criminal elements."

The President says nothing. He watches the Director consult files he must know by heart; the licking of his fingers as he turns the pages, the adjustment of his eyeglasses, are all rituals measured to unsettle, before he states, "Miss Marilyn Monroe, a.k.a. Miss Norma Jeane Baker a.k.a. Miss Norma Jeane Mortensen. A former pornographic model. The former wife of a communist sympathizer."

"If Marilyn Monroe represents a potential threat to national security, then you must investigate her, Mr. Director."

"I'm gratified you agree, Mr. President."

"And one would hope that the investigative prowess of the FBI might eventually produce evidence more admissible than guilt by association."

The Director is unaccustomed to sarcasm. He shifts in his chair. "Mr. President?"

"In the absence of proper evidence, I recognize no threat to national security."

Mr. Hoover shuffles his files. He clears his throat.

"Mrs. Judith Campbell. Known sexual consort of Mr. Francis Albert Sinatra. Known sexual consort of Mr. John Roselli. Known sexual consort of Mr. Sam Giancana a.k.a. Mr. Sam

Flood. Mrs. Campbell has traveled with these gentlemen and co-habited with them in various luxury hotels in Las Vegas, Nevada and Miami, Florida."

The President does not flinch.

Mr. Hoover states, "These men are thugs, vermin. They would debauch our national character. The woman is a common prostitute."

The President says, "If you've got pictures, you'll see she can hardly be called 'common.'"

"I have never in all my years of service, sir, had cause to lecture a President on the morality of his sexual conduct."

"Nor will you lecture me, sir."

"Then, Mr. President, may I respectfully seek reassurance that appropriate action will follow?"

"I've been advised, Mr. Director. That will be all, thank you."

After the Director has left, the President drops his pugnacious expression. The appointments secretary enters, but he sends him away. He sits for a long time gazing at his own reflection floating in the veneer of the table.

The next time Judy calls, he begins, "I'm sorry, kiddo. I can't see you again."

"Jack?"

After a short silence, the President says, "Has anyone been saying anything about us?"

"Who?"

"Has anyone said anything about your seeing me?"

"Some people know. Obviously."

The President measures another tense silence and then he says, "Who's he been talking to about us?"

"'He'?"

"You know who I mean." The President stares across the South Lawn, wondering if anyone's listening in on this conversation, wondering if Frank now thinks of him the way he thinks of some movie actor who's fallen out of favor and stops getting auditions.

At the other end of the line, Judy is sobbing. "There's a problem, Jack," she says.

"What kind of problem?"

"A . . . medical problem."

He doesn't miss a beat. "You need to have it fixed," he says.

"I know, Jack, I know . . ." she sobs.

"You should've taken precautions."

"I know, Jack, I know . . ."

"If you need money . . ."

"I know a doctor," she says.

He says, "It's for the best."

Then Judy says, "Can I never call you again?"

"I'm sorry, kiddo. Take care of yourself. And I'm sure I don't have to remind you that national security considerations apply."

The moment affects him less than other men. He's dumped girls on countless occasions. A wall goes up.

# THE BATS

THE END OF a liaison is not something in which the subject takes pleasure, since a conquest who has graduated into a regular sexual partner will invariably be one who is physically appealing and socially adroit, while unsuitable partnerships he ends early, often after the first encounter, though he will usually persist with a seduction even in the knowledge the woman is unsuitable on account of her physical attractiveness or his heightened appetite at the time. Judy has been an enjoyable addition to his circle, and losing her leaves a hole to be filled, or, more accurately, deprives him of one.

Since the subject is also beginning to tire of Fiddle, Faddle and Fuddle, lovely girls though they are, his temptations are beginning to stray beyond the safe confines of Washington political circles. Naturally he must resist such temptations, or else there is a very real danger he will fall back into old habits; any attractive woman who catches his eye is liable to be propositioned, with potentially disastrous consequences for his political reputation.

Needless to say, he isn't remotely concerned that some kind of press scandal would ensue, but instead that the lady herself, or her possessive husband, boyfriend or father, would seek to place damaging confidences in the hands of political enemies. While it's true the press has no jurisdiction in the personal lives of public figures, an unscrupulous opponent can always find some rationale by which to convince the newspapers that a personal matter lies in the public interest.

While the subject misses Judy, at least he can sleep easy in the knowledge she can do no harm. But it is imperative that he tread carefully, so the present scheme whereby the Beard escorts women into and out of the White House in the guise of his own personal guests must be fiercely protected, not least because their other regular accomplice, the President's brother-in-law, sulkily refuses to cooperate.

The President is constantly on the lookout for new conquests, and therefore he's delighted when a demure young woman appears in Mrs. Lincoln's office having suffered a canceled appointment with the First Lady. The young woman is a final-year student at the First Lady's alma mater who had been granted the promise of an interview for the school newspaper, only to be turned down at the last minute because the First Lady is complaining of a head cold, although she is currently on the White House tennis court rallying with her Secret Service agent. The President wanders casually into his secretary's office on the pretext of scheduling a telephone conference with the Secretary of Defense, whereupon he draws the blushing young woman into conversation, expressing his sympathy at the missed interview, and makes up for it by asking one of the staff to arrange for her to receive an internship at the White House, which she will take up on graduation. The girl blushes with delight, though naturally the President forgets her instantly, as it will be some months before he sees her again, if indeed she decides ultimately to take up the appointment.

Salvation arrives in the form of a pert blonde from a rich, bohemian New York family, whom he recognizes at a luncheon as a girl who was peripheral to his social circle two decades ago and again just after the war when her husband and the subject worked together briefly. He can't remember her name, of course, but she says, "Mr. President, we danced together one night about a hundred years ago." The President was in college, or even still in prep school, and cut in on her dance, but she moved on gaily, and he can still remember her glance back over her shoulder, the look of a woman amused by her power over young men. She must be ten years older than the First Lady, but she has aged well, and she reveals she's attending the luncheon as a guest of her sister and brother-in-law, the brother-in-law being a prominent newspaper editor.

The President says, "Where's your husband?"

"I have no idea," she says. "Divorced," she says.

She has already stopped addressing him as "Mr. President." They talk for a few minutes about old times before his aides signal he has business waiting, but not before he gets one of them surreptitiously to obtain her name.

The First Lady has instituted the practice of hosting periodical dinner dances at the White House, widening the circle from obligatory invitees of previous administrations to include more exotic creatures—artists, musicians, authors and the like—together with the beautiful people of Washington and New York society. Both Mary—she being the President's former acquaintance—and her sister are familiar to his wife as predecessors at Vassar, so it takes only the subtlest of nudges from the President to ensure they appear on her radar, receiving invitations to the next dinner dance, at which the First Couple greet guests in the East Room with a cocktail reception, followed by dinner in the State Dining Room, at which he spots Mary, seated at a neighboring table, her face radiant with laughter, and finally to the Blue Room, wherein resounds the infectious beat of the Lester Lanin Orchestra, though, on account of his back, the President avoids dancing and instead wanders from group to group bearing a constant flute of champagne that, on account of his stomach, warms in his hand. Eventually he appears to happen upon Mary, but on striking up a conversation he soon feels like the youth she abandoned on the dance floor twenty years before, as she shows the body language of a shimmering fish that knows it will slip the hook.

The President invites her to view a painting in the Red Room, slipping his hand round her waist; she lets it rest there for a moment before turning from the painting, a champagne flute to her lips as she glances back with a quizzical look. She bears rather an ethereal mien, and, as a man accustomed to ingenuous secretaries translating the widening of their eyes into a commensurate widening of more southerly parts, he finds her hard to decode.

He says, "Didn't you like the painting?" and she says, "You're so obvious," then before midnight she slips out to a waiting cab.

Normally the subject doesn't care a damn if a woman turns him down. Usually there's a plausible excuse—she's married, or she's too close to his wife. But the fact that he can't fathom a single good reason for Mary to say, "No," bugs him so much that, instead of exploring pastures new, he determines to try again at the next opportunity. In the meantime, he returns to his usual White House partners, including, obviously, from time to time, the First Lady, with welcome variety occasionally being provided by one of the Beard's impressionable young escorts handpicked from the back offices of Washington, D.C., some of whom are agreeable enough to splash about in the White House pool with the President while the Beard watches from the side in bare feet with his trousers rolled up to the shin, holding a set of towels at the ready.

At his weekly physical, the President credits these pool interludes with the recent improvement in his back, albeit referring only to the swimming and stretching exercises. The President buttons his shirt while Adm. B. records his findings in the medical log, but then he hangs the pen in the air, strokes his chin as if in contemplation, and says, "It's my duty as your physician, Mr. President, to comment upon the wisdom of certain practices you've been employing."

The President hesitates over the next button but then quickly goes ahead and fastens it. "What do you mean, Admiral?" he says.

"Personal visits by the backdoor, Mr. President. Secret sessions."

"I don't regard this as medically relevant."

"The visitor is a medical practitioner, is he not, Mr. President?"

Relieved, the President loops his tie nonchalantly.

The Admiral continues, "And you've been in receipt of various treatments by this 'practitioner,' have you not, sir?"

"Various, yes."

"These treatments are not prescribed by the vast majority of respectable practitioners in the management of a back complaint."

"I don't care if he's injecting me with horse piss, Admiral—it works."

The next day the President receives a letter signed by Adm. B., Dr. T., Dr. C. and Dr. K., all expressing their disapproval in the matter of Dr. Feelgood's methods, with especial concern being leveled at his inclusion of amphetamines in the formulation of tonics and elixirs, drawing the President's urgent attention to the numerous side effects associated with that particular class of substance, though naturally, in their habitual pomposity, they fail to note the parallel with the medicinal steroids that have obliterated the subject's adrenal glands, ulcerated his stomach and eroded his spine. They conclude with the observation that unpredictable agents, irresponsibly prescribed, pose a danger to the President's mental efficiency, and it would be their duty as medical practitioners to take any necessary measures to prevent an insult to his well-being: in short, a thinly veiled threat to communicate his medical problems outside their confidential circle, reigniting the preelection rumors about his chronic ailments, a threat the President takes sufficiently seriously to cancel the forthcoming appointment with Dr. Feelgood, and instead to scheme an arrangement whereby the good doctor will see the First Lady and she will take possession of any treatments that need to be smuggled to her husband in times of crisis.

The Admiral is naturally delighted when the President informs him he will no longer be employing Dr. Feelgood's services, though he goes on to attest that, following discussion with the President's other physicians, small revisions to his medical regimen are required. The principal change, instigated by evidence of muscle weakness and weight loss, is to commence a course of testosterone injections.

The President says, "I never felt I was short of testosterone."

"It's for muscle weakness and weight loss," the Admiral repeats, preparing the first injection.

The President denies any immediate effect, although at the end of the afternoon, he does ask Mrs. Lincoln to retrieve Mary's number from the files kept by the Secret Service on the guests from the last dinner dance. She puts him through and he says straight out, "Don't you like me?" to which Mary says, "I hate what you did in Cuba," and for once he has no rejoinder to cover the insistent static that hums between them.

A SORE FESTERS in America, and its name is race. Our economy was built on the blood and bones of slave labor, and for a civilized republic we were rather late in dispensing with the practice, yet emancipation led not to universal liberty but to an economic and social apartheid that our fellow Western democracies struggle to comprehend, through which every single pronouncement on the value of liberty around the globe is undermined, causing many among the dark-skinned peoples of the world to regard the United States as a nation of hypocrites, the political cost being a loss of influence among those nations most susceptible to anti-American ideology.

Any southern politician will pontificate on the political dangers of granting equal civil rights to nonwhites, a threat almost as great as that which led to secession, but the time has come for the Union to treat all its citizens equally, and in that cause the President must lead, although the course ahead will be perilous, and his instinct is that the least constitutional damage will be done by effecting change through gradualist policy-making. Yet he also appreciates that such an approach will incur the wrathful impatience of those citizens who suffer under this ghastly American apartheid, and they will quite properly accuse him of failing to confront the issue in purely moral terms. Any parent would be proud if their son grew up to be President, but dismayed if he had to become a politician in the process.

The unpleasant truth the President faces is that a bill granting equal civil rights to all would never pass Congress, the result being increasing frustration and resentment among those pressing for those rights and violent schism between North and South. In his opinion, the worst outcome of failure to pass effective legislation would be the confirmation to observers here and abroad that the United States government connives in the systematic dehumanization of one-tenth of its own citizens, some of whom fought courageously for their country in opposition to the poisonous ideology of a master race and yet returned home to experience similar subjugation. His predecessors have long promised to act, but their approach reminds him of an old Chinese proverb: "There is a great deal of noise on the stairs but nobody comes into the room."

The President could turn his back on his fellow man, as countless predecessors have done, retreating behind a smokescreen of pragmatic gradualism, or he can take up arms in the struggle. Despite leading a life of material privilege, he is not unfamiliar with bigotry. His ancestry and religion have provoked outrageous slurs. The first Catholic to win the presidency, the first from immigrant stock, he represents proof that the electorate can be persuaded to overlook creed or class, and this charges him with the determination that one day they might see past color.

He begins in a quiet way, by issuing an executive order against racial discrimination in federal employment, by appointing talented black politicians to high office, by appointing black judges, and by demanding an ethnic census of all government departments (the result being predictably monochrome), after which he personally instructs members of the Cabinet to diversify their recruitment policies. The President invites the young son of a black government official to join the White House schoolroom alongside his own children.

Next he tackles voting rights. In many southern states, only a fraction of eligible nonwhite voters are permitted to register, the scandalous practice being to deny their intellectual competence to vote, exemplified by the case of a black voter obstructed from registration on account of his alleged inability to interpret the meaning of certain passages of the Constitution to the satisfaction of an electoral clerk, the voter in question holding a doctorate in political science and the clerk having only a high-school diploma. Previous Presidents have turned a blind eye, but this one orders the Department of Justice to file suits against any county operating such a policy, while at the same time encouraging a voting drive among black southerners, knowing that once they are permitted to vote in sufficient numbers, politicians will have no choice but to consider them in their policies or else fail to win reelection. Violence flares when the federal government attempts to desegregate bus terminals and airports, but the prospect of civil unrest does not deter him. President Lincoln was prepared to lose half the country in the cause of his moral conviction, and, should the moral imperative arise, this current President must act in the image of Abraham Lincoln summoning his wartime Cabinet to a meeting on the Emancipation Proclamation. "I have gathered you together," Lincoln said, "to hear what I have written down. I do not wish your advice about the main matter. That I have determined for myself." Later, when he went to sign, after several hours of exhausting handshaking that had left his arm weak, he said to those present: "If my name goes down in history, it will be for this act. My whole soul is in it. If my hand trembles when I sign this proclamation, all who examine the document hereafter will say: 'He hesitated.'" But his hand did not tremble, nor will this President's.

The subject ensures Mary's name appears on the guest list for the next White House function, this time a luncheon, and when he once again maneuvers her into a private encounter, he asks her directly if she would like to visit one evening in the Residence when the family is weekending out of town. "I've started seeing someone," she says.

"Is he a head of state?" he says.

"Sure," she chuckles.

"Does he have a big country like I do or some tin-pot banana republic?"

"He doesn't even have a country," she says.

"So," he says, "what's he got that I haven't?"

"Mystery."

The First Lady appears in the hall with a summoning expression. He says, "Apparently I can be read like a book."

"Which one?" his wife says. "*Vanity Fair*?"

"Nowhere near so challenging," says Mary, and the two women laugh.

Sometimes the subject must ponder whether his wife is complicit in his womanizing. She never disapproves openly of his consorting with attractive women—in fact, at times, appearing to facilitate it, for example in the seating plan for today's luncheon, which is a matter she insists on deciding herself, whereby the President finds himself seated between two vivacious ladies, whom he will be amply motivated to charm (or at least attempt to), whereas the First Lady would be aware of the struggle he would face if his immediate neighbors were a pair of old crones.

When he burrows into the company of a good-looking woman, sometimes he glimpses his wife drawn, say, by the woman's laughter or his, and the expression that momentarily plays on her countenance is not one of jealousy but of pride, presumably in the observation that she possesses a husband capable of charming other women rather than being saddled with a cretinous bore. Perhaps she watches him maneuver toward a conquest with the same swings of pride and disgust as she would if he were winning a fistfight.

Moreover the subject questions whether on occasion she designs his fornication to ensure a partner of whom she approves. Aesthetics are so important, after all. Perhaps he succeeds in his philandering, in part, because she wants him to. She has surrendered fair portions of time in which he can pursue private interests, and, while these are almost totally political endeavors, a few hours here and there in a week are devoted to womanizing. Fornication would be infinitely more challenging to schedule were it not for her willingness to leave him to his own devices, which, given his suspected proclivities, is such a patent risk that one may conclude she is affording him these opportunities rather than countenance the unambiguous hurt and conflict of catching him in flagrante delicto.

This is one possible explanation for her decision, by way of example, not to attend the fund-raising concert at Madison Square Garden in celebration of the President's forty-fifth birthday, at which Marilyn is billed to sing.

Marilyn draws a gasp from the audience when she slips off her fur. For an instant, he too is fooled into thinking she's naked before the light catches her skin-tight, flesh-colored dress. She croons a breathy version of "Happy Birthday" that brings a lump to the pants. The after-show party takes place on the Upper East Side, where she flirts with half the men and attempts to impress the other half with her political savvy. She quietly asks the President how her audition's going.

"What audition?" he says.

"For First Lady," she says.

Later she gets drunk and in an upstairs bedroom wiggles her tail at agents stationed on a neighboring rooftop. As the party winds down, the President invites her to accompany him to his duplex atop the Carlyle. Either it's the dress or the testosterone shots.

As usual, he aims to avoid displays in front of the staff or Secret Service, the plan being for his guest to travel independently across Park Avenue, but she is a little garrulous, so he decides the safer course will be to keep her where he can see her. In the Beard's absence, he's forced to pick out one of the aides with whom she flirted earlier tonight; he wore the look of a child who'd never been to Coney Island before. The President orders him to accompany her to the Carlyle in a yellow cab, while the President travels in the limousine and takes the elevator to the thirty-fourth floor; the aide brings her up to the apartment where the President intends to thank him with a drink, but Marilyn stretches out invitingly on a chaise longue, spilling a splash of wine down her dress, and both men gaze momentarily at the damp patch soaking through to her nipple.

"Thanks, Kenny, goodnight," the President says, and shows him the door.

"Poor guy," Marilyn laughs. "I think he was hoping for a ménage à trois."

"It's a federal requirement that they be able to count at least that high."

"Swell suite, Jack."

This pied-à-terre's been in his family for years. He perches at the window overlooking Central Park. Cars are ants crawling on the streets below, the beams of their headlights like probing antennas. He prefers for her to believe this is just another ad hoc presidential suite because he needs the comfort of personal barriers. He doesn't want her picturing him here in other assignations over the years, or shooting the breeze with his dad over a nightcap. In the end, it will dispel her fantasy of usurping his wife.

His head throbs and possibly it's an effect of the testosterone but his prostate feels inflamed. For two hours now, he's experienced a singular desire to have sex with Marilyn. She could be the most unpleasant personality imaginable and he'd still suffer this surging physical compulsion. He stares at her lying on the chaise longue, her dress clinging to the pout of her breasts and the curve of her belly, and he feels fit to burst.

"That's some dress," he says.

She says, "Thank you, Mr. President. And it might interest the President to know I needed quite some help getting it on, and I think I just might need some getting it off."


Some women complain it's over so fast, while others must be grateful it is. Sometimes he wonders what they do after he falls asleep. Perhaps they stare at the ceiling, or curse him, or deliver a heartfelt monologue oblivious to his narcosis till the interjection of the first hoglike snore.

That night the President was awoken by a ringing at the door. Marilyn snuck to the bathroom while he dealt with the interruption, which came from the same agent who showed his disapproval at their first presidential tryst at the Beverly Hills.

The agent said, "I'm sorry, Mr. President, a security problem is ongoing in the hotel and my orders are to confirm your location and notify your safety."

"I'm safe, thank you," the President said sleepily.

"Very good, Mr. President." The agent keyed his lapel microphone and transmitted, "Lancer secure."

The President heard a chuckle echo in the bathroom and suppressed a grin at the suggestive code name. "What's the security problem?" he said.

"It's delicate, Mr. President."

"Scandalize me."

"Mr. President, a gentleman claims his wife is being corrupted. The agents stationed in the lobby are attempting to calm him down."

"A simple phone call would have given you the information you require."

"The lobby captain telephoned, Mr. President. No one picked up."

"I must've been asleep."

The agent gazed back at the President inscrutably.

"The gentleman in the lobby . . ."

"Yes, Mr. President?"

". . . he would be my guest's ex-husband?"

"He would, Mr. President."

"I want no charges against him. Put him in a cab and make sure he gets home safely."

"Yes, Mr. President."

The agent fixed a sober expression and withdrew into the hall as the President shut the door. Marilyn emerged from the bathroom wearing an untied toweling robe open from neck to knees.

"That was sweet, what you did," she said.

She twirled the loose ends of the belt, making her body ripple. Suddenly the President was wide awake again and surfing toward her on a wave of hormones.

Afterward she laughed, "You *are* corrupting me . . . Lancer!"

"Perish the thought," he said.

"You know, Jack, Joe's harmless," she said. "He gets upset, is all. He's still kind of protective. It's sweet, in a way."

"'In a way,'" the President said, yet, as soon as he had pictured Marilyn's ex causing a disturbance in the hotel lobby, his instinct was to be sympathetic, if only because former athletes also live in pain.

Back in Washington, the President summons the head of the Secret Service for a short meeting at the end of the day, at which he inquires if there are any continuing security concerns. "No, Mr. President," comes the reply. "The gentleman made no threats to your person, and, in their reports, all my agents concurred that he appeared embarrassed by his conduct almost immediately on the night in question. He became extremely apologetic."

"Were your agents able to make out the substance of his grievance?"

"It seemed Mr. DiMaggio was under the impression he was meeting the lady for dinner after the concert in Madison Square Garden."

"How would he know where she was and with whom?"

The head of the Secret Service shifts uncomfortably. "With respect, Mr. President, I have concerns regarding the security smarts of the lady in question."

"She told him?"

"I believe she must have, Mr. President. My guess is she informed the gentleman when she broke their date to accompany your aide to the Carlyle Hotel."

"I see. Thank you."

The President moves to dismiss him, but he holds his position. "With respect, Mr. President, may I continue? My field agents have expressed their concern at presidential guests being permitted to circumvent standard security protocols. I needn't stress the potential jeopardy to your person, particularly your defenselessness if you fall asleep in their company."

The President says, "I appreciate your concern and shall do my best to cooperate."

The head of the Secret Service sets his jaw the way his agents do, then leaves, after which the President takes a swim, alone for once, to reflect on the stupidity of his latest tryst with Marilyn, which he knows will only encourage her delusions. She called him the morning after because her ex-husband was worried he was going to be watched from now on.

"It's fine," the President snapped. "We let him go out of respect for his services to baseball. There's a rule you can't be a threat to national security if you made a fifty-game hitting streak twenty years ago."

"This isn't funny, Jack," she bit.

"No?" he bit back.

"It was fifty-six games."

"I do apologize."

"Lancer, are you jealous?"

She avoids conflict by flirting, and he fell for it before, but not when he called her straight after the meeting with the Secret Service chief.

He said bluntly, "It was a mistake your telling him about us."

"What's the big secret, Jack?" she said. "Everyone knows."

"My private life is sensitive. There are national security considerations."

"You know what I mean, Jack. I mean everyone knows who's in the know. Our thing is like Rock Hudson and Tab Hunter's thing. Everybody knows but nobody knows."

"They only know because you tell them about it."

"You sound calm, but I feel you're angry with me."

"I'm not angry."

"I'm so happy you're not angry with me."

"Swell."

Without a pause, she shifted the conversation. "I know there's a problem with me making movies," she said. "I couldn't be a movie star and First Lady. Look at Grace. She had to give it up."

"You're right. It would be a problem."

"I'd give it up, for you, Jack."

"But wouldn't you miss it too very badly?"

"I wouldn't miss too very badly being treated like a piece of meat every goddamn day."

As he soaks in the hot water, reflections of the overhead lights twinkle on the surface, reminding him of the shimmering beads she wore that night in New York. He hopes Marilyn will recognize his low regard for her, yet the next day Mrs. Lincoln logs two calls (unreturned) and three more the next day (also unreturned). The President has assumed she has become so accustomed to fawning attention that his nonchalance would work, but he has reckoned without the psychological damage of her upbringing, which has conditioned her to expect rejection from everyone. He imagines his own daughter being bumped from one loveless relative to another, and it brings him so close to a sense of guilt that the next day he returns her second call.

He tells her, "I don't think it's a good idea for us to see each other anymore."

"I know—we've got to keep things quiet till after the election. Then we can be together."

"No. We won't be together."

"You *are* angry. I'm sorry, Jack—"

"This has to stop. I hope you understand why. And, please, no more disclosures about our relationship."

He has been feeling nauseated for days, and, after the call to Marilyn, it peaks. He squats in the head suffering pain that pulsates through his gut as he struggles to let the bats out of the cave.

The next morning, he undergoes a regular consultation at which he has ordered all his official physicians to attend and asks them, "Are you quite convinced of the need for testosterone injections?"

"Quite convinced, Mr. President," says Adm. B.

"Quite convinced," says Dr. T.

"Definitely the most effective therapeutic option," says Dr. C.

"I concur completely," says Dr. K.

The President says, "I'm nauseous a lot of the time."

"That's a common side effect," says Adm. B.

"We can prescribe something to control it," says Dr. T.

And all four nod in synchrony.

The President spends the next three days in meetings and on the phone dealing with economic matters, and formulating an executive order to ban discrimination in housing projects, which for years has been used as an unofficial method of preventing integration of black families into white neighborhoods.

Meanwhile in a Cabinet meeting, some of the Joint Chiefs start banging the drum about South Vietnam. The Chief of Staff of the Air Force says, "We've got to show them we've got balls."

"Show whom, General LeMay?"

"The communists. The godless world. Show them we won't take any of their shit, Mr. President. Bomb the jungles back to the Stone Age and keep the Reds out. Hell, invade North Vietnam while we're there, take the whole country."

"We'd lose a lot of men in those jungles," says the President. "And what would we be fighting for exactly, General?"

"Our balls," he says.

At their regular consultation the following week, Adm. B. reports that the President's blood tests haven't demonstrated the desired improvement, and therefore all the physicians agree the testosterone dose must be increased.


GOVERNMENT AIDES ARE concerned that the President's support for civil rights has led to a drop in his popularity, a perverse indication of the sensibilities of the electorate, who rejoiced in the imperialist fiasco across the Gulf, who enjoyed the rhetoric at the Berlin Wall, but disapprove of showing common humanity toward their fellow citizens.

"We're worried this is a vote loser," the aides say.

The President's closest circle suggests easing up on civil rights programs until his popularity has bounced back.

The President says, "I refuse to abandon the principle of equal rights for all citizens—" but sudden nausea grips his stomach. He turns pale and glistens with a glaze of sweat.

Later that day, his physicians confirm that the testosterone is responsible for his nausea. "It comes in waves," he says. "I can't control it."

"We can," they answer. "If the pills aren't strong enough, we'll start injections."

Adm. B. asks the President to drop his pants and, as the President lies facedown on the sofa by the fireplace, the Admiral jabs in a needle. Once he's decent again, Mrs. Lincoln informs the President that Marilyn has called half a dozen times in the last couple of days. She didn't pass on the messages at first in the hope the calls would stop. The President sighs and says, "Let's just change the God-damned phone number."

"Very well, Mr. President," says Mrs. Lincoln.

The next day, in between the afternoon meetings and early evening swim, she enters somberly to say, "There were two more calls today, Mr. President. She's been calling the main switchboard number and asking the operator to put her through to your office."

"Advise the operators not to put her through."

"Very well, Mr. President," says Mrs. L., but the next day she enters at the customary time, the flexible window between the last postmeridian meeting and the therapeutic swim, and reports, "I'm afraid she's created rather a fuss, Mr. President. Raised her voice to the operator. Threatened to cost her her job. The operator didn't like to say, but she sounded drunk."

"I think I'm forming quite the vivid picture," says the President. Drunk and high, she is berating the White House switchboard with the question "Do you realize who I am?" before furnishing the answer: "I'm the movie goddess the President's been screwing the past two years." It's the same line she's been reciting around Hollywood, until now a tantalizing show-business morsel of gossip served on the same dish as egregious facelifts, clandestine abortions and lubricious all-male pool parties, but, should she maintain the disclosure, the material might become fissionable. Her fallacy has aggrandized the anemic anecdote of the showgirl used and discarded by the prince into a full-blooded melodrama in which she claims the President and the Blonde are promised to each other after the next election, casting him as the scoundrel who goes to the polls as a family man but intends to govern as a playboy. Ordinarily the President would have no concerns, but she is no ordinary woman, instead being one of a profession that respires the oxygen of publicity, so ultimately the denouement may balance on the frank economics of the plot, whether presidential mistresshood commands more bountiful box-office lucre than that wind-assisted flash of legs and panties, the iconic cinematic moment serving as proof she valued her career beyond her union with the prudish former baseball legend, this being the singular demonstration that her pursuit of the bigger, better deal might surpass the dissolution of an inconvenient celebrity marriage with the downfall of a president.

The President's brother-in-law breaks his sulk to call. "She's telling everybody out here she's your mistress," he warns. "Unless we do something, it's going to find its way into a gossip column."

"I appreciate your concern, Peter," the President says evenly.

"I can talk to her, Jack, make her see sense."

"It's very kind of you to go to the trouble, Peter," the President says in the same even tone.

"I'm only thinking of the election."

The President knows he's only thinking of Frank, of course, and of the quid pro quo incumbent upon this little favor. So he says, "Let me give it some thought, Peter."

The President stands some way short of the midpoint in his first term in office, yet his staff's concern over his popularity together with Marilyn's belief that his disaffection relates to fears for the election rather than sexual ennui prompt him to appraise the limited time remaining to pursue his life's work. The prospect of losing the election terrifies him. He fears vacuum more than death. He calls his brother-in-law right back.

Next morning, Peter calls the President's private line in the Residence. He spoke to Marilyn the night before as planned, and she seemed to understand what was required. "Say goodbye to Jack," she said. "Say goodbye to yourself." Early this morning her housekeeper found her in the apartment, naked on the bed, pill bottles broken open and the contents scattered everywhere about the place.

The suicide does not imbue the subject with guilt, nor should it. That particular weakness proves utterly destructive to the philanderer. He decides to regard this tragedy as a test of his womanizing prowess, a test not in the traditional sense that would come to the mind of the fornicating ingénue or the conventionally monogamous male, both of whom would imagine that challenges only take the form of difficult conquests or intricate concealments, whereas the subject appreciates from experience that periodically one is penetrated at the most interior shell of one's compassion, and the womanizer who has thus far complacently deflected the suffering of a scorned lover or jealous wife comes to realize the ultimate demand of his chosen path. He must play the sociopath, unless he has the good or ill fortune, depending upon your viewpoint, of being one already.

The philanderer faces regular tests of nerve, taking forms as mundane as his willingness to lie to people who trust him or his willingness to proposition the wife of a colleague, and a man who succeeds in these small endeavors comes to regard himself as a guiltless engine of seduction. But he deludes himself. The true examination arrives when the man understands the limits of his capacity for inhumanity, or, more properly, understands that it must be limitless. Not a night goes by that the subject doesn't reflect on the appalling suffering of the Cuban Brigade, with no compulsion to disregard this feeling; in fact, he persists in harassing the State Department and the Justice Department to secure the men's release. But however reluctant he is to shed more blood, he must still, as Commander-in-Chief, be prepared to do so in defense of this country he has sworn to serve. And as a womanizer, guilty misgivings must never be allowed to stop him from satisfying his urges. The conquest of guilt is the foundation of the subject's success as a fornicator.

On his wedding day, he experienced transcendence before the totems of continence. The vows acquired some sudden seductive power, and he floated in the serenity of guiltless sex, the advertisement of monogamy having temporarily brainwashed him, precipitating the moral struggle of a month or so later, upon their return from the honeymoon, when his inevitable itch for sex with other women became quite maddening. He chose to scratch, with an old girlfriend whose discretion was assured, after which he found it straightforward to overcome the guilt from breaking his marital vows.

When his hedonistic cruise around the Mediterranean coincided with his wife's confinement abruptly producing a stillborn infant girl, he urged himself to seize upon the situation as an examination of his capacity to endure guilt. To survive its limit was the key to conquest. His companions were adamant the subject should return at once to the United States, whereas he exhibited a determination to continue the vacation, with its regular parties on deck hosting various nubile young women who were delightfully amenable to being escorted below. After all, he urged himself to think, what difference would it make?

His heartlessness appeared shocking, puzzling his shipmates with what they interpreted as an utter lack of sympathy for his wife's condition, but his true intention was to demonstrate an impermeability to the emotional distractions that attend the career of any moderately successful philanderer. Once one admits those confounding spirits, they will gather thick and fast, in guises far less haunting than the death of a child. Soon he would become hostage to his wife's jealousy, or her embarrassment, or her loneliness.

So he refused to fly home. He partied. The next morning, his closest friend among the party advised him he would almost certainly face a divorce if he did not go to his wife's side, and at this prospect he relented, but returning in the knowledge that he had achieved what few men have, the certainty of the depth of his will.

"She's dead," Peter relays over the telephone, repeating the details of Marilyn's naked body and the scattered pills. "Suicide," he says, after which the President thanks him and advises him not to call directly about the matter again.

Tales of mutilating cruelty to blacks can sometimes bring the President close to tears, but, after the report from his brother-in-law, the President takes a meeting with the chairman of House Ways and Means to discuss a tax cut, and then, after his swim, he reads Caroline's bedtime story, kisses John, Jr. good night, before dining in the Residence with the First Lady, an ordinary evening except that perhaps he takes an extra minute over choosing the wine.

THE NEXT DAY, the President learns that a black student has been denied enrollment in the University of Mississippi despite being academically qualified, his exclusion deriving from an illegal local policy of segregation sanctioned by the state governor himself, who took it upon himself to visit the university, flanked by armed police officers, and personally turn the student away on his third successive day of seeking registration.

Once again, his aides remind the President of the divisive effects of involving himself in civil rights issues. He would be entitled to regard these events as a matter internal to the State of Mississippi. Instead he asks his secretary to call the governor's office.

Down the line, the President says, "Governor, there is no legal reason to obstruct this student's entitlement to enroll."

"Well, Mr. President, there's never been a Negro admitted to Ole Miss before, and I see no reason for that arrangement to change."

"It must change, Governor," the President says.

"The State of Mississippi will not surrender to the evil and illegal forces of tyranny."

The President takes a calming breath before saying, "I understand this young man served nine years in the United States Air Force and now he wants to better himself through a college education."

"He can have college, but not Ole Miss."

"I'm afraid, Governor, it appears we're in a hole, you and I, as I'm given to understand he's rather stuck on the idea."

"Mr. President, this is an intolerable intrusion into the affairs of the State of Mississippi."

"Then at least we agree about one thing, Governor. This is intolerable."

The President's aides show him newspaper photographs of the mobs in Mississippi, armed police officers interspersed among citizens expressing their civic concern by wielding baseball bats and metal pipes and baying vile insults at the small peaceful crowd gathered in support of the importunate student. A sickening photograph of a police dog lunging at a black woman is wired around the world. For the first time in the President's life, he is ashamed to be an American. One of his advisors remarks, "It's just one student. Pretty soon he'll give up and go home. Then we're off the hook."

The President's expression sets hard. Part of him wants to get on a plane down to Mississippi and walk that young man into the enrollment booth himself. He wants to call him up and hear him express incredulity that someone from the President's office is phoning him, and for the President to say, "Actually, Mr. Meredith, this isn't someone from my office, this is the President," and then explain how much he admires his guts, and how the bigots must be defeated, but the President knows there'll be a pause at the end of his rhetoric in which the student will want to hear a promise, and the President can't make one, because he can't guarantee not losing, and that's why he can't make the call.

But the President orders his aides to quit worrying about popularity. He says, "We face a moral question and we must answer it morally."

In the Oval Office, the television cameras point toward his desk as the President takes a final sip of water before easing into his chair. An assistant brings a mirror so he can confirm the magnificence of his hair, then he broadcasts to the nation:

> "This nation was founded by men of many nations and backgrounds. It was founded on the principle that all men are created equal, and that the rights of every man are diminished when the rights of one man are threatened. It ought to be possible, therefore, for American students of any color to attend any public institution they select. It ought to be possible for American consumers of any color to receive equal service and it ought to be possible for American citizens of any color to register to vote. It ought to be possible for every American to enjoy the privileges of being American without regard to his race or his color. Every American ought to have the right to be treated as he would wish to be treated, as one would wish his children to be treated. But this is not the case. The Negro baby born in America today has about one-half as much chance of completing high school as a white baby born in the same place on the same day, one-third as much chance of completing college, one-third as much chance of becoming a professional,

twice as much chance of becoming unemployed, a life expectancy which is seven years shorter, and the prospects of earning only half as much."

The President tunes out the insidious whir of the camera. In the lens, he sees reflected a tiny motion of the curtain behind him, caused by a draft from a window open to keep the room cool despite the TV lights, and in the gaps between the film crew he glimpses aides shifting silently.

He glances at his notes, swallows and continues:

"Difficulties over segregation and discrimination exist in every city, and it is better to settle these matters in the courts than on the streets, but law alone cannot make men see right. We are confronted primarily with a moral issue. It is as old as the scriptures and is as clear as the American Constitution. The heart of the question is whether all Americans are to be afforded equal rights and equal opportunities, whether we are going to treat our fellow Americans as we want to be treated. If an American, because his skin is dark, cannot eat lunch in a restaurant open to the public, if he cannot send his children to the best public school available, if he cannot vote for the public officials who will represent him, if, in short, he cannot enjoy the full and free life which all of us want, then who among us would be content to have the color of his skin changed and stand in his place? Who among us would then be content with the counsels of patience and delay?

"One hundred years of delay have passed since

President Lincoln freed the slaves, yet their heirs, their grandsons, are not fully free. They are not yet freed from the bonds of injustice. They are not yet freed from social and economic oppression. And this nation, for all its hopes and all its boasts, will not be fully free until all its citizens are free. We preach freedom around the world, and we mean it, and we cherish our freedom here at home, but are we to say to the world, and much more importantly, to each other that this is the land of the free except for the Negroes; that we have no second-class citizens except Negroes; that we have no class or caste system, no ghettoes, no master race except with respect to Negroes?

"Now the time has come for this nation to fulfill its promise. We face a moral crisis as a country and as a people. It is time to act in the Congress, in your State and local legislative body and, above all, in all of our daily lives. Those who do nothing are inviting shame as well as violence. Those who act boldly are recognizing right as well as reality. In this respect I want to pay tribute to those citizens North and South who have been working in their communities to make life better for all. They are acting not out of a sense of legal duty but out of a sense of human decency.

"This is one country. It has become one country because all of us and all the people who came here had an equal chance to develop their talents. We cannot say to ten per cent of the population that you can't have that right. I think we owe them and we owe ourselves a better country than that."

After the President's speech, the staff gathers to receive news of its reception across the land. The President doesn't join them. Instead he meets with officials of the Justice Department to draft legislation to put before Congress that will enshrine equal civil rights in the Constitution, and then the following morning he federalizes the Mississippi National Guard, who march onto the Ole Miss campus to secure the registration of an ambitious young American who happened to have been born black.

A STAR IS born, briefly it shines, and then it falls. They inter Marilyn during a quiet funeral in Westwood, the whole ceremony orchestrated by her ex-husband, who bars her Hollywood friends, even Frank, blaming them all for corrupting her to their fast living, and orders fresh red roses laid in her crypt three times a week. Every swish of his baseball bat swears retribution against any man who helped dim her light.

As dusk falls, the fins of the presidential motorcade become bats' wings arched in the color of death. His limousine cruises out toward the Potomac en route to an assignation with Mary, but the events of recent days have seeded fears he could lose the next election, truncating every single one of his plans and programs.

Other men's lives are a marathon, while he must regard his as a sprint. He has promised change, and though eight years may not even be enough, four years will certainly be too few. His legacy must exceed the works of one man and become the works of a whole people—that is the grand scale of the subject's existence—yet his life itself is commensurately that much less than three score and ten, and instead must be measured by his years left in the White House, for a President is capable of achieving more in one day in office than in all the subsequent decades given him on earth.

The hopes and opportunities he has promised for all, this new spirit of limitless achievement he has proclaimed, all are grains of sand trickling through the hourglass.

Westward, across the river in Arlington, the headstones turn corpse-grey under the setting sun.

The President looks in, and says to the driver, "Turn around," and he goes back to work.

# THE SCHLONG

THE PRESIDENT'S APPROVAL rating has plunged to its lowest number yet, so clearly his predecessors' inaction was born of their insight that one can never underestimate how much the American people hate blacks, but Mary is an enlightened voter who's come to appreciate the President's stand on human rights, and, although he's disappointed more citizens don't share her view, he's gratified by her conversion.

Moreover, she demonstrates the often disregarded aspect of the subject's fornicating habits, namely that a fair number of his passes target married ladies or divorced ladies near his own age; as a younger man he often regarded the bedding of a woman in the immediately senior decade to be quite the badge of honor, since such a lady must be scrupulously tasteful in her choice of lover in case the country-club matrons purloin her secret.

But now that the subject is a man in middle age who, it has to be said, has come by a certain position, the questions of taste apply to *his* paramours, and, while beauty is the sine qua non, one must concede that a modicum of vulgarity attends a uniform pageant of girls whose years fall short of their bra size. In a cer-

187

tain way, he's rather proud of his epicurism, because the only characteristic common to all the women he's chosen is that they interest him on some intellectual or psychological plane, his wife (who else?) being the epitome.

The subject enjoyed his first success at a dinner two nights following the civil rights address to the nation, when Mary distinguished herself from the vast majority present by appearing to occupy a space nearer to his own than in the past, in contrast to those beaten back by the inferno of boats and bridges that surrounded his presidential personage that week, and that Friday, with the wife and children weekending in Virginia, she finally visited him in the White House as a guest of the Beard.

"Given your stand on human rights, Mr. President," she said, "may I assume you're also in favor of the Women's Movement?"

"Sure I am," he said. "I hate it when they just lie there."

After a light supper and bottle of Côtes du Rhône, the Beard retired and the President lit an Upmann.

"You got any pot, Jack?" she said.

He shook his head, grinning.

"No pot in the White House," she said. "Whatever is the world coming to?"

When she services him the following week, he rewards her with a joint, scored and rolled by the Beard from a dealer about whom the President doesn't ask and the Beard doesn't tell, and when she passes it back to him as she reclines on the Lincoln bed, he takes a short drag but, on account of his office, doesn't inhale.

Before she leaves, she says, "What would your wife think of what we're doing?"

"The pertinent question is, what do *you* think of what we're doing?"

"I think I'm a whore."

"I rather hope not. I couldn't afford you."

Her smile is thin, her skin pale. She says, "How does she put up with you, Jack?"

"I guess she must love me," he says.

In recent weeks, the First Lady has been in one of her mysterious phases, the cause of which he appears unable to decode. A few days ago, his secretary interrupted the President between meetings. "I'm very sorry, Mr. President, but I thought you should know that the First Lady has taken ill."

From her tone, the President understood immediately the type of illness afflicting the First Lady, that peculiarly evanescent malady that prostrates her at the time of an official appointment but from which, half an hour later, she bounces back, onto the tennis court or into a dress fitting. His brow turned all the darker when Mrs. Lincoln added, "It's the mentally handicapped children," knowing this particular charity was of personal importance on account of his sister, and a cause upon which he'd pressed the First Lady to become involved.

"When are they due?" he said.

"They're in the Green Room now, Mr. President."

"Put my eleven-thirty back to noon."

"And this afternoon's schedule, sir?"

"Don't change it. I shan't swim at lunchtime."

He opened the Oval Office doors onto the West Colonnade, bringing the agents to attention. They followed at a respectful distance as the President strolled between the white marble pillars to the South Portico, whereupon the President proceeded alone via the Blue Room, entering the Green Room in which a group of about a dozen youngsters sat with their teachers.

The President said, "I'm afraid the First Lady has taken ill, but I hope I'm an adequate substitute."

The teachers formed a line and the official photographer asked if the President minded pictures, and then he met the children, who ranged from about six to about sixteen, though it's often hard to tell age when their problems are severe, before the principal inquired nervously if the President would care to remain for the show they'd prepared. The President took a seat and the first performer gave a short violin recital, which won loud applause from the President.

The second performer was a young boy who had to be cajoled into standing up but was so nervous that his voice was inaudible as he attempted to recite a passage of poetry. The President asked the photographer to stop flashing, as he thought it might have been distracting the boy, and then the President crouched beside the lad to hear his poem.

The President said, "Shall we read it together?" and he enunciated the first few words, the boy following, till the boy's voice got strong enough to lead, and, when they reached the end, to wonderful applause from the teachers and small number of White House staff, the President shook the boy's hand in that big way one does with children. The President left feeling as he always does, that, despite the unrelenting pain of his back, which only intensified that afternoon since he was forced to omit his midday swim, one must not dwell on one's own situation when there is far, far greater misfortune in the world.

That night over dinner, the President decided to challenge his wife on why she had missed the engagement, having learned from her assistant (under considerable duress) that the First Lady spent the day in dress fittings, followed by lunch with a girlfriend, followed by a closed visit to a boutique, to which she said, "I was ill."

"With what?"

"My stomach."

"You know how much it meant to me."

"I do, Jack," she said, and lit another L&M, staring defiantly through the cloud of smoke she blew in his direction.

AFTER MARY HAS gone, he decants a glass of water and pops a couple of painkillers before breaking out onto the balcony overlooking the south grounds. By now, every second set of lights on Constitution is a taxi.

The First Lady's Press Secretary came in some distress earlier, as a consequence of unsettled accounts with various fashion designers and jewelers, the First Lady's creditors nearing the brink of embarrassing the White House through legal proceedings, whereupon poor Pamela became embroiled in the potential scandal. That morning, she opened a folder to show the President a clutch of unpaid invoices totaling close to a hundred thousand dollars.

These episodes occur periodically in the subject's marriage, when his wife becomes a cat that buries its shit. Usually the subject is only aware of an arcane tension in their relations, until the day he excavates her copropolis. He will write a check on Monday, and his wife will utter not a word of thanks; her equilibrium will be restored, and she will return to her obligations as First Lady.

But the President's fury has simmered all day, and now he thumps the marble balustrade with his palm. It isn't her money she's spending, nor his exactly, but their family's, money that will provide for the children's education, for their future, their homes and vacations, and, as well as being angry, he's hurt, because her lack of values mock any gift he ever gives her, a dress he buys or a mare, because she values nothing material if frittering a hundred grand is something she can do without compunction.

Unable to sleep, the President makes work calls for hours, waking aides at home in their beds, until Adm. B. arrives in the early hours, having been informed that the President is sleepless and agitated, but, before administering a sedative, he wants to ensure the President takes all his medication, in particular the testosterone, which he missed earlier on account of relentless meetings.

"I feel pent up," the President says.

"You'll be fine, Mr. President," the Admiral says.

"I think it's the injections."

"You'll be fine, Mr. President," he repeats before he leaves.

The President doesn't sleep. He's still angry with his wife. Since reading the poem with the mentally retarded boy, he's been thinking a lot about his sister. Normally he hardly thinks about her at all. In his family, she's best never mentioned, given it raises the uncomfortable issue of culpability. He wonders how she sleeps. He wonders if her blank look continues day and night and if her nurses grow so disturbed by those staring eyes that they drug her just to close them.

In the end, he calls Fuddle, since she lives nearest, who drives over, albeit grudgingly, signed in by the Beard whom he's also woken, and, when she slips into the bedroom, he throws open the covers and tells her he won't be able to sleep unless she gets a grip on his problem.

He rises at first light and works alone in the Oval Office, reading reports and dictating memoranda into a machine, though when he wants to step out into the Rose Garden for some air, he finds the patio doors locked. He taps on the glass to beckon the agents, but they don't react. Maybe they don't recognize him in sweater and slacks. He taps again. He turns away wondering if they really don't hear or if they've been ordered not to let him out, but when he calls for Marine One, it comes without delay, transporting him rapidly out of D.C. and over rural Virginia to the ranch.

The First Family eats lunch outside, and the President makes a fuss over the children. John toddles around the table always with a hand on one of the legs, though when he reaches his father, he is so overcome with excitement that he drops onto his butt and bursts into tears. The President can't lift him from a sitting position so the First Lady must round the table chewing a mouthful of ham and hoist him onto his father's knee, slapping dust off the seat of his dungarees. The President feeds him a sliver of ham, but the eggs only provoke an expression of disgust. Caroline gabbles news of her pony rides to which her mother interjects an occasional correction or clarification, but the President notes she is terser than usual and making limited eye contact.

Before long, the subject's eyes itch and he starts to sneeze. He is afflicted by grass pollen and horse hair and dog hair. Even his son's rocking horse with its authentic mane precipitates an allergic reaction. By the time they put the children to bed, there's a low wheeze to the subject's breathing. His chest pulls tight and his sinuses clog. His wife disregards the symptoms steadfastly until her provocation makes him flare in anaphylactic anger.

"A hundred thousand dollars," he snaps. "God damn it. I'm not made of money."

"You can afford it," she says.

"That's not the point!"

"Tell me the point, Jack."

"You're not at liberty to spend my money willy-nilly."

"I'm not 'at liberty.' But you are."

"I'm what, Jackie?"

"'At liberty,' Jack."

"They were going to make a scandal out of the unpaid bills."

"Sure they were, Jack. They figure it's good for business if all their clients know how indiscreet they can be when they put their minds to it."

She lights a cigarette, knowing it will only make his chest tighter.

He retreats to the doorway. He glimpses a shadow move through the hall, and assumes it's the nanny. When she's gone, he says, "I need you to stop spending so God-damned much, Jacqueline, that's all, for Christ's sake."

She says, "You know why I spend, Jack," then turns away to smoke by the window.


AT NIGHT, THE wind rustles the dark trees that ring the ranch. His wife brings the children every couple of weekends depending on the season, and more often than not he joins them sometime during the Saturday, staying till after lunch the next day, before returning to work, and usually an assignation, on Sunday evening. He watches the trees rock, their darkness opening and closing.

Marilyn's ex could hide out there, his bat swishing through the leaves, as could some of Frank's goons slinging Berettas.

Frank sent a generous gift for the President's birthday, a strikingly embroidered rocking chair that the First Lady decided was tasteless, in keeping with her general execration of Frank as "a boorish hood," so, despite finding it comfortable and rather appealingly outré, the President was forced as always to accede on matters of décor, hence the chair's donation with churlish haste to a children's hospital, although in truth it was convenient that a connubial intervention would provide cover were Frank to cite his gift in rapprochement.

The truth is, he may sometimes treat his entourage abominably, but he was always generous to the subject, and often, particularly when the President reflects upon that dinner at the White House where Frank's coarse overfamiliarity offended many guests, especially the First Lady and her coterie of society ladies, he concludes that most likely they were merely witnessing the effects of liquor in combination with the excitement of a slum kid who grew up to be best friends with the President of the United States, and this was the reason he kept calling the President by his first name when all the other guests observed the general convention whereby only his wife calls him "Jack" in public.

Yet on this particular night, peering out toward the dark trees massing in the distance, the subject recalls a past occasion on which Frank addressed him as "Mr. President" and the President said, "'Jack.'" He wonders if the memory can be real. Whether Frank's volubility meant he was intimidated by the subject's status or felt comfortably equal to it, the subject has chosen to presume the latter, and be affronted. But when he thinks of Frank, as he is doing tonight, he misses him.

In the sitting room, a black telephone rests on the hook while nearby an agent reads a biography of Northumberland under flashlight—a book the President pulled off the shelf and recommended to him—and, after asking him for some privacy, the President dials Santa Monica.

"Who is it?" Peter slurs.

"It's Jack."

"Jack, shit, what time is it?"

"Peter, I need you to call our friend."

"Now?"

"Sure, now."

"It's late."

"He'll be awake."

The President reads blue files till his brother-in-law calls back a half-hour later.

"They won't put me through," he says. "I'm persona non grata, persona nota-ona-da-lista."

"Does he know it's coming from me?"

"I left a message."

"OK. Well. Good night."

The President finishes the blue files and starts on the red. His son stirs, and he goes to him before he wakes the First Lady or the nanny. The President listens in the doorway without putting on the light as the boy babbles to himself semiconsciously, emitting urgent but incomprehensible noises. He lifts him out of the cot to make sure he's not wet or smelly, after which the boy grizzles in his father's arms for a few minutes before dropping back to sleep. Then the President eases him down onto the mattress and pulls the blankets up to his chin.

The President lays a hand over his chest and stoops to kiss his head. If the subject loses the election, his son will remember nothing of these years; his recollections of his father in the White House will vanish behind the mist that obliterates our infantile consciousness. His father, the President, will become a ghost.

The phone doesn't ring, so the President tries Frank's numbers himself, first trying his place in L.A., then Palm Springs, from where one of his entourage laughs and asks if it's Vaughn Meader making a prank call, to which the President replies, "Mr. Meader is busy tonight so I called myself," after which there is a short pause, and then the stooge very respectfully informs the President that his boss is playing in Vegas, connecting him to the private line in his suite at the Sands.

A girl answers. "Who's calling?" she says.

The President hesitates.

"Who's there?" she says.

"Jack," he says.

"Lemmon?" she says.

"Kennedy," he says.

"Oh, my God!" she says before exhorting Frank to the phone.

"It's kind of late, Jack," he says nonchalantly, enjoying the ambiguity.

"The way I remember, it's only about now you're getting over the previous night's hangover."

"I got a hangover cure now."

"What's that?"

"Stay drunk."

The President laughs, "I miss you, Frank," he says.

"I miss you, too, Jack," says Frank.

But then an awkward silence follows. The President says, "Thanks for the birthday present."

"Don't mention it, man," Frank says.

And now the President gets irritated again. He recalls the first time Frank called him "man"—at the Palm Springs compound, when there were a couple of grand hookers in the pool (grand being not a compliment to their splendor or dignity but how much they cost each), the girls challenging the men to join them, prompting Frank and the senator to shed their polo shirts and shoes, whereupon Frank dropped about three inches in height, creating an awkward moment between them, as to that point the subject never had definitive proof he used lifts, and he dared to feel the more desirable as they gazed down at the giggling girls pointing their glistening breasts, dared to crown himself the alpha alpha, until Frank dropped his pants to uncage a brutal schlong, winked darkly and said, "This makes me first, man," before leaping into the pool.

The President waits for Frank to sense his affront and offer something conciliatory, maybe invite him back out to the Springs one time, but there's only tense silence on both ends of the line. Through a gap in the curtains, the President sees the agent with the flashlight off and his eyes scanning the trees. His breath condenses in the night air. The Secret Service circle the farmhouse, and the President observes a dark figure carry a flask of hot coffee to another agent on patrol by the dirt track that leads out toward the highway. But the President can think of nothing to say down the line to Frank, instead radiating the hesitation of inchoate feelings.

"You don't sound too good, Jack," he says.

*"Mr. President?"*

The President wakes in his rocking chair with red files open on his lap. He realizes he must have fallen asleep. Neither man will swallow his pride for the other, despite Frank's desire to mingle with power or the President's to once more transcend the twenty-five-foot fences of Palm Springs, there to have his pick of bathing beauties frolicking in the pool, their bodies slick and complaisant, their mouths opening and shutting on demand.

"Mr. President?" the agent repeats. He stands over the President, the book shut in his hand with the page marked by his index finger, saying, "I apologize for waking you, Mr. President, but your orders are never to let you sleep like that because of your back."

"Thank you—yes," the President says dreamily, but soon the pain is so excruciating it takes five minutes with the agent's help to rise from the chair.

He needs crutches to get to the bedroom. His wife's eyes open in the gloom, but she remains motionless as he balances on the crutches to take the weight off his spine. He fears she'll turn over and pretend to be asleep.

He murmurs, "You know I can't do this by myself."

She says not a word in getting out of bed and untying his brace, and still not a word as she helps him onto the mattress.

In the morning, the trees drop beneath his feet as the helicopter bumps into the air and the children wave from the porch. At once, he misses them. He longs to stuff them in his pockets and carry them to work.

Past the highway, the country falls back into a plain, over which the helicopter tracks the 50 east to D.C. In Washington, the President receives an urgent call from the Pentagon, in which the Secretary of Defense reports that the Soviet Air Force has jumped to a high-alert state and that there appears to be a surge of naval traffic, particularly in their nuclear fleet. The

President orders him to utilize all means at his disposal to determine the cause of the Soviet action. Calls bounce back and forth all day between the White House, the State Department and the Pentagon, with the result that the President remains in the Oval Office, either in conference or at the end of the phone, every minute of the day, unable to escape to the pool for a swim, so that he must conduct his stretching exercises as best he can in the short intervals between calls and meetings, and he hesitates to visit the head, even though his stomach is turning over and he suffers an episode of painful diarrhea midafternoon.

The Joint Chiefs gather to brief the President and the Defense Secretary at about 6 P.M., all of whom disavow any knowledge of the motivation for the enemy alert.

The President says, "Do we think they're building up to an offensive action?"

"We don't know at this time," they say.

"Are their movements toward Berlin?"

"There's an armored division moving toward the city."

"There are subs outbound from Murmansk."

The President remains on edge all evening. He paces the Residence. His back is rigid and he passes blood. If the phone doesn't ring for half an hour, he calls the Pentagon and the State Department to demand situation reports. He's tempted to call for a Dr. Feelgood tonic, but Adm. B. visits instead to ensure he's ingested all his medication.

Then at midnight the Secretary of Defense calls. "It was us," he says.

After a night sleepless with rage, in the morning the President summons the Chief of Staff of the Air Force to explain why one of his (the President's) nuclear bombers flew a dry bomb run into Soviet airspace two nights ago.

"The mission was successful, Mr. President," the general says. "Our planners have extrapolated a seventy-five percent chance of an effective preemptive strike."

"I don't want to make a preemptive strike," the President says.

"A preemptive strike capacity must be part of strategic defense planning, and now you know the Air Force could provide one if you needed it, sir."

"And now the Soviets think it *is* in our plans. They went to DEFCON 3."

"Exactly, sir. That's why there's been no diplomatic protest. They don't want the world knowing we can get our bombers in. *They're frightened.*"

"God damn it, General—*I'm frightened.* Kindly desist from this brinksmanship of yours, both with the Soviets and with your Commander-in-Chief."

The general hesitates. He appears perplexed by the President's tone. At length, he says, "Yes, Mr. President, sir," and takes his leave.

Later the President tests the door to the Rose Garden, but this time buzzes his secretary to have someone bring the key. Eventually an agent he's never seen before arrives to open the doors with a deferential word or two, releasing the President into the Rose Garden, where he gasps the summer air. Men's working relations are complicated by their animal nature, and it's plain the Air Force Chief of Staff is a man unimpressed by the President's status or intellect or by the physical attributes that qualify him as a bona-fide alpha male.

When Frank took off those custom-made shoes, on the Olympic podium he stepped down from gold to silver, but his retaliation penetrated to the heart of a man's psychological vulnerability, and, although someone of his crude bent would take the matter literally—often at parties initiating a pecker contest wherein male revelers are challenged to vent their flies, a parade he invariably expects to win—in the past this has not been a matter to which the subject has ever given much thought, yet now he finds himself in a risible competition. The penetrating psychological effect of Frank's poolside exhibitionism embarrasses him still, embarrasses an educated, mature male for whom such atavism should be meaningless, yet it isn't, of course, because males are naturally competitive, and the primal symbol stabs them all. Frank knows that no matter how many women the subject has, the subject always remains smaller, and this thing that should not matter matters a great deal. Perhaps this is the secret power the general feels he wields, that the missiles are splendid, gleaming phalluses, and they're his, not the President's.

Fortunately it is fine weather today, as the President officiates at a medal ceremony on the South Portico, where the guest of honor will be our current Last Man in Space. This astronaut is a diametric opposite to our First Man in Space, at every opportunity proclaiming his devotion to God, country, mom and apple pie. There's something about Our Last Man in Space the subject finds unsettling, although he's charming and courteous enough during the ceremony, speaking graciously to the First Lady, and it's only later as the subject recalls the glassiness of his eyes as they peered back that he decides he's another man who considers he's better, not just because he's flown farther and longer in space than any of his predecessors, but because he exerts as much control over his hungers and ambitions as he does over the switches and levers of his space capsule. Apparently the spacemen down in Florida party with fast cars and even faster women, and the President has had some of them come visit Palm Beach for an informal barbecue, where it's plain every man present has eyes for tails that aren't necessarily attached to enemy jets, except Our Last Man in Space, who's prepared to risk his life in a rocket ship but not slip the surly bonds of monogamy.

Finally, at the President's regular medical consultation with Dr. T., he's surprised to receive not just Dr. T., but Adm. B., Dr. C. and Dr. K. too.

"How's the nausea, Mr. President?" the Admiral wants to know.

"I don't seem to be suffering as much."

"That's good news, sir," he says.

"Good news," says Dr. T.

"Because, looking at the numbers," says Dr. C., "we need to up the testosterone."

"Not a big increase," says the Admiral.

"Fifty percent, is all," says Dr. C.

"Are you sure?" the President asks, and they all nod the same nod.

His final meeting the next day involves some advisors from the State Department. He suggests Fuddle drop by afterward, taking advantage of the First Lady's late return from Virginia, and invites her back to the Residence for dinner.

She says, "I'm afraid I've got plans already, Mr. President."

"I won't keep you long," he says.

"If you insist, sir," she says, "then obviously I need to make quite inconvenient changes to my schedule tonight."

"I'd prefer it wasn't a case of insisting," he says.

She shifts uncomfortably.

He rises from the rocking chair, whereupon she stands in obeisance of his office, until he says, "Then that's it, then, isn't it?"

"I've gotten engaged," she says.

"Congratulations, er . . ." he says.

*"Diana."*

He strolls back to his desk. She remains ill at ease on the far side of the office by the fireplace, unsure if this is a signal for her to sit down again. One might expect the situation to be somewhat commonplace for a young mistress to experience an epiphany, but in actual fact these girls develop insight less frequently than one would ever imagine. The signs of ruthless sexual exploitation are conspicuous, so many of them must continue in denial, or possibly they feel powerless to alter the fundamentally unilateral nature of the arrangement.

For a moment, the subject contemplates apologizing for recently calling on her abruptly in the middle of the night, only in an effort to retain her sexual servitude, but he realizes that in essence he doesn't especially care for her, particularly when one calculates how many of her type are churned out each year by exclusive schools and colleges.

He says, "You understand national security considerations apply."

Tears cloud her eyes.

"Thank you," he says. "Goodbye."

She wipes her nose and appears momentarily capable of regaining control of herself, but doesn't, and hurries out with a hand across her face.

After some work calls, he reads reports on the situation in Southeast Asia, all of which appear to slant toward military intervention. Strategic minds sound convinced that an American war in Vietnam will be short and victorious, but that's what they said about Cuba. He digests all the reports in sufficient time to permit himself a swim.

The Beard accompanies him down to the pool, helping untie the brace, then sits at the side while the President exercises, after which he inquires if the President would like him to bring one of the secretaries down to join them. The President worries that the Beard is becoming temerarious in his zeal to serve his country. The release of orgone energy ensures the President's well-being, and perhaps the Beard has extrapolated that more frequent trysts will make him an even more effective leader. The President applauds the desire to oblige, but remains anxious to avoid the embarrassment of importuning an unwilling or (worse) indiscreet woman, and so he declines, reminding the Beard that the First Lady returns to town tonight.

In the Residence, he finds her in a much improved mood from the previous weekend. No doubt she is cognizant of her debts having been settled by the President's banker. The children have arrived semiconscious from the drive, so the three of them—the President, the First Lady and the nanny—attempt to transfer them to their beds with the same care one would use in handling unexploded bombs. He bends gingerly to kiss their foreheads. John twitches his nose before rolling over to sleep. They give the nanny a whispered dismissal and spend a moment in silent contemplation of their sleeping progeny.

He extends his hand toward hers and he's thankful she lets him take it, after which he draws her close and kisses her on the cheek, smelling her scent and nuzzling her thick dark hair, and then they edge through the yellow Oval Room into their private sitting room, where they kiss.

"I've missed you," he says.

"I've missed you too," she says.

That night, they make love, and two months later, to their mutual joy, his wife falls pregnant.

# THE GULF (2)

THE FIRST LADY'S pregnancy brings the subject's marital sex life to another abrupt hiatus. As usual, the medical advice they received was unhelpfully equivocal, but they both suffer an overriding anxiety toward precipitating the 50 percent chance of losing the baby based on the First Lady's obstetric history of one miscarriage and one stillbirth out of four pregnancies. The subject is grateful for the continuing services of Mary, and occasionally Fiddle-Faddle—though he's tiring of them both and would welcome their moving on to another office and another philandering boss (there are plenty to choose from in this town)—plus other impressionable young ladies of D.C. pimped by the Beard. These trysts are less frequent than he would like owing to the levels of circumspection on which he insists, even when complemented by periodic encounters he manages to manufacture upon his travels, usually in the form of old girlfriends whose discretion is assured, so it's with some interest that he notes the arrival on her internship of the girl from Farmington—Marion or Monica—who came to interview the First Lady for her school magazine, but his excitement over calculating a seduction is overtaken by events, when his breakfast in the Residence is interrupted by a defense advisor, who begins with the word, "That thing we've been worrying about, Mr. President—it looks as though we really do have it to worry about."

The advisor relays analysis by experts at the National Photographic Intelligence Center of a recent U-2 spy plane reconnaissance of Cuba that reveals the presence of Soviet SS-4 medium-range ballistic missiles capable of carrying nuclear warheads over a thousand miles, a matter of some concern given Cuba lies a mere ninety off our southeastern coast, so the President immediately orders a full meeting of what he christens the Executive Committee for as soon as the key members can be assembled.

Naturally the matter of the missiles preoccupies the President throughout his morning schedule—with the latest Last Man in Space and his family, followed by a short walk across the hall to the Fish Room, where he meets with members of the Panel on Mental Retardation, and then to a luncheon in the Residence in honor of the Crown Prince of Libya—and he remains preoccupied, even while he plays for a short while with Caroline, who shows him pictures she has drawn before sitting for a while on his knee to ask when the new baby will be ready to be born, if it will be a boy or a girl, if it will be good, like her little brother, or naughty, like her little brother, until the aides and advisors begin to assemble in the Cabinet Room. He kisses her goodbye, reluctantly handing her over to an aide to escort back to the Residence, before the committee sits, every member receiving the same briefing on the presence of the missiles, which have been established on the orders of the Soviet Premier, in league with his Cuban counterpart, not merely for the defense of that island, but to establish a devastating offensive threat against the United States. While the President challenges the intelligence advisors on every point they make regarding identification of the missiles and the establishment of their readiness for action, he cannot help but imagine that the Soviet Premier is once again testing him, that he has known for some weeks now that the day would come when the American President would wake to this monster in his backyard and thereafter never sleep soundly again.

By the end of the first meeting, the President has made clear that he will not receive any information or advice without giving it the most forensic interrogation and insists on every point of policy being discussed in a collegial atmosphere. A clear understanding forms among the President's committee that the missiles might be launch-ready within a few days, probably ten, this time line limiting options to a surprise air strike to destroy the weapons, full invasion, or direct confrontation with the Soviet Union, while protracted diplomatic efforts might inadvertently provide time for the weapons to be made operational and possibly used in defense of an air strike or invasion.

The President gives initial orders for further reconnaissance of the missiles and Cuba's air defense systems and for planning to commence on air strikes and invasion, yet, lest the press and the Russians become alert to these deliberations, the appearance of normal political life must be preserved, with scheduled meetings and engagements continuing uninterrupted. Hence the President motors to the Department of State Auditorium to give a speech and then returns to the White House for talks with the Crown Prince before reconvening the Ex-Comm meeting for another couple of hours into the evening, after which, still on edge, he finds himself hosting a dinner in the Residence with the First Lady.

As he small-talks with dignitaries, consuming bland fare and avoiding the wine for fear of reigniting a peptic ulcer, one track of his mind considers the appalling consequences of a failed air strike: such an action might precipitate deployment of those nuclear missiles when otherwise they would have slept in their silos, and, while the Soviets would be compelled to use weapons of mass destruction in this region on account of the overwhelming superiority of our conventional military, precisely the converse situation applies in Berlin, where any Soviet retaliation by their vastly stronger conventional forces could only be resisted by a rapid escalation to nuclear exchange.

These remain his thoughts as the guests depart, oblivious of the perilous affair unfolding across the Gulf, and then the President and First Lady go up to bed, where he takes his regular medications plus a sedative to break his mental fever, and, as he tries to sleep, finally, he thinks of Mary, and the Intern, but in the morning the latter is nowhere to be seen about the West Wing, even though he keeps a lookout for her during the arrival of the West German Foreign Minister.

Instead the President invites Mary to join him for "lunch" in the pool, after which he returns to the committee's next session in rebalanced mood such that some members who don't usually see him more than once in the same day compliment the refreshing properties upon his personage of a midday dip.


LATER, IN THE Oval Office, while the President prepares to go to the airport for a scheduled campaign trip, he spies the Intern flitting between Mrs. Lincoln's office and the Press Office, but, before he can calculate a pretext on which to intercept her, Adm. B. enters to check on his physical condition.

"Acute stress can have a dangerously destabilizing effect on your endocrine status," the Admiral says.

He feels the presidential pulse and listens to the presidential heart.

"We must increase your corticosteroid dosages," he says, after which he presses the presidential belly, and then he checks off the medication ingested today, administering the testosterone shot himself, and before he leaves he says, "We can't have you cracking under the pressure, can we, Mr. President?"

Then the President's aides arrive to accompany him in the limousine. The President glimpses a pair of military uniforms slipping into the vehicle behind, the Football swinging in their hands, and then he sees it again on the airplane, and then it waits inside as he gives a short speech to the press on the tarmac at Bridgeport, Connecticut, and follows him on the next two stops on the stump before he returns to Washington later that evening, going straight back into the Cabinet Room because the NPIC have analyzed the latest batch of aerial photographs.

The President is told the analysts have detected forty-two medium-range nuclear missiles in the process of being rendered operational by a labor force working day and night, as well as additional sites designed for intermediate-range nuclear missiles capable of reaching every major city in the United States bar Seattle. The Defense Secretary puts it most bluntly when he states, "Those missiles could hit Washington D.C. forty-five minutes after an order from Moscow. The Cubans have got weapons of mass destruction that pose a threat to the security of the United States."

The Air Force Chief of Staff says, "My advice to you, Mr. President, is that we cannot stand by and let these missiles become operational. The threat must be eliminated, not just now, but permanently, by destroying the Cuban military and invading the island. You wouldn't be in this hell of a fix if Cuba One had been followed through."

The President flushes with anger, but says calmly, "You're in this fix with me, General, in case you hadn't noticed," which wins sufficient laughter around the table at the general's expense to rescue the situation.

After further discussion, the President calls for a show of hands in favor of air strikes. Without hesitation, all the men in uniform thrust their arms in the air. The President says, "God help us all if the Soviet missiles go up that fast," to quiet chuckles, giving a second to scan the faces of those men who wear fruit salad on their chests, and he sees eyes eager for the fight. Further hands go up, giving a majority in favor of a military offensive.

But the President says, "It would constitute a surprise attack against a smaller power, which goes against everything for which I believe this country should stand. We had the moral high ground when we suffered the attack on Pearl Harbor, and we would do so again were a tragedy of that scale ever to be visited upon this nation in the future. I would like to explore another method of preventing those missiles becoming operational. With our domination of air and sea in this region, can we not cut off the supply of matériel to the island?"

"A blockade," says the Defense Secretary.

* * *

WHEN THE PRESIDENT returns to the Residence, the First Lady is already asleep. He limps into his son's room, where he finds John sleeping. Caroline, in the next room, has bundled her blankets into a heap with her legs sticking out at the bottom and her chest at the top, so he spreads the covers over her again, and she turns with a snort and buries her face in the pillow. He brushes her hair and kisses her cheek. She smiles a semiconscious smile. "I love you," he whispers, and she whispers back, "I love you too, Daddy," and continues to slumber.

The valet helps him out of the back brace so as not to wake the First Lady. The valet checks off the numbers as the President counts out rows of tablets and adds another line of tiny white cortisone pills in accordance with the higher dose prescribed by his physicians, which he swallows with slugs of water, then, after the valet has withdrawn, he doubles the dose of antidiarrheal and anti-indigestion medication because his stomach has been in turmoil for about forty-eight hours, ever since he saw the photographs of the missiles, and when he lies down in bed, he feels his stomach acid roll up into his gullet, stinging so strongly it makes him gasp.

He watches his wife's dark outline rise and fall with her slow breathing, and then he reaches out briefly to lay a hand on the bulge of their unborn child pushing up through the blankets. He needs an extra sedative to put him to sleep, before his eyes close against visions of their baby being born into a world of ash and radiation.

THE FOLLOWING MORNING, the President flies to the Midwest for more campaigning on behalf of the Party, starting in Ohio and then proceeding to Illinois, where he takes time out to place a wreath at Lincoln's Tomb.

Fall has stripped the green off the trees, making them skeletons gathered around the memorial. They say President Lincoln foresaw his own death ten days in advance, in a dream that began with the sound of weeping emanating from somewhere in the White House, which he followed to the East Room, where he found a catafalque, on which rested a corpse wrapped in funeral vestments, and around it were stationed soldiers and a throng of people, gazing mournfully upon the corpse, whose face was covered. "Who is dead in the White House?" Lincoln asked one of the soldiers. "The President," was the answer, "killed by an assassin."

In the crypt of Oak Ridge Cemetery, the President considers his counterpart of one century past, as oblivious in Ford's Theatre, moments before the bullet blasted the back of his head, as the smiling, deferential faces here today. Meanwhile, all over the globe, nuclear triggers click.

The President remains in constant contact with aides en route to Chicago, receiving hourly bulletins on the state of preparations for the blockade, troop build-up and reconnaissance reports, which he endeavors to put out of his mind during his address this evening to the Cook County Democratic Party, after which he rushes to the telephone once again, speaking to his closest circle one by one, ensuring every single one is examining the situation critically and furnishing him with candid opinions, because, though we are a democracy, in periods of international conflict the leader of our nation becomes a de facto dictator, all too eager to imperil our soldiers' lives.

When the President retires to the Blackstone, Dr. T. and

Adm. B. await, concerned that today's schedule may have upset the delicate balance of the Commander-in-Chief's medication, so they prescribe muscle relaxants for his back, inject painkillers into his sacroiliacs, and administer a combination of pills and emulsions to combat his nausea, dyspepsia and diarrhea.

In addition, the subject is back on antibiotics, following an exacerbation of prostatitis, which has flared up recently owing to the lack of drainage that accompanies his wife's pregnancy, and he must pop a couple of headache pills, because it's two days since his postpool shower with Mary and he dreads suffering a crippling headache tomorrow, which is inevitable, given his quartan toxemia.

The Intern has been invited to accompany the presidential excursion, ostensibly to furnish her with experience of the campaigning duties of his office as Leader of the Party, and so it occurs to him at this hour, one before midnight, to invite the staff for a nightcap in order to position her where he can engineer a private encounter. As it happens, the matter is simplicity itself, as the Signal Corps has transferred a folder of photographic reports from Washington for his perusal, which he directs the Intern to convey to the presidential suite, and to wait therein while he finishes a short briefing with his Press Secretary, after which he takes the elevator with a Secret Service agent to the twenty-first floor, finding the Intern guarding the folder from the NPIC.

He invites her to mix a daiquiri while he speed-reads the reports, once again finding himself let down by the Farmington syllabus as she requires instruction in the recipe and combines the constituents so tremulously he fears there'll be more rum on the rug than in his glass, then he invites her to sit and wait with a notepad, and, on completing the folder, he dictates, "POTUS examined material period no change in course period," and then he smiles, work finished, and offers her a drink, which she politely declines. Her skin is pale and unblemished, her hair thick and straight, but she is quite nervous.

"Are you sure?" he says. "Maybe we both need to relax at the end of a day like today."

"I don't know, Mr. President," she says.

"Well, I certainly need to relax," he says.

She gazes at him for a few seconds, unsure of his meaning. He thinks she must be worried she'll be asked to mix another drink.

"You must be tired, Mr. President" is her eventual reply.

His fingers drum on the armrest of his chair. He decides to say, "Do you think you could do something to help me relax?"

She is shaking with nerves. "I'll see what I can do, Mr. President," she says, and exits.

He awaits her return, a little perplexed, but hugely excited. The presidential rocket starts its countdown.

The telephone rings, Room Service, saying one of his aides has asked them to send up a masseur. He declines, pleading tiredness, and phones Fiddle (or Faddle), whom the Beard thoughtfully packed as backup, to be broken out of her wrapper in an emergency.


CAMPAIGNING IN THE Midwest is scheduled to continue through the weekend, but the President becomes anxious about being away from Washington during the crisis, so his Press Secretary issues a statement that he has come down with a cold—not rhinitis or sinusitis or urethritis or prostatitis or any of the infections he *does* have at this particular time—to facilitate abbreviating the trip without arousing suspicion.

In the morning, he motors to O'Hare, flies to Andrews, boards the helicopter for the hop back to the White House, and then limps across the South Lawn into the Oval Office before proceeding through his secretary's office, saying "Good morning" to Mrs. Lincoln, and into the Cabinet Room, where the Executive Committee stand to attention waiting for the President to sit before they do so themselves, and around the table they go straight to work on the fine details of strategy.

The session continues intermittently over the whole weekend and through Monday, with breaks for lunch and dinner, plus any long-standing diary commitments the President must meet, such as talks with the Ugandan President, to maintain an air of business as usual. Once again in the debate, he faces strong calls for air strikes and invasion. The Air Force Chief of Staff suggests planning a preemptive strategic nuclear strike against the Soviet Union.

In meeting with senior senators of both parties, the President outlines the discovery of the missile bases and his proposed response. Almost to a man, they insist he abandon restraint and order our forces into action in Cuba and Berlin.

Meanwhile, in his time away from the Ex-Comm, the President hurries to his wife and children. He glimpses them in the playground, so he shambles out into the south grounds to join them, as countless fathers must also be doing across the country on this apparently unremarkable Sunday in October.

The President has appreciated having his family close by over this tense period, yet he has become accustomed to a regular Sunday evening assignation. Routinely he would have a snack with the Beard and the girl, and then use her quickly in the Lincoln Bedroom, ensuring the Beard had her off the premises by 7 P.M., before his wife and children would return from out of town. Tonight the four-poster lies empty, and the President's toxemia simmers.

The following night, he goes on air. Gloom has settled in the windows of the Oval Office by the time he's installed behind his desk, cleared of all documents save speech notes, even the photographs of the First Lady and their children having been scooped into a box. He fixes his eyes on the middle camera of three and says:

> "Good evening, my fellow citizens. This Government, as promised, has maintained the closest surveillance of the Soviet Military build-up on the island of Cuba. Within the past week, unmistakable evidence has established the fact that a series of offensive missile sites is now in preparation on that imprisoned island. . . ."

The President outlines the evidence, the strategic threat posed by the missiles, and the proposed naval blockade. He takes a breath. His stomach aches. If he were capable of producing adrenaline, there'd now be a cold sweat trickling down his brow. Instead he appears cool and controlled. His tan is flawless and his hair splendid.

> "My fellow citizens: let no one doubt that this is a difficult and dangerous effort on which we have set out. But the greatest danger of all would be to do nothing. Our goal is not the victory of might, but the vindication

of right—not peace at the expense of freedom, but both peace and freedom, here in this hemisphere, and, we hope, around the world."

Once the cameras cut, the President gives thanks to a few members of the television crew before slipping into the head to vent stinging poison from his knotted gut. Adm. B. and Dr. C. are waiting in the sitting hall when he comes out.

"Fine speech, Mr. President," says Adm. B.

"Very fine, sir," says Dr. C.

"Thank you," he says, admitting them to the Oval Office.

"How are you tonight, sir?" says the Admiral.

"My belly's on fire," he says.

"That will be down to the corticosteroids," says the Admiral.

"The increased dose will upset your gut metabolism," says Dr. C.

"Then shouldn't you reduce the dose?" the President says.

They shake their heads simultaneously. "Now we've increased it," they say, "it would be catastrophic to reduce it."

The doctors have instituted an even stricter regimen of bland food and passed their orders to the chef, so, while the First Lady enjoys an appetizing repast that evening in the Residence, the President's plates bear wan offerings scarcely distinguishable from the china.

Tonight they dine alone, hardly discussing the speech or the situation, because he's told her most of it already, and instead they talk about the children and forthcoming engagements. But his anxieties continue unspoken, which she comforts with a hand on his or a brush of his cheek.

After dessert (hers—none for him, on doctors' orders), she

declines a coffee, because she wants an early night. As she stands, she holds her swollen belly, and then they cross the sitting hall to their bedroom.

The President sent the Soviet Premier a copy of the television address via the embassy, Mr. Khrushchev's reply being cabled to the White House the next day, and the President studies the translation in the Oval Office with his aides.

> Dear President Kennedy,
>
> Just imagine, Mr. President, that we had presented you with the conditions of an ultimatum which you have presented us by your action. How would you have reacted to this? I think that you would have been indignant at such a step on our part. You are threatening that if we do not give in to your demands you will use force. No, Mr. President, I cannot agree to this, and I think that in your own heart you recognize that I am correct. I am convinced that in my place you would act the same way.
>
> The Soviet Government considers that the violation of the freedom to use International waters and International air space is an act of aggression which pushes mankind toward the abyss of a world nuclear-missile war. Therefore, the Soviet Government cannot instruct the captains of Soviet vessels bound for Cuba to observe the orders of American naval forces blockading that island. Our instructions to Soviet mariners are to observe strictly the universally accepted norms of navigation in International waters and not to retreat one step from them. And if the

American side violates these rules, it must realize what
responsibility will rest upon it in that case. Naturally
we will not simply be bystanders with regard to
piratical acts by American ships on the high seas. We
will then be forced on our part to take the measures
we consider necessary and adequate in order to protect
our rights. We have everything necessary to do so.

Nikita S. Khrushchev

The President looks up from his rocking chair to see all his
aides' heads still down reading the printed pages. Most will have
read only a paragraph in the time he takes to scan a page. He raps
on the armrest, waiting, while with every passing minute the
Soviet technicians laboring on the Cuban missiles come closer to
making them ready to blow up American cities.

Naturally the Soviet Premier's response does not cause the
President to waver, and the Navy proceeds as ordered to establish
a quarantine zone around Cuba, under instruction to intercept
and inspect any inbound traffic and to turn back those bearing
offensive weapons. In Washington, the President waits for the
first encounter between one of our warships and a Soviet vessel, a
situation already grimly anticipated by the Ex-Comm, whereby
everyone shares the fear that the Soviets would resist being
boarded and there would ensue an armed exchange between the
two vessels involved, which either side could consider an act of
war, and thereafter the two great powers of the planet would
pursue a course of apocalyptic escalation.

As he swims that noon, he considers the millions who will
perish, and those who'll never grow up, among them his own
children.

The Defense Secretary has arranged a meeting in the Fish Room with the Chairman of the Joint Chiefs and the Air Force Chief of Staff, which the President attends in the afternoon. Between the two generals sits a man in his late twenties who never meets the President's eyes even when they shake hands. The Air Force Chief of Staff says, "Our boy John is the best brain we've got on nuclear exchange."

"Game theory," says the Chairman.

"Explain to the President, John," says the Air Force Chief of Staff, and John says, "Mr. President, game theory attempts to analyze behavior in strategic situations, where an individual's performance in decision-making depends on the actions of others, such as nuclear war between the United States and the Soviet Union, in which event game theory can help decide the validity of a first strike, second strike and so on. For the purpose of my own analysis, Mr. President, I've assumed nuclear war is a zero-sum game."

"Meaning what, exactly?"

"Meaning, Mr. President, that our success must be at the expense of our enemy, or vice versa, since the two sides can't both win a nuclear war."

"We can both lose one," the President says.

"Not this way, Mr. President," says the Air Force Chief of Staff. "Tell him, John."

"Certainly, General. Mr. President, in peacetime, the most mutually successful strategy is cooperation, in which neither side launches a strike, and both survive. However, in war, the most effective game-theoretic model at our disposal is Hawk-Dove, the game informally known as Chicken, and in this case the most mutually beneficial course is an anti-coordination matrix in which the players choose different strategies. In anticoordination games, the resource—in this case the world—is rivalrous but nonexcludable and sharing comes at a cost, or negative externality. In Chicken, the cost of swerving is to lose the game, but appears preferable to the crash which occurs if neither player swerves; however, in nuclear war, the cost of swerving may be national extinction, a consequence approximately equal to an internecine full exchange. An unstable situation exists with more than one equilibrium. The evolutionary stable strategy for Chicken is a mixed strategy, that is random polarization between playing Hawk or Dove—in short, unpredictability. The scenario of nuclear war resembles Chicken on a game-theoretic level because it would appear that a rational person would swerve to avoid collision, but a mixed strategy must of necessity include the option not to swerve, that is, to crash, or else the opponent will always win. However, although the evolutionary stable scenario for Chicken is this mixed strategy, I have calculated a superior strategy that I call Daring with Probability. If one side is prepared to engage in a preemptive strike, the probability is that the enemy will suffer enormous losses to its retaliatory capability, as a consequence of loss of population, destruction of infrastructure, electromagnetic pulse and so forth. I have calculated that the probability of victory for the side that executes a preemptive strike is eighty-five to ninety percent."

"There it is, Mr. President!" says the Air Force Chief of Staff.

"There's what, General?"

"Well, what else, Mr. President?—the argument for striking first, before the Soviets do."

"My worry, Mr. President," says the Defense Secretary, "is the Soviets may already be thinking along the same lines."

"They don't have the math we have!" says the Air Force Chief of Staff, and pats John on the back.

"Gentlemen," says the President, "our national game is baseball. I believe theirs is chess."

"But this is the clincher, Mr. President," says the Air Force Chief of Staff.

"And what would that 'clincher' be, General?"

"Why, Mr. President, *mathematical proof,* of course!"

The President thanks them and dismisses them. The next day, his aides announce that the Cuban missiles appear to have become operational. The President spends a half-hour in the head, having overdosed on Lomotil to control his diarrhea, precipitating rebound constipation. He feels bloated enough to explode.

He sits over the pan studying the Game Theorist's calculations of the end of the world based on some obscure rules of probability. Next the President reads another report in which physicists have been polled to predict the weapons used in the Third World War, to which one responds that he doesn't know, but he can be sure in the Fourth we'll use stones.

That night, his wife and children sleep, but he doesn't. He stays up in the Oval Office discussing strategy. By dawn he suffers a nagging headache and it is only then, having been so absorbed in the crisis of Cuba Two, that he counts the days.

The President takes a couple of aspirin to kill the headache, but they don't touch it and have the side effect of inflaming his peptic ulcers so that, when he finally manages to squeeze out a motion after breakfast, it's black with digested blood.

In desperation, the President orders the Beard to borrow one of the secretaries' swimming costumes so the Intern can join him in the pool.

She's nervous as the Beard ushers her from the changing room, but the President beckons from the water, and she descends the ladder.

"It's so warm, Mr. President," she says.

"Some like it hot," he says.

"No, sir, I— It's pleasant. Only I expected to feel cold."

"It's a good way to start the day, don't you think?"

"Yes, sir, thank you, Mr. President."

"Let's swim," he says, waving to the Beard so he lays out some towels before disappearing discreetly.

The President and the Intern go a couple of laps and then at the edge she stands up to sweep her wet hair off her face.

"So how are you enjoying the White House?" he says.

"It's such a wonderful opportunity for me. I'm so deeply grateful, Mr. President."

He feels blood pounding in his head and a throb prodding his temples, and he looks at this girl whom another man might be nervous of corrupting, but a philanderer must seize women as empires seize countries. He closes on an intercept course with clear intention to board, when the Beard returns at a trot.

"I'm very sorry, sir, but there's an urgent call from the Department of Defense."

He says, "Convene the Ex-Comm," and leaves at once. The Intern remains in the pool, disconcerted, but the Beard will arrange for her to go back up to the West Wing, while the President towels off quickly and dresses, helped into his back brace by his valet, and then he hurries up to the Cabinet Room, where they tell him that Soviet troops are moving on Berlin.

"They're on a war footing," says the Secretary of Defense. "If we hit Cuba, they'll take Berlin."

Later the President finds out that, as soon as he heard the news, the Chief of Staff moved the Air Force to DEFCON 2 for the first time in its history. Missiles and bombers were put on high alert without the President's knowledge from a decision made by generals bunkered underground in Omaha. In a flux of fear and fury, the President telephones the Defense Secretary and orders him to make it plain to the military commanders that only the President has the right to declare war, no matter how eager they are to start one, but he knows they've gone behind his back because some of them think he lacks the balls for this job; they believe it takes courage to ordain death and destruction.

During the President's final meeting of the day, Adm. B. sits outside in the hall with the men coveting the Football, and, when the presidential advisors disperse in the early hours, the Admiral carries out a short physical to assess his patient's heart and blood pressure, etc., during which the President expounds his various dyspeptic symptoms, and then the Admiral administers some painkillers and muscle relaxants and hormone replacements.

"We need you in shape for war, sir," he says before he goes.

The President goes to his wife and children in their quarters, finding them all sound asleep. He kisses them and then retires to the Lincoln Bedroom, where the Beard has prepared a late supper of cheese sandwiches, which the President eats with an extra dose of aspirin to fight his headache. Mary got back to town tonight, at last, and the President, virtually blinded by a migraine, has ordered the Beard to escort her to the White House.

"Are the First Lady and the children going out of town early this week?" the Beard asked.

"No, they're here."

"But . . ."

"I know, Dave."

"You want me to bring Mrs. Meyer to the Residence?"

"I do, Dave," the President said.

"Aye, aye, skipper," said the Beard, and went to his task with alacrity, appreciating that the fate of the world depends on draining the President's poison.

Despite his crisis, the President is still thinking with the clarity of the practiced philanderer. He does not call his wife via the internal switchboard and, say, inform her he's going to take a nap in the Lincoln Bedroom before the next session of the Ex-Comm. Instead he strolls through the East Sitting Hall calm in the knowledge the family bedrooms lie at the far end of the Residence, interconnecting with the West Hall, and if his wife happens to see him, he will wave and call "Hi" but vanish through the door without further explanation.

An agent mans the entrance, with orders that the President is not to be disturbed. The Beard appears a few minutes later and, having confirmed the coast is clear, slips Mary into the room.

"My God, Jack," she says, seeing the President prostrate on the bed, but he doesn't want to explain the problem, only for her to cure it.

Afterward she smokes, and they talk. He ought to worry about his wife at the end of the hall, in case she comes looking, but he's in such a state of blissful torpor he won't even need sleeping pills tonight.

"It was a hell of a risk," Mary says.

He says, "Sex is rivalrous but nonexcludable."

She dresses in the window, gazing out across the capital. "I keep fearing I'll see rockets," she says.

"I hope my phone would ring first," he says.

"Is it inevitable, one day?" she says.

"Everything ends," he says.

"Well," she says, "if the world's got to end, this is the way to go."

She smiles her ethereal smile, but she knows he wouldn't be with her then; he'd be with the woman along the hall, their children huddled in their arms.

When she goes, he slumps into sleep. One of the conditions of the defense alert is that nearly two hundred bombers stay airborne constantly, flying a course toward the Soviet Union loaded with thermonuclear bombs—to allow our forces a second-strike capability, so we can still inflict an apocalyptic retaliatory blow even if the homeland has already been obliterated—and those bombers keep on flying till they receive an order to come home, or else they will press on and deliver their holocaust to Soviet cities. But when the Defense Secretary asked the President if he wanted to ground the bombers, he ordered them to stay up, so his Soviet counterpart will know, whatever the mathematics of a preemptive strike, he'll burn in hell just the same, though, as the room goes dark, the President wonders if he too sees those bombers crossing the sky like a thousand metal crosses on the graves of each million dead.

Loud knocking wakes the President. Initially disorientated, he can't remember if Mary is still here. "I want to see my husband," he hears the First Lady demanding, and the door swings open. The Beard peers in fearfully while the agent adopts a gaze neutral to the President's fate if his wife catches him cheating.

"Jack, I was worried," she says, her eyes scanning the room.

"I needed a nap," he says, rapidly becoming wakeful, seeing his date has vanished without a trace.

"I was worried," his wife repeats, and he forces a smile, thankful color never drains from his pathologically tanned face.

# THE LETTERS

SOVIET VESSELS APPROACH our warships. The moment of collision will inevitably arrive, unless one or the other decides to swerve. The arcane ramblings of game theory spin through the President's mind as he descends to the basement under the West Wing of the White House, where military and intelligence staff have assembled in the wood-paneled Situation Room to coordinate naval action. They stand as the President arrives and he orders them to continue at their posts, and, while he takes his seat, he imagines his counterpart in some bunker under the Kremlin confronting the same terror. The President must imagine him to be sane, if only so that he may make sane decisions himself, for if the Premier is a madman, then we're all doomed.

This morning, the President read further reports commending the advantage of a preemptive nuclear strike against Cuba and the Soviet Union simultaneously, and he wonders if Mr. Khrushchev is receiving identical counsel from his generals, men in the autumn of life who no longer dread death.

The Chief of Naval Operations reports, "Some of the Soviet

traffic has slowed down or changed course, Mr. President, but some shipping continues to sail toward the quarantine, and, in accordance with our rules of engagement, the *Essex* and the *Gearing* are now under orders to intercept."

The President keeps silent as he observes the encounter unfold through the R/T of the naval commanders, in which with each passing minute they report ranges closing, until the point nears where the *Gearing* and the *Essex* position to fire upon the Soviet vessel. He stands to stretch his back, pacing the room. This time, none of the officers stand in deference.

The Chief of Naval Operations says, "Perhaps you'd be more comfortable upstairs, Mr. President," but the President shakes his head and retakes his seat, to the CNO's evident chagrin.

A few moments later, the President hears a naval officer report that both our ships are in visual contact with the Soviet vessel and awaiting orders to inspect it. The Chief of Naval Operations is about to give the order.

"Wait, would you, Fleet Admiral?" says the President.

"Mr. President?"

"Wait."

The Chief of Naval Operations glares.

"Ask the Soviet ship to identify itself," the President says.

"Mr.—"

"Ask it, Fleet Admiral."

"Yes, Mr. President."

The message passes to the ships, who in turn challenge the Soviet vessel. The Soviet Premier, if he is not a madman, if he is a man who values life as the President does, will have ensured his captains are under orders to respect the quarantine insofar as the etiquette of the high seas. While interception and boarding remain a different matter, there is no loss of national prestige involved in a vessel identifying itself.

The President's fingers drum on the armrest of his chair. His teeth grind. He feels a lurch in his gut that would ordinarily send him scurrying to the head but now, in this crisis, he endures the spasm that pulls taut lines on his brow. He has endured days of stomach pains and Spartan meals and feels ready to faint, but it passes, and one of the officers relays the message: "It's the *Bucharest*."

"A tanker," says the Chief of Naval Operations. "Mr. President, we must act with decisive force. I shall order our ships to board and search the *Bucharest*, and, if they are met with resistance, to respond accordingly."

Such eventualities have been debated repeatedly in the sessions of the Executive Committee, with each option and outcome explored, and still no consensus yet exists on what constitutes reasonable force in attempting to board a vessel of a sovereign power, or what loss of life, on either side, would meet the threshold for an act of war, or whether American ships should attempt to disable or sink a Soviet vessel that flouts the quarantine, and at what point a synecdochic encounter hundreds of miles out at sea may morally be permitted to detonate hostilities that will consume the nations of this earth.

The President asks, "Who lies in firing position, Fleet Admiral Anderson, the *Essex* or the *Gearing*?"

"The *Gearing*, Mr. President."

"Put me through to the captain."

"I'm sorry, Mr. President, that isn't possible."

The President says, "It is entirely possible, Fleet Admiral, and you will do it now."

One of the wood panels on the wall is swung open by a naval officer, a telephone is brought to the President's station and, in a matter of seconds, patched into the radio telephony loop of the Situation Room.

The President says, "Captain, this is the President of the United States calling you from the Situation Room of the White House. Do you copy?"

A short delay intervenes as the messages are relayed via the communications network, and then the President hears a distant voice through the speakers built into the panels of one of the communications stations: "I read you loud and clear, Mr. President."

"Captain, please ask the *Bucharest* to declare its cargo."

"Aye, aye, Mr. President."

While the Situation Room awaits the Soviet response via the *Gearing*'s Signal Officer, the President says, "Captain, in your judgment, is there anything suspicious about the *Bucharest*?"

"Please specify, Mr. President."

"We're naval men, Captain. Does the ship look like a regular tanker and its crew look like a regular crew?"

The Chief of Naval Operations gasps in dismay, but the President ignores him.

"Do you follow me now, Captain?" the President says.

"I do, Mr. President. It looks like a regular oil tanker, sir."

"Thank you, Captain. Are you a family man, Captain?"

"Yes, Mr. President, I am."

"I hope when all this is over you and your family will come visit here at the White House."

"That would be an honor, Mr. President."

Now they wait, but the President knows the captain of the

*Gearing,* if he hadn't already, is picturing his wife in her loveliest frock and his children in their Sunday best on a White House lawn bathed in perfect East Coast sunshine, and he is now wondering what will become of them should the world blow up. His voice is softer when he comes back. "I have a response from the *Bucharest.*"

The Chief of Naval Operations intervenes and radios, "This is CNO Anderson. What is his response, Captain?"

"He declares his cargo is oil, sir. Nothing but oil."

The Chief of Naval Operations glares at the President, but he cannot escape logic. Eventually he says, "Let him pass, Captain."

"Yes, sir."

The President exits the Situation Room, joining up with an agent who waits by the door, and then they go back up to the first floor via the elevator, where the President convenes a meeting with his closest circle in the Oval Office, in which he orders that henceforth all strategic military command take place via the Situation Room.

American ships and Russian ships dance and swerve and sensibly avoid crashing into each other, but with each passing hour the Cuban missiles near readiness, and it appears as if the only means of removing them will be an invasion, prompting Soviet retaliation either locally or globally. This will be how the inferno sparks.

The President wanders the halls of the White House, visiting staff who are working late so that they know he is working late also, facing what would seem to be a stalemate.

Members of the Executive Committee have cleaved into small alliances. The President glimpses the Chief of Staff of the Army exchanging intense whispers with the Vice President about the prospect of a postinvasion Cuban democracy reconstructed by American corporations.

He returns briefly to the Residence, where the First Lady is waiting for him. "Mrs. Lincoln said you were on your way," she says brightly, but he takes it as a warning shot that he is being watched. Ever since she burst into the Lincoln Bedroom after his assignation with Mary, she has tracked his movements and shown more interest than usual in whom he is meeting and what he is up to.

"Ex-Comm have dispersed for a few hours," he says by way of explanation for his presence.

"Aren't you the busy boy?" she says.


BY THE TIME midnight comes around, the President receives a response to his protocol suggestion in the form of a letter from the Air Force Chief of Staff, who declines the President's "kind invitation" to the Situation Room as if he's RSVPing his distant cousin's wedding, declaring that his own mission is best served by his staff underground in Nebraska, with one paragraph that reads:

> In this crisis, Mr. President, I would ask you to consider the humble counsel of one who has contemplated Apocalypse for most of his professional life, and resist the assumption that it is infinitely more wicked to kill human beings with nuclear bombs than by busting their heads with rocks.

Tonight, the President doesn't sleep. He takes sedatives, but they cannot close his eyes to the abyss opening beneath his feet.

In the morning, in the Cabinet Room, the Chairman of the Joint Chiefs says, "If we are to strike, we can only strike *before* those missiles can be launched. If we strike after, then we may precipitate the very situation we have taken action to avoid—ballistic missiles raining nuclear bombs on American cities. Mr. President, I urgently recommend invasion."

During a lengthy summary of the situation by the Secretary of State, the President crosses in front of the windows to the book alcoves at the far end of the room, and, when the Secretary of State has finished, the Chairman of the Joint Chiefs says, "If nuclear war is inevitable, then we must fire first, on Cuba and on the Soviet Union."

"Nuclear war is *not* inevitable!" the President says. For the first time, he has raised his voice. "It is not, gentlemen, and I reject the idea not just intellectually but morally. These weapons cannot be our masters."

Later the President receives an urgent call from the State Department. A letter from the Soviet Premier is sent via air pouch. With his closest advisors, the President hovers around the teletype and reads the translation as it spools out.

> Dear President Kennedy,
>
> I think you will understand me correctly if you are really concerned about the welfare of the world. War is our enemy and a calamity for all the peoples.
>
> I see, Mr. President, that you too are not devoid of a sense of anxiety for the fate of the world, and not without an understanding of what war entails. I have participated in two wars and know that war ends when it has rolled through cities and villages,

everywhere sowing death and destruction. You are threatening us with war. But you well know that the very least which you would receive in reply would be that you would experience the same consequences as those which you sent us. My conversation with you in Vienna gives me the right to talk to you this way.

I don't know whether you can understand me and believe me. But I should like to have you believe in yourself and to agree that one cannot give way to passions; it is necessary to control them.

You have now proclaimed piratical measures, which were employed in the Middle Ages, when ships proceeding in International waters were attacked, and you have called this "a quarantine" around Cuba. I assure you that on those ships, which are bound for Cuba, there are no weapons at all. The weapons which were necessary for the defense of Cuba are already there.

You have asked what happened, what evoked the delivery of weapons to Cuba? You have spoken about this to our Minister of Foreign Affairs. I will tell you frankly, Mr. President, what evoked it. We were very grieved by the fact—I spoke about it in Vienna—an attack on Cuba was committed, as a result of which many Cubans perished. You yourself told me then that this had been a mistake. I respected that explanation. You repeated it to me several times, pointing out that not everybody occupying a high position would acknowledge his mistakes as you had done. I value such frankness. It is also not a secret to anyone that the threat of armed attack, aggression, has constantly

hung, and continues to hang over Cuba. It was only
this which impelled us to respond to the request of the
Cuban Government to furnish it aid for the
strengthening of the defensive capacity of this country.

If assurances were given by the President and the
Government of the United States that the USA itself
would not participate in an attack on Cuba and would
restrain others from actions of this sort, if you would
recall your fleet, this would immediately change
everything. Then, too, the question of armaments
would disappear. Then too, the question of the
destruction of the armaments which you call offensive
would look different.

Mr. President, I appeal to you to weigh well what
the aggressive, piratical actions, which you have
declared the USA intends to carry out in International
waters, would lead to. We and you ought not now to
pull on the ends of the rope in which you have tied
the knot of war, because the more the two of us pull,
the tighter that knot will be tied. And a moment may
come when that knot will be tied so tight that even he
who tied it will not have the strength to untie it, and
then it will be necessary to cut that knot, and what
that would mean is not for me to explain to you,
because you yourself understand perfectly of what
terrible forces our countries dispose.

Nikita S. Khrushchev

The President expects everyone to take enormous encourage-
ment from the proposal to remove the missiles in return for a

nonaggression pact with Cuba, but none of the Joint Chiefs takes the letter at face value, insisting it's a ruse to buy time for the Soviets to arm the Cuban missiles in preparation for a preemptive strike, so the United States should invade anyway and get ready to go nuclear on the back of it.

It is probably only then that it strikes the President that perhaps the Soviet Premier is wandering the halls of the Kremlin too, just as the President was after the invasion of Cuba, asking himself how he could have been so bloody stupid as to let the generals talk him into basing nuclear missiles in Cuba.

THE INTERN, THE subject notices, has evolved a dramatically smarter look during the current tension; she wears more fashionable dresses and has found time to have her hair styled, the overall effect being to give her a more mature appearance, and needless to say the subject interprets this development as an effort to command his attention, based on his suspicion that to this point she has naïvely remained incredulous of his interest in her, given her own (accurate) self-estimation that she is a young woman from solid but hardly noble stock with winsome looks that fall short of dazzling. Or perhaps she looks no different at all, and the subject is merely experiencing the tensile equivalent of beer goggles, but the fact remains that her most alluring feature is her proximity, firstly because his desire is repeatedly reinforced by glimpses of her in the halls or gliding in and out of Mrs. Lincoln's office with folded arms nuzzling a file of photostats against her chest, and secondly because he feels he can count on a certain amount of loyalty from West Wing staff, sparing the temptation of reckless speculations further afield.

Regardless, the subject senses that she at long last appreciates she's caught the presidential eye—the fact she didn't reach this conclusion the instant she was offered an internship personally despite having no secretarial skills whatsoever is testament to her erstwhile naïveté—and, while she herself might not be dazzling, the subject imagines that, given his personage, she finds herself dazzled. Now that he has determined, to his own satisfaction, she is interested and available, it only remains a matter of facile calculation before he has her.

Though the First Lady appears to have moved to DEFCON 2, he remains confident nonetheless that he will elude her reconnaissance as he has done at other times in their marriage when her suspicions were piqued. His plots turn variously to a pool setting or to an invitation to cocktails, until the President's plucky mood is punctured by notification of a new dispatch from the Soviet Premier, the translation arriving only a few minutes later in the form of photostats laid by the Intern at each place on the Cabinet Room table. She saves a smile for the President as she lays the squared and paper-clipped pages in front of him, a smile which he disregards in favor of focusing on this urgent development, and he doesn't even admire her from behind as she makes her meek exit.

Dear President Kennedy,
    I understand your concern for the security of the United States, Mr. President, because this is the primary duty of a President. But we too are disturbed about these same questions; I bear these same obligations as Chairman of the Council of Ministers of the U.S.S.R. You have been alarmed by the fact that we have aided Cuba with weapons, in order to

strengthen its defense capability—because whatever weapons she may possess, Cuba cannot be equated with you since the difference in magnitude is so great, particularly in view of modern means of destruction. Our aim has been and is to help Cuba, and no one can dispute the humanity of our motives, which are oriented toward enabling Cuba to live peacefully and develop in the way its people desire.

You wish to ensure the security of your country, and this is understandable. But Cuba, too, wants the same thing; all countries want to maintain their security. But how are we, the Soviet Union, our Government, to assess your actions which are expressed in the fact that you have surrounded the Soviet Union with military bases; surrounded our allies with military bases; placed military bases literally around our country; and stationed your missile armaments there? This is no secret. Responsible American personages openly declare that it is so. Your missiles are located in Britain, are located in Italy, and are aimed against us. Your missiles are located in Turkey. Yet you are disturbed over Cuba. You say that this disturbs you because it is 90 miles by sea from the coast of the United States of America. But Turkey adjoins us; our sentries patrol back and forth and see each other.

I think it would be possible to end the controversy quickly and normalize the situation, and then the people could breathe more easily, considering that statesmen charged with responsibility are of sober mind and have an awareness of their responsibility combined with the ability to solve complex questions and not bring things to a military catastrophe.

I therefore make this proposal: We are willing to remove from Cuba the means which you regard as offensive. Your representatives will make a declaration to the effect that the United States will remove its analogous means from Turkey.

Nikita S. Khrushchev

Suddenly the situation has worsened. For some reason the President cannot immediately fathom, his Soviet counterpart has linked a peaceful solution with a betrayal of a long-standing defensive commitment to one of America's front-line allies, an option that would be insupportable even if not under duress. He feels the blood drain from his face followed by an agonizing gut spasm, but all around the table he sees only lambent faces.

The President limps across the South Lawn to the playground. Caroline asks him to push her on the swing, and he takes over from the nanny, who places John Jr. on the seesaw. Caroline swings back and forth, her coat buttoned up to her chin to resist the cold. She says, "Can we go to the sunny house this weekend, Daddy? It's so cold here."

The sunny house is their place in Palm Beach, Florida, no more than three hundred miles from the missile sites in Cuba. He says, "That isn't a good place right now, honey."

"Are we going to the ranch? I can ride my pony!"

"I'm not sure where you and mummy and your brother are going this weekend. Maybe some place new this time."

"Where, Daddy?"

"Somewhere safe," he murmurs.

"Where's safe?" she says.

Plans exist to evacuate the First Family to the Presidential Bunker at Camp David, but that isn't the answer. There is no true answer for her. But he says, "I'll find somewhere," and then they all walk back across the lawn to the Residence before it gets dark.

THE EX-COMM SESSION extends late into the evening, but the President leaves the Cabinet Room briefly to ingest a glassful of milky emulsion to douse the flames of his volcanic ulcers, and then he goes back in, this time to give his express order for the United States military to ratchet up to Defense Condition 2 worldwide, in every base on every continent, on every ship, with the knowledge that intensification to DEFCON 1 is now only one step away: global nuclear war.

When he gives the Committee a half-hour break for supper, he wants to walk to the Residence via the West Colonnade but he finds the door to the outside locked with everyone at hand disclaiming knowledge of the key's whereabouts. He must breathe air musty with dust and dander that makes his eyes itch and blocks his sinuses. He limps up to the Second Floor, finding his children asleep but his wife waiting in the Family Dining Room. As soon as he sits, they receive starters of fish soup. He lets out a sneeze and dabs his runny nose with a handkerchief, the First Lady being so accustomed to his myriad allergies she now barely acknowledges his symptoms with a "Bless you," but she is keenly attuned to his downcast mood and reaches across the table to lay her hand on his.

"Do you want me to take the children?" she asks.

"I hear Nebraska's lovely this time of year," he says.

She says, "Do you think it's going to happen?"

He says, "I ought to be the one to say, oughtn't I? But—honestly—I don't know."

She goes pale. They finish the soup in silence, and their empty bowls give way immediately to the entrées, as the staff have been briefed about his abbreviated break.

Her eyes flick to his and around. She's studying the tense lines on his brow and about his eyes. "Are you in pain?" she says.

"Always," he says. "You know."

"I know," she says.

She knows he can never give in and again be the bedridden little boy alone with his history books while all the other children gambol on the lawn. She reaches across the table and grips his hand again. He smiles at her, and before he returns to the Cabinet Room, he embraces her and kisses her mouth and her cheek and her hair.

"You need me," she says. "You'll always need me, Jack." Then she walks away, not looking back.

The generals who regard nuclear war as an inevitable auto-da-fé lie deep in their subterranean bunkers or orbit the Great Plains in refitted transport airplanes that serve as platforms for a permanent airborne command post, not only planning but desiderating the day the civilian race is vaporized and they assume control of the country, or rather what remains of it, perhaps even the Chief of Staff of the Air Force, for it will be he who declares himself President of the Ignited States of America, forming a Cabinet comprising the Secretary of Rubble and the Secretary of Ash and the Secretary of Radiation, and the war will have been their Flood and the Great Plains their Ararat.

When the President reviews the two letters from the Soviet

Premier, he suspects the hand of the Kremlin generals in the second, it being the same tone he hears in the recommendations of his own hard-liners.

After his swim, the President returns to the office to study any remaining papers. Mrs. Lincoln has left a letter on his desk from a ten-year-old girl in Indiana:

> Dear President Kennedy,
>     Of course you are a busy man, but I just wanted to send you this letter to cheer you up a little. We are praying that all your decisions will be right. Everybody is hoping that we will have peace. We know that the situation is critical, however, we have confidence in you. God bless you daily.
>
>                                     A young citizen
>                                     Betsy Pieters

He suddenly stops and takes a breath. Afterward, Mrs. Lincoln makes a copy and sends a standard acknowledgment, while he folds the original into his inside jacket pocket.

His daughter has not slept well the past four nights. Caroline has been waking every few hours complaining of nightmares, and it's the nanny who's been getting up to her, but tonight when he goes through to visit the children around midnight, though his son is fast asleep, his daughter does seem unsettled. He decides to carry her through to the big four-poster in the bedroom along the hall so she can sleep with him. She is semiconscious and fretful as he rolls her under the covers and then he slides in beside her.

Within a few minutes, she is anxious. He senses she feels

overpowering dread, the terrible fear faced by all the adults she knows having taken the form in her childish imagination of a bogeyman hunkered in the shadows, and it is not a dissimilar vision to the one that haunts him, of an infernal monster waiting to pounce come the sleep of rational men.

He whispers, "Daddy's here. Nothing is going to hurt you. Daddy will protect you."

He holds her close and she falls asleep. In the morning, he finds her curled in the fetal position with her fair hair jumbled across her face and her thin arm limply embracing his shoulder. Leaving her breaks his heart.

Over breakfast in the Cabinet Room, the Executive Committee receives a briefing from the CIA. They have detected a communiqué from the Cuban dictator to the Soviet Premier. The CIA director reads out the message:

> "'Chairman Khrushchev,
>
> "If the imperialists invade Cuba, the danger that that aggressive policy possesses for humanity is so great that following that event the Soviet Union must never allow the circumstances in which the imperialists could launch the first nuclear strike. That would be the moment to eliminate such danger forever through an act of clear, legitimate defense, however harsh and terrible the solution would be, for there is no other.
>
> Fidel Castro.'"

The CIA Director repeats, "'. . . *for there is no other* . . .'"

"There it is, Mr. President," says the Chairman of the Joint Chiefs. "They're planning a first strike. It's them or us."

The President looks around the table, and everyone is looking back at him.

The President returns to the Oval Office with an urgent need for a stroll in the Rose Garden to clear his head and his sinuses, but the door is locked and he ends up pacing like a caged beast, before it occurs in a flash that the solution to this deadlock still lies in his hands. He snatches a pen and paper from his desk and begins to scratch out a set of proposals for the attention of the Soviet Premier, but disregarding the second letter contaminated by the aggressive posturing of the old guard, and concentrating on the personal common ground of the first.

"Screw the generals," he mutters.

Then he calls in his secretary, to type out his rough handwriting, which only she and the First Lady appear able to read, with the door closed, no interruptions, and no disclosure about what they are up to.

"People will talk, Mr. President," she says with a glint.

"Let their imaginations run wild," he says.

She types quickly and he proofreads just as fast, and then the letter is dispatched on his urgent order to the State Department for translation and transmission to the Kremlin.

Dear Chairman Khrushchev,

    I have read your letter of October 26th with great care and welcomed the statement of your desire to seek a prompt solution to the problem. The key elements of your proposals—which seem generally acceptable as I understand them—are as follows:

    1) You would agree to remove the ballistic missile

systems from Cuba and undertake to halt the further introduction of such weapons systems into Cuba.

2) We, on our part, would agree (a) to remove promptly the quarantine measures now in effect and (b) to give assurances against an invasion of Cuba.

If you will give your representative similar instructions, there is no reason why we should not be able to complete these arrangements and announce them to the world within a couple of days. The effect of such a settlement on easing world tensions would enable us to work toward a more general arrangement regarding other armaments. I would like to say again that the United States is very much interested in reducing tensions and halting the arms race; and if your letter signifies that you are prepared to discuss a détente affecting NATO and the Warsaw Pact, we are quite prepared to consider with our allies any useful proposals.

But the first ingredient, let me emphasize, is the cessation of work on missile sites in Cuba and measures to render such weapons inoperable. The continuation of this threat, or a prolonging of this discussion concerning Cuba by linking these problems to the broader questions of European and world security, would surely lead to an intensification of the Cuban crisis and a grave risk to the peace of the world. For this reason I hope we can quickly agree along the lines in this letter and in your letter of October 26th.

John F. Kennedy

Darkness settles on the south grounds. The lawn becomes a black lake. He makes it to the Residence, where he steps out onto the balcony and peers into the penultimate night of the world. In the morning, if there is no agreement, or even no reply, the President must order the invasion and his counterpart must order retaliation. They must both act and set in train the events that will carry the world into permanent dark because there is no escape from power, and power of this magnitude creates obsidian compulsions.

Tonight his daughter sleeps with her mother, to keep her nightmares at bay, the two of them intertwined beneath the covers, with his daughter curved around her mother's bump. He lifts John from the cot and carries the soft, fragile sack through to the bedroom, and then he lowers himself into the rocking chair. He holds the boy asleep against his chest, his face nuzzled into his father's neck, while he watches over his girls, waiting.

At dawn, no word has come from Moscow, and the President wonders if there has already been a military coup. He summons the Executive Committee, and they gather over breakfast to plan the war. He issues his inventory of apocalypse, and, in the afternoon, while Ex-Comm hurls the war plan into operation, the President meets in the Fish Room with the executive committee responsible for civil defense, and discusses the prospect of mass evacuation of cities and the availability of shielded subterranean bunkers capable of housing essential personnel.

By nightfall, the atmosphere in the West Wing is funereal. The President drops by the Oval Office to send his secretary home, and, in the hall outside, the girls linger—Fiddle, Faddle and the Intern—wondering which of them will be chosen, but he doesn't even glance their way, instead shambling in the opposite direction, to the Residence.

Tonight the children sit with their mother and father at dinner, then afterward their parents read them their stories, side by side, before retiring to the Yellow Oval Room, where for once the President sits on the sofa with his wife, with the curtains left open so they can gaze out at the city lights for the last time, because tomorrow they will be blacked-out to hide from the bombers, or they will be melted by fire.

Later his wife helps him up from the sofa, before taking sleeping pills with her to bed. She knows he will not be able to sleep tonight. She kisses him, and her hand lingers on his before she turns.

In a jacket hung in the closet, he discovers the letter from the little girl in Indiana, and uses a sheet of White House stationery to handwrite a reply. He folds the letter in half and slips it into an envelope he addresses himself, and then he goes into the hall, the uniforms carrying the Football jumping to attention and following as he pads along to the West Wing, where he finds a secretary still at work and gives her the letter to stamp and mail tonight.

"Tonight, Mr. President?" she says. "Do you want a courier, or can it wait for the mail room in the morning?"

He says, "Perhaps you'd be kind enough to drop it in a mailbox on your way home?"

"Yes, er . . . of course, Mr. President, if that's what you want."

He lumbers from office to office, saying goodnight to the staff, and urging those remaining to go home to their families. Soon the halls are deserted save for close aides and their administrative assistants.

The President acknowledges the two uniforms seated in the lobby coveting the Football. The Football is a black vinyl satchel containing the launch codes for the nuclear arsenal the President alone holds the authority to employ. They will follow him as they do every night, waiting in halls or lobbies, the ghosts at his parties, only tonight they will be that little bit closer.

In this atmosphere, the subject's conduct proves to be rational and natural. In times of stress, the sex drive increases. The teleological explanation is that a peril that may substantially reduce the population must be answered by abundant reproduction in order to ensure survival of the species. The Intern must have begun to shed misgivings regarding the repercussions of a tryst since in her heart she wonders if there will be anyone left alive to care a damn what she got up to with the President. Like the nuclear bombers perpetually cruising toward Russia, a couple of East Wing secretaries have been kept in a holding pattern since DEFCON3, as part of the Beard's plan for a preemptive strike against presidential stress. Instead, observing the President's interest, he tells the Intern, "The President needs you," and with patriotic solicitude delivers her to the Oval Office.

"Come in, would you, er . . . ?" the President says, settling behind his desk.

The Beard withdraws discreetly, closing the door that adjoins the secretary's office, while Mrs. L., bless her, keeps her gaze firmly fixed on the sheet of paper rolling out of her clacking typewriter.

"It's a tense time for everyone," the President says.

The pressures of the subject's office encourage the young woman to believe that she is not simply falling prey to a powerful, middle-aged fornicator, but instead she is charitably sympathetic to his lonely struggle against the dark forces of the planet, thereby granting a momentary release from the tension as would a nurse administering a painkiller. On this foundation, he constructs a moral highway to bypass a girl's chastity.

"Very tense," he says. "Slip down under the desk, would you?"

For a moment, she acts as if he cannot have said what he's actually just said, or else she hesitates.

"No need to be shy," he says.

She stammers, "I don't, er, don't quite know what to say, Mr. President."

"Consider it a service to your country, though it's not a question of conscription."

She takes a few moments to consider, during which he peers straight at her quite neutrally. He expects the Intern to be more eager to comply, given his assumption that she is dazzled by him. Given her virtually complete absence of secretarial skills, no eyebrows would be raised if he dismissed this intern and got a better one. He makes a mental note to do just that assuming Cuba Two is ever concluded, when she spares them both the trouble by descending beneath the desk.

"Now that's the ticket," he says.

BEFORE DAWN, AN aide summons the President to the Signal Office, in which he finds many of the staff whom he'd thought had gone home. A letter from Moscow has been wired to the embassy and is now being translated.

The Ex-Comm regroups in the Cabinet Room, where like expectant fathers they wait for the teletype to give birth to the first page. The President snatches it in his fist and scans in a headlong rush.

> Dear President Kennedy,
>     In order to eliminate as rapidly as possible the
> conflict which endangers the cause of peace, to give an

assurance to all people who crave peace, and to reassure the American people, who, I am certain, also want peace, as do the people of the Soviet Union, the Soviet Government, in addition to earlier instructions on the discontinuation of further work on weapons construction sites, has given a new order to dismantle the arms which you described as offensive, and to crate and return them to the Soviet Union.

I regard with respect and trust the statement you made in your message that there would be no attack, no invasion of Cuba, and it is for this reason that we instructed our officers to take appropriate measures to discontinue construction of the aforementioned facilities, to dismantle them, and to return them to the Soviet Union. Thus in view of the assurance you have given and our instructions on dismantling, there is every condition for eliminating the present conflict.

Nikita S. Khrushchev

He quickly shuffles to the end and sees that the translator has noted the original is signed by the Soviet Premier himself.

The nuclear powers have stepped back from the abyss. While some of the men around the table have mixed emotions, most are delighted by the outcome. They interweave handshakes, but the President whispers to the ones he trusts, "Get every single one of the Joint Chiefs on the phone. I want them to confirm they understand we're not going to war."

He waits in the Oval Office for each call to come through, and will only relax when every single one of the generals promises, no doubt through gritted teeth, that he won't start the war anyway.

The last to call, unsurprisingly, is the Chief of Staff of the Air Force, via a tinny speakerphone from his rabbit hole in Nebraska, who is not only dismayed by the absence of nuclear apocalypse but also by the news that his boy, the Game Theorist, has been institutionalized for paranoid schizophrenia.

The President feels sudden elation in the certainty he shall see his children grow up, but, before he goes to wake his wife and give her the news, he intends to celebrate by cracking open a nineteen-year-old intern.

He meets her in the small private study adjoining the Oval Office. He shuts the door into the hall and holds it closed, while from this position he keeps a lookout through the internal door toward Mrs. Lincoln's office, whose door is also closed. Afterward, when he has strolled casually back into the Oval Office, she rubs her sore knees and rinses her mouth at the small service sink.

Mrs. Lincoln's door swings open and the First Lady strides into the Oval Office. "You did it, Jack!" she says, and throws her arms around him.

"I did it," he says, momentarily peering over her shoulder into the private study but unable to see if the Intern is still in there.

"Everybody's been out of their minds with worry," she gabbles, strolling around the room, perilously close to the study.

"We made it," he says, and she says, "Yes!" and throws her arms around him again.

They kiss for a few seconds before he asks, "Are the children sleeping?"

"Like tops," she says.

"You should go back to bed, rest."

"I will," she says.

"I'll be over in a few minutes, I've just got a couple of—"

"Of course, of course," she says, and smiles, and then leaves.

The President inches toward the private study. Pressed up against the outer door, the Intern crouches on the floor.

"Go now," he says.

The President leans on his desk. The first light angling into the south-facing windows spreads round him, and from behind he must appear to be a man alone with the weight of the world on his shoulders. He hangs his head and contemplates how near he came to the brink of destruction.

# THE DESSERT

As a politician, the subject has become accustomed to a certain narrow definition of popularity, which relates directly to his approval by the electorate and extends to other members of the government, and, following the successful resolution of the crisis, he finds himself in a position of unprecedented authority by virtue of the respect won from voters and colleagues.

There exists a small faction in government and in the military who choose to conclude that the President's only achievement was to prove what they knew all along, that the only way for America to deal with the outside world is to act tough, yet the President takes comfort from the fact that this hawkish cabal is small and, he hopes, disenfranchised by the constructive settlement of the situation.

For most of the subject's life, he's considered popularity purely from the viewpoint of social attractiveness, and the crisis has also served to enhance that important attribute, since, having received widespread plaudits for his statesmanship, at social functions—whereat the President and First Lady have always projected considerable cachet—a new and profound deference for his authority obtains, a common viewpoint being that the sub-ject has come of age as a President, at this point more than half-way through his first term, and can safely look ahead to reelection.

The effect on the subject's philandering, with the First Lady's pregnancy advancing as it is, has been a welcome potentiation of his powers of seduction. The woman who wishes to play nurse, draining the bulging abscess of world tension, has now had a recent insight into the grave prognosis for mankind of untreated infection, and offers her ministration with an even greater sense of serving the national (and global) interest, while the woman who enters the traditional contract of paying sexual tribute to a man of power and attainment finds herself encountering a figure who is possibly unsurpassed at present in regard to those twin attributes, which certainly serves to pleasantly lubricate the transaction.

Going about the daily business of Leading the Free World with authority, confidence and brio, the President finds himself somewhat frustrated by the pickings on the various floors of the White House. It appears as if he has consumed the juiciest fruits on the branches of government, and he now holds that he de-serves to gorge on the apples, pears and tomatoes that this and other cities have on display. These perquisites are everywhere, walking around, standing, sitting, squatting and lying, offering their tributes to men who have done nothing for their safety and security, and it feels unjust to be at the zenith of his political career without enjoying a parallel ascent in the career of fornicator.

The subject has never exploited his office for the dividend of family or supporters, or favored lobbyists to boost his personal emoluments, or endeavored to accumulate wider powers than those granted by the Constitution to prosecute questionable enterprises at home or abroad, yet he does intend to uphold the modest sexual perquisites his position attracts. Initially the presidency had a calamitous effect on the subject's womanizing, but he accepted the sacrifice in service of his country; now the country owes him a sacrifice in return.

While the President swims lengths of the White House pool, the Beard appears, with trousers upturned and necktie loosened, and muses about a friend called Bill, who has an acquaintance called Bob, who is the expert at matching girls to the discreet requirements of leading politicians and businessman.

"What d' you say, Skipper?" says the Beard.

The subject's own use of prostitutes has been occasional rather than habitual, although it was the method by which he lost his virginity as a seventeen-year-old boarder, on a trip to New York with a schoolmate, an experience he would not describe as enjoyable, instead being a rite of passage after which he felt a novel confidence with girls deriving from the knowledge that there would be nothing in their underwear by which he might be flummoxed. Ever since, the subject has subscribed to the view that men don't pay prostitutes for sex: they are paid to leave and not talk afterward.

The President says, "I guess it wouldn't hurt to see what he can do."

The Beard says, "I'll get right on it, Mr. President," and smiles his smile of vicarious gratification.

Tonight the First Lady is out of town with the children. The family has reverted to its normal routine, with the President joining them for part of Saturday and/or Sunday, returning in time for a Sunday evening assignation before his wife and children return. The First Lady's suspicions appear to have abated, or perhaps even she is showing gratitude for his bravura handling of the Missile Crisis.

However, it is too much to expect Bill, Bob and the Beard to provide anyone at such short notice, so the President finds himself on something of a lookout as he conducts the day's engagements, most being the normal run of on- and off-the-record meetings with senators and congressmen, at which there's no opportunity to encounter a female target, but to his delight this is certainly not the case at the presentation ceremony held in the East Room in the afternoon, at which he bestows a second oak leaf cluster on one of his generals (who appears to be on our side, remarkably), wherein he soon spies two or three distinguished young ladies escorted by their distinguished fathers or distinguished brothers.

At the short reception after the ceremony, the President maneuvers toward the women with the same graceful disguise one adopts in pursuing a tray of canapés, finding himself in conversation with an attractive blonde of about twenty-seven, guest of her colonel father, with whom he exchanges brief pleasantries.

As he turns to move on to the next distinguished guest, the President slips his hand briefly onto the small of her back and says, "Don't go."

The reception breaks up a few minutes later, but as he departs, he spots the colonel's daughter lingering over her exit and sends the Beard to invite her to the Residence for a private meeting. A few minutes later, the Beard shows the girl into the Lincoln Bedroom, offers the President and his guest drinks, and withdraws.

The President says, "I'm so glad you could join me."

"Thank you, Mr. President. I think my father's a little perplexed about what's happened to me. I guess I am too."

"Are you?"

He moves toward the bed.

She says, "I guess not."


THAT EVENING, HE has Mary too. His gut aches and his back aches and he feels permanently hungry from the bland diet the doctors have him on, but at least one body part still works normally.

Afterward, Mary smokes a joint and says, "There are other girls too, aren't there?"

"Some," he says.

"A lot?"

"Some."

"Tell me about one," she says.

"None come to mind," he says.

"Doesn't it play havoc with your schedule?"

"Less than the Beltway traffic."

She laughs. "How do you woo them?"

"Generally I just ask."

"You meet a girl and you just ask her for sex?"

"Some have the look like they might rather like some."

"Do they all say 'Yes'?"

"Not all."

"Most?"

"Enough," he says.

She inhales deeply and passes the joint. This time he inhales too.

"But they're *not* 'enough,'" she says.

He doesn't answer because, while he's extremely fond of

Mary, as he is of many of the women he sleeps with, the only woman whose emotional terrain he's prepared to negotiate is his wife's. It's common for the subject's mistresses to feel a little sorry for themselves sometimes and to accuse him of using them, yet there's nothing devious in his exploitation, since he always makes plain that he loves his wife and has no desire to divorce her. Moreover, the constancy of the subject's commitment to his family spares the mistress any guilt regarding her potential to split children from their parents, and he never expects his mistresses to be faithful to him. However, he finds these arguments never exert much mollifying effect.

He passes the joint back and she says, "No one's enough for the big hero."

She's taken to calling him "the big hero." She said, "You're the big hero now that no one cares a damn about your first Cuban 'adventure.'"

"Some do," he said.

"You?"

"I'm one of them."

She looked across with those pale, distant eyes. "Something bothering you, Jack?" she said.

Following the successful solution to Cuba Two, it wasn't many days before his thoughts returned to the Brigade, the survivors of those men blasted to bits on the beach imprisoned ever since in Havana, whose release he has repeatedly pursued through the Department of State and the Department of Justice. Having pledged not to attempt another invasion, the President saw an opportunity to reopen negotiations on the grounds that State could promise the released prisoners would not be supported in further military endeavors to recapture their homeland, but now the men are due to go on trial charged with treason, the expectation being that many of their number will be sentenced to death or life imprisonment. The President has made representations through State and the UN that the men should be treated in a manner more resembling the management of prisoners of war under the Geneva Conventions, whereas the Cuban authorities have insisted that the invasion was a criminal act and that the men be dubbed "enemy combatants," denied the rights of POWs, proving that only a crass dictatorship would flout international law in order to inflict dehumanizing punishment upon military men fighting in their nationalist cause.

However, the regime is not ideologically inflexible (fortunately sharing the moral relativism on which we pride ourselves in Western democracies), for they do appear enticed by a ransom for the prisoners, though the President's aides are becoming concerned that any failure to secure the Brigade's freedom will be perceived as a disastrous blow to his prestige so soon after the triumph of Cuba Two, and therefore not worth the risk.

The President says, "Those men are rotting in jail after a mission I sent them on."

"That's why we're advocating a low-profile approach," says the Press Secretary. "Consideration we give to the Brigade's plight only draws attention—"

The President raps his fingers impatiently on the armrest of the rocking chair, and his Press Secretary shuts up.

"Mr. President," says the Secretary of State, "a rescue effort reminds the public of a failure the administration's put behind—"

"I'm not going to abandon them to their fate in case not getting them out makes me look weak. I want those men home for Christmas, damn it!"

An embarrassed silence falls, truncated by a few murmurs of "Yes, Mr. President," and then he dismisses them all with a wave of his hand, after which he sits on the head spraying a Niagara of foul effluent.

Though the crisis has been over for weeks, he remains on the same high steroid doses, which his various physicians refuse to reduce.

Adm. B. says, "Abrupt withdrawal of the treatment will precipitate an Addisonian crisis."

"'The administration lurches from one crisis to another.'"

"Very good, Mr. President, keep your spirits up."

"They're not up, Admiral. Far from it."

He says, "I suppose we could try tapering the dose at five milligrams a week."

Dr. C. says, "We also need to monitor your cholesterol, Mr. President."

"What's this now about cholesterol?"

"Our routine blood tests have demonstrated a morbid hypercholesterolemia."

The President sighs. "I suppose you need to do more tests to diagnose the cause."

"Oh, no, we know the cause, sir. It would be all the testosterone we've been prescribing."


LATER THE PRESIDENT helicopters to Philadelphia to watch the Army-Navy football game, sitting in the Navy end of the stadium for the first and second quarters then being marched across the field to the West Point Commandant, who sits him among the Army brass for the third and fourth. When the crowd hushes for the national anthem, he thinks he can hear the sound of his arteries hardening and the bruit of blood struggling to squeeze between the clumps of cholesterol.

The President has chosen to reward a few close aides with seats on the trip, but as they fly back, he notices the maudlin expression of one special advisor who is newly estranged from his wife. There have been three broken marriages so far during this administration, all through the husbands' infidelity, one going so far as to get a secretary pregnant.

Occasionally the President wonders if he's served as role model to his circle, who've borne witness albeit distantly to his extramarital adventures, perhaps receiving an epiphany regarding the bleakness of monogamy, and have attempted to emulate his practices but collectively failed to emulate his success.

The subject is sorry to hear of his aides' misadventures but stops short of sympathy. A philanderer whose marriage disintegrates, whose children become estranged, whose colleagues feel pity, is a sorrowful figure indeed, no matter how notched his bedpost: he's the hothead who crashes on the first bend while the champion goes on to win the race. No doubt each contributed to his demise in his own way, although failure of concealment is only one part of the likely downfall, there being the unforeseen psychological trial of guilt that sometimes precipitates a confession, often followed by a futile plea for forgiveness, or, worse, the delusion that the mistress is more loving or beautiful than one's wife. Although he expresses regret for these men's shattered personal lives, in truth he feels they have treated the business of fornication far too lightly and suffered their just deserts.

It may appear that the subject is the impetuous vessel of priapic impulses, but that is to misapprehend the degree of calculation inherent in his dalliances, which is not to say that the enterprise is not precipitated by arousal, a case in point being the recent tryst with the colonel's daughter. Consummation took only a few minutes, yet years of apprenticeship contributed to the flawless targeting of a young woman accustomed to the habits of powerful men, someone of sufficient class and discretion to understand the limits of the transaction, and one who would convincingly play her part when returning to her father with an account of having been invited to the Residence for a short viewing of artworks in which she'd expressed interest during her brief conversation with the President at the post-medal-giving reception. In years to come, she might confide her story to one or two close friends, for which he would bear no grudge, in contrast to a siren such as Marilyn, whose strumpet obsession with celebrity compelled her to trumpet her confidences around Hollywood, and no doubt if the opportunity had arisen to embarrass her President, she would have put self-promotion before civic responsibility.

The subject would tutor the three sorry members of his administration that a complete abandonment of continence will vitiate the art of fornication, but he never discusses his trysts. His method is to act as if they don't exist: he didn't depart the Lincoln Bedroom after the colonel's daughter's visit with his face contorted by the grin of the Cheshire cat (nor did she act like the cat who got the cream), yet his adulterous aides couldn't resist displaying the spoils of sex, returning to their colleagues and, ultimately, to their cost, their wives, bearing the smugness of mysterious achievement.

Tonight, after flying to the Marine Terminal at La Guardia, while motoring into New York City the President orders his limousine to back up to a young woman he witnesses struggling to hail a cab on Madison Avenue. He lowers his window and says, "Perhaps you'd appreciate a ride?" Rain spatters the windshield as the President makes witty small-talk with the young woman, a junior secretary in an advertising agency, before darting his hand up her skirt. Her eyes pop. Her knees lock. She falls abruptly silent, and he hears her breath quicken. He orders a detour to the Carlyle for an unscheduled interlude, during which the girl remains quiet but never utters the word No. He overcomes his disappointment in her frigidity, then proceeds as planned to a charity banquet in aid of cancer research, after which he returns to the thirty-fourth floor of the Carlyle with the wife of a stockbroker who caught his eye (the wife, not the broker), and who signaled her openness to a proposition by complimenting the President on the rich chestnut color of his hair, the two of them stealing brazenly into a restroom without the government falling or the cuckolded husband shooting from ten paces at dawn.

In the morning, the President returns to D.C., where his first meeting in the Oval Office updates the convoluted haggling between State, Justice and the Cuban government over a ransom package of essential humanitarian goods such as pharmaceuticals and baby food in exchange for the release of the Brigade's prisoners, the cost of which seems to rise ten million dollars every week.

"I don't care about the money," he says. "Just get those men out."

"If the expense leaks out," says the Secretary of State, "we're going to look pretty desperate."

"Those men are sick and starving," says the President. "They look pretty desperate too."

Late morning, the First Lady and children rejoin from Virginia, so he lunches with them in the Residence after his midday swim, before completing his afternoon's schedule and enjoying the evening ritual of reading to the children as they put them to bed, and then dining privately with his wife and some close friends. In bed afterward, the President and First Lady exchange news, though obviously he omits accounts of his excellent sexual victories.

They kiss, and then she rolls away onto her side to sleep, leaving him wide awake to wonder if his wife doesn't seize with feigned reluctance the alibi of pregnancy. She huffs as she hefts the weight of her gravid belly, but aside from that there is no physical distinction from the customary rejection roll familiar to so many male incumbents of the marital bed, although on occasions the maneuver may derive more from indifference than from outright rejection. Yet he cannot help recalling how it took only a matter of weeks from the onset of intercourse for the regularity to stretch from nightly to weekly, not through any overt renegotiation of the contract between them, but through an insidious process of pleading tiredness or discomfort, until a couple who couldn't ever wait to be alone together have transformed into one who have sex once every week or two, and for periods of their marriage for various reasons they go as long as a couple of months without. Accepted, not all marriages are alike, but in theirs he feels the impetus to reduce the frequency of coupling came from his wife and she persisted with it until the new pattern was firmly established. Ever since, neither of them has done much of anything to change it.

The equilibrium prevails because she rejects him regularly enough to deter nightly pestering but not so many times that he becomes discouraged from ever trying. Yet little is acknowledged regarding his constant struggle to rebound from rejection, while all the time, through the natural processes of ageing and familiarity, his wife becomes incrementally less arousing. Sometimes he thinks she ought to be more grateful that he still bothers to try.

In bed, still unable to sleep, he recalls the midday swim, at which the Beard announced he'd got through to Bill who said Bob would be honored to supply certain perquisites who'd discreetly service presidential needs. The subject has enjoyed his recent ventures outside the safe circle of regular girlfriends and White House secretaries, and, in truth, those liaisons were beginning to adopt the texture of a stable polygamy—which sounds exciting but actually isn't much better than monogamy except for taking a while longer to follow the rule of diminishing returns. Given that only a new addition to the harem can revive arousal, it seems inviting prostitutes into the White House would be a harmless method of modulating the subject's orgone energy.

The Beard schedules the first party for Friday night, when the First Lady and children will be heading out of town for the weekend, and, after drinks and something to eat, the President and guests all end up naked in the pool, eight girls with four men— the President of the United States, the Beard, and Bill and Bob.

The girls are utterly professional, so the men can count on them providing their services with complete discretion. Afterward, the Beard tells the President Bill and Bob have offered to waive their usual fees for the girls, but he orders the Beard to insist on payment. "To avoid any accusations of impropriety," the President explains.

In the morning, the President flies down to Palm Beach to join the family. He takes the children sailing, while the First Lady, reticent on account of her pregnancy, remains ashore with magazines and cigarettes.

Over the weekend, the President hears of a breakthrough with the Cubans, the government having accepted the ransom of humanitarian goods, and the following week he returns to Florida to welcome the Brigade home, a ragged, sickly, emaciated but proud group who have concealed their flag throughout imprisonment, which they present to the President during a mass celebration at the Orange Bowl.

When he gives thanks for their safe return, one of them breaks ranks to give him an embrace.

THE PRESIDENT AIMS to engender a national feeling of having come through a crisis and becoming not only stronger but more just, so from this platform he returns to the ideals set forth throughout his time in office, instituting programs to help the poor and provide opportunities for all regardless of class or color, meanwhile advancing toward a legitimate breakthrough in test-ban and nuclear-disarmament negotiations with the Soviets.

In pursuit of the latter, he flies to the Bahamas for a conference with the British Prime Minister, where they quickly agree on an Anglo-American proposal regarding enforcement of a moratorium on the testing of nuclear weapons. The PM is in good form as ever, sending his good wishes to the First Lady on her pregnancy, though when the President reciprocates regarding the good health of his wife, the PM is courteous but unforthcoming. But the atmosphere remains convivial, particularly as the PM has included his charming Secretary of State for War, an Old Harrovian who served with distinction in the war, who shares the President's first name.

On the second day of the summit, in private, the Prime Minister says, "Naturally, Jack, you'll have to live with the economic consequences."

The President says, "I prefer the country to take all that money we spend on death and spend it on life."

"It takes courage to remodel the military-industrial complex, Mr. President," says the PM.

On the President's departure, the PM walks him out to the limousine and glimpses the Intern hiding on the backseat. But the Prime Minister waves him off with a smile, and only when he glances back does the President see his face fall into troubled reflection.

WHEN THE PRESIDENT returns to the White House, he finds time to drop into his secretary's office.

"Good morning, Mr. President," she says.

"Good morning, Mrs. Lincoln," he says. "I wonder if you could be so kind as to furnish me with a transcript of President Eisenhower's Farewell Address."

"Certainly, Mr. President," she says.

The President heads out into the Rose Garden to officiate at Boys' Nation, where he greets a line of high-school juniors being taught the practices of federal government, shaking hands with a strikingly confident youth from Arkansas named Bill.

When he returns to the Oval Office, the Intern provides the requested transcript.

"Thank you for including me in the official party to Nassau, Mr. President," she says.

He searches the transcript.

"Prime Minister Macmillan is such a gentleman," she says.

The President finds the phrase that's vexed him ever since he heard it:

"Until the latest of our world conflicts, the United States had no armaments industry. Now we annually spend on military security alone more than the net income of all United States corporations. This conjunction of an immense military establishment and a large arms industry is new in the American experience. The total influence—economic, political, even spiritual—is felt in every city, every Statehouse, every office of the Federal government. We recognize the imperative need for this development. Yet, we must not fail to comprehend its grave implications. In the councils of government, we must guard against the acquisition of unwarranted influence, whether sought or unsought, by the military-industrial complex. The potential for the disastrous rise of misplaced power exists and will persist. We must never let the weight of this combination endanger our liberties or democratic processes. Only an alert and knowledgeable citizenry can compel the proper meshing of the huge industrial and military machinery of defense with our peaceful methods and goals, so that security and liberty may prosper together."

When the President looks up again, the Intern has not budged. In the Bahamas he used her less than expected, because the Beard said Bill said Bob said he knew a couple of terrific girls over there.

She says, "Sorry, Mr. President, I wasn't sure if you wanted me to stay."

She wears a slightly needy expression. The door is shut, and, glancing down at his watch, he counts five minutes till the next appointment.

"Be quick," he says, hurriedly making room for her under the desk.


WHEN THE SOLDIER of Brigade 2506 broke ranks that day in the Orange Bowl, the President reacted initially as did the Secret Service agents, instantly reaching for their sidearms, and the President tensed, feeling suddenly scared and vulnerable, but the man had no intention of punching or stabbing or whatever violent speculations flashed through everyone's mind. Instead he threw his arms around the President and murmured thanks. The President's momentary seizure must have appeared to result from physical fear, when his true condition was emotional confusion. This man spent almost two years in a Cuban dungeon because of an incompetent operation. The President's strenuous efforts to secure his release and the release of his comrades were merely restitution for the appalling offense the President had committed against their person.

Yet this man's lips trembled and his eyes welled with tears, causing the President's confusion in the face of such abject gratitude for what had been, in the President's own estimation, the minimum act of human decency of which a national leader was capable, that of recognizing the suffering generated by war. When the generals speak longingly of the next battlefield, the President sees those jungles only as future slaughterhouses of American youth. They list projected troop requirements and offer reports from the Pentagon that predict casualties running into thousands but conclude the risks are acceptable in order to stem the spread of anti-American ideology.

In the war, after losing his boat—two men dead and eleven surviving by the skin of their teeth—the President endured the proclamations of hawkish admirals. When they said we'd fight for years and sacrifice hundreds of thousands of lives if we had to, he always checked from where they were talking. It was seldom out in the Pacific. They turned the deaths of thousands into drops in the ocean, but, if those tens of thousands wanted to live as much as those eleven had done, the admirals would've swallowed their words.

In the privacy of the Oval Office, the President sits by the fireside with the Vice President. "You've seen the reports calling for greatly increased U.S. involvement in Vietnam," he says.

"Yes, Mr. President," the VP says.

"What's your conclusion, Lyndon?" he says.

The Vice President temporizes. "What's yours, sir?" he says.

"I'm opposed," the President says.

The VP nods sagely. "I agree with you, Mr. President," he says.

THE PRESIDENT AND the British Prime Minister finalize their proposal on a nuclear-test-ban treaty, but the Soviets have become mistrustful again. The President is due to give a commencement address at American University, where he'll be awarded an honorary doctorate (which is a good deal easier than having to study for one), and he chooses this occasion to transmit a message home and abroad.

A podium stands on the university lawn bathed in sunlight.

Thanks to the usual painkilling shots, he bounds up the steps to the platform with his customary display of vigor and gazes out over the rows of students, academics and officials, spying military uniforms in prominent positions, with the two who bear the Football and the Secret Service endeavoring to be more discreet, and then he begins:

"'There are few earthly things more beautiful than a university,' wrote John Masefield in his tribute to English universities—and his words are equally true today. He did not refer to spires and towers, to campus greens and ivied walls. He admired the splendid beauty of the university, he said, because it was 'a place where those who hate ignorance may strive to know, where those who perceive truth may strive to make others see.' I have, therefore, chosen this time and this place to discuss a topic on which ignorance too often abounds and the truth is too rarely perceived—yet it is the most important topic on earth: world peace.

"What kind of peace do I mean? What kind of peace do we seek? Not a Pax Americana enforced on the world by American weapons of war. Not the peace of the grave or the security of the slave. I am talking about genuine peace, the kind of peace that makes life on earth worth living, the kind that enables men and nations to grow and to hope and to build a better life for their children—not merely peace for Americans but peace for all men and women—not merely peace in our time but peace for all time.

"I speak of peace because of the new face of war. Total

war makes no sense in an age when great powers can maintain large and relatively invulnerable nuclear forces and refuse to surrender without resort to those forces. It makes no sense in an age when a single nuclear weapon contains almost ten times the explosive force delivered by all the allied air forces in the Second World War. It makes no sense in an age when the deadly pollution produced by a nuclear exchange would be carried by wind and water and soil and seed to the far corners of the globe and to generations yet unborn.

"Some say that it is useless to speak of world peace or world law or world disarmament. But that is a dangerous, defeatist belief. It leads to the conclusion that war is inevitable—that mankind is doomed—that we are gripped by forces we cannot control. We need not accept that view. Our problems are man-made—therefore, they can be solved by man."

The President sees looks of surprise flicker on the faces ranked before him at the direction he's taking. Then he says:

"No problem of human destiny is beyond human beings. Man's reason and spirit have often solved the seemingly unsolvable—and we believe they can do it again.

"I am not referring to the absolute, infinite concept of peace and good will of which some fantasies and fanatics dream. World peace, like community peace, does not require that each man love his neighbor—it requires only that they live together in mutual tolerance, submitting their disputes to a just and peaceful settlement.

"It is an ironic but accurate fact that the two strongest powers are the two in the most danger of devastation. All we have built, all we have worked for, would be destroyed in the first 24 hours. And even in the Cold War, our two countries bear the heaviest burdens, for we are both devoting massive sums of money to weapons that could be better devoted to combating ignorance, poverty, and disease. We should all have a mutually deep interest in halting the arms race, for, in the final analysis, our most basic common link is that we all inhabit this small planet. We all breathe the same air. We all cherish our children's future. And we are all mortal.

"To make clear our good faith and solemn convictions on the matter, I now declare that the United States does not propose to conduct nuclear tests in the atmosphere so long as other states do not do so. Such a declaration is no substitute for a formal binding treaty, but I hope it will help us achieve one. Nor would such a treaty be a substitute for disarmament, but I hope it will help us achieve it. Our hopes must be tempered with the caution of history—but with our hopes go the hopes of all mankind.

"This generation of Americans has already had enough—more than enough—of war and hate and oppression. We shall be prepared if others wish it. We shall be alert to try to stop it. But we shall also do our part to build a world of peace where the weak are safe and the strong are just. We are not helpless before that task or hopeless of its success. Confident and unafraid, we labor on—not toward a strategy of annihilation, but toward a strategy of peace."

Some of the audience rise in applause, but he glimpses others exchanging curious looks, and the military officials appear indistinguishable from the Secret Service, expressionless as they whisper into their hidden microphones.

THE SUBJECT HAS made use of prostitutes at various periods in his life, when suited by the convenience arising from the predictability of the arrangement and from its finite nature, not only in that he's spared the challenges of seduction, but more importantly delivered from the management of the aftermath: one does not need to tell a whore one won't be seeing her again, nor to suffer an explanation that, although the encounter possibly promised more in her eyes, it was actually just a lay, nor even to endure the tedium of having to account for oneself morally for being an adulterer, which is by far the most enervating postcoital discussion, almost enough to put one off sex altogether. Such questions are as otiose as a bartender asking why his customer wants to order a drink. And so in the subject's current position and state of mind, he decides to frequent a particular style of bar, where the drinks come ready-poured, and go down very easily.

His current favorite is a German girl, Ellen, a recent new arrival as hostess at Bob's gentlemen's club—Bob recommended her to Bill who recommended her to the Beard—a strikingly beautiful brunette, good for pool parties and private dinners, who has become the hottest party girl in town. She made her first impression on the President in the pool, after which he ordered the Beard to ask Bill to ask Bob to make sure he sent her again next time, which duly eventuated the following week, whereupon Ellen and the President shared drinks and *hors d'oeuvres* in the Residence before retiring. Though at dinner he was forced to abstain from fine wine and rich food, in the Lincoln Bedroom he helped himself to a generous serving of dessert.

Some men, in their dealings with prostitutes, endeavor to discover something sordid in the practice, and eventually succeed. They experience the usual shame or guilt associated with philandering, but in this particular form of fornication discover a greater abundance due to the pecuniary arrangement. The whore will serve any client who furnishes her fee, so the man does not feel the customary fillip to his self-esteem, and possibly comes to compare himself to all those halitotic lonely-hearts who employ her of necessity. Analysis of the subject challenges all these arguments vigorously, first on the grounds that there is certainly room within the relationship between a man and a prostitute for him to believe that she is providing special service based on his looks, charm or status, but moreover a man deludes himself if he regards every conquest as an idealized conjunction of his beauty/ wit/cologne with the lady's exquisite taste, when many men experience the good fortune of successful seduction as a result of the lady's emotional vulnerability or plain drunkenness. The inveterate fornicator must not dwell on these hard truths, nor should the man who enjoys the services of prostitutes.

Inarguable exigencies obtain in his situation. The obligations of office—which the subject discharges assiduously—limit the time and opportunity for philandering but not the desire. As with the President's sound management of the economy, he regards it as a simple matter of supply and demand, and party girls like Ellen are imports essential to feed his esurient libido.

Nevertheless, as noted by Rabelais, though it is doubtful he was the first, the appetite comes with eating, so it certainly isn't the case that the reliable services of Ellen *et al.* divert the subject from maintaining dalliances with the Intern, other women he encounters in the course of presidential engagements, and Mary. Mary continues to attract him because she remains mysterious, like his wife. Monogamy engenders ennui because it swaps mystery with repetition, but the allure of women like the First Lady and Mary is that they cannot be accurately decoded.

Yet it's Mary who says, "You surprise me."

"How?" he says.

"I thought you were an asshole."

Of course, he laughs.

She says, "I thought you were a pawn like all the others. That's how you looked when you agreed to invade Cuba the first time. Now you're proving they can't control you."

"I guess I'm full of surprises."

"If only people knew."

"The voters?"

"For one."

He takes the cigarette from her mouth and stubs it out in the disposable ashtray that the valet trashes without fail lest the lipstick-stained butts are discovered by the First Lady.

She says, "Seriously, Jack, don't you ever think you ought to be more careful?"

He takes her hand and moves it down to where he wants it to go. "I am careful," he says.

# THE PUSH

As HER PREGNANCY moves nearer term, the First Lady withdraws from Washington life to assume the position of Cape Cod's magazine-reading smoker-in-residence, where she can keep her blood pressure down and her swollen ankles up, returning once every week or so to attend the more glamorous social events in the White House diary, a cause of some embarrassment when she cites medical advice as her reason for declining stuffier engagements. On a number of occasions, the President is obliged to write letters of apology in the hope the recipient will appreciate that the First Lady is otherwise employed making her own personal contribution to the gross national product. However, her anticipated delivery of a future high-band taxpayer is offset by a considerable deficit to the marital balance of payments. The President wonders if his wife's uninterrupted expenditure on items of fashion and interior design reflects the current mores in his private life, as the First Lady speculates on his methods of release following their caesura of connubial congress. Yet, since he has been, as always, utterly scrupulous in concealing evidence and gossip, he would hope that her speculations only lead her back to the conclusion that he has merely confined himself to the closest method at hand.

Her suspicions are a transient diversion, albeit so far a diversion running to tens of thousands of dollars. Naturally the fragility of her condition prevents the President from confronting the matter until after the baby is born, and perhaps she observes an equal armistice, since he suffers no objection to carrying on what is perforce a bachelor life for days on end between her visits. When possible, he travels to be with his family, and sometimes he keeps the children here in Washington under the nanny's care, eating breakfast and lunch with them, occasionally taking them for a swim or to the playground when his diary allows, and endeavoring to be present every bedtime to read their stories and plant their goodnight kisses. However happy they are as a family, the subject's perception of his own physiological needs is immutable, so naturally when the opportunity arises, he will pick up a date or throw a wild party with girls courtesy of the Beard's Bob-via-Bill connection. At other times, the President takes buddies sailing in the presidential yacht, or plays golf; they hang out down in Palm Beach, playing cards and messing in the pool with girls, with no pecker contests required to determine who gets first dip.

The President has become a king. If he wants to sail, a retinue of guys and girls follows to the harbor; if he wants to watch a football game, they all troop to the TV, bringing drinks and hot dogs. On whim, they go walking in the rain, or he challenges them to diving contests, while as judge he reclines in his brace sipping a daiquiri. Only when one of the guys throws him a magazine does he realize after whom he's been taking.

Frank slumps on a sofa with his necktie loose, nursing a scotch and cigarette, while his new girl, a leggy blonde dancer, arches her back to emphasize her cleavage. She tells the reporter shyly that it's too early to mention marriage. The magazine photos capture Frank smiling softly, but there's a hard glint in the eyes of knowing that when he's through with this number he can cast a net on the Strip and land six more just the same. Every couple of months, the President sees pictures of him with some girl or other, Hollywood starlets with dolls' faces and figures that could launch ICBMs. He tries to convince himself they're all as needy and self-absorbed as Marilyn was, but suddenly a White House Intern has never seemed so ordinary.

She's hanging in the hall, finding excuses to stay late to tempt him into inviting her into the Oval Office, but he signals to the Beard to shut the door on her, and even though it's late, he tells him to get Bill to get Bob on the phone because he wants Ellen tonight.

THE POLITICAL OUTLOOK for the world, the country and for the President has never appeared brighter, yet behind this shining moment lurks a black specter. At times, he recognizes it as an outward phenomenon, a darkening in the expressions of the military and agents who greeted the hope and idealism of his first year in office with warm smiles and admiring eyes but who now stare blankly, seemingly at the walls, or into space, and sometimes, when he steps out into the hall or the garden, he glimpses doors closing or curtains being drawn behind quickly receding dark figures.

Adm. B., Dr. T., Dr. C. and Dr. K. arrive together at the end of the day to examine the President in the Residence. They ask, "How has your mood been lately, Mr. President?"

"Good," he says.

"Have you felt low or despondent in any way?"

"No," he says.

"Have you had difficulty sleeping?"

"No."

"Or loss of appetite or libido?"

"No."

"Have you heard voices?"

"No."

"Or seen things that aren't there?"

*"No,"* he snaps.

"I'm sorry, Mr. President," says Adm. B., "but we have certain anxieties about further reducing your dosages of corticosteroids."

"They've been reduced by five milligrams per week over the last month," says Dr. T., "and often patients report asthenia or dysphoria," says Dr. C.

"My stomach and back have been feeling better since I started on lower doses," the President protests.

"We might just increase again," says Adm. B., "as a precaution against withdrawal symptoms," says Dr. C.

The President follows their orders and energy returns and his mood lifts a little, and now, when he glimpses the spectral presence of the military and the Secret Service, he recognizes it as the discreet activity of those individuals who serve America so faithfully, and eventually he realizes that the cause of his dolor must be the First Lady's absence.

For the past two and half years, they have grown closer than ever before in their marriage, which he ascribes to the children. He looks back at his selfish conduct when she lost their first baby and cringes at his callousness. Now that they are a family, the wrinkles between the subject and his wife have been tacitly ironed out, and his responsibility as a father has created an emotional center of gravity that never previously existed.

His optimistic outlook is further enhanced when the State Department receives a positive response from the Soviets regarding the proposed ban on nuclear-weapons testing, so the President and the British Prime Minister dispatch their respective delegations to Moscow. Agreement is soon reached by all parties and the treaty signed.

The following evening, the President goes on TV to address the nation:

> "Since the advent of nuclear weapons, all mankind has been struggling to escape from the darkening prospect of devastation. Yesterday a shaft of light cut into the darkness. Negotiations were concluded in Moscow on a treaty to ban all nuclear tests in the atmosphere, in outer space, and under water. The achievement of this goal is not a victory for one side—it is a victory for mankind. We have learned in times past that the spirit of one moment or place can be gone in the next. But now, for the first time in many years, the path of peace may be open. According to the ancient Chinese proverb, 'A journey of a thousand miles must begin with a single step.' And if that journey is a thousand miles, or even more, let history record that we, in this land, at this time, took the first step."

The test ban is yet another triumph for the President's considered approach to foreign policy, and the delegation returns from Moscow with genuine optimism that the Soviets are now amenable to opening talks on nuclear disarmament. For the first time in the Cold War, the world can look forward to an easing of tensions, a safer planet for everyone, and one in which the vast resources spent on weapons of war can be diverted toward ameliorating hunger, disease and ignorance.

The President sends a memorandum to each of the Joint Chiefs outlining his plans for détente, but receives only curt acknowledgments in return, while the Chief of Staff of the Air Force writes a convoluted missive on the perils of appeasement. His boy, the Game Theorist, remains too heavily medicated to operate a slide rule, so the Pentagon has appointed a replacement to configure the mathematical expediency of attempting to obliterate most of our planet east of the Caucasus.

Our British allies are equally delighted with the treaty, though the President's most recent conversation over the telephone with the PM developed toward a more despondent tone.

"I rather fear storm clouds are gathering," the PM said.

"Over what, Harold?"

"Over Jack's sexual escapades."

The President swallows, momentarily discombobulated, until he realizes the PM means the British Secretary of State for War, whom he met in the Bahamas. Jack Profumo is alleged to have enjoyed a short affair with a prostitute, and the President has instructed the London ambassador to keep him apprised. In the House of Commons, Profumo denied any impropriety, but the British press is continuing to investigate the matter, even though the word of a gentleman should be sufficient.

"It's all highly unseemly," the PM continues, a few days later, when prompted for more gossip. The President can't help but be titillated. "One must keep private matters private. We certainly managed."

The President detects a note of rancor in the PM's voice, and says, gently, "I wasn't aware, Harold."

"My wife and I have dealt with the matter; one expects that to be an end to it."

"Yes, of course. Forgive me for prying."

"Jack's been a complete arse," the PM continues, and once more the President is unsure whom he means.

So much gossip has been generated at such a high level by the British scandal that the CIA has given it the code name Bowtie. The ambassador has cabled a classified report detailing all the allegations in the British newspapers and a photograph of the girl, a very pretty brunette. The War Secretary had an affair lasting only a few weeks, which became known in high circles last year, but naturally the press wasn't interested since a politician's fornication is of no relevance to public life. Things changed when journalists discovered the girl had also been sleeping with a Soviet naval attaché and Mr. Profumo was forced to account for his conduct in the House of Commons. One presumes that press and Parliament were concerned that the Soviet attaché was feeding her questions to put in pillow talk, but the idea is preposterous that the Secretary wouldn't become suspicious to the point of lockjaw at being quizzed on NATO strategic nuclear configurations by a vacuous party girl, let alone actually divulge them.

While he has the ambassador on the phone, the President says, "Just between us, David, is something going to come out about Harold Macmillan?"

"How do you mean, Mr. President?"

"The affair," he says.

There is a pause, and then the ambassador says, "That's his wife, sir. She's been sleeping with another politician for years. God knows how he puts up with it, or why."

THE DIRECTOR OF the Federal Bureau of Investigation requests a meeting, and, by the time the appointment comes round, the President's gut and back are as sore as ever, exacerbated by the reinstated steroid doses. He spends a half-hour in the head spitting blood from either end before crossing the hall to the Fish Room, where the Director stands with his customary queer deference to shake hands before introducing a colleague at his side, a balding, bespectacled lawyer.

"I've appointed my Special Investigator to uncover any American officials who might be incriminated by Bowtie," says the Director, "and I'm pleased to inform you, Mr. President, that, insofar as his investigation extends to date, no American officials appear in our reports."

The President says, "I wasn't aware you were investigating Bowtie."

"I investigate anything and everything which might threaten the security of the United States, Mr. President."

"How reassuring, Mr. Hoover."

"One becomes alarmed, Mr. President," he says, ignoring the sarcasm, "when one hears of our principal ally's highest-ranking defense official being pumped for nuclear secrets."

"There may have been pumping, but I doubt she got any secrets." The President flicks his eyes to the Special Investigator to see if his thin lips shape into a grin, but he remains as blank as his boss.

"In this vein, Mr. President, I've tasked my Special Investigator with identifying any similar security breaches within our own government. Kenneth."

"Thank you, Mr. Director." The Special Investigator adjusts his glasses and then regards a clutch of close-typed pages in his file.

The President interrupts, "There are channels, Mr. Director. I don't see that this is a matter for presidential attention."

"You will, Mr. President," he says, and this time his mouth does curl into a sick grin.

The Special Investigator says, "I have detected a risk to national security involving an East German national and a politician occupying very high executive office. The East German national appears by day to be the respectable wife of a sergeant in the West German Army stationed at their embassy here in Washington D.C., but by night she plies a lucrative trade as a glamorous club 'hostess,' charging two hundred dollars or more for sexual favors. We have good reason to presume that this prostitute is in fact working as a communist spy."

The Director takes a photograph from the file and spins it on the table. The woman's black hair is piled high and stylishly and she wears a dark floral halter-neck dress. Her full lips are turned in an understated smile. "Ellen Rometsch," says the Special Investigator.

"And the very high-ranking official, Kenneth?" Mr. Hoover says knowingly.

"That would be the President of the United States, Mr. Director," he says.

"You recognize the woman, Mr. President?" the Director says.

The President looks up calmly and says, "If she's a spy, she didn't learn much."

The Director says, "We infer the woman's mission is to acquire information embarrassing to this government and this nation, a mission which appears to have borne abundant fruit."

The President's eyes fix on the file. Documents have been paper-clipped into several bundles, with a different woman's photograph topping each, overlapping so he can't see more than sections or slices but enough to make out worryingly familiar features.

The Director says, "Mr. President, have you had sexual relations with that woman?"


"JACK'S GOT TO resign."

Every time the President hears someone mention his name, he jolts, thinking at first the speaker refers to him.

The President is stuck on the telephone talking to a congressman about his constituents' anxiety that the local plant is going to close, because the plant manufactures the aerocasing for a model of intercontinental ballistic missile, one of a growing list of such calls he's now fielding since the signing of the Test-Ban Treaty. Over many years of lobbying, there is not a single state of the Union that isn't home to communities dependent upon the defense industry for their livelihood. Politicians and corporations have sliced up the pie in a way that means, if it's taken away, everyone goes hungry.

The door into his secretary's office is ajar, and he glimpses the Intern arriving with a set of documents before collecting a bundle of typed letters to file. The President is beginning to feel about her the same way he came to feel about Fiddle-Faddle-Fuddle. He still takes her down to the pool or into the office, of course, but the rest of the time he'd rather she remained invisible. When she does appear, she never looks sure how to carry herself, sometimes trying to shoot the President a seductive gaze—once even flashing the top of her panties—and other times endeavoring to seem aloofly indifferent. In any case, when she now looks briefly in his direction, he doesn't pause to read her as he's too involved in the phone conversation to make eye contact.

One of the staff passes in the hall, saying, "Jack's shamed his office."

Later the President makes a call to a party donor whose company makes the washers for the pistons for the hydraulic pumps for the bomb-bay doors for our nuclear bombers, and he hears a voice at his end say, "Jack's shamed his party."

In the end, Jack resigns. Historically the President would have chosen numerous reasons to disown his namesake, for the world seems to be so full of clumsy philanderers, while the best prosper invisibly. No doubt the President would have noted a cruel distinction between the two of them regarding the facts of his baldness and his not-particularly-tallness, to the effect that he was so proud of having claimed a gorgeous young thing that he did far too little to conceal it, but such detachment is no longer completely possible when he reads the files and watches the news reports.

Mrs. Profumo clings to her husband's side as he gets in and out of limousines and goes in and out of engagements—or maybe *he's* clinging to *her*—with a mob of press calling out impertinent questions and ranks of photographers exploding flashbulbs in their faces. His bald head is always slightly bowed and penitent, while the wife attempts to hold hers up. She was an actress before they married, a glamorous socialite partnered to a rising star of the British establishment. Now, away from the reporters and the photoflashes, a door closes and the clamor abruptly cuts out, leaving the two of them standing alone in a silent, empty hall, the obloquy hushed as if by an airtight seal, replaced by shame, with this their prison and his "crime" their mutual life sentence.

And this is what the President must have been thinking as he sat in the Fish Room with the Special Investigator flashing photographs while the Director listed their names, some of whom he recognized but couldn't place and some he could place but couldn't name.

On his next trip to Europe, the President meets unofficially with the British Prime Minister, at Birch Grove, his private country residence. In the evening, they drink whiskey and smoke while the President rocks in his chair. The PM appears suddenly old and weary. He says, "Things have changed, Jack, almost overnight. They've got the taste for it."

"For what, Harold?" the President says.

"Scandal," he says.

It won't let up. The people understand that Mr. Profumo can't be the only politician to have lurid secrets hidden in his private affairs, so they want to hear more, and to justify the titillation, the press contends it's now in the public interest to oblige. The emperors of Ancient Rome knew that public contentment required not just bread, but circuses. Having been guilty of taking a prurient interest in the scandal himself, the President too is seduced by the divertissement proffered by low urges in high society. To the less informed and less observant, the discovery that the rich and powerful are equally in thrall to their animal instincts must be an amusement akin to that of the crowd in Hans Christian Andersen gifted with their emperor's incongruous nudity. A scandal would not be news if the news had not crossed the divide between information and entertainment, and the press in Britain have discovered a new and powerful force in the market and as a result have never shifted so much newsprint.

"Scandal sells," the President says, but too late.

Soon the Prime Minister resigns as well, on the grounds of ill health, but he looked as if his sickness was induced by the passing of old values that demarcated a man's achievements in office from his exploits in the boudoir. His War Secretary has been reckless, but his culpability resides only in the appearance of things: he misled Parliament, yet the utilitarian denials of a philanderer are only to be expected in such circumstances, to protect the feelings of his wife and son and to preserve the decorum of society. The Prime Minister has every reason to be nauseated by this flagrant breach of the rules of public etiquette, as is the President. Perhaps he even became anxious that, since everyone's affairs are now fair game, snide diary columnists might begin referring to his cuckolding. In any event, he has chosen to leave public life rather than remain under this new—though, one hopes, transient—regime, one that ordains it no longer entirely matters whether a man discharges his office competently; he must also suffer a life of impeccable sexual continence.

On that melancholy evening at Birch Grove, the PM said pointedly, "A man stands naked in his bedroom window because he can't see anyone looking in. He thinks he's invisible."

He peered across his whiskey glass at the President with his first and last expression of disapproval. "But people *are* looking, Jack," he said.

THE DIRECTOR SAID, "Mr. President, did you have sexual relations with that woman?" and that afternoon the President told the Beard to tell Bill to tell Bob not to send any more girls. In the evening, the President hosted a small reception for the Italian Foreign Minister at which his younger sister stood in for the First Lady, whose policy continues to be only to interrupt her Cape Cod convalescence for royalty or the French.

Mary featured on the guest list along with a couple of other women he'd added with the aim of seducing. He merely engaged the two possibles in pleasant colloquy, but kept his options open for the future by suggesting he might have them back later in the season.

Mary visited the Lincoln Bedroom for a short assignation, after which, as she was about to light a cigarette, he broke up with her. On reflection, she might have taken the news better if he had signaled his intention beforehand, but these situations develop their own momentum.

"I'll get someone to call you a car," he said.

"I don't want a God-damned car, Jack," she said.

Later the Beard relayed that the Secret Service found her wandering across the Ellipse with a rain-soaked dress clinging to her skin, carrying one shoe with the other missing. Fortunately one of the agents recognized her despite her smeared makeup and sodden hair, and they found a blanket and got her in out the rain, or else she might have stumbled down as far as Constitution

Avenue and been hit by a car or picked up by D.C. Metro. She was too tearful to make much sense, but when the agents asked her what was wrong, she said, "I can't tell you. I can't tell anyone. All I can do is go quietly mad."

Often the subject is surprised by how hard some girlfriends take a breakup. Usually he concludes that distress on their part results from their having succumbed to a liaison with a happily married man, and, once the futility of their situation becomes obvious, pride dictates they must issue an ultimatum for him to leave his wife or else they will withdraw their services, but his preemptive strike delivers the *coup de grâce* to their self-esteem. Of course, the loss of affection plays some part. Although he's sometimes quite fond of the girl, he treats that emotion as he does the philanderer's other foe; like guilt, it can only increase the risk of detection. He prefers a policy of asympathy to a girl's ostensible sorrow. According to his brother-in-law, both Marilyn and Judy professed their anguish to Frank, who seized the opportunity to offer to have Peter's legs broken, this being the best he could muster given the numerous security obstacles barring administering corporal punishment to the President of the United States, although he did promise Marilyn's ex he'd discuss the matter with subterranean elements who might be able to come up with some better ideas.

The President pays scant attention to such rumors, as, in the present situation, he has neither the opportunity nor the inclination to dwell on the emotional consequences of deboning the presidential cupboard.

Then, in the Oval Office, among his papers he finds a sealed personal envelope bearing an internal postmark. The letter inside is handwritten, with lines crossed through and overwritten.

Dear Handsome,

I really need to discuss my situation with you. We have not had any contact for weeks. <u>Please do not do this to me.</u> I feel disposable, used and insignificant. I understand your hands are tied, but I ~~just~~ want to talk to you and look at some options. I am begging you <u>one</u> last time ~~from the bottom of my heart~~ to please let me ~~come see you~~ Visit Briefly Tuesday evening. I will ask Mrs. L. Tues. afternoon to see if it is o.k.

—M

He rips it up and throws it in the trash, unsettled by the writer's distraught style and the fact that she must be one of the West Wing staff with an access pass so she could slip the letter into his mail, as his secretary would certainly have intercepted it. The matter continues to perturb the President as he takes the chopper to Andrews AFB, and it is only on the connecting flight to the Cape to join the family for the weekend that he realizes "M" must be the Intern's initial.

In intimate moments she'd taken to calling him "Handsome," but he never appreciated that it was intended as a pet name. Now he clearly remembers her using it one time in the Oval Office after she emerged from beneath his desk. By the time he lands at Otis AFB, he has dismissed the letter as the emotional lability of a spoiled sophomore, best ignored.

When he descends the ladder, Caroline and John scamper across the tarmac. For a moment, he feels an overwhelming impulse to gather them in his arms and swing them in the air, before the sorrowful reminder he's not blessed with the same back as regular fathers, so instead he simply hugs them and kisses them and then walks hand in hand with them to his beautiful wife, who waits by the limousine that carries them all to the beach house.

The First Lady is now only a few weeks away from delivering and is so protective of their unborn child that she declines to join the children at sailing. In bed, she lies on her side, hot and uncomfortable, struggling to shift the weight while he is similarly immobile on account of his back.

They discuss names. He suggests naming a boy Joseph for his dead brother and a girl Kathleen for his dead sister, but reminders of death strike the wrong chord. She cries and he holds her until she falls asleep.

Over the weekend, he takes only a small number of work calls, affording time to take the children to the beach to build sand castles, while the First Lady lies in. She agrees, as the ocean is flat calm, to take lunch on the deck of the presidential yacht, after which all four of them enjoy ice-cream cones.

The ice cream numbs the pain of his stomach ulcers, which have reignited under the high dose of steroids, but later gives him diarrhea. The First Lady helps him count out the pills and check them off on the prescription list, noting his physicians have added another painkiller (back), a course of antibiotics (skin abscesses) and a stronger antacid (ulcers), the abscesses being an uncomfortable and unsightly development Adm. B. ascribes to the steroids impairing his immune system.

Although they haven't seen each other for over a week, they slip into the easy physicality of their marriage, touching, hugging and kissing frequently during the course of the weekend. Unavoidably he experiences an urge for sex, but his wife lies on her side like a beached seal and soon emits stertorous music.

Before the sedatives take effect, he wonders how the Profumos are sleeping tonight, if they even share a bed now. Apparently, Mrs. Profumo stands by her husband. No wife ought to endure her husband's infidelity against her will, but neither should she be forced against her will not to endure it.

The British ambassador has relayed that the President's namesake has relinquished all the entitlements of office and now serves penance in the East End of London by slopping toilets for a charity for indigents. One imagines him returning every evening in his coveralls so that not even in his own home can anyone be left uncertain of the feculence of his downfall. The President's concern for himself is not so much that the FBI aims to shame the office of President, but that the British scandal will prick political opponents into inoculating the American body politic with the same germ.

"Did you have sexual relations with that woman?" the First Lady will ask.

In the moonlight, he gazes at her. To keep cool, she opened the window and pulled back the blankets, and now, while the curtains ripple in the breeze, he watches the tidal rise and fall of her outline as she breathes. He brushes her cheek lightly with his lips and smells her hair, but all the time knowing, for her sake too, he must *never* be undone by guilt.


THE SUBSEQUENT WEEK in the White House reminds the President that he has been returned to the morbid frustration of his initial period in office, as if he's slid down the longest viper in a game of snakes and ladders. He goes about his daily business unable to enjoy a momentary diversion from the pressures of leadership by inviting a nubile secretary into his office or a tipsy socialite up to the bedroom.

The Intern lingers in the halls of the West Wing for him to notice, but the President pretends not to connect her with the heartfelt letter pleading for his attention. Once he even hears her next door crying on Mrs. Lincoln's shoulder. He hopes his secretary told the girl to stop making a fool of herself, but neither party—the President nor Mrs. L.—considers such a conversation within the purview of their professional relationship.

Always solicitous, the Beard worries for the President's health. The effect is as dangerous, the Beard carks, as the abrupt withdrawal of an addictive drug. The pool parties have halted since the FBI smugly revealed one of the girls worked for the Warsaw Pact.

"What evidence have you gleaned she's a spy?" the President demanded.

"That investigation remains ongoing, Mr. President," the Director said.

The President said, "It's merely a tenuous supposition, isn't it, Mr. Hoover?" and in their initial silence he saw vindication.

Then the Director continued, "With respect, Mr. President, Bowtie demonstrates that the *potential* for a security breach is equally damaging as an actual breach."

The President said, "If she's a threat to national security, have her deported."

The Director gazed back inscrutably, while the Special Investigator bit his lip and polished his spectacles tensely.

The President said, "Find out whom she's attempted to compromise, if anyone. Find out what she's learned, if anything. Then chuck her back over the God-damned Wall."

"Is that an executive order, Mr. President?" said the Director.

"It is, Mr. Director," said the President.

Then the President told the Beard to tell Bill to tell Bob to offer the girl some money to keep her mouth shut. While on the one hand many voters would be incredulous (bless them) that a contented family man with a beautiful young wife would suffer the temptation to stray, let alone with a whore, on the other the virulence of the scandal is almost impossible to predict in this present miasma.

They discussed figures and, while the Beard gravely relayed that Bill had gravely informed him that Bob had gravely informed him that that particular service wouldn't come cheap, the President didn't balk at spending what was still considerably less than his wife's current outstanding bills to various New York boutiques.

The successful fornicator must be prepared to do what is necessary without compunction, and the facts of this particular case are no different in nature from the normal acts of concealment, though possibly in degree. The philanderer chooses sex with a prostitute since it simplifies the potential difficulties relating to the woman's temptation to gossip or to linger after sex.* It seems to the President that paying the woman a multiple of her normal fee extends the mutually agreed transaction to include not gossiping to the grand jury and not lingering in the country.

---

*The Beard and the President joke about the latter all the time, especially when the Intern had desperately endeavored to extend postintercourse intercourse. "You'd better run back up to the office," the President would say, floating in the pool with his head still cushioned on the side. "They'll be missing you, kiddo."

"They know I'm gone a while," she would say in return, caressing the hairs on his chest. "Can't I stay, Handsome, and swim a little?"

After he got rid of her, he said to the Beard, "Dave, you know the difference between an intern and a turd?"

"I don't, Mr. President," he said.

"At least if you lay a turd it doesn't follow you around all day."

On a flight down to Texas, the President reads the FBI reports that have finally landed on his desk. No evidence has been found that Mrs. Rometsch is or was an East German spy, plus the woman herself dutifully denied ever having met any prominent officials in the United States government, whereupon a judge was swiftly persuaded of her status as a common prostitute and found in favor of deportation.

In the past, men in his position never had to consider how they conducted themselves behind closed doors, for they knew they would be judged on what they delivered to the people. The only exception would be acts of criminal depravity, and, as far as he is concerned, fornicating with consenting adult females does not constitute depravity. He must answer to the higher moral imperative of office. He believes that there is much left to be done, and he has much more to give, in terms of ending the Cold War and devoting the resources of this great nation to helping families out of poverty and providing a wealth of opportunity for all and not merely the privileged few.

The stewardess who serves an orange juice is one of the good-looking ones, and the President is sure he's had her before, though obviously he can't remember how many times or her name.

"Thanks, honey," he says.

She says, "You're welcome, Mr. President," and smiles over her shoulder as she walks away wiggling her tail.

The President pops a couple of headache pills to deal with the mounting crisis inside his skull since the FBI declared they were watching. When he first took office, he never anticipated it would work as a fabulous aphrodisiac. Although his digestive system and spine are undergoing excruciating relapses, the Addison's has never been so well controlled: he bears the trimness of an athlete, with firm, tight flesh where there once were jowls; his tan is less yellow and his hair even more splendid than usual. The stewardess ostentatiously makes a right into a private cabin, then from the threshold gazes back while she pops her top button. The President is on the verge of closing his files and receiving her in-flight service when he wonders if she's on the Bureau payroll.

The Boeing lands in El Paso, where the Vice President and the state governor greet the President, then they conduct a number of official engagements before retiring to the Cortez for dinner, at which they discuss next year's election campaign. The VP appears to be in fine form, sunning himself outside of the shadow the President casts in Washington, repeatedly reinforcing his credentials for attracting the southern vote. Southern whites are disenchanted with the President on account of his stand on civil rights, and, while he despises their redneck prejudices, he might need their votes, so the VP is eager for the three of them to agree on a return to Texas in November, taking in some of the major cities such as Austin, Houston, Dallas and Fort Worth.

When the Governor departs, the President and his deputy retire to the presidential suite for a private discussion. But then the phone rings and, when he answers it, one of the agents informs the President his next appointment has arrived in the hotel lobby. "Send her up," he says.

Muscles twitch in the VP's cheeks, but he dutifully picks his hat off the stand.

"Sorry, Lyndon," the President says. "I'm sure we'll take this up tomorrow."

"I look forward to it, Mr. President," the VP says, shuffling out the door. In the corridor, he makes an effort to square his shoulders before striding toward the elevator.

A few minutes later, a Secret Service agent taps on the door, and the valet admits the President's guest.

After resisting the stewardess, the President encountered yet more flirtations and invitations when he went about his engagements earlier today, in the form of lingering handshakes and suggestive glances. Now that his proclivities are known in certain circles, he attracts the pick of state aides or local aristocracy, from whom he fled, swallowing more painkillers to dull the pangs of celibacy chipping chunks off the inside of his skull.

His guest works for the Governor as one of his campaign managers, with a particular expertise in strategies focused on major urban areas. They spoke briefly at one of his engagements earlier in the day whereby he deduced she wasn't a honey trap on account of her complete lack of flirtation. Through an aide, he suggested she come to the suite after dinner to continue the discussion. Though she's a voluptuous bottle-blonde in her late thirties, she appears to have taken the President at his word, arriving in the same sober attire as earlier, bearing a bundle of charts.

She takes a seat on the couch, opposite the President's rocking chair, while the valet waits discreetly for orders.

The President says, "Would you care for a drink, er, honey?"

"No, thank you, Mr. President," she says.

"It's been a long day. I'm having one."

"Please don't hold back on my account, Mr. President."

"Sure you won't join me?"

"I'm sure, thank you, Mr. President."

"You're going to make me feel bad."

She clears her throat nervously. "I wouldn't want to do that, Mr. President."

"Good," he says. "A glass of wine?"

"A small one, Mr. President," she says reluctantly. "White, please, Mr. President."

"Coming right up. A daiquiri for me, George. Leave the wine bottle—we can help ourselves if we want more."

The valet makes the drinks and then withdraws, while the pressure inside the President's head cranks up a notch.

She waits tensely for him to show interest in the charts, and then she launches into a rehearsed address. "You're more popular in the urban areas than the rural areas in the South, and therefore it's important to approach the two communities differently, by an effort to consolidate support in the cities and to win swing voters in the boondocks."

The President says, "You know you're a very attractive woman."

She blushes. "Thank you, Mr. President."

From nerves, she's drunk most of her wine already.

He says, "Let me top up your glass."

"Really, Mr. President, I shouldn't."

He hoists the bottle out of the chiller and pours it regardless, then seizes a seat beside her on the couch.

She edges away to make room.

He touches her knee.

She shifts again and says, flustered, "Did you have a good dinner with the Governor and the Vice President?"

He says, "I ate up all my dinner," and, drifting his gaze downward from her face, adds, "and now I deserve two big scoops of dessert."

Suddenly the President finds himself lying on the floor with pain knifing through his back and down his legs. She is standing over him, crying, "I'm a respectable, married lady," but he can barely hear her for the currents of agony electrocuting his lower body. "I came here in a respectful, professional fashion. Do you know what it's like for women?" She continues to vent her outrage until she seems to come to her senses and says, "Can you get up?"

"Call George," he gasps. "Quickly."

She strolls to the adjoining room and calmly asks for the valet, who comes running.

"I must've caught my foot and tripped," the President says.

She peers down, and he wonders if she's enjoying his distress. Although she doesn't correct his excuse, she certainly doesn't appear remotely apologetic.

"I'll just need a minute . . . it's my back . . ."

"I better go now, Mr. President," she says coldly. "I wouldn't want my husband to become concerned."

The valet ushers her quickly to the door and then invites in a couple of agents so that between the three of them they can plant pillows to support the President's neck, spine and legs while a doctor is called.

The President isn't sure exactly what happened, but he thinks that after he put his hand on her knee he might have tried putting it someplace else and she pushed him or bumped him off the couch. When he hit the floor, he jarred his back and for all he knows the metal plates have jolted off the screws that fix them to his spine. But his clearest recollection of that moment is the look on her face as she stood over him, a look of outrage as she demanded, "Do you have any idea what it's like for women?" and he can only assume he had no convincing answer.

# THE CHAMBER

"HAVE YOU HAD sexual relations with this woman?" says the Special Investigator.

His pale eyes swim behind the lenses of his spectacles and, behind him, swim the aquarium-dwellers of the Fish Room.

"Mr. President?" he pushes.

The President says, "On what grounds is this case a matter of national security?"

"Mr. President, you've made the case yourself. After all, is it not true that, in demanding the silence of mistresses, girlfriends and casual sexual partners, you quote 'national security considerations'?"

The President realizes the FBI has tapped his phone. He glares across the table at the Director, whose head is downturned, making notes on sheaves of narrow-lined paper.

"Mr. President," says the Special Investigator, "this is a voluntary statement made under the terms of the Bureau's internal investigation into Bowtie. For the purposes of this statement, a person engages in 'sexual relations' when the person knowingly engages in or causes intentional touching, either directly or through clothing, with the genitalia, anus, groin, breast, inner thigh, or buttocks of any person with an intent to arouse or gratify the sexual desire of any person."

The Special Investigator's finger rests on the tape recorder documenting the conversation. In the hush of the Fish Room, the tape only picks up the scratching of the Director's pen as he makes more notes, and then he finally looks up in expectation of the President's answer. The Special Investigator pushes, "Mr. President, did you have sexual relations with that woman?"

The President says, "If this statement is voluntary, then I'm entitled to decline to answer."


FOLLOWING THE INJURY in El Paso, the subject has been fitted with a rigid body brace that immobilizes his back from the shoulder blades down to the groin. He explained to Dr. T. that he caught the edge of a rug in his suite at the Cortez and lost his footing, and her subsequent examination revealed a torn groin, almost certainly because his back went into a rigid seizure as he fell, and the twisting or shearing motion caused by contact with the floor ripped an agonizing slash in the cramped muscle.

To rise from his seat in the Fish Room, the President must grip the edge of the table and hoist himself upright before limping out with a rigid back and pelvis. Each painful step across the hall recalls that dismal encounter, and, in the Oval Office, he spares a few minutes to reflect on events in the days since returning from Texas, beginning with the news that the woman has not only taken great umbrage at the advance but wishes to register a formal complaint. The Bowtie inquiry started by investigating U.S. government officials involved in the British scandal, but its remit appears to have expanded exponentially.

The President's secretary came into the Oval Office at the end of the day and said, "Mr. President, I think you ought to know that the FBI are interviewing all the women and asking if you've ever made sexual advances."

"I trust you said you've always resisted," he said, but neither of them could muster even a smile, and the President struggles to determine how this process could serve national interests.

Mrs. Lincoln leaves with him a handwritten log of telephone messages from White House women warning that they have been subpoenaed by the Special Investigator. He sends no replies. He wads up the list and hurls it in the trash.

The next morning, a story appears in a newspaper called the *Star* under the headline "High U.S. Aide Implicated in British Scandal," in which one of the prostitutes involved in Profumo's downfall suggests one of the other party girls is a former "paramour" of an official who holds "very high elective office" in the United States government, the girl in the picture looking worryingly familiar, and later that afternoon the White House Press Secretary fields an inquiry from the journalist who filed the story, pursuing the girl's claim that the President took her for dinner at "21" in New York City before the election: "Is it true?" the *Star* man wants to know.

The *Star* is a Republican newspaper dedicated to criticizing the President and his party. The British Prime Minister appears to have been prescient in his warnings, and the President reacts with the same disgust that overwhelmed the PM. The press is prepared to provide a platform for prostitutes and other good-time girls to launch allegations against men of vision who serve their country, allegations that do not involve incompetence or corruption or even depravity. The Press Secretary reports, "He insisted the public bears a right to know a politician's character, since a man who cheats on his wife may be dishonest in office. By concealing sordid affairs, the President is guilty of deceiving the American people about his true character."

The President snaps, "Tell the bastard, 'Altiora peto,'" but then, as the Press Secretary frowns and turns to exit, he says, "Sorry, Pierre, wait."

The President recalls his interrogation in the Fish Room, in which the Bureau's Special Investigator tunneled through a list of White House women—Fiddle, Faddle, Fuddle, the Intern, various secretaries and junior administrators, some of their names being beyond the President's recall, and even some of their faces—whom he had already interviewed regarding alleged dalliances with the President of the United States.

"No comment," the President said, embarrassed, in answer to the Special Investigator's question.

"Let us be clear in our understanding, Mr. President," he said, "that you do not deny having sexual relations with this woman, as defined under the terms of your statement." He brandished a photograph of the Intern.

"Yes," said the President.

"And this woman . . . ?" He waved a photograph of another of the White House women, Fiddle (or Faddle).

"No comment," said the President.

"You do not deny having sexual relations with this woman, as defined under the terms of the deposition?"

The President was angry and resentful but above all embarrassed. He murmured, "No comment."

The Director stopped making notes, and the Special Investigator adjusted his spectacles. The Director said, "Thank you for your cooperation, Mr. President."

"May I ask, Mr. Hoover," the President said, "for whom you're gathering these depositions?"

"For our files, Mr. President," he replied ominously. "For our files."

The President limped out of the Fish Room and back to the Oval Office, where he now finds himself in the company of the White House Press Secretary, who is awaiting the President's response to the man from the *Star*.

The Press Secretary says, "Pretty soon, sir, they'll be asking if it's true the FBI are looking for female White House personnel you've seduced."

The President says, "I shall answer questions on my record in office, for which I'm accountable. But I decline to respond to questions about my private life. They are questions no American would ever want to answer, nor should he ever have to answer. I claim that same right."


As usual, the President breakfasts in the Residence, this morning with an aide who briefs him on present developments in the quest for détente, and then he takes the elevator—avoiding the stairs—and limps along the hall to the West Wing. His back has not been this bad since the Pacific.

In those days, naval training followed by the endless hours at sea aggravated his football injury so much he couldn't even sleep in a bunk, instead having to lie on a plywood board, a condition made gravely worse when a Japanese destroyer rammed his boat and the impact hurled him against a hard, metal bulkhead before the boat split in two and the crew tumbled into the water. Six of them clung to one half of the capsized hull. The President led two of the strongest swimmers out into the dark ocean where they could hear the voices of other crewmen shouting for help, bringing back first the most severely wounded man, the engineer, who'd suffered extensive burns and couldn't swim, so the President had to tow him, and then he dove in again to bring back two more, so that between them they saved five, two never being recovered, presumed drowned.

The men hung on to the hull till daylight, when they could make out a distant strip of land, toward which they swam, with the President towing the engineer by biting the ties of his life vest between his teeth. It took five hours against strong currents to reach land, and once his men were safely installed on the island, the President swam another hour out into a strait through which their boats regularly sailed, in the hope of flagging one down, but none came and he was forced to swim back to the island, sometimes losing consciousness through pain and through not having slept for two nights.

As soon as he lay down to rest, his back muscles locked in spasm, but the next day he swam again, this time to another island, where he found water and a canoe, bringing them back to his thirsty crew, and soon after, they were discovered by natives, who conveyed a message scratched on a coconut that led to their rescue after seven days as castaways, by which time his back was immovable. That's about as bad as it feels today, as he limps into the Oval Office and takes almost a minute to work himself down into his rocking chair, before an hour's meeting with a congressman who has heard of the President's reluctance to involve our forces in Vietnam and wishes to express his concern because the biggest plant in his district makes the ammunition for our government-issue machine gun.

The next meeting, with a committee concerned that the Test Ban will limit development of deadlier nuclear weapons, is interrupted by his secretary with an urgent message from Cape Cod. The First Lady has gone into premature labor and is en route via helicopter to the hospital at Otis Air Force Base; he cancels all his meetings and takes the chopper from the South Lawn to Andrews and then joins the SAM Boeing for the one-hour flight to Otis.

He sits starboard and peers out the window at Philadelphia passing under the wing, then, as the aircraft climbs, he stares out into the flat, grey waters of the Atlantic. The stewardess brings a glass of water, and he doesn't even look up to see whether it's one of the good-looking ones.

The eternal spires of New York City glide beneath the wing and the SAM begins its descent toward Massachusetts. The President can barely make it down the steps because his back is so tense inside the new brace, but he won't wait for a cherry-picker, letting it hurt; it hurts so much there are tears in his eyes as he gets in the car waiting to speed from the strip to the base hospital, and the driver must think the President is already crying for fear of the fate of his wife and child.

His arrival creates the usual deferential chaos, meaning the base CO is waiting at the hospital, as is the Chief of Medicine, but the President doesn't take in what they say, though he assumes it's simply that they offer their services if anything can be done to make the First Lady's stay more comfortable.

"The First Lady is in surgery, Mr. President," the Chief of Medicine says. "She's undergoing a cesarean section, sir."

"How is she?"

"There appear to be no complications, Mr. President, but the obstetrician will send someone out to report to you as soon as there is definitive news."

"Do you know anything about the baby?"

"Yes, Mr. President. Congratulations. The First Lady gave birth to a son."

Neither the Chief of Medicine nor the CO is smiling.

"What's wrong? How is he?" the President demands.

The Chief of Medicine says, "Your son is nearly four weeks premature, Mr. President. He weighs less than five pounds and the pediatricians installed him at once in an incubator."

"But he's doing well?"

"I wish I knew more at this early stage, Mr. President, but the pediatrician will report to you as soon as he can."

"I want to see him."

For a moment, the Chief of Medicine wants to treat him as any ordinary expectant father, but the look in the President's eyes tells him not to. "Yes, Mr. President," he says.

The Chief of Medicine leads the President through a door and along a hall. An agent shadows the President. Some of the staff recognize the President and don't know how to react. They come stiffly to attention and some salute and others don't, neither faction being certain of the protocol. The President presses on grimly, head down, the hard floor sending painful shockwaves into his pelvis and back.

In a locker room, the Chief of Medicine advises the President he must change into surgical scrubs. He is acutely embarrassed at having to make the President undress, and the situation is made worse when he sees his discomfort in removing his jacket.

The President says to the agent, "I'd be deeply obliged if you could assist me."

"Yes, Mr. President," he says, and helps him off with the jacket and shirt, revealing the rigid body brace supporting the President's torso.

The Chief of Medicine blushes in deep embarrassment at forcing his supposedly vigorous young Commander-in-Chief into displaying such obvious infirmity, and then they must suffer the greater social discomfort of helping remove his shoes and trousers.

THE PRESIDENT'S NEWBORN son is the tiniest shred of life he has ever seen. His skin is translucent, pierced by minute medical tubes, and his chest is a tiny stretched balloon pumping up and down in rhythm to the bellows driving oxygen into his lungs via a ghastly pipe that runs down his throat. The doctors and nurses, who must be the pediatricians, stand to attention around the incubator, not daring to speak.

"May I?" the President says tremulously, reaching out toward the incubator.

One of them steps forward to answer but does not know how to answer.

"May I touch the glass?" the President clarifies.

"Yes, Mr. President, the exterior surface of the incubator is not sterile."

The President lays his fingertips against the glass, inches away from his son. He wants to weep in the face of the baby's fragility, but he manages to say, "How is he doing, please?"

"Mr. President, premature infants are at risk of respiratory problems resulting from the immaturity of their lungs."

The one who has answered is the one who stepped forward earlier. The President doesn't look at him. "My son has this condition?" he says.

The pediatrician says, "Yes, Mr. President, I'm afraid so. We have put your son on a ventilator to help him with his breathing, but, Mr. President, this is no more than a regular Air Force hospital."

"You're of the opinion my son should be transferred to another facility?"

"Yes, Mr. President, I believe your son would receive more specialized care if he were transferred—that is my sincere advice to you, sir."

"Travel won't harm him?"

"We can transfer your son in the incubator, Mr. President. No, he won't be harmed."

"You believe the benefits outweigh the risks?"

"Yes, Mr. President, that's precisely how I would characterize the situation."

"Make the arrangements, please, Doctor."

"Yes, Mr. President."

"How is my wife?"

The Chief of Medicine moves to the President's side. "If you come with me now, Mr. President, we can see if it's possible to see the First Lady."

Before the President leaves, he tells the pediatric doctors and nurses, "Thank you all for what you're doing for my son."

They say, "Thank you, Mr. President," but he notices nearly all of their eyes are downturned and their voices wavering.

The President and the Chief of Medicine trudge back through the hall, shadowed by the agent.

"What are my son's chances, do you think, doctor?" the President asks.

"It's a very specialized area, Mr. President. I really wouldn't like to speculate."

Thereafter they walk in silence.

AN OBSTETRIC SURGEON emerges from the operating room and the President notices large patches of sweat dampening his scrubs.

"Good news, Mr. President," the obstetrician says: "the First Lady is doing well following her surgery."

"There were no complications?"

"There was some bleeding, Mr. President, requiring that we transfuse the First Lady with two pints of blood, but her blood pressure is very good now and you'll be able to speak to her, sir, as soon as she comes around from the anesthesia."

"Our baby is going to be transferred. Is the same required for my wife?"

"I don't think that would be wise, Mr. President," he says, though the President notices he is trembling from the rigorous interrogation at the hands of his head of state, however competent he may be under normal pressures. "Your wife's—excuse me, sir—the First Lady's condition is stable at present but moving her might jeopardize her recovery."

The President turns to the Chief of Medicine. "I want my wife to see our son before he's transferred."

"She won't be well enough to ambulate for at least seventy-two hours," the obstetrician advises the Chief of Medicine.

"Then bring my son to her!" the President snaps.

The two doctors glance at each other.

"Yes, of course, Mr. President," they say.

THE FIRST LADY is pale from her hemorrhage and groggy from the aftereffects of the anesthesia as she lies in a private room, where she is given no more than a few seconds to glimpse her infant son in his little glass box and denied even touching him or holding him before he is transferred to the ambulance. Her agony is so primal that the President almost does not recognize his wife in that moment, her face twisted in torment and her voice rasping in a cry of anguish more raw than he's ever witnessed in this otherwise impeccably reserved woman, and each of her choked, drowning gasps is the stroke of an ax that quickly gouges open his armor.

He grips her pale, weak hand and sobs; they both sob and tears cloud his eyes, but he doesn't wipe them or blink them clear so that, instead of facing the pitiless machines feeding the stricken body of the woman he loves, he surrenders to a fuzz of light and dark.

In the afternoon, she falls asleep. The surgeon remains concerned though confident her condition is stable. The President doesn't want to leave her, but a chopper transfers him to the airstrip where the presidential Boeing waits to launch. Apologetic aides have work matters to discuss, but he shuts himself away the whole flight, hoping desperately that when he lands in Boston the doctors will have better news about his son.

He even prays. For five hours, he dragged a wounded man across the ocean to safety. Surely that life saved earns an equal gift for his little lad.

But at the Children's Hospital the news is not good. The President's son requires a tracheostomy so that his breathing tube can be moved from his mouth and inserted directly into his windpipe, to better maintain the inflation of his lungs.

The Secret Service has cleared the fourth floor of visitors, so the President walks through long, deserted halls, as if in a dream. Medical staff avoid him twice over, out of nerves, and out of what they must know of his baby's prognosis.

A waiting room is converted into a makeshift presidential suite, rapidly outfitted with a rigid bunk for his back, a rocking chair, a desk and direct phone lines going in and out. Out the north window, he witnesses dusk settling on the city, from Longwood up to the bridges over the Charles, and his alma mater, on the other side of the river, fading in the gloom.

He can't stay in this room waiting. The agent who guards the door walks him back along the hall. He finds a doctor who tells him his son's tracheostomy has been successful but only time will tell whether it's sufficient to keep his lungs working through the critical days to come.

"If his lungs can mature, Mr. President," the doctor says, "then he'll make it."

The President doesn't ask what will happen if they don't.

Father sits with son when he comes out of surgery. The brutal pipe that went into his mouth now disappears into a dressing stuck to his throat. Even so young, such a little scrap of a being as he is, he struggles to cling to life. The President imagines him fighting for his breath and his struggle makes him start to weep again. He presses his hand against the glass of the incubator wishing he could do the breathing for him.

On his behalf, the President's staff have taken the presidential suite at the Ritz-Carlton, and the doctors suggest he go there and get some dinner and rest. They want him out of their hair, and one of them says, "There's nothing you can do here right now, Mr. President."

"I can be *with him*," he says with an edge that's more pain than anger, but the poor fellow cringes as he takes a step back, whimpering, "I only meant—I—I sincerely beg your pardon, Mr. President."

"I know you're doing the best you can," the President mutters, and in truth he suspects the medical team is practicing less bungling and obfuscation than the usual run of their profession.

Later he does take the limousine to the Ritz-Carlton, showering and eating and putting on a change of clothes, but he becomes restless and unable to sleep, so he recalls the limousine and returns to the hospital. En route he orders the Secret Service to exercise more compassion this time and not on his account to remove parents visiting their sick children, and when he limps through the halls, he sees faces ashamed of their curiosity peering out from windows and doorways.

There has been no change in the baby's condition. The tracheostomy hasn't improved his respiration but the doctors want to give it more time. The President lies on the hard bunk in the waiting room, his back feeling as bad as it did shipwrecked in the Pacific after nights without sleep. He takes more painkillers, but they only fire up his ulcers, so he's grateful for Dr. T. coming up from New York and prescribing an intense course of anesthetic injections into his lower back.

Earlier he asked the doctors if his son would be in pain. "We don't believe infants are conscious of their own suffering in the way we are," the pediatrician said.

"I mean do the needles and tubes hurt him?" the President insisted.

The pediatrician hesitated gravely. "Yes, Mr. President," he said. "We believe infants feel pain."

The President lies on the stiff mattress as the needles prick his back. Tears fill his eyes. For father and son, every living minute is agony.

After midnight, he limps back along the hall with an agent to find a doctor or nurse because he wants to be with his son again before he tries to sleep. Through a doorway, he sees a dark room in which a child of about ten lies propped up on pillows with a catheter inserted into the side of his neck, the child having an enormous head and wasted legs. He stares at the President blankly, not recognizing him at all, so he can only smile at the child and move on.

When he comes back later, the hydrocephalic boy is not there anymore, and he wants to ask where he's gone, because he thinks of his sister institutionalized in Wisconsin the last twenty years, who was lobotomized and shut away, while he only grew richer, happier and more successful, but instead he returns to the make-shift room and lies on the hard bunk staring at the wall till first light brightens the east window.

In the morning, the doctors announce they want to try placing the President's son in a hyperbaric chamber. "It's possible the high pressure will force oxygen into his lungs," they explain.

"Are there any further treatment options?" the President says.

They shake their heads. "No, Mr. President," they say.

He gazes at the fragile scrap of life clinging to existence and feels pride in his struggle. His son shows in his few hours of life what every human being should. He seizes every breath. Like his father, he suffers a life of pain but he never surrenders.

The President flies back to Otis for a few hours to be with the First Lady. She remains weak but appears out of danger.

"We should name him," she says.

"Patrick?" he says.

"Patrick," she says.

"He's a fighter," he says. "And he's the most beautiful little boy, with the most beautiful brown hair—"

His voice breaks. He puts his arms around her and their shoulders heave.

BY THE TIME he shuttles back to Boston, Patrick has been moved to the hyperbaric chamber located in the hospital's basement. This time the President can't leave even to shower or change. Each hour he awaits news, and each hour a senior physician comes up to the fourth-floor waiting room to deliver a progress report, the only words of which that register are "serious," "grave" and "critical," until in the early hours of another sleepless night the Chief of Medicine stands in the room and says, "Mr. President, I think you should come down and be with your son now."

He explains the situation as they walk to the elevator, and then they make the descent. The President tries to be strong, but he hasn't slept in two nights and his back shoots bolts of pain down his legs, and each floor the elevator counts down seems to rip away chunks of Patrick's future. The President sees football games and baseball games; he sees beach vacations and sailing trips; and from each one the image of the handsome brown-haired lad is being torn.

His son is blue and his breaths are slow and the doctor says, "I'm deeply sorry, Mr. President, but we're losing him."

The President cannot even speak, sorrow chokes the words, and he slumps into a chair while the doctors disconnect the tubes and then lift the baby out of the chamber, wrap him in a blanket and carry him out. They lay him in his father's arms and his father rocks him gently as his breaths become slower and slower. The President finds his son's hand and puts his finger into the baby's palm. The hand is blue and cold and barely squeezes his, and he knows the child is surrendering. He wonders, when his own end comes, how long he will fight, and if he will give in, and if he will show the courage the boy has shown, his beautiful, beautiful son.

There is a story the President has been reading to his children lately, a simple fairy tale beloved by John, and he attempts to whisper it now. "Once upon a time, Patrick, there was a chicken called Chicken Licken, and one day something fell, bump, on his head. 'Goodness gracious me,' said Chicken Licken, 'the sky is falling down . . .'"

The President tells his son as many stories as he can recall, until the child slips into cold sleep. Tears run down the President's cheeks and onto his son's, as he kisses him and tries to say good night, but he can't speak, he can only croak, and then he doesn't want people seeing their President crying anymore, so he pulls himself together and goes back up to the fourth floor and shuts the door.

\* \* \*

BEFORE DAWN, HE flies back to Otis to be with his wife when she wakes up. The land lies blank and bottomless below. He struggles to comprehend why something he loved so dearly should be taken away. Then, in the first rays of sunrise, he recalls the babies lost that he never spared a thought for. A lifetime of fornication, while he takes for granted those who love him, is finally being punished.

# THE BRACE

Although the responsibilities of office mean his work schedule must return to normal at once, the President visits his wife at every opportunity during her recovery in hospital and then during her convalescence in Cape Cod. Each time he goes, he takes her a present, sometimes only flowers, other times delicate jewelry, and soon the normal routine of family life has subtly changed, for they no longer spend part of the weekends apart, instead clinging to each other's company every hour available, until his wife feels well enough to return to Washington, after which they are together each evening as well.

The children were so excited about getting a new brother that the President has bought them another dog and another horse, which they love, though he must double his dose of antihistamines. It is not only the sorrow of their loss that has glued them together, but also the fact that he no longer needs to schedule regular intervals apart since abstaining from fornication.

His son was taken and his wife, if a few circumstances had been only slightly different, might now also be gone. On the urgent flight after he first got news of her labor, he feared he might lose her, and the thoughts became insistent, until he realized that all these years he's lived in denial of what it would mean if he did lose her, not through death, but through divorce.

When she is strong enough, he takes his wife to visit Patrick's grave, which lies upon a cold, lonely hillside outside of Boston, and there they both weep, as he did alone the day of his funeral, clinging to the tiny white casket as though he could never let him sink into the earth.

Summer has ended in death and, though death visits the trees, turning their leaves dry and brown and baring their branches, they understand it is the cycle of nature; life will be born again, a process that begins awkwardly but tenderly in their bedroom some nights later.

Grief draws him west. In his wife's company, he flies out to Wisconsin and then motors through the forests to an isolated building in prairie not dissimilar to the wild hillside on which their baby rests. The nurses in their starched uniforms stand at attention on the porch, where the First Couple greet each in turn, before the Mother Superior leads the President and First Lady down long halls to a large room redolent with fresh flowers in which a middle-aged woman sits in an armchair by a window overlooking the prairie.

"It's Jack," he says, "and this lady is my wife, Jacqueline."

"Hello, Rosemary," says the First Lady, "it's so nice to meet you at last," and she steps forward to offer her hand.

The President's sister stares at them incuriously and then at the floor. He remembers her as a young girl, running and laughing on the lawn. From his bedroom window, he watched the ambulance come and go, following the winding road down toward the highway. He knew, but did nothing.

Later she speaks but it's demented gibberish. Nonetheless they stay for an hour and he talks to her about their family and eventually he remarks that he's now the President of the United States, though she doesn't respond. "But I'm still the same old Jack," he says.

The nurses stand to attention and wave as the presidential limousine coasts back over the prairie to the airport.

"I'm not," he whispers.

"Not what?" his wife whispers back.

"The same old Jack," he says.

Out the window, they gaze at tall grass bending in the breeze; his hand creeps across the seat to find hers, and his wife grips his in return as they travel gratefully home from the wilderness.

In Washington the next day, the President chairs a meeting of the Cabinet at which it soon becomes apparent that during his compassionate leave the business of government has continued uninterrupted, though not necessarily after a fashion faithful to his policies. The Joint Chiefs announce that a plan now exists to conduct as U.S.-led invasion of North Vietnam starting almost as soon as the next election is won.

"Within a year there could be as many as half a million American fighting men in Vietnam," the Chief of Staff of the Army says, and the President sees each of the other Joint Chiefs nod bullishly.

Later the Press Secretary seeks a private meeting in the Oval Office, and, as the President rocks in the chair by the fire, he hears that the man from the *Star* won't drop his inquiries. He doesn't have a story yet, but he's on the hunt for one.

"They see what happened in England," the Press Secretary says, "and they smell blood. He knows about the interviews of female White House personnel."

The President rocks, tapping his fingernails on the armrest, before he eventually says, "How does he know?"

"I don't know, Mr. President," comes the reply.

The President recalls his predecessor's warning that only an informed citizenry can stop the rise of the military-industrial complex, but the electorate won't be able to consider the important issues of our time if a tendentious press diverts their focus toward the sex lives of public figures. He cannot flinch in the face of scandal, as to do so will only give strength to those influences in our society who seek to employ this sordid stratagem: should they succeed, democracy itself would be in jeopardy.

That evening after he reads his children their stories, the President and the First Lady dine with close friends in the private dining room of the Residence, though as usual he is forced to eat plain fish and potatoes while the others enjoy carré d'agneau lubricated by burgundy. In the bedroom, the First Lady releases the straps of his body brace, and when it comes off, there are welts where it has pinched his flesh. Then he lies on the carpet as his wife puts on their old Victrola to play tunes from *Camelot* while massaging oil into the tender regions of his back.

Scandal brought down a Prime Minister across the Atlantic, and it now seems obvious that the President's political opponents, both inside and outside the government, have taken inspiration, not only feeding allegations to the press but also endeavoring to change the prevailing climate in favor of targeting the private lives of public figures. The press will declare their inquisition takes place in the public interest, while in truth it only serves the aims of political factions.

The next morning, his secretary informs the President that the Director of the FBI has requested a lunch appointment. The two men eat in tense silence interrupted by strained pleasantries until Mr. Hoover consumes his entrée, whereupon he says, "I've shown respect for your office, Mr. President, in not being accompanied by my Special Investigator."

"Your respects are always appreciated, Mr. Hoover," the President says, taking a sip of water. With a nod, he dismisses the staff from the President's Dining Room, and the two men face each other privately across the table.

Mr. Hoover says, "Mr. President, a gubernatorial aide in Texas alleges you molested her; the Federal Bureau of Investigation has uncovered a member of White House personnel willing to testify that you and she conducted an inappropriate sexual liaison."

"Who's the girl?" the President asks.

Mr. Hoover says, "Her name isn't important, Mr. President. She's a very junior member of the West Wing staff who feels extremely bitter at being sexually exploited. But, from a legal standpoint, it's just her word—and a story that beggars belief."

The President shifts with discomfort. He takes another sip of water. "Go on, Mr. Hoover," he says.

"These women, Mr. President . . . these allegations . . . they not only inflict irreparable harm on the office of President, but also on America. For them to become public is not in the national interest."

Mr. Hoover toys with the cutlery and clinks his fork down on his plate. A member of the staff appears, mistaking the sound for a summons, but the President waves him away instantly.

Mr. Hoover says, "Sir, it would be a service to your country if you were to resign before the election. You might consider citing ill health. Your reputation could only grow, were it felt you went too soon."

The President makes no reply.

Mr. Hoover adds, "In case the other side gets hold of this."

"'The other side'?" the President repeats. "Who's on 'the other side'?"

The Director dabs his lips with a handkerchief. "Mr. President, if the facts regarding your personal life ever become public—"

"My personal life is no one's business but my own."

The Director of the FBI says, "Mr. President, you, sir, are an immoral man, and you must resign."

The President says, "No, sir, I have a vision for America as the moral leader of the world, and I shall not resign, I shall see it through."

The President stands.

The Director stands. "I see, Mr. President," he says. "No doubt we shall confer again on this matter."

"You'll forgive me, Mr. Director, if I fondly hope we don't."

The President watches the Director lumber out into the hall, then the President retires to the Oval Office, where he gazes out across the South Lawn toward the Washington Monument casting a long shadow in the low autumn sun. In the past, it has been said that only a good man makes a good king; the President scorns the presumption that an adulterer cannot help but treat his office with the same reckless insouciance as he treats his lovers.

The philanderer should tell as much truth as possible in order to practice his art, which applies equally to the politician. When interrogated by the Special Investigator, the President's answers met the same criterion whether he responded as a politician intent on holding office or as a loving husband desperate to hide painful secrets from his wife. The President's responses may have been evasive, but the good he can achieve in office outweighs his private peccadilloes, and the integrity of his marriage outranks partisan political loyalties. He found himself embarrassed at considering whether his trysts constituted sexual relations.

His memory flashed back to that assignation with Marilyn in the penthouse above the Carlyle the night she'd sung "Happy Birthday" wearing a shimmering skin-tight dress. She'd said, "It might interest the President to know I needed quite some help getting it on, and I think I just might need some getting it off." He'd undone her zipper and the garment had slid off like snakeskin; she'd reclined on the couch as the living apotheosis of a Rubens nude. "It's your birthday, Mr. President," she'd said. Any man on earth would have killed for this chance. "Do anything to me you want," she'd said.

But there was nothing he could have done to her. As a regrettable consequence of his back condition, the subject's trysts are restricted to limited sexual acts being performed upon his person.


THE PRESIDENT LIMPS between the pillars of the West Colonnade, glimpsing gloomy figures peering from high windows. Every morning, he wakes beside his beautiful wife, and every noon he swims alone or in the company of male aides, and every evening he puts the children to bed and dines with his wife either in public or in private, and then they retire to their room and sleep side by side. They have never been closer, or more in love, and he has never been more miserable.

He craves the new intern who's replaced the old one. He craves the new secretary who works in the Signal Corps. He wants the ambassador's wife who sat beside him at lunch. He wants the socialite he met at a reception. He wants rid of the poisons that pollute his blood, inflame his tubes and hurt his head. If the fulfillment of desires is the essential requirement of contentment, then he is not, nor can he ever be, a happy man. One woman, even the one he loves, cannot save him. She assumes he grieves for their dead baby, or he's haunted by the visit to his demented sister, but his sorrow is not for either of these lives lost, only his own.

All his ailments worsen. Despite stupendously high doses of steroids, his Addison's disease fails to respond, leaving the President permanently listless and nauseated. Next his thyroid falters: he is lethargic, constipated and hoarse. His skin coarsens and cracks. Even his magnificent thatch turns lifeless. And all the time his ulcers rage, his bowels blister, his tubes burn and his back buzzes.

All his physicians attend a case conference, at which they dispute drastic and conflicting interventions. In an effort to rescue his thyroid function, the President is prescribed such large amounts of hormone replacement that his hands tremble; he can barely hold a set of speech notes.

A week later, the physicians reassemble in camera. The President's numbers are even worse.

"I think," says Adm. B., incredulously, "he's dying."

The President no longer views his condition with the nonchalant fatalism of youth. There is so much work left to do, and so many who will be left behind. Caroline will be six in November, and John only three. Caroline will remember, but John will not.

In the Oval Office one evening, he begins a letter to his son, to be sealed until after his death:

> You are reading this because I am no longer here. Each passing day, your young memory will fade a little bit, until I am gone. You will want to know about your father. Your sister will remember me a little, but listen to your mother: she will know best. Others will have many stories about me, some true, some not true, but this that I write comes from my heart.
>
> I have loved you more than anything in the world. I have played with you every day I could, even when the fate of the world lay in my hands.
>
> I have read you stories and you have stared at me with curious eyes, not believing a word. You are ticklish. I tickle you and you giggle. I say, "If you don't giggle, I won't tickle," but you only giggle more.
>
> Sometimes in the evenings we watch TV. You squash against me on the couch drinking your milk with your cheek pressed on my arm. You lay your little hand open on my lap for me to hold. I hold it and you hold your milk in the other.
>
> I take you sailing. We sit on the boat in the sunshine eating ice cream. Whichever flavor I offer you, you always say you want mine, and I always let you have it.
>
> Some days we walk hand in hand to my office. We play hide and seek between the pillars.

Sometimes you want me to throw you up in the air. Your mother won't let me, because I have a poorly back, but, when she is not around, I sometimes do it anyway, even though it hurts me a little bit, just for the way it makes you whoop with laughter.

Sometimes, when you have had a bad dream, I lie in the bed nearby. I watch over you until you fall asleep.

HE STOPS THERE, his eyes misted by tears, promising to continue the message at a later date. His head is pounding. If he can't have a woman soon, it will burst.

OUTWARDLY THE PRESIDENT endeavors to appear his old self. At functions he takes center stage amid a coterie of admirers, both male and female, who rejoice in their charismatic leader's persiflage. Unnoticed, his deputy awkwardly hugs the periphery, etiolated by the President's shadow. This particular evening, the VP says, "See you in Texas, Mr. President," as he bids goodnight before shambling out alone, all gazes remaining in tribute to the President; a burst of laughter that the Vice President hears echoes down the hall. His shoulders sink and he turns out of sight.

A few minutes later, the President rejects a pouting redhead who drunkenly suggests an assignation in a restroom guarded by a blank-eyed Secret Service agent.

In the Residence, his wife helps him out the body brace, and they lie together listening to music ahead of the early flight in the morning.

He struggles to sleep. He could have the Beard call up the redhead, and she'd be smuggled into the White House within the hour. Having sex with her isn't merely a matter of desire. Tonight might be the night the Bomb blows up the world, or tomorrow morning may be the morning his back finally gives out and he'll spend the rest of his life in a wheelchair, incapable. But he must make this sacrifice not just for his family but for his country. In the wake of a scandal, who knows what figurehead the moral monogamists might choose? He pictures the ranks of narrow-eyed opportunists who preach Creation but practice destruction, who profess the sanctity of life but unleash death.

The President rises with the same headache. He takes aspirin to numb the pain, but the pressure never shifts, and then the First Lady seals him into the carapace that immobilizes him from neck to tail.

They eat breakfast with the children, and then a chopper carries them to Andrews, where they board the SAM, flying down to Love Field and then embarking on a motorcade downtown to a trade mart. Crowds line the streets, with more than a few banners waving disapproval of the President's support for civil rights, though his advisors fear he will face trenchant hostility as the tour progresses.

Against the bright sunlight, the First Lady dons sunglasses but he asks her to take them off so the crowds can see her face. She laughs, "Whose idea was it to ride open-topped? It's playing havoc with our hair."

"The people need to see us," he says.

He spends his life indoors. He relishes the fresh air.

The President asks the driver to slow down so he can greet a group of nuns, and then a few minutes later he asks for another stop so he can offer good wishes to a group of schoolchildren.

As the motorcade turns onto Main Street, a young man waving a banner rushes the car and Secret Service agents block him and drop him. The President sweeps his hair from his eyes and keeps on charming the rows of well-wishers packing the sidewalks. He picks out a banner that bears his mug shot overscored with the word TRAITOR.

The presidential motorcade makes a sharp right followed shortly after by a sharp left and then they coast through an open, grassy plaza toward an underpass. The day is hotter than forecast and his skin is becoming sweaty and itchy beneath the body brace, but he keeps on smiling and waving.

Suddenly pain explodes in the President's back and throat and he starts choking. He feels like his baby must have felt struggling to breathe, and a thought flashes one last time of his courage, which still makes his father so proud. Blood pours down his front and the First Lady cries, "Jack! Jack!"

He struggles to duck. He pitches and pivots in panic; the hard edge of the brace cuts into his skin, but it is built to hold him straight. It will never give.

This man wrecked his back saving a wounded comrade, but this is only part of the story; the condition was exacerbated by his philandering in a hotel room in El Paso, and for these two inseparable reasons he wears a brace that holds his head high when otherwise he would be able to duck the next shot.

His wife screams again but the second bullet lobotomizes the President, relieving his headache at last. The final sound he hears is not the crack of gunfire, or the cheers of the crowd turning to screams, but his wife's voice, crying his name. That is her sole comfort, that he died in the arms of the only woman he loved.

# BIOGRAPHICAL NOTES

JOHN FITZGERALD KENNEDY was born into a wealthy, political family on May 29, 1917. He overcame lifelong medical problems to serve with distinction in World War II and then in the United States Senate. Elected President in 1960, his achievements included defusing the Cuban Missile Crisis, supporting equal civil rights for African Americans, securing a ban on testing nuclear weapons and setting the goal of a manned moon landing. He was assassinated in Dallas on November 22, 1963, survived by his wife, Jacqueline Bouvier Kennedy, and their two children, Caroline and John Jr.

Reliable sources allege President Kennedy conducted numerous extramarital affairs while in office, though many of his liaisons are beyond independent verification. In addition, a number of the President's confidants reported that he suffered withdrawal symptoms from sex, most notably the British Prime Minister, Harold Macmillan, in whom the President confided, "If I don't have a woman for three days, I get terrible headaches." It is fascinating to speculate how a contemporary sex scandal would have affected the Kennedy Administration, and what epitaph it would have inscribed on his presidency.

President Kennedy's womanizing was not widely publicized until more than a decade after his death, resulting in an initial diminution of his political reputation. However, in recent years, historians have recognized the extraordinary vision of his presidency, the unique optimism he imbued in his nation, his personal strength of character—particularly in relation to his chronic medical complaints—and the eloquence, erudition and wit of his speeches. As a result, the President ranks, after Franklin D. Roosevelt, as the most highly regarded President of the United States in modern times, a reputation that grows as successors continue to fall short.

JACQUELINE KENNEDY ONASSIS, an alumnus of Miss Porter's School at Farmington, Vassar College and George Washington University, enjoyed a privileged upbringing before she married Senator John F. Kennedy in 1953. Mrs. Kennedy was only thirty-one when she became First Lady, fast becoming a global style icon. Despite allegations from White House staff that she could be willful, spoiled and aloof, she stands as the most admired First Lady of modern times. Five years after her husband's assassination, the First Lady married Aristotle Onassis, the richest man in the world, but was again widowed in 1975.

Sources close to the former First Lady have revealed that she was aware of her first husband's promiscuous infidelity throughout their marriage, but no recorded comment on the subject from Mrs. Kennedy Onassis herself has ever been publicly released. Upon her death in 1994, she was interred beside the President, in accordance with her wishes.

NUMEROUS INSTANCES OF artistic license pertain to the details and chronology of events depicted in this novel. Interested readers will find unabridged texts of the President's speeches at the John F. Kennedy Presidential Library Web site, www.jfklibrary.org, where they will also find the President's day-by-day White House Diary. Full texts of letters exchanged by President Kennedy and Chairman Khrushchev can be read in an online volume of the *Foreign Relations of the United States* at www.state.gov, accessible via a link from the JFK Library.

# BIBLIOGRAPHY

Readers interested in the authentic history of the characters and events which inspire this story are recommended to consult the following excellent works which proved invaluable in my own research for the novel:

Adler, Bill, ed. *The Eloquent Jacqueline Kennedy Onassis: A Portrait in Her Own Words.* New York: HarperCollins, 2004.

Dallek, Robert. *An Unfinished Life: John F. Kennedy, 1917–1963.* New York: Little, Brown, 2003.

Dallek, Robert, and Terry Golway. *Let Every Nation Know: John F. Kennedy in His Own Words.* Naperville, Ill.: Sourcebooks, 2006.

Exner, Judith, with Ovid Demaris. *My Story.* New York: Grove Press, 1977.

Giglio, James N. *The Presidency of John F. Kennedy.* 2nd ed., rev. Lawrence: University Press of Kansas, 2006.

Harris, John F. *The Survivor: Bill Clinton in the White House.* Random House, 2005.

Hersh, Seymour. *The Dark Side of Camelot.* New York: HarperCollins, 1997.

Kennedy, John F. *Profiles in Courage.* New York: Harper & Brothers, 1956.

Klein, Joe. *The Natural: The Misunderstood Presidency of Bill Clinton.* New York: Broadway Books, 2002.

May, Ernest R., and Philip D. Zelikow, eds. *The Kennedy Tapes: Inside the White House During the Cuban Missile Crisis.* New York: W. W. Norton & Co., 2001.

Schlesinger, Arthur M., Jr. *A Thousand Days: John F. Kennedy in the White House.* Illustrated and abridged ed. New York: Black Dog & Leventhal Publishers, 2005.

Smith, Sally Bedell. *Grace & Power: The Private World of the Kennedy White House.* New York: Random House, 2004.

Smith, Sally Bedell. *For Love of Politics: Bill and Hillary Clinton: The White House Years.* New York: Random House, 2007.

Sorensen, Ted. *Counselor: A Life at the Edge of History.* New York: HarperCollins, 2008.

Vidal, Gore. "Thirteen Green Pages with Hindsight Added." In *Palimpsest: A Memoir.* London: André Deutsch, 1995.

# ABOUT THE AUTHOR

JED MERCURIO trained as a doctor and joined the Royal Air Force while at medical school. He received extensive flight training before resigning his commission to practice medicine. While a resident in internal medicine, he wrote the groundbreaking medical drama *Cardiac Arrest* for the BBC. His first novel, *Bodies,* published in 2002, was nominated by the *Guardian* as one of the top five debuts of the year. He adapted the novel into an award-winning drama series for the BBC. His acclaimed novel *Ascent* was published in 2007. Mercurio lives outside London.